UGLY COOKIES

A NOVEL

UGLY COOKIES

A NOVEL
FRAN METZMAN & JOY E. STOCKE

PELLA
PELLA PUBLISHING COMPANY, INC.
New York, NY 10018-6401
2000

UGLY COOKIES

A NOVEL

Library of Congress Control Number 00-123456

ISBN 0-918618-77-0

Cover Design by
GERDA ALBERT

Also by Joy E. Stocke
Poetry
THE CAVE OF THE BEAR

Acknowledgments in Alphabetical Order:
Merrie Allison, Ken Bingham, Lili Bita (me poli agapi), Victoria Brownworth,
Vilma deBrun, Zola Bryen, Andrea Dasaro, Betty Ann and David Fellner of the
Sedgwick Cultural Center, Bill Fox, Constance Garcia-Barrio, Denise Larrabee,
Steve Lieske, Talia deLone, Richard Marek, Kelly McQuain, Moorestown
Library, Dennis O'Donnell (our faithful editor), Paul Rubinstein, Sarah Schuman,
Joyce Spindler, Amy Stocke-Burns, Peter and Dorothy Stocke, Polly Toll,
Jeanette Tryon, Shirley Weinerman, Sharon Wohlmuth

PRINTED IN THE UNITED STATES OF AMERICA
BY
ATHENS PRINTING COMPANY
337 West 36th Street
New York, NY 10018-6401

For Carla and Ross

My wonderful children, who have given me strength,
dedication and love. FM

For Fred and Sarah

With love. JES

"When in doubt, laugh."
Boon-Dan-Tan

Chapter 1

BRIDGET BERNSTEIN'S HAND trembled as she inserted a key into the lock of her ex-lover's apartment door. She had to hurry. He'd be home in half an hour. She heard the whir of the elevator down the hall and threw herself against the door. It flew open.

She stumbled inside and quickly shut the door. If she hoped to reconcile with David, it had to be today, their third anniversary. David loved romantic surprises. Just last year, on their second anniversary, while she was still at work, he had decorated her apartment with beeswax candles and vases of pale white gardenias. To her delight, when she got home, he waited in her bedroom wearing only a gardenia behind his ear. Candles glowed on her dresser. A bottle of champagne rested in a silver bucket on the nightstand. Surely, he'd forgive her tonight for trespassing.

Cautiously, she moved through the dim hallway, a thick knot in her throat. If she found signs of a new girlfriend, she'd leave without a trace. Barring that, she'd try to set things right.

She remembered making love with him on the lush Turkish carpet that covered a pine plank floor, gazing up at rough-hewn beams, secure in his arms as if they were on a voyage together. Now the apartment, once a Victorian dressmaker's loft, looked dusty and neglected. His beat-up sneakers lay askew on the living room carpet next to an empty soda can. She wedged her feet into them, held out her arms to an imaginary David and waltzed across the floor.

Tripping over the soda can, she bumped her shin against the coffee table. Regaining her equilibrium, she massaged her aching shinbone, then stepped out of the shoes. David had never let his place run down like this. Maybe he was working overtime trying to forget her.

In the hall, she opened the closet beneath his bedroom loft, fear-
ing she might find an unfamiliar frilly robe or silky nightgown. A
quick search revealed only David's clothes hanging on the rack.
She brushed her hand across his nubby brown tweed jacket, the
one he'd worn the night she moved her things out of his apartment.
She dipped her fingers into his jacket pocket, then stopped. A chill
ran through her bones. What was she doing?

There were women who steamed open their lover's mail or
checked their phone bills, but she never dreamed that she'd stoop
so low herself. She tried to will her fingers out of his pocket, but
they continued grazing the soft material until she was sure it was
empty. She sniffed his shirts. No foreign perfume. Hallelujah.

In the bathroom, she saw an old tube of her lipstick on the sink.
David's toothbrush hung alone in a porcelain holder. The usual
items lined the shelves of the medicine chest. On a hammered
brass tray near the tub sat the bottle of chocolate liqueur she and
David had shared when they took baths together. She lifted the
bottle, unscrewed the cap, remembered tasting the sweet liquid on
David's lips and drank. A surge of confidence shot through her
body. It was obvious he still missed her. Why else would he leave
such intimate reminders?

She checked her watch. Time to go upstairs. David would be
home from teaching his sociology class in fifteen minutes. In the
loft, she turned on the lamp. David's nightstand drawer was ajar.
Just like him, always rushing somewhere. She sifted through loose
change, scraps of paper, a few packets of the condoms they'd used.
Everything had a light coating of dust. It sure looked like his sex
life was as boring as her own.

At the foot of his bed, she ran her fingers over the quilt she had
bought for him. She smiled, remembering how he had laughed
when he found the naked couple she'd embroidered in the corner.
Tracing her finger along the feathery thread outlining their bodies, she imagined him climbing the stairs, undressing, slipping into
bed beside her, whispering, "Glad you're back, babe."

"I still love you," she said, pressing her mouth to his pillow.
Giddy, she sat up and removed her raincoat, blouse, skirt and
stockings. She had worn his favorite red lace bra and matching

bikini panties. Before snapping off the light, she carefully folded and stacked her clothes on the floor.

His spicy scent enveloped her as she sat on the edge of the bed and drew the quilt around her shoulders. She peered eagerly through the railing where she had a perfect view of the living room below.

She had to make him understand why she hadn't immediately accepted his marriage proposal, why she had panicked and run to her Grandmom Ruth in Florida. David wasn't sure he wanted children and she had never pushed him on the topic. When she brought the subject up, he would change it, later, bringing her flowers or making her dinner. They'd go to a movie, and her desire to hammer out issues would vanish with the opening credits.

While in Florida, she thought about how they both loved the theater, art, movies. They had shared so many ideas that had made her feel close to him. They could work out the issue of children when she got home.

She had called him from the airport before her return flight. "I'm ready to work things out," she said. She heard him suck in his breath.

"Do you know how many women would jump at the chance to be my wife? You were the one I asked and you chose to run away." He slammed down the receiver.

At first she thought his response arrogant, but on the plane she decided that she had deeply hurt him. When she returned, she didn't argue when he insisted that she move her things out of his apartment and return his key. But first, she made a copy just in case he changed his mind and became his old self again.

In the days that followed, she wandered the streets on her way home from work. Sometimes, she found herself in front of his office at the University or on a bench at the bus stop across from his apartment. She'd stare up at his windows, happiest when the lights were off imagining him alone in the dark, missing her.

She stopped going out at night and sat by the phone, his telephone number flashing on and off in her mind. Once, she disguised her voice pretending to sell subscriptions for Bride Magazine, but he had hung up. That's when the idea struck her. She'd do something dazzling to get him back.

A noise broke the silence in the loft. The door squeaked open. She held her breath, leaned forward and peered over the railing. David's familiar footsteps reverberated on the wooden floor. Her heart pounded. He flipped on a light switch, filling the room with a soft yellow glow. Hair mussed, shirt wrinkled, he looked tired. She couldn't wait to comfort him.

He turned back to the door.

"Come on in," he said.

A tall, attractive woman entered carrying a grocery bag. Her honey colored hair fell just below her shoulders in a simple flip. Long, shapely legs carried her willowy frame into the room. David, at five-foot eight, clasped his hands around her waist and stared up at her. He barely reached her nose.

Sweat filmed Bridget's forehead. She was trapped. How could she have been so stupid?

The woman scanned the apartment. "Nice place, but it's a bit dusty."

"What do you expect?" David kissed her neck. "We've been hanging out at your place since Valentine's Day."

His words thrust like an ice pick into Bridget's gut. That meant he'd been staying at the woman's apartment for a month.

The woman smiled and handed David the grocery bag. He took it into the kitchen.

Bridget drew the quilt tightly around her shoulders. She heard a spoon clang against a pot. The woman sat on the sofa and stretched her legs beneath the coffee table.

Soon, the pungent smell of freshly chopped garlic wafted up to the loft. The chocolate liqueur churned in Bridget's stomach. She put her hand over her mouth to stop herself from gagging. The woman looked relaxed and in control as though she and David had been together for years.

David came back to the living room carrying a wine bottle and two glasses. He twisted a corkscrew into the neck and slid out the cork.

Bridget felt the air in the loft grow leaden. Lamplight illuminated David and his girlfriend. They seemed miles away in their own safe world.

"A toast to us." David sat down. His hand skimmed the woman's thigh.

"And to your new book," she said, leaning forward to kiss him.

Book? The woman's words startled Bridget. After publishing two papers last year, David had said he needed a break from writing.

David clinked the woman's glass and grinned. "The University Press wants my manuscript as soon as I can finish it. It's my turn to join the big leagues."

The woman ran her fingers through his hair. "Your idea is brilliant. Aging baby-boomers will love having state-of-the-art cooperative housing available in the city. No one wants to live in a nursing home, anyway."

Bridget bit her lip to keep from shouting. The kind of housing he talked about was her idea. She had shared her work with him and he had tried to convince her that baby-boomers were too self-absorbed to buy the concept. Now, he sat smugly ripping her off. Her arms and legs ached, but she dared not move.

David refilled the glasses and smiled. "Dinner's almost ready. Be right back."

The woman removed her shoes, hiked her skirt and smoothed her hair.

David returned, balancing two plates of fettuccine in his hands.

He lifted a strand and fed it to her as if he'd performed the ritual many times. The woman leaned against the armrest and smiled. "This sauce is as luscious as you," she purred.

Bridget eased herself from the bed. She had to find a way out before they came upstairs. She stuffed her foot into her pantyhose and ripped the nylon, nearly kicking over the nightstand.

Through the living room window, she saw the rooftops of adjacent apartments, the ghostly shapes of water towers, and beyond, illuminated in blue neon, the Benjamin Franklin Bridge. She wanted to leap out the window, dive into the Delaware River and swim until she reached the Atlantic Ocean.

When she looked down again, David and the woman had set their plates on the coffee table and were undressing each other. They'd be upstairs any minute. She looked for a place to hide, her eyes alighting on the space beneath his old roll-top desk. Carefully, she crawled across the floor, trying to remember which floor-boards didn't creak.

She huddled in the well beneath his desk top, sat on a thick book and looked through the railing again. David and the woman weren't coming up after all.

The woman lay on the sofa, her hair fanning against the arm-rest. David, his tongue hanging out like a dog in heat, flung himself on top of her. She guided his movements with authority. Bridget turned away, but disbelief compelled her to look again. The woman pounded her heels into his back, her voice echoing against the apartment's brick walls.

"You taste great. Oh, touch me there. Pinch hard. Yes! Squeeze. Move your head." The woman barked orders like a drill sergeant.

Bridget gritted her teeth. David looked like a derrick mechanically pumping oil. What had happened to the tender lover she remembered?

Soon, the lovebirds nestled in each other's arms. The woman grazed David's cheek with her fingertips and dreamily closed her eyes.

When Bridget realized they were falling asleep, she saw her chance to get out. Although her legs felt like metal weights, she crawled from her hiding place and gathered her clothes, slipping on her shoes and raincoat. Clutching her blouse and skirt under her arm, she cautiously rose and took a step forward, then stopped dead in her tracks. She knew she should leave, but something compelled her back to David's desk.

Light filtered up from the living room. She flipped through papers. Next to a reference book, she found a manuscript. She positioned the document to catch the faint light, squinted and read the introduction. Word for word, it was everything she had researched about cooperative housing.

Numbness vaporized into anger. Her hand shot out. The paper felt cool and silky, oblivious to David's treachery. How had she been so blind?

Her fingers curled around the manuscript. She hesitated, lifted the pages, then flung them over the railing. Papers rained down.

She grabbed the reference book and tossed it. The book hit the floor with a thunderous crash.

Suddenly, the apartment blazed with lights. She hurried across the loft.

"Who's there?" shouted David.

She reached the landing. He stood naked at the bottom. "Bridget? What are you doing here?"

"It was our anniversary. I'm sorry. I didn't know you had someone else. I'm going." Her words tumbled over themselves.

"Who is it?" shouted the woman, crouching on the sofa.

"My ex," he said, his voice icy. "Call the police." He came up the stairs and met Bridget at the top.

Bridget gripped the railing. "I didn't mean to hurt anyone. I aimed the book at the floor."

The telephone receiver banged against the wall in the kitchen. The woman's voice rang out. "Help! A madwoman is attacking us. Come right away. Apartment C-1, the Sussex House at Third and Arch."

Bridget tried to rush past David. He grabbed her raincoat by the shoulders and pulled until it shook free. They stared at each other. She blinked, embarrassed by her underwear.

"You're pathetic," he burst out.

Anger burned her throat. "Not pathetic enough to stop you from stealing my ideas." She grabbed her coat, but David held fast, blocking her way.

"You're not leaving until the police come."

"Just let me go. It will never happen again."

"What's going on up there?" called the woman.

"Be careful," said David. "No telling what she'll do next."

"That's ridiculous," said Bridget.

The woman came to the bottom of the steps and glared up at her. She had put on her clothes. Her skirt was twisted, her blouse half-buttoned.

"Just give me my coat." Bridget jerked the fabric.

He pulled it back and stumbled.

Bridget yanked the coat from his hands.

"Shit," he cried, as he lost his balance.

"No," screamed Bridget.

"David," shrieked the woman, backing away. But it was too late. He tumbled down the steps.

Bridget imagined the crack of bone as David barreled into the woman and knocked her to the floor.

"My leg," he cried.

"Help," yelled the woman. "Where are the police?"

Bridget angled her way down the steps. Someone knocked at the door.

"Open up," a voice commanded.

"I'm so sorry." She reached toward David.

The door crashed open. Two policemen stepped in, guns drawn.

"What's going on here?" boomed an officer.

"I'm dying," groaned David. "My leg's crushed and she did it." He pointed his finger at Bridget.

"You've got to help him," said Bridget. Her ankle ached. She looked down. The woman held her foot in a vise-like grip.

"Let go of me," she said, and tried to pull away.

"Arrest her, officer," shouted the woman. "She just tried to kill us."

"Against the wall, lady." The officer pointed his gun at Bridget's heart.

"It's not true. I'm gonna be . . ." Bridget's stomach heaved. She doubled over. With one great spasm, her throat opened, and a fountain of chocolate vomit spewed over the lovebirds as they tried to roll away.

The air in the police station smelled faintly of mildew. Bridget sat in a green metal chair below a ceiling fan and trembled. She had never received a speeding ticket, let alone been arrested for assault and battery. In the frenzy at the apartment, she had dropped her clothes. The kind matron sitting beside her had given her a sweater. Over the sweater, she wore her raincoat.

"Ms. Bernstein," whispered the matron. "I've had my share of trouble with the opposite sex. I can tell you're a nice girl. I'd bet my paycheck your man did you bad."

Bridget clutched the matron's hand. She wished her friend Claire was here, but Claire was in Columbia with the Peace Corps. Claire had been raised by an activist mother and knew how to handle crises when they arose.

She watched the arresting officer hang up the telephone. He dropped his feet from his desk and walked over.

"This is the story, Miss," he said, politely. "Since there's no way around the fact that you broke into your ex-boyfriend's apartment, we had probable cause to arrest you. We called the Municipal Judge at home. He issued a temporary restraining order."

"What does that mean?"

"It means that until your court date next week, you can't go near your ex. After that, maybe you can't go near him ever again. First off, get yourself a criminal attorney."

"Criminal attorney?" She felt herself slipping from the chair.

The matron pulled her back. "Sit up straight, girl. You'll be fine."

"We talked to your boyfriend in the ER," continued the police officer. "He says he's willing to drop the assault charges if you agree to the restraining order. If I were you, I'd still get myself an attorney."

"I'll do whatever I need to get out of here."

He plucked at a button on his shirt. "The next thing you need is a court date. I'll tell you one thing, if your boyfriend ever reports that you violated a restraining order, you'll wind up back in court, maybe jail."

"Which lawyer do I call?" Her voice quivered.

The matron put her arm around Bridget's shoulder. "Don't

worry. There are hundreds of 'em out there."

Touched by her kindness, Bridget rested her head against the matron's soft flesh. Why had she been so blind to David's faults, always cutting him a break? What had she seen in a man who could turn on her so viciously?

"Miss," said the Matron. "Do you have a momma?"

Bridget nodded, remembering the times she and David had visited her mother's ugly cookie factory. Not many people got along with her mother, but David knew the right buttons to push. He loved telling her mother about his research. Her mother, in turn, loved showing-off a large map stuck with colored pushpins highlighting the markets that sold her ugly cookies. David would cheer her on each time she added a new pin.

In those moments, she felt connected to both David and her mother, temporarily forgetting the void left by her father's death.

"You're lucky to have such a successful young man to take care of you," her mother would say.

She had convinced herself that her mother was right. She needed a strong-willed man like David. And he needed her.

The Matron touched Bridget's cheek. "Sweetheart, you're free to go. Maybe, you should call your momma first and tell her what happened."

Bridget almost smiled. If the Matron knew her mother, she would never make a suggestion like that. There was a good chance her mother would never speak to her again. She sat up. In that case, telling her mother might not be such a bad idea, after all.

Chapter 2

CARSON MCALISTER PULLED his silver Jaguar into the parking lot of Ball and Jack's Electronics Emporium. Twenty-five years before, cornfields had surrounded the company on the outskirts of Madison, Wisconsin. Now, the building anchored a small industrial park that bore the family's name.

He parked and looked up at the company's emblem, a thirty-foot tower that supported a revolving ten-foot wide ball and jack. His father had built the tower in tribute to the company's first million dollars in sales.

When Carson was a kid, at least once a month, in all kinds of weather, his dad would pick up a pizza and take the family to the tower. Munching on slices, cheese oozing over thin crust, they'd sit in the car and watch the lights go on, the ball and jack glittering, spinning round and round through the night air.

"Someday, I'll turn over a successful organization to you kids," his father would say, pointing a finger at Carson, his older brother, Jack Junior, and their adopted sister, Lisa.

Carson remembered his father's wide grin, his mother's indulgent smile. Corny, yeah. But, at that moment, no one was prouder than he to be the son of Jack McAlister.

He stepped out of the Jag into a dull March morning and closed the door. He had already called the leasing company and told them to pick up the car in six weeks. It wasn't his style, anyway. His brother had talked him into leasing it, rather than the Subaru he wanted for camping trips he never had time to take.

In the lobby, he stopped at the marble fountain. His father had imported it from Italy the previous spring just before he died. He dug into his pants pocket, fished out a quarter. Between his decision to quit the family business and his broken engagement, he'd never felt more on edge. "Help me, Dad," he whispered. And tossed the quarter into the blue-tiled depths. The fountain gurgled impassively.

Upstairs, he joked with the receptionist and asked her to buzz his brother into his office. If he didn't tell his brother that he was quitting this morning, his nerves would shatter. He had asked his sister to be there, too, for moral support. She had declined.

"Jack and I are at each other's throats half the time," she had said. "He'll think I set this up. Remember, from now on I'll have to deal with him alone."

The image gnawed at Carson. "It's not fair to dump Jack on you. Maybe I shouldn't leave."

"Forget it. Things might work out better when Jack doesn't have you for a scapegoat." He remembered her forcing a smile. "Don't think I won't miss you like hell."

He loved her all the more for making him feel less guilty about leaving her in the lurch. She understood that the only moment of joy he'd experienced since the day his dad died was when he had accepted a banking job in Philadelphia. No longer would he walk in his brother's shadow.

He turned the handle of his office door. A hand landed squarely on his shoulder. "What's up?" said Jack. "I hear you're looking for me." They walked into Carson's office.

Jack had his father's square, solid build, and wore his dark hair cropped short. Carson always marveled at how different he was from his brother. He took after his mother's side, tall and rangy with a high forehead and square jaw.

Jack walked past him to the window. "Hey, take a look. The steel frame's up for the new warehouse. There's our future, Bud. I bet Anne can't wait to decorate the plant manager's office."

Carson slumped into his desk chair. "We broke off our engagement last night."

"Impossible." Jack looked incredulous.

There was no way to explain it. Carson knew in his gut when he spoke to her and saw a blank shadow cross her eyes. What Anne loved most was the idea of marriage and the image of them at the country club while the nanny took care of the kids. He drew in a deep breath. "I broke it off because I'm leaving. I'm giving notice today."

Jack's body stiffened. "That's ridiculous. This is your life. Your heritage."

"I don't expect you to understand, but I need to make this change."

Jack paced the length of the narrow office. "You can't give up in the middle of the expansion. The company's on a roll. Besides, you're a damn good Chief Financial Officer."

Carson folded his hands on top of his desk blotter wishing Jack had said those words years ago. "Lisa's willing to take over. I'm sure she'll do the job better than I will. She works almost as hard as you do."

"Has she been in on this from the beginning?" Jack walked to Carson's desk and leaned forward, his nose an inch away from Carson's face.

Carson backed away. "No. I'm taking a banking job on the East Coast because I need a change. I only talked to her after I made the decision."

"I bet you did. She'd love to see you go so she can get enough power to kick me out."

Carson diverted his gaze from the anger in Jack's eyes. He felt his heart race and tried to calm himself. "You can trust Lisa. She's our sister. She wants the best for all of us."

"Bullshit. She's adopted, not blood. I'm the only one protecting the family's interests."

Carson picked up the contract he had been working on the day before. The numbers blurred in front of his eyes. "This place is your life, not mine. I don't want to be your lackey anymore."

Jack softened his voice. "I'm sorry if I fly off the handle sometimes. You're like Dad. Too soft. I hoped you'd develop a hard shell by now. But, I'll back off if that's what you want."

"I've made my decision."

Jack looked exasperated.

Carson wished Jack understood him better. Just because he preferred going to an art opening instead of a Terminator movie didn't make him a wimp.

"Don't zone out on me now," said Jack. "This isn't a Shakespeare drama. This is real life. I've worked my ass off to make us number one in the Midwest. And this is how you thank me? Everything

Dad built was going down the tubes when I took over. If it hadn't been for me . . ."

"What the hell are you talking about? If it wasn't for Dad, there wouldn't be a Ball and Jack's."

"Don't give me that crap."

"So Dad made a few mistakes. If he had lived, he would have pulled out of them. Give him some credit."

Jack's face reddened. He grabbed the contract from Carson's hand. "Dad nearly destroyed everything with his so-called friends at the country club, falling all over himself for their attention. Look at all the free merchandise he gave to those idiots, and the loans they never paid back. If I hadn't hung around day and night, there'd be no business."

"I'll stay for six weeks."

"Get out now."

"I said six weeks."

"I don't care what you said."

Carson shot to his feet. Jack lunged across the desk. Before Jack could hit him, Carson lifted his fist and punched Jack square in the nose.

Horrified, he watched blood stream over Jack's lip. Jack pressed the contract to his face. A red stain seeped into white paper. Carson's knees turned to liquid. What had he done?

*   *   *

Since his flight to Philadelphia was delayed, Carson had overindulged in O'Hare's repertoire of fast food: pizza washed down with Coke, frozen yogurt dipped in chocolate, two hot cinnamon-sugar pretzels. The sugar had given him a buzz that had dissolved into a raging headache.

His mother and sister had driven him to the airport. Now, he sat at his gate wondering if he could pull this off. Through gray fog, he saw the blurred headlights of planes landing and taking off, and the bright yellow outlines of the trucks running luggage to cargo holds. It seemed impossible that tomorrow he'd be far away from everything familiar.

An elderly man sat in the seat next to him, unfolded a newspaper and smiled. Carson nodded and turned away trying to banish the knot of grief that had formed in his throat.

He remembered Jack's silence during the trip to the hospital. The next day Jack had looked like a prizefighter, his eyes black and blue, his broken nose swollen beneath bandages. How could one punch do so much damage? He had stayed six weeks like he'd promised Jack, barely speaking to him, except to say he was sorry.

The day before he left, Jack broke the silence. "I think you should turn over your third of the business to me before Lisa manipulates it from you. It should stay with the real family."

Carson jammed his fists in his pockets. "Lisa is real family."

Jack insisted on rewriting history, striking out the day their parents had adopted Lisa.

Carson, too, had been surprised when his parents announced that a long-lost friend, a widow dying of cancer, had called and requested that they adopt her sixteen-year-old daughter.

From the moment Lisa arrived, he had liked her. She fit into the family with her quick humor and her ability to adapt to the family's quirks, putting a buffer between him and Jack. She had a delicate, pale look, and with her fair hair and light eyes, she blended into their Midwestern community.

Jack resented her immediately. "She's sneaky," he said. "Look how she wraps Mom and Dad around her finger. We hardly see Dad, but who does he talk to when he comes home? Lisa."

Carson chalked Jack's anger up to the fact that he had lost his standing as the oldest in the family. In some ways Carson understood. Lisa's energy and sense of humor had completely charmed their father.

"Flight 567 to Philadelphia now boarding." The announcement cut through his reverie. Lifting his carry-on bag, he slipped into line, flashed his boarding pass and stepped on the plane.

A flight attendant came by offering magazines. "So, you're traveling alone?" she said softly, a half smile crossing her full lips.

"Yup. I've been run out of town." Her Minnesota accent melted his shyness. He wanted to cling to its familiar twang.

She waved her hand as if dismissing his remark. "Can't imagine that."

He smiled, basking in the warmth and attention.

A second flight attendant passed by and tugged at her sleeve. "See you when we bring the beverages." She continued down the aisle.

Her departure made him feel lost. For a moment he wanted to bolt off the plane. Then he remembered all the reasons why he had left, especially his unhappiness with Anne. The emptiness in their relationship had become clearer than ever when he accepted the new job. Not for a second had she considered coming with him. He understood how tied she was to her family and lifestyle. But he couldn't make clear to her the kind of passionate bond he yearned for.

He wished the stewardess would come back and talk with him. Just a couple of well-placed words on his part and he would arrange to see her again. But an initial shyness with women plagued him and flirting didn't come easily.

He straightened his shoulders. The new job came first. The plane lifted off the runway. He set his briefcase on his lap and opened it.

Chapter 3

FROM HER PERCH ON the cracked marble steps of the Mother Mary Convent, Bridget watched an old woman walk toward her pushing a metal shopping cart full of groceries. "Hello Angel," she called.

Angel maneuvered the cart past a pile of trash, her plump frame straining the seams of an old-fashioned black cotton dress, her legs sturdy in their lisle stockings and black oxford shoes.

Bridget had grown up in this South Philadelphia neighborhood of red brick row homes near Angel's family and the convent. When Bridget was a child and the nuns still ran the convent, Angel had been a fixture in the Italian Market a block over on Ninth Street where she sold produce from a brightly painted wooden stand.

Ten years ago, when the Diocese put the convent up for sale, Bridget's mother had bought it and now used it solely for storage. But Bridget remembered when roses grew in the convent's tiny front yard and the front door was open to anyone who wished to worship in the small chapel.

Whenever Bridget was troubled, she came to sit on the steps and think. This morning, she needed to make a decision about David. He had sent her a flyer inviting her to one of his lectures at his favorite hangout, the Zen Caffeine-Free Coffee Bar. He had signed it, "See you there." They hadn't spoken since the restraining order went into effect three months before. Why had he invited her now? To make peace or to trick her?

Angel stopped her cart at the foot of the steps and clucked her tongue. "I recognize your lovely face, but I can't exactly place you." She squinted at Bridget as she adjusted a black crocheted snood over a thick silver bun. "It's a shame, but my head don't work like it used to."

Bridget leaned closer, smelled the heavy scent of tea rose perfume, a popular brand among the grandmothers of her youth. She smiled, remembering how its sweetness had permeated the front parlors of the neighborhood row homes. "Give you a hint. I'm the annoying kid who used to knock on your door asking for donations for the convent's soup kitchen. In the summer, you gave me bushels of tomatoes and peppers from your produce stand. Remember, you taught my grandmom how to make real Italian gravy?"

Angel's dark, watery eyes flickered with recognition. "Of course, Bridget Bernstein. Your Nonna always followed behind you like a mother hen. Now, she was a pistol."

"Still is," said Bridget.

"I remember the time your Nonna put on the potato pancake party right here at the convent. Mama mia. I can still see the piles of grated potatoes. Then she taught us that dance. What's it called?"

"The hora." Bridget raised her arms and snapped her fingers.

Angel chuckled. "We all kicked our heels around the dining room table that night. I was sore for days. I remember Sister Mary Anne had just come back from a pilgrimage to the Holy Land and knew all the steps."

Angel touched Bridget's cheek with her roughened fingertip.

"Oh you gave us a laugh, the little Jewish girl who wanted to become a nun. I remember how you begged to move in with our family and learn how to be a Catholic." Her smile deepened the wrinkles netting her face. "When you told your Mama that Jesus was Jewish and that he was your shepherd, she went right through the roof."

"No kidding," laughed Bridget. "I was in your kitchen helping with the meatballs when Mom stormed through the door yelling that she had picked my name in a moment of insanity. She had no intention of me becoming another Saint Bridget and if I didn't stop my nonsense she was going to change my name to Miriam and send me off to the Hebrew Academy." Bridget hugged Angel's full, soft frame. Angel held tight before letting go.

"God bless you Bridget." Angel's expression darkened. She waved her gnarled hand at the overgrown weeds and the tires littering the convent yard. Graffiti swirled up the three-story building. Dirty cardboard panels covered broken windows. "Isn't it sad to see how it's changed around here? Your Mama could keep the place nicer. Now she's gone and put up a for-sale sign. Who's gonna buy it? There's enough trouble in the neighborhood what with the gangs of kids hangin' around makin' problems for everybody."

Bridget stared at the broken bottles and cans littering the yard. She remembered when the nuns still lived in the building. There had been a vegetable garden in the back and a clothesline where white sheets billowed in the wind.

She felt time spooling backward. The convent had been the focal point of the neighborhood. Grandpop had loved to play Canasta with the nuns on Sunday evenings. And Grandmom never tired of sending new recipes to the soup kitchen.

It seemed to Bridget that they had all been part of the nuns' family until the Order moved to upstate New York. For a while a handful of sisters remained, tending to the changing ethnic composition of the neighborhood. When they finally left, her mother bought the building for a song from the Archdiocese and quickly filled it with spare machinery from the factory.

Now she expected to sell it and make a profit. Bridget sighed. The building had lurked in the back of her mind as a possibility for her cooperative housing. She'd often fantasized about asking her mother to donate the building to her.

"It's a miracle you picked the first of May to visit," said Angel. She crossed herself, dug into her pocket and withdrew a pouch, which held a set of pink crystal rosary beads. "Me and a few of the other old-timers still get together to give an offering to our blessed Virgin." She nodded to a chipped concrete statue of the Virgin Mary. The statue's hands stretched toward them from behind a bent chain link fence.

Angel smiled. "It's the Virgin's special day. When I was a kid, we would bring her branches from a fig tree my pop had planted in our backyard. It was big day for young men to propose to their girlfriends."

She pointed down the street. Bridget saw two more women walking toward them dressed like Angel. Grandmom called it the widow's uniform. Something she had refused to wear when Grandpop died.

"Tina over there," said Angel. "Her husband proposed on the first of May. He gave her sixty years of marriage and she gave him seven beautiful bambinos."

Angel held up her beads. "Let's you and me say a few prayers together before the other ladies get here."

Bridget shrugged. It had been a long time.

"You haven't forgotten the Hail Mary, have you?"

Bridget remembered kneeling with Angel's grandchildren in front of a small altar in the living room. The words came back to her. "Hail Mary full of grace." She smiled.

"Molto bene," said Angel.

When the other women joined them, Angel had already said prayers on three rosary beads and seemed to have moved into a trance. The others nodded at Bridget. Without a word, they withdrew their beads. Oblivious to the honking cars, the traffic, the litter, they joined Angel in their ancient ritual.

Bridget bowed her head and marveled at the neighborhood version of the Wailing Wall. She didn't know whether to laugh or cry. If she ever needed the power of prayers, it was now.

Lulled by the women's soft voices, she thought about the restraining order. It had decreed no telephone calls, no physical contact, no correspondence and no communicating with David's mother. Why would she bother? She'd never interfered before when his mother sent him underwear and toilet bowl cleaner. She looked at the women, heads bowed, beads clicking and envied their unshakable faith. She would pray with them a while longer, gather strength, then go to the Zen and ask David to lift the restraining order. Maybe the flyer was David's way of calling a truce.

* * *

When she reached the Zen Caffeine-Free Coffee Bar, Bridget cautiously peered through the window. Young corporate types crowded the room sitting at low tables sipping herbal teas and decaf soy milk cappuccinos from brown mugs. Cones of incense burned in white china bowls. A woman in a gold kimono bowed before setting a tray of steaming cups on a table. She saw David sitting in the center of a group of students and backed away from his line of vision.

Only a few months ago, she had been part of the group, basking in his warmth. In hindsight, it hadn't always been perfect. Sometimes when she voiced her opinion, he would gently explain to her how and why she was wrong. Back at his apartment, she'd make her point again and he'd reluctantly agree with her. It struck her that he mostly validated her opinions when no one else was around.

Her mother's voice echoed in her head. "You have a big mouth, Bridget. Do you want to be a spinster for the rest of your life? You should have been sweet until you got David to the altar, then you could have told him a thing or two."

She watched David gesture to a young woman, then lift his gaunt, poetic face. Fighting an urge to run, she opened the door and stepped inside. He noticed her immediately and hobbled toward her leaning on an ornate cane, its silver-tipped head carved into the shape of a lion. "You've got nerve showing up like this," he called. His voice drowned out the sound of chimes hanging from the ceiling.

She sucked in her stomach and straightened to her full height at the sight of his exaggerated limp. What was his problem? He'd acted the same way in court, prominently displaying his splinted leg on a chair, smirking as his hysterical girlfriend spouted lies about how she had beaten them up. Her lawyer had told her to calmly wait it out. She had no chance of winning.

David stopped and pointed his cane toward her. "What do you want?"

She unfolded the flyer, waved it in his face. "The bigger question is what do *you* want?"

"I didn't send out the flyers. My secretary did. I don't pay attention to her every move."

"Then whose handwriting is this?"

She studied the exaggerated way he raised an eyebrow feigning innocence. A fleck of cappuccino foam clung to his lip. "Not mine."

"Forget it." She lowered her voice. "I want you to lift the restraining order."

"Why? Are you seeing someone?"

"Who would date me? You've convinced everyone we know that I'm a madwoman. I'm afraid they'll find out at work. Why can't you tell the truth?"

He shook his head. "You should be thankful that Cecilia's family kept the story out of the papers. Why didn't you call me instead of showing up at my apartment and violating my privacy?"

"I tried, but you wouldn't take my calls."

He rapped his cane against the wood floor and paused. "If you think this has been easy for me, you're wrong. You're behavior is completely erratic. I want you to stay out of my side of town, that means anything east of Broad Street, especially places we used to go together like the Italian Market."

His words stung. Was he taking his new girlfriend to all their favorite places? Had he shown her the convent? "The court gave me an order that I intend to follow, not your bullshit," she said. "No one can arrest me if I go to the market."

"You're in no position to dictate to me. Any time we're accidentally in the same place, all I have to do is tell the police you're stalking me and they'll lock you up."

She wanted to kick the cane out from under him. "I'm not the only one who committed a crime. You plagiarized my idea."

He narrowed his eyes. "If you spread lies about my book, you'll wind up in worse trouble than you already are. You've got the Java High Bookstore on your side of town. Hang out with all those slackers you like so much."

She saw his motivation in a flash. He'd use this to blackmail her into silence. She let her voice grow cold."You're a control freak and a plagiarist. It's too bad you can't handle women who have ideas." People around them stared.

"Don't menace me," he whispered. "Count your blessings that I don't have you arrested."

"I've counted them. And the biggest blessing is that I'm no longer involved with you." She reached for the handle, thrust open the door and strode down the street toward the corner.

*   *   *

She stopped walking when she reached Walnut Street and the Belle Epoque Thrift Shop. In the two years she and David had been together, he never threatened her. But she had never really challenged his ego either. While he appeared supremely confident, she saw now, it was only a façade. What kind of war had she started and what were the rules?

A couple strolled by hand in hand. She watched them look into each other's eyes, fingers entwined as if they spoke a secret language. She had thought that she shared that language with David, but it had been an illusion.

She entered the Belle Epoque, stepped inside and parted beaded curtains. The heady scent of patchouli oil drifted through the air. She and Claire had shopped here as teenagers on the prowl for trendy bargains, sitting for hours in the dressing area on two orange bean bag chairs, trading stories and dreams about what they would become when they grew up.

Claire's life had been far more exotic. Her mother, Bev, had been raised in a wealthy, conservative white family on the Main Line, and had gone to private schools. At Bryn Mawr College she had joined the Civil Rights Movement and traveled to Georgia where she met Claire's father, Wilmer, a black Baptist minister.

"The rest is history," Claire used to say. Her mother and father fell in love at a protest rally. When Bev got pregnant, they agreed it would be a mistake to marry so she came home and had Claire, raising her in a garden apartment near the Art Museum.

Claire had taken a cue from her mother, making life changes as easily as drinking a glass of water. Bridget wished she had more of that quality herself. She stopped at a rack of dresses.

"Hey, this would look real cool on you," said a young sales clerk dressed in a black spandex mini-dress. She stood on three-inch platform heels and held a teal blue linen shift in her arms.

"Just got it in. Calvin Klein. Check it out."

Bridget fingered the smooth fabric. "It's not my usual style."

"Come on, it's made for a great figure like yours." The sales clerk led Bridget toward the dressing area, marked by a loop of rusted pipe. Hanging from the pipe was a dusty, green, crushed-velvet curtain.

The clerk drew open the curtain and peered at Bridget. "You look upset. Problems at work?"

"Just a broken romance."

"I've got something to cheer you up. The perfect shoes for that dress. Be right back."

Bridget stood in her bare feet on a matted, gray shag rug in front of a cracked mirror. She slipped the shift over her head. It fell in a fluid column to her ankles. She studied her image. The girl was right. The dress gently skimmed her hips and the color emphasized hints of apricot in her wavy, dark brown hair.

She checked the price, forty dollars, glanced again into the mirror and saw the girl return.

"Catch this," said the girl. "The bargain of the century. Joan and David. Squeeze your foot in, Cinderella, 'cause they're only twenty bucks."

Bridget slipped on the simple silk flats and felt a little better.

"Whatever guy you meet next time will flip when he sees you in that dress," said the girl.

Bridget flinched. Rumors spread fast in this city. Anyone who knew her story would be wary about dating her. "I haven't been in the singles scene for a long time. I don't have a clue."

The girl pushed a lock of green-tinted hair behind her ear. "I met the coolest guy through the personals in The Philadelphia Rag. Some real hip guys show up in there. Sure beats the losers in bars."

Ten minutes later, Bridget stood in the take-out line at the F & J Diner waiting to order a salad. She carried her dress and shoes in a brown paper shopping bag and a copy of the Philadelphia Rag under her arm. The line inched forward. She unfolded the Rag and turned to the back pages where the personal ads were listed. She had to be crazy reading the personals, although she'd heard of other people who had lucked out.

Everyone wanted the same thing: long walks, romantic dinners, quiet evenings, travel. Everyone said they were smart, good looking, and had great careers. They sounded too good to be true. Still, she hated spending all those evenings alone in her apartment.

She paid for her salad and walked out into the late afternoon sunlight. It drenched her face, its warmth uplifting her. Life had options after all. She'd write her own ad, aim for somebody different from the arrogant, authority figures that had attracted her in the past. No longer would she act like a chameleon adapting to the men in her life. Next time, her needs would be addressed equally.

Across the street, Saturday shoppers peered into the windows of antique stores. She saw David standing in the midst of the crowd, leaning against his cane like a suave gentleman. He must have followed her.

She walked toward him, determined to tell him off. He held up his hand and wagged his finger. It appeared to be a mild rebuke, but she knew better. His threat of arrest echoed in her head. Pretending indifference, she flipped her hair over her shoulder and headed in the opposite direction, crossing a small playground and doubling back down Smedley Street. She suspected that David could walk much faster than he let on.

When she finally glanced over her shoulder, David was nowhere in sight. She slowed her pace and watched the pattern of light slanting through the wrought iron gate of a townhouse across the street. She began writing an ad in her head.

Accomplished woman with a restraining order against her, seeks a man who's not afraid of a fatal attraction.

She hoped the kind of guy who answered it wouldn't be too upset if David decided to have her arrested and hauled off in handcuffs on their first date.

Chapter 4

CARSON DEVOTED MOST Saturdays to work, but on Sunday mornings, he jogged along the River Drive to clear his head. It surprised him that he liked the city so much. He enjoyed the restaurants and the museums in Philadelphia, but found it hard to meet people. Especially women.

He'd seen interesting women sitting on the benches by the snack bar, adjusting the laces of their running shoes. Once in a while, someone would smile at him. He'd try to screw up his nerve to say hello, but wound up jogging by, heading instead, to a greasy spoon where he scarfed down his new favorite food, a Philly cheesesteak with extra fried onions.

Today, after his run, he planned to check out the Archeology Museum. His boss had reminded him that he might meet someone more his style at places he himself enjoyed.

He huffed his way along the path, his sneakers showing wear from pounding the asphalt. His new job was stimulating, but at the end of the day his brain was fried. Some nights, he barely had enough energy to drag himself home to his empty apartment. Still, in the last month, he'd felt surer of himself. He'd just set a division record for new revenue. As a reward, his boss had promised him an assistant. Once he trained someone, he'd get out more often in the evenings.

He watched the scullers ply the Schuylkill River, bright light bouncing off the ripples made by their oars as the boats skimmed the water. The crush of people running, roller-blading, biking against the backdrop of fresh green leaves and bright rhododendron blooms energized him. Behind, the city skyline jutted into the horizon. Lissome women whisked by on roller blades, their hair blowing behind them, their bare shoulders glistening with perspiration.

His preoccupation with the dazzling, sweaty bodies confirmed the obvious. He was horny. An attractive woman whizzed by on her roller blades, giving him a big smile. This was the sign he'd been waiting for. No more wimping out. He sprinted in her direction trying to keep up. He would have lost her, but she slowed her pace to avoid running into the onslaught of bikers and skaters coming from the other direction. A quarter mile later, when he thought his lungs would burst, she stopped at a dip in the path and he finally caught up.

"Excuse me," he called. A sharp pain stabbed his side. He doubled over. Although he was in good shape, he didn't have the stamina to keep up with a hotshot roller blader.

The woman skated toward him. "Are you okay?"

Another cramp gripped him. He looked up, trying to breathe through it. People glanced at them as they whizzed by.

"I'm . . ."

She took his hand and led him from the path. "Sit on the grass and put your head between your knees."

He sat down and closed his eyes. Slowly, his cramp subsided. She dropped down beside him and shook out her legs. He gathered his breath, digging hard for something witty to say, then looked up at her. She took off her sunglasses and studied him.

Surprised, he saw lines radiating from the corners of her blue-green eyes. He realized that she was at least ten years older than he was. So what. She had a pretty face and a great body. Maybe someone older and wiser was what he needed.

"You're a great roller blader," he managed to say. He paused and stared at a patch of dirt. "I guess you figured out that I was following you."

She threw her head back and laughed. Strands of gray glinted through dark red hair. "Were you trying to hit on me?"

He dropped his face into his hands. "When you smiled, I flipped. I'm new in the city and you seemed so friendly, I thought I'd take a chance."

She brushed a blade of grass from her shorts. "I'm flattered. I'll be fifty next month." Her smile radiated warmth. "Wait till I tell my husband that a hunk was after me."

Carson's breath eased. "Some hunk. I just made a perfect ass of myself."

"No you didn't. If I were a few years younger and single, I'd put the make on you myself. You need to get out and meet women your age."

"Wish it were that easy for me." He stood up and helped her to her feet.

She slipped her sunglasses on. "I don't know you from Adam, but I bet you'll have no trouble finding the right woman."

He smiled.

"Good luck," she said, before skating toward the boathouses.

* * *

Forty minutes later, he stood in the courtyard of the University of Pennsylvania's Archeology Museum and leaned against the shoulder of a bronze, muscular Bacchus. A breeze ruffled the flowers of the rhododendron bushes surrounding the pool. The woman's kindness had made him feel lonelier than ever. But she was right. He had to get out on the dating market—or would it be more like a meat market?

He missed his mother and Lisa. They understood his reserve. Lisa would draw him out, introduce him to people. That's how he had met Anne, at one of Lisa's bashes. He and Anne had ended up alone at the beer keg. As he filled Anne's glass, she had impulsively kissed him. He'd been so flattered that he asked her out. After that they were a pair.

He jogged up the steps two at a time into the museum. Another flight brought him into the muted light of the rotunda. A statue of the Buddha drew him across the floor toward its wide, almond-shaped eyes and peaceful face. He wished for a tenth of the Buddha's serenity. Maybe then he would find someone different, strong-willed and independent. But would that kind of woman want him?

He headed toward the Egyptian wing, past a case containing a large crystal sphere cradled in a pewter wave. On the cases of mummies in their sarcophagi, he studied the hieroglyphics: an eye, a bird, a sun. Then, in a small diorama featuring everyday life in ancient Egypt, he saw something that intrigued him. Two women carried baskets on their heads. Long black hair fell to their waists.

He imagined himself in that scene, unloading wheat from a ship, a woman gazing at him. "Who are you?" she would ask.

He would tell her that he wanted to sail with her down the Nile to see the pyramids in a golden sunset. He smiled to himself. It sounded like an Egyptian personal ad. That was an interesting idea. He'd already been reading ads in the Philadelphia Rag. Why not try one?

Children's voices interrupted his reverie. A family stood in front of a statue of a seated woman with the head of a cat. "It's a goddess," the mother said to her daughter.

"A weird goddess," said the father.

Carson smiled. The family looked content, comfortable with each other. That's what he wanted someday. But he also wanted a woman who would be stimulating and exciting. Marriage didn't have to be dull. His parents' marriage never was.

He walked toward the statue of Buddha. "Tell me old boy," he whispered. "What do you think of this ad: horny, shy banker seeks higher plane with intelligent woman who can reveal her innermost thoughts and listen to his, too."

The Buddha seemed to blink.

He bowed in thanks. If the Buddha was with him, he had to be onto something.

Out in the courtyard he breathed in the summer air and wondered if the endorphins from jogging had pushed him over the edge.

* * *

SWF–32–Attractive in an ethnic way. Seeking down-to-earth guy for a committed relationship. Social worker with mind of her own loves to cook, read, enjoys good conversation. No pseudo-intellectuals from Philadelphia need apply. Box 6265.

SWM–34–Newly relocated from America's heartland. Shy, at first, but have a sense of humor. Financially secure, seeking free spirit with traditional values. Box 5786.

Chapter 5

JAZZ WAFTED THROUGH the book stacks from invisible speakers in the Java High Coffee Bar and Bookshop. Formerly, a candy factory, its old-fashioned brick facade, carved cornices, large leaded-glass windows and busy outdoor cafe distinguished it from the neighboring buildings.

Java High attracted intellectuals, college kids, writers, people on the make, and even a few homeless folks who sometimes crashed on a black vinyl sofa near the front door. Bridget felt most at home here, as if she could move in and no one would mind.

With her index finger, she traced a line down a row of self-help books. She'd read more than a few lately. She tucked a book of spiritual advice beneath her arm and walked to the coffee bar. Behind the polished chrome counter, next to the cappuccino machine and a stack of white china cups, a clerk sat perched on a stool reading a comic book. He looked up and smiled.

"Hi, Edward," she said when she reached the counter. "A cup of coffee, please."

"How 'bout I give you a free ethpretho, 'cauth "I'm feeling good today."

"Make it a double." She shuddered at Edward's latest addition to his never-ending face and body-piercing program. He had planted a fourth stud in the middle of his tongue and had inserted a hollow rod in the middle of each earlobe.

In spite of his posturing, Edward, who had arrived in January, was a sensitive soul. He had just dropped out of college depressed about his parents' recent separation. She'd liked him immediately and had appointed herself as his second mother.

Devilish at times, Edward liked to play practical jokes with orders, putting maraschino cherries on cappuccinos, serving lemonade in martini glasses he brought from his apartment. No one really minded.

"For heaven's sake," she said. "You should take those studs out of your tongue. How does your girlfriend stand it?"

Edward grinned and stuck out his tongue as he frothed the milk. Light glinted off the gold studs. "She liketh it, ethpethly when I kith her in thertain places."

"Try to behave yourself," she said, as he handed her the cup. "You haven't been around for a while. I really mithed you."

The cup warmed her fingers. "Well, I'm back with a vengeance. I've got a date tonight. Would you believe that I met him through a personal ad?"

"Hope he'th hot. But thtick around for a minute. Got thomething to tell you." Edward turned to fill an order.

While she waited for Edward to finish, she thought about her phone conversation with Carson McAlister. He had just moved here and didn't know a soul. A good sign. She had seen his ad, too, and was just about to answer it when his reply came. He claimed he wanted a free spirit. Did he know what he was in for? She imagined herself saying, "By the way, Carson, did I ever tell you how I almost killed my last boyfriend?"

Anyway, if the date didn't work out, she still had Java High, her only refuge in the city.

Edward leaned across the counter. "I hate to tell you thith, but your ex wath in thith afternoon athking for you. He wath here a couple of timeth latht week, too."

Her hand began to shake. Coffee sloshed over the rim of the saucer. She remembered the smug look on David's face when she told him about her ruined social life. He definitely wasn't letting her go.

Edward handed her a napkin. "He thaid he wath only pathing through and doethn't plan to come back."

"Like hell he doesn't. He's backed me into a corner so he can find me whenever he wants."

"He won't cauth trouble ath long ath I'm here," said Edward.

She leaned over the counter, kissed Edward's cheek, and dropped a tip into a paper cup on the counter. In the cafe, she sat at an empty table, her teal linen shift brushing her ankles.

If David was trying to get a reaction from her, she'd better stay cool. One misstep and he'd have her at his mercy. She watched the people sitting nearby. At the next table, two goateed young men played chess.

Along the bank of computers at the rear, three men and four women stared at monitors. Everyone looked confident, as though they knew where their lives were going.

She opened her book, something Claire had recommended. It was called, Tracing the Road Map of Your Mind and Heart, by the local guru Boon-Dan-Tan. "Practice life with an open heart," she read. "Take risk with hands outstretched. Be not afraid of love ..."

*   *   *

Carson hurried up Pine Street. His meeting had run late. He'd barely had time to stop home and change before his date with Bridget Bernstein. He wore a fresh, white, oxford cloth shirt, open at the neck, and had changed into a pair of chinos. Over the shirt, he wore his favorite vest.

He toyed with the vest's brass buttons as he walked. The vest had belonged to his father and he'd decide to wear it at the last minute for good luck. He hoped some of his father's charm would rub off on him tonight.

Bridget had sounded smart and sexy on the phone, just the kind of person he wanted to meet. He had suggested they go out to dinner at a nice restaurant, but she'd insisted on meeting at a coffeehouse. No doubt it was easier to end a date over a cup of coffee than a bottle of wine. Besides, she had warned him that she was coming off a bad relationship.

Remember, McAlister, he admonished himself. Be polite. If the conversation flags, don't be shy. Ask questions. Take it slow. If he got through the first few minutes, he'd be fine.

Up ahead he saw a giant coffee cup outlined in pink neon. In the center glowed the words, Java High Bookstore and Coffee Bar. The kitschy sign amused him like so many other things in this crazy city. He liked soft pretzels with mustard and laughed when his co-workers said they were going "down the shore," although they meant they were going to the beach.

He pushed open the door and walked into the noisy cafe. Scanning the crowd, he saw a dark-haired woman reading a book, a lock of hair caught in her fingertips. She wore a teal dress just like the one Bridget had described. His breath came up short. She was great looking. He worried that he would stutter when he began talking to her. His dad's advice came to him. "Charm the ladies, son. Be snappy and witty and it will get you the best of 'em. It got me your mother."

Indeed it had.

*   *   *

When she glanced up from her book, Bridget saw a tall man with light, sandy brown hair scanning the tables. He caught her eye and strolled toward her. His easy gait made her think of a summer day in a field, the two of them spreading a red-checked blanket under a tree, eating a picnic of fried chicken and corn.

"Excuse me," he said, when he reached her table. "Are you Bridget Bernstein?"

She nodded and nearly groaned. Over his shirt, he wore a vest on which swam dozens of embroidered whales.

He sat down and crossed his legs.

Still, he was very attractive, broad-shouldered, but trim. She could tell he worked out. But that vest. She'd never seen anything so silly, although maybe it didn't look so bad on him. She twisted a lock of hair around her fingertip and began counting whales.

He leaned back in his chair. "You're staring at my vest. My dad wore it on his first date with my mother. I thought I'd wear it to see if you found it funny. My mom always got a kick out of it."

She smiled. "If I don't, have I flunked our first date?"

"Not by a long shot." He flinched slightly. "I guess the idea was pretty dumb."

She studied him, saw intelligence in his eyes. He didn't seem as innocent as she first thought. Why waste time, though. "Can I ask you a few questions?"

"Go ahead."

"Are you married? Ever been married? Do you have children, weird fetishes or sexual deviations?"

Carson kicked his foot against the table leg and laughed.

"Depends on what you think is weird, but in general I'd say no."

He felt adrenaline pump through his veins, tilted his head and glanced at the book lying on the table. "You're reading about road maps. Are you planning on taking me somewhere?" She looked puzzled, then he saw her face brighten. She got the joke.

"Depends on you. It's a self-help book."

"Truth is, I expected you to read something different, like The Bridget of Madison County." He slapped the table and laughed.

He was cornball, but sweet, and his nervous gestures echoed her own anxiety. "Pretty funny."

He reached into the sugar bowl and pulled out a blue packet. "I'm having a hard time relaxing. You're dazzling me and it's making me tongue-tied."

Dazzling? She'd been more aggressive than dazzling. What kind of women had he been involved with before?

From the corner of his eye, he observed how she sat in her chair, her head tilted forward. Her wavy dark hair framed high cheekbones and shimmered with highlights ranging from apricot to the richest chocolate. Her almond-shaped eyes seemed to penetrate his own. He glanced at her slim neck, her small shoulders, and the swell of her breasts beneath her dress. Too bad the table stopped his line of vision at her waist.

"I was wary about placing a personal ad," he said. "But I lucked out on my first try. You remind me of a beautiful Egyptian princess."

"My mother calls me her Jewish Princess."

"Either is fine with me."

She noticed that his eyes were dark blue like the water she had seen from the nude beach the time she and David went to Martinique. She had watched the waves, the curve of coastline, trying to look cool and uninterested in the naked men parading back and forth. For a second, she imagined a naked Carson walking along the beach, the hot sun shining on his tanned back. She almost giggled. Could he feel the heat coming from her body? Here she was lusting after a stranger. She cleared her throat. "What did you mean when you asked for a free spirit with traditional values?"

"I don't know. I was trying to sound clever. What about you? No pseudo-intellectuals from Philadelphia?"

Her muscles tensed. "I wasn't too successful with that type. This time I wanted a nice down-to-earth guy . . ." She hesitated.

He grazed her arm with his fingertips. She felt a quickening in the pit of her stomach, imagined brushing her fingers across his lips. When he smiled, she noticed he had the tiniest, sexy cleft in his chin. "Were you transferred to the East Coast?"

"Nope. My family owns a business back home. My brother and I didn't get along so I made a change. I hope I did the right thing." He flattened the packet of sugar with his palm. "I'm sure I did the right thing." He sighed deeply. "Tell me about your work."

"My work?"

"Sure. When you told me you were the director of a nursing home, I thought to myself, now there's a tough job. What made you decide to work with old people?"

He watched Bridget lace her long, slim fingers together, imagined them touching the papery skin of an old person's cheek. Then he imagined them stroking his own cheek.

"My grandmom Ruth helped raise me. I feel comfortable with older people, although I know a lot people our age don't. There are so many myths about the elderly."

"Such as?"

"Like all old people are senile. Some of the residents at the nursing home are so sharp they put me to shame."

"Truth is," said Carson. "I haven't had much contact with older folks. My grandparents died when I was young." He leaned toward her.

She smiled. He seemed interested in her answers, almost daring her to be audacious. "Did you know that lots of older folks have a strong sex drive, even without Viagra."

He exaggerated a gulp.

She laughed. "My friend Claire, who used to work with me, wrote a manual to help the more passionate residents with their sex lives. It didn't go over well with the administration."

"Did you ever have to call in the vice squad?"

"The vice squad loved us. They sent us all their retirees." She liked the way his humor contradicted a reserved manner.

He shifted in his chair and crossed his legs. His calf muscle curved nicely against the fabric of his chinos.

"A nursing home's not the ideal living situation for everyone," she said. "Some of the residents feel like they're in prison." She paused. "I have this idea for cooperative housing. I even have a building in mind. We'd have our own space, but share food, utility and transportation costs. At first I thought it would be just for the elderly, but now I'd like to see it become inter-generational."

"Excuse me," a familiar voice rang out behind her. Her blood chilled. She turned. David sat at a table in the corner by the book stacks. How long had he been there?

He rose, placing his cane in front of him. With measured steps, he walked over.

"Did I hear you mention cooperative housing?" His voice was deliberately sweet.

She watched Carson look from her to David.

David turned to Carson. "Isn't Bridget's enthusiasm infectious? I'm Doctor David Angsdorf. I'm sure she's told you about me."

Carson caught a look of fear in Bridget's eyes. Her face had gone chalky.

She saw an odd expression suddenly cross Carson's face.

"Who's that guy standing behind you?" he said.

She quickly turned her head.

A young man wearing a green tank top and an obviously fake beard reached over her shoulder and grabbed her coffee. "I noticed you weren't drinking this delightful beverage," he said. "Mind if I finish it?"

"Put that down," said Carson.

Bridget tried to grab the cup. Coffee spilled into her lap, inky liquid seeping through the fabric of her dress. Silently, they watched the man bump into tables as he fled toward the door.

"Are you burned?" said Carson.

"The coffee was cold," she said, wiping the stain with a paper napkin, lint clinging to her skirt.

David cleared his throat.

Carson ignored him, picked up another napkin and handed it to her. "Who would steal a cup of coffee? Look, there he is, standing at the window grinning like an idiot."

"He's the Java High Coffee Bandit," she said softly. "He's harmless, but they can't keep him out of here. He always wears ridiculous disguises. I don't even know what he really looks like. It's sad in a way."

"Someone should report that creep to the management," said David.

She dabbed at her dress. "Why don't you just leave."

"But I like it here."

"You're soaking wet," said Carson. He warily eyed David. "I'll take you home."

She rose quickly, letting Carson take her elbow and guide her toward the door. David was crazier than the Coffee Bandit. And Carson was a nice guy, but he'd never be able to deal with her and all the chaos she attracted. She must have been out of her mind to place that personal ad.

Outside, the evening air felt cool and fresh. She gazed up at Carson and imagined his clients trusting him with their money simply because his eyes were clear and honest.

"Who was that guy?" he said.

"Just an annoying ex-boyfriend." She tried to act nonchalant and turned from his gaze.

"Obviously he's not over you."

"Well, I'm over him."

"I hope so." He didn't sound convinced. "Would you like to meet here again tomorrow night?"

She marveled that he wanted to see her again and here of all places. "I've got a better idea. There's a great little theater near my apartment that shows old movies. They're playing Zorba the Greek. Want to go?"

He leaned forward and kissed her cheek. "My mother was in Greece last spring. Why not?"

Chapter 6

BRIDGET WALKED PAST the pet shop and stopped. Tiny white poodles nestled into one another as they slept in the window, their bodies puffing up and down like furry balloons.

She watched them sleep, envying their innocence. One of the poodles lifted its head and blinked its eyes sleepily at her. "What's your opinion, pooch?" she said. "Why is David hounding me? Sorry for the bad joke." The dog blinked again and went back to sleep. She began walking. Maybe the puppies had the right idea. She should just ignore David. As far as she could see, there was no logic to his behavior.

When she reached the Belle Epoque Thrift Shop, she stared at the worn and chipped mannequins. She looked down at the stain on her dress. What a waste. Carson had been a good sport about the whole thing. If David would just leave her alone, in time she'd explain everything to Carson.

She longed, too, to tell her mother. Maybe, for once, her mother would listen with compassion, advise without judgement, hug her and love her unconditionally. Fat chance.

She checked her watch. Almost seven. Her mother would be leaving the cookie factory any minute. She found a pay phone on the street and dialed the factory. To her surprise, her mother picked up in the middle of the first ring.

"Sarah's Ugly Cookies. Sarah here, I'm on my way."

"On your way where?" said Bridget.

"Bridget, is that you? I'm expecting a call from Gordon. I'm heading up to his warehouse. He just got in a shipment of orange flower water at the best price I've seen in years."

Heavy street traffic sped by. Horns honked. "I was hoping we could have dinner together. Do you have an hour?" The smell of hot dogs wafted in the air. Bridget heard her mother pause.

"What's that? I can barely hear you."

"Let's have dinner tonight," Bridget shouted.

"Oh. That's real nice. We can do that. Come to Gordon's with me. Manny's Deli's up there. We'll grab a corned beef sandwich. Where are you?"

"Near Java High." She paused. Manny's was on David's side of town, but she knew her mother. They would never sit in the restaurant and chat. More than likely, they'd eat their sandwiches on the way to Gordon's. "Can you pick me up in front of Java High?"

"That ratty coffee house?"

"Mom." Bridget tapped the receiver with her finger.

"You're on Pine, right? Walk over to Broad. I don't want to get caught in that traffic. I'll meet you in ten minutes."

Her mother's idea of ten minutes was more like half an hour. At Broad and Pine, she sat on the steps of the old art school to wait. Up ahead, she saw an Atlantic City casino bus idling at the curb. A man and woman got on. She thought of her father, how every Wednesday for almost twenty years he had taken the same bus to the casinos. She imagined him mounting the bus steps on the day he died, dressed in his baggy gray suit, wearing a white polo shirt beneath.

He would have left her mother's cookie factory and boarded the four o'clock special, his eyes trained reverently toward the east and the craps tables at the casinos. How ironic. If he hadn't tried a new casino, he would still be alive today.

She pictured her father standing at the craps table, the man next to him nervously fingering his chips, all his money riding on her father's toss of the dice. They'd been winning big on number eleven.

Her father cupped the dice, lifted both hands for the fifth toss. "Come on eleven. Come on eleven." He shook the dice above his head, leaned forward and threw them across the table.

"Seven."

"We lost," screamed the man.

She still had nightmares about what happened next. A pistol pulled from the man's waistband. Her father's unbelieving stare.

The gun leveled at his head. A shot ringing out. Her father falling dead over his chips onto the table.

The funeral parlor had overflowed with the buddies from his gambling club, all decked out in their trademark tuxedos, a pair of dice stitched onto the lapels. At the funeral they had made her laugh through her tears with their casino stories. They swore that entering the pearly gates after a craps game was a badge of honor. Her mother wailed and moaned, forgetting that she had fought with her father about his gambling nearly every day.

Bridget shook her head. She missed her dad. For all his faults, she had adored him. She imagined Carson's background as very different from her own, his father sitting on the terrace in a crisp Brooks Brothers shirt, his mother in a casual cream colored silk dress, a golden retriever wagging its tail and barking as Carson came up the walk.

Her mother, who preferred Jewish professors from Penn, wouldn't understand what she might see in Carson.

* * *

David opened the drawer of his nightstand and searched for a condom. He had a date with Cecilia and didn't feel like stopping at the drugstore. In the back of the drawer he found a packet of colored condoms. Cecilia would never go for them. They were a bit silly; especially the hot pink ones. But Bridget had liked them.

He blew into the drawer. Dust floated into the air. He whisked his hand through the cloud and watched it dissipate. Examining his empty hands, he remembered making love with Bridget, the heat rising from her skin, how he had stroked every inch of her body. She was so concerned with herself and her plans that she had never taken the time to see how much he had loved her.

He leaned over the railing and imagined her sneaking into his apartment, sitting beneath his desk watching him and Cecilia make love. He hoped she remembered how good he had been in bed.

When he saw her at Java High this evening, his stomach sank. He had hoped to find her alone, but she and that guy were really into each other. She was practically drooling all over him.

Why did she have to run off to Florida? Had she stayed, things would have been different. They would have been planning their wedding and he would have dedicated his book to her.

She had known from the beginning that he wasn't the type to have children. Why had she insisted on denying it? She should have understood that it had taken all his nerve to propose. But, no. She had to react in her typical impulsive manner and run to her grandmother.

Breaking and entering. That's how she wanted to make up with him? She didn't know him at all. Which was just as well. Never again would he reveal his inner life to another woman until he trusted her one hundred percent.

Cecilia wasn't the right woman for him, anyway. But, she had other things, social standing and barrels of money. Plus, she put no real demands on him. Once he became recognized as an authority in the field, he would take a long sabbatical, see if he could stay at Cecilia's family's place in the Bahamas, kick back and write more books.

Bridget claimed that he stole her idea. Maybe he had borrowed pieces of it. His spin simply made it unique. He racked his brain. What was his spin exactly? Statistics, of course. You could manipulate numbers to do anything you wanted.

He grabbed his cane and hurried down the steps. In the bathroom, he splashed water on his face and decided not to shave. Cecilia thought stubble was sexy. After drying his face, he reached for Bridget's lipstick. He had deliberately placed it on the shelf to make Cecilia jealous. He gently pressed the cool metal tube to his cheek, imagining Bridget kissing him, parting her mouth.

Why had she been so brazen in public when they were together? Questioning his theories in that soft, little girl voice. He had hated it. Underneath her docile guise lay a quiet aggression that unnerved him. Bridget needed more of her mother's traits. Sarah knew how to make a man feel important. She understood his position. Bridget should have known that sharing her concepts with him was vital to their mutual success.

He slipped on his loafers and wondered if Bridget understood the consequences of her arrogance. He would block any move she made especially her new relationship. Maybe she'd see the error of her ways and come back to him.

He perched his glasses on his nose, carefully mussed his wispy brown hair and reached for his jean jacket. The perfect absent-minded professor. He checked himself in the mirror and smiled with approval. Cecilia would be all over him the minute he walked through her door.

* * *

Half an hour later, Bridget saw a truck pull up to the corner. Painted on the side panel was a picture of a grinning woman wearing an Amish bonnet, spreading her arms to embrace the world. Above her head floated the words, "Sarah's Ugly Cookies."

Bridget marveled that her mother had turned a business making misshapen cookies into a small empire. The sweet, cherubic face on the truck faintly resembled her mother, except that her mother's Eastern European features, a longish nose and full mouth, had been softened by the artist.

Bridget resented how the ad agency insisted that her mother impersonate an Amish woman.

Her mother loved the idea. "Why not?" she had said. "I'm a plain woman making ordinary cookies."

The real Sarah leaned her head out the window. "Get in," she called. Bridget climbed into the cab. "Buckle up," said her mother. "What in the world happened to your beautiful dress?"

"I had an accident." Bridget pleated a fold of fabric over the stain.

Her mother pulled away from the curb. "Did you drop a latte or whatever you drink these days in your lap? Not that I mind you drinking all those frappaccino-cappuccino things. I shouldn't complain. Cookie sales have gone through the roof since they opened all those places. Why don't you go to Starbucks? It's cleaner."

"It happened at work." How easily lies flew when she wanted to keep her mother off her back.

"That's terrible. You should keep extra clothes at the office. I do. It's not nice for the nursing home director to look like a slob."

Bridget noticed a smudge of flour on the left shoulder of her mother's designer-discounted suit. "Thanks for the tip."

"Okay. I understand. You had a stressful day. Take it from me, the life of a high-powered career woman ain't no picnic. Now listen, when you get home, put some pre-soak on the stain and set your dress in a sink of cold water overnight, then . . ."

Bridget watched the city roll by her window. The three-story colonial houses of Society Hill, the factories of Old City, now turned into stylish loft apartments. Her heart pounded. David lived on Arch Street. This was the first time she'd been near his place since the restraining order.

They passed beneath the Ben Franklin Bridge, crossed Spring Garden into the old Eastern European working-class neighborhood of Northern Liberties.

She remembered David telling her that if she had half her mother's business sense, she would have already set up her own nursing home. Sure, with him running it.

Her mother's voice brought her back to the present. "Here's our first stop." She made a quick, bumpy turn.

Ahead, Bridget saw the large black and white sign advertising "Manny's, The Best Corned Beef in Town."

"Wait here while I run in," said her mother. "Don't open the doors for anybody. It's a shame. I used to come up here with Grandmom on Saturdays. She'd trade her knishes for Manny's corned beef. The neighborhood's gone to seed with all the rockers and dopers and hippies moving in. You want a corned beef special or one of those cottage cheese diet plates?"

"I always order a turkey sandwich, remember?"

"How am I supposed to remember? You sound just like your grandmom expecting me to keep a thousand things in my head. I know you had a rough day and all. Old folks can be tiring. Remember after your grandpop died, whenever I visited Grandmom, she just wanted to sit on the sofa and look through photo albums all the way back to when she came over on the boat to meet him. She even cut pictures out of a magazine taken by that guy, what's his name? Staglitz? You know. He married the lady who painted flowers that look like women's private parts."

Bridget leaned back in her seat and sighed. "Alfred Stieglitz and the lady was Georgia O'Keefe."

"Right." Her mother opened her door and stepped out. "Well, your grandmom put copies of Mr. Staglitz's photographs in her scrapbook. 'Look at these people in steerage,' she tells me. 'I was in lower class, too. They treated us like dirt.' She sure became a big Yankee Doodle. Look how she spoiled you."

Bridget rolled her window down. "Why? Because she listened to me?"

Her mother walked around the truck. "I'm listening to you, too. But, I've got a business to run. So stay in the car and I'll make sure Manny gives you extra corned beef."

"I said turkey. I don't like corned beef."

"Since when?" her mother called over her shoulder.

"Since I was a kid!"

Across the street, the bells in the steeple of the Ukrainian church chimed eight o'clock. Bridget watched her mother bustle into Manny's, her feet encased in tired black leather pumps. She fingered the stain on her dress, angry that she'd set herself up for disappointment again.

The sky darkened to a deep mauve, clouds fading into hot pink streaks. And the way her mother and grandmom fought, it was a wonder she didn't get an ulcer growing up.

The scent of onions and warm bread rose from the restaurant's exhaust fan, reminding her of Grandmom's knishes. She closed her eyes and thought about the time her mother decided to expand the cookie business and include knishes, how she'd bundled her up on a cold, November afternoon and taken her to Grandmom Ruth's apartment for a baking demonstration. Knishes. What a disaster that had been. Her mother and grandmom were the most competitive people she knew, but that afternoon they had topped themselves.

She remembered standing in the familiar warmth of Grandmom's kitchen chopping onions. Across the worn, black and white checkerboard linoleum floor, Grandmom had dumped flour on a gray, Formica table and glared at her mother. "You don't want the knishes to get sticky."

Her mother flicked her fingers through the pile of flour and glared back at Grandmom.

Grandmom had taught her mother everything she knew about baking. But Grandmom demanded perfection; the perfect thickness of cookie dough, the proper lightness of cake batter. Years ago, her mother had rebelled, deliberately smashing cookies. Her ugly cookies were an instant hit and she had made a small fortune, but it wasn't enough. She was determined to master the art of making knishes.

Steam billowed from a large pot of potatoes toward the ceiling of the kitchen in the old apartment Grandmom and Grandpop Nathan had lived in since before Bridget was born.

Bridget silently prayed that her mother and Grandmom wouldn't fight. They squabbled over everything: whether the moon was full or not, whether vinegar or ammonia cleaned windows better, whether you would wreck your teeth if you brushed them with baking soda.

"Now, Sarah," said Grandmom, bustling toward the stove. "Don't you dare ruin my knishes and make them ugly just like you did with my cookie recipes."

Grandmom scooped up the onions and set them in a pan of sizzling butter. "You diced these perfect, Bridget, just like I showed you." She drained the potatoes.

Bridget's mother was a younger, slightly taller clone of Grandmom, flesh beginning to hang on thick arms, another roll forming beneath her dimpled chin. She set her hands on her hips.

"For your information, Ma, my daughter learned how to follow directions from me."

"Your cookies look like dog do-do. And that husband of yours, taking money from you and gambling."

"Gus can spend his salary any way he wants." Her mother glanced at Bridget. "If you keep insulting him, I'm leaving. And my daughter goes with me."

Grandmom leaned over and hugged Bridget.

"I'm staying," said Bridget.

"I'm the boss," said her mother.

"All right," said Grandmom. "From now on, I keep my mouth shut."

Bridget watched her mother and grandmom work silently,

mashing potatoes with the onions, salting, peppering, smacking
dough flat on the table. They dusted their rolling pins with flour.
Bridget held her breath.

Grandmom opened her mouth, shut it, and opened it again. "You
were a smart girl, Sarah. Why did you marry that bum?"

Her mother glared at Grandmom and smacked the rolling pin in
her hand. "You're never satisfied. I have a nice house. Bridget's
college tuition is in the bank. And didn't I give you money so you
and Pop could move to Florida next year?"

"You said that money was for my cookie recipes. Royalties. I'll
give your money back."

"What will I do when Grandmom leaves?" Bridget stepped in
front of her grandmom. "Don't make her go."

"You see what you've done to my daughter?" said her mother,
raising her voice. "You've taken her away from me."

"You did it yourself, working all the time."

Tears sprang to Bridget's eyes.

"Don't start crying," said her mother.

Bridget wiped her eyes on the sleeve of her blouse.

"Come here, doll," said Grandmom. "Grandpop and me, our old
bones can't handle the cold anymore. You can visit us in Florida
anytime you want."

Grandmom rolled out the ball of dough. Her mother followed,
moving like a conductor. Grandmom sprinkled flour on the board
as though bringing a violin section to a crescendo. Her mother
rolled too hard and tore the sheet. She pinched it back together.
Grandmom stared disdainfully. Then she continued rolling, each
push forward exactly the same distance as the last. Folding her
paper-thin sheet of dough over her rolling pin, Grandmom held it
in front of her mother.

"Ma," said her mother. "Stop with the competition."

"No competition. I'm in charge of this kitchen!" Soon a series of
dumplings lined up across the table. "Look how perfect they are,"
said Grandmom. "No one can resist my recipes. Why do you think
your cookies taste good? It's no thanks to you and that good-for-
nothing husband."

Bridget backed into a corner, recognizing the angry look that appeared in her mother's eyes when Grandmom pushed her too far. Her mother reached over and picked up a handful of perfectly formed knishes. "I'll show you how to make these ugly." She raised an arm and paused, cradling the dumplings in her fist. One by one she threw them against the wall. Bridget slid to the floor and hugged her knees.

"How can you ruin all my hard work?" said Grandmom. "Clean up this mess."

"The hell I will." Her mother picked up another handful, tossing knishes against the wall where they stuck briefly before hitting the floor. The filling oozed out.

"A curse on you and your business," said Grandmom, bending beneath the table, picking up the knishes. "Bridget, get a baking sheet from the cupboard."

Bridget forced herself to stand up.

"A curse from you is a compliment," shouted her mother, tossing another handful of knishes against the wall.

Bridget helped Grandmom pick up the mangled dumplings and set them on the baking sheet. She tried to press the lumpy mess back together.

Grandmom raised her hand and pointed a trembling finger at her mother. "Don't worry you No Goodnik," she shouted. "I'm baking these damned things and you're taking them home."

Grandmom slipped the tray into the oven. "Stupid daughter."

"Get our coats, Bridget," said her mother.

"No," said Bridget.

"You're not leaving until the knishes are done," said Grandmom, her voice cold.

"I've got to go to the bathroom," said Bridget.

"Then go," said her mother. "And don't stay in there for an hour."

"Six pink squares, six black squares," sang Bridget. She sat on the toilet seat holding her stomach, counting the porcelain tiles that surrounded the tub. "Big squares, little squares, Camay soap and a sponge. I'm not going out there until the knishes are done." She locked the door.

When she smelled the rich aroma of pastry and potatoes, she

cautiously opened the door. In the hall she brought down her wool coat and her mother's old cape.

When she reached the kitchen, Grandmom had removed a tray of half-baked knishes and was setting them on a sheet of foil, wrapping the packet closed. She dropped the bundle inside a shopping bag.

Her mother stood at the door, waiting for her coat.

"Please, Mom," said Bridget, staring at the floor. "Let's take the knishes with us."

Her mother leaned forward and straightened Bridget's collar. "For you, my darling, I'll take them."

Grandmom thrust the bag at her mother and frowned.

Her mother hesitated, then grabbed the handle.

"Remember, Sarah," said Grandmom. "Next time ease up on your rolling pin, and keep turning the dough. That's how you get perfect knishes."

Her mother rolled her eyes. "Thanks for the advice, Ma." She stiffened her shoulders and reached for Bridget's hand. "Come along," she said, as they walked down the steps into the cold air.

Chapter 7

"I'M BACK."

Bridget's eyes flew open as her mother unlocked the door of the truck and settled into the driver's seat. A strong smell of corned beef, peppercorn, bay leaf and garlic filled the space between them.

"You poor thing," said her mother. "You look so tired. We'll get the orange-flower water in a jiffy, and I'll drive you right home so you can soak your dress and eat your sandwich in peace. Corned beef for me and turkey for you, just like you asked."

Bridget bit her lip. "Could we sit here a few minutes and eat?"

"Gordon's waiting for us." Her mother gunned the engine. They turned down an alley beneath the highway.

"Mom," said Bridget. "Why didn't you ever make ugly knishes at the factory?"

"Too much labor, my darling. I couldn't turn a profit on them. And to think your grandmom and I almost killed each other over the recipe." She laughed.

"It wasn't funny."

"Have you ever seen a mother and daughter fight more than us?"

"I hated it."

"Don't dwell so much on the past. Grandmom and I always forgive and forget." Her mother stopped the truck in front of a red brick building before backing into a loading dock. "Mothers and daughters have bad days now and then. Grandmom and I had our share." She looked at Bridget. "Funny, I don't remember any with you." She swung open her car door and hurried up the warehouse steps.

Bridget got out of the car and followed her mother to the factory door. Her mother rang the bell below a polished brass plaque that read, "La Maison Foie Gras, Gourmet Purveyors to the Trade."

Gordon and her mother had known each other since high school.
He had owned the bakery where her mother had invented Ugly
Cookies. Four years ago, after Gordon's wife died, he and her
mother had grown closer.

The door opened. Gordon stepped out on the dock. He had a
pleasant round face, close-set brown eyes and steel gray hair held
back in a short ponytail at his neck. Multi-colored marking pens
bristled from his breast pocket. "Come in, Sarah, my Queen," he
said, and kissed her cheek. "Ah. Bridget. What a nice surprise. You
get more beautiful each time I see you."

Bridget smiled. The scent of rosemary, sage and mint enveloped
her as she stepped into Gordon's warehouse.

"Bridget had a terrible day," said her mother. "It's all gone
downhill since she broke up with her professor boyfriend."

Gordon winked at Bridget. He knew her mother as well as she
did.

"So you got the goods?" said her mother.

"Sure do, babe. Wait till you smell the orange flower water. It's
to die for. We also got a shipment of Madagascar cinnamon. I'll give
you a sample. It'll be heaven in your oatmeal raisin cookies."

Her mother beamed. "And maybe something to cheer up my
Bridget?"

"Anything for your beautiful daughter." Gordon ushered Bridget and her mother past shelves laden with tins of olive oil, jars of
vinegar, peppers, mushrooms. They angled their way through an
aisle where different lengths of sausages hung in neat rows. Bridget was fond of Gordon. She marveled that her mother had found
a truly nice man when she couldn't keep a single boyfriend.

"Now, I prescribe chocolate for your troubles," said Gordon.
"We've got fabulous chocolate chips from Belgium. Pricey, but
worth every penny. You'll take a pound home with you."

Less than an hour later, her mother pulled the truck in front of
Bridget's apartment. On her lap, Bridget cradled a gold foil-
wrapped box containing the chocolate chips.

"It's good we spent the evening together," said her mother.
"Dinner on the run's not so bad. You can think of me when you eat
your sandwich later. Remember when you were a kid? Grandmom

made dinner for you most nights. By the way, she's coming up next week for some routine heart tests."

"Why didn't she tell me? Is she all right?"

"She feels fine. It's a good excuse for her to visit us." Her mother reached into the deli bag, took out a sandwich for herself and handed the bag to Bridget. "So did you make up with David yet?"

Bridget gritted her teeth. "He's not the wonderful, lofty person you think he his."

"Oh, no? If you ask me, your generation is so picky, never satisfied. No wonder you're not getting married. At the rate you're all going, you'll be too old for babies."

"With guys like David, that's a good thing."

"Oh sure. He's only a Doctor Professor. But, what do I know? Instead of putting all your money into fixing up your apartment, you could have bought something wonderful with him."

"Speaking of which," said Bridget. "I should get going. I've got painters coming tomorrow morning before I leave for work."

"See what I mean," said her mother. "You could have saved yourself a couple hundred bucks right there."

Bridget stepped out of the truck. When she entered her apartment, she closed the door and leaned against the bulky frame. One day she'd stop going to her mother and setting herself up for disappointment. The woman would never change.

She was glad to be in her own place, glad that the painters were coming. Edward knew them from the University and had recommended them. It was time to make her place really special. Then, she'd invite Carson over.

She put the sandwich on the hall table and brushed at the coffee stain on her dress. The stain had dried hard as cardboard. She remembered her mother's advice about soaking the stain. Love came from Sarah in the form of nuts and bolts practicality.

In the bathroom, she slipped out of the dress, kicked off her shoes and reached under the sink for a bottle of pre-soak. She filled the sink with cold water and thought of Carson. If he saw how she and her mother communicated, it would scare the living daylights out of him.

Chapter 8

"GREAT APARTMENT," said Max, brushing the palm of his hand across his dark crew cut. "Nothing like working with real plaster. I hate plasterboard. Soaks up too much paint."

Bridget forced a smile. Only recently had she begun to appreciate the elegance of her apartment, its fine walls and leaded-glass casement windows now open to let in the breeze. She had hardly slept here when she was seeing David.

She pushed a strand of hair from her forehead, picked up a color-chip and held it up to the painters.

Larry, tall and lanky, adjusted his paint-spattered cap over a greasy blond ponytail and dipped his brush into the can. Paint the color of pale, raspberry cream stained the brush.

"Looks good," she said, remembering when Claire worked at the nursing home and had painted the reading room Chinese red.

Claire had insisted that older adults needed private areas for romance, and had lobbied for months to make the room something special.

At first, their boss, Andrew Jacobson, had vetoed it. Finally, after the residents signed a petition in favor of what they called their Cupid room, he relented. "Just one coat of paint," he said. "And make sure there's only conversation and music in there."

Bridget had passed the lounge one morning and skidded to a halt in front of a sign that read CUPID'S RETREAT.

"Hi Bridgie," Claire called from behind an old record player. "Listen to this." She set the needle on the record and turned on the machine. Strains of music filled the room, Pavarotti singing Pagliacci.

Claire had decorated the room with Rock Hudson and Doris Day posters. She had even managed to find old posters of Jane Fonda dressed as Barbarella and Burt Reynolds posing nude for Playboy. On the shelf where the Readers Digests once sat, she had set up an array of potions, Kama Sutra Love Oil, Peppermint Foot Oil, Intimate Encounters Spray, and edible Honey Dust Powder. It all seemed so long ago.

Bridget watched the boys apply the raspberry paint to the walls. The morning Andrew dismantled Cupid's Retreat, she had been away for a meeting. He had found a cache of sexy videos beneath the black velvet sofa and fired Claire on the spot.

"It's time for a new direction, anyway," Claire had said. Shortly after that, Claire joined the Peace Corps. Bridget remembered the last thing Claire told her before she left. "Watch yourself around Andrew. He likes to mess with your head."

Bridget and Andrew had been lovers. She had let him seduce her with his self-confidence and drive. At first, he neglected to tell her that he was married. When she found out, he tried to convince her that his wife was just as unhappy as he was. They planned to divorce soon. Bridget had serious doubts, but she couldn't untangle herself from Andrew and the attention he gave her. When he finally ended their affair, she almost quit, but Grandmom convinced her to stay.

"The man's a coward, but he did you a favor breaking it off," Grandmom had told her. "You do good work at the nursing home and those patients need you. It's terrible to mess around with a married man, but why should you throw your career away? He made you Director. Stay. He'll find himself another chippie soon enough. That kind always does. And someday when you meet your maker, you'll hold your head high and say, I didn't steal a husband and father."

A splash of paint fell to the floor.

She looked at Larry.

"Don't worry," he grinned, almost leering. "We know what we're doing." He stared at her as if he could see right through her dress.

"Hey, Larry," called Max from his perch across the room. "Stop flirting and get back to work."

"I'm taking good care of our customer," said Larry. His eyes swept brazenly over Bridget, making her cheeks burn.

She stepped back.

"Don't mind him, Miss," said Max, carefully brushing a thin layer of paint on the wall. "The joker thinks he's Casanova. He even hit on a nun once."

"Just watch the paint splatters," said Bridget. She headed into the kitchen in search of aspirin.

Why did men think that brazen flirting enticed women? She opened a drawer next to the sink, withdrew a bottle of aspirin and shook two tablets into her hand.

At the sink she filled her glass with water and swallowed the tablets. She wouldn't have minded hearing that kind of flattery from Carson.

She heard the painters' laughter and conversation in the living room and realized how much she missed the easy repartee of friends.

"This one's been our nicest customer so far this summer," Larry was saying.

"Yeah," said Max. "Remember that blonde we worked for on Delancey? What a nut case. Changing the color on us four times, then watching our every move."

"But, what a bod," said Larry.

"Is that all you ever think about?" said Max. "What about her jerky boyfriend telling us what to do every three minutes." He turned to Larry. "What a moron, making us call him Doctor Angsdorf."

Air thickened in Bridget's lungs.

"I'd know how to make that blonde happy," said Larry.

"She was way out of your league," said Max. "And that story about the doctor's ex-girlfriend breaking in and attacking them with a baseball bat while they were doing it."

"Wow," said Larry. "That scene must have been wild."

Bridget hurried into the living room. "Cut the conversation, please." The guys stood in the corner mixing paint. She reached for the ladder to steady herself. It swayed. The paint pan wobbled and tipped over the top rung. She screamed. A shower of pink liquid poured over her head. The pan clattered to the ground.

Larry stared at her, stifling a laugh. "You look like a raspberry ice cream cone." He leaned closer.

"Don't come near me." She pushed him out of her way.

"Sorry," he said. "It's only water-based paint, anyway." He backed up, lost his balance and landed on the empty pan. "Ouch!" "Just finish the job." She headed into the bathroom.

At the sink, she studied her image in the mirror. Paint laced through her hair, dripped over her face, tipping her lashes pink. If her knees weren't shaking so much she might laugh at herself.

From the living room, she heard the clank of cans and the painters whispering as they cleaned up the mess. She and David were definitely on a collision course.

*   *   *

Carson rested his forehead against the cool glass of his office window and gazed across the parkway. Late afternoon sunlight bathed the Art Museum's Greek Revival facade a delicate orange. Beyond the museum, he saw the Schuylkill River winding west. Cars hurtled along the highway.

Thirty minutes from now, he'd sit next to Bridget in a darkened theater watching a movie. He'd never talked to anyone about his innermost feelings, but something about her was different. Already, he felt he could trust her.

Since leaving Madison, he'd spent most of his idle moments thinking about what he had left behind. His mother's voice on the telephone hinted at sadness. No wonder. Her beloved husband was dead, her sons fighting, and her daughter was stuck holding up more than her fair share of the business. Lisa had promised him that all was going well, but how could he be sure when he'd let them all down?

Meeting Bridget had diminished the pain of leaving home. Nothing white bread about her. He didn't want to screw this up. They had just started to make a real connection when her weird ex and that coffee nut interrupted them.

*   *   *

"Great movie," said Bridget. "Are you ready to run off to Greece with me?" She pulled Carson to a stop beneath a street lamp, lifted her arms and snapped her fingers.

"Sure, Zorba," he laughed. "But I'm tied into the bank for at least a year." Her offer was tempting. While they sat in the theater, her head resting against his shoulder, he had imagined them boarding a ferry for an island, a breeze lifting her hair, sun-brightened strands brushing his face as they headed into open sea. That had been his mother's dream, only she'd never had a chance to share it with his father.

Bridget slipped her arm through his. "Life in the village was hard for women. Zorba and his boss had all the freedom in the world, but the women were punished for asserting themselves. It ticked me off."

He savored the huskiness of her voice, the furrow in her brow, the warmth of her skin. "It exists here, don't you think? I've seen chauvinism against my sister in the family business, people second-guessing her opinions. I see it at the bank, too. We demand that men and women excel, but sometimes when women get assertive, we accuse them of growing . . ." He stopped.

"Balls?" she smiled ironically. "Which we don't need, thank you."

He pulled her close. "What can I say? Men are jerks. But I'd still run off to a Greek island with you."

She relaxed against his shoulder. He seemed to appreciate women, but would he be so generous when she told him about David? She didn't want to blow the Greek island fantasy just yet. For once, she'd heed her mother's advice and keep her mouth shut.

They turned the corner. She sighed.

Carson drew her closer. He glimpsed a softness in her demeanor that he hadn't seen before. He thought of Anne, how he'd been seeking gentleness in their relationship. He'd been a coward the way he pushed Anne to break off with him. Truth was, he'd abandoned her. What would Bridget think if she knew?

He toyed with a lock of her hair. "Maybe we could try cooperative housing in Greece."

"I'm amazed you remembered."

"Why? Because I'm an insensitive macho pig?"

She poked his ribs with her elbow. They headed up Spruce Street and stopped in front of her brownstone. Although she wanted to invite him upstairs for coffee, the place smelled like a paint factory. She found a tissue in her pocket, and brushed the city dust from the faded marble step before they sat down.

He touched her knee, caught a whiff of scent, floral mixed with her own fresh essence. "Tell me more about your idea."

She studied his clear blue eyes and open face. "I want to find a building, gather a group of mainly older folks, pool our resources and form a household."

"Sounds like the sixties when communes were in vogue. A lot of them failed."

She measured her words carefully. "That's not what we're trying to do. Claire and I have tossed the idea around for years. We've seen elderly people deteriorate because they feel out of touch with the world. If older folks are mobile and have their senses, they flourish in a community of mixed ages. We can trade responsibilities, provide daycare for working mothers. Things like that.

"Aren't older people better off in retirement complexes?"

"Not always. In a cooperative home, everyone would have a voice and stay productive."

He wondered if she'd given serious consideration to the bottom line. "What about the financing?" he asked cautiously.

"That could be a problem. I've done a lot of research. The big piece is finding a building in a suitable location."

"Don't forget renovation. I've seen those costs demolish the best plans."

"Yeah. That's a biggie, especially with ramps and special bathrooms."

"See what I mean. The bucks add up real fast."

"No kidding," she said abruptly. "But, there's the non-profit route, too."

He touched her shoulder. "Sorry to show my practical side, but I work with numbers for a living."

"I'll figure something out." She lifted her hand, touched his palm, pressing fingertip to fingertip.

He held her fingers tight, saw passion in her eyes. "You've set yourself quite a goal, but I think you just might do it. And since we can't steal away on that Greek ferry yet, how about having coffee at Java High tomorrow night?"

She smiled. This was too good to be true, although David was a problem. There wasn't much she could do about it, unless she chose to remain a hermit. "Coffee sounds great."

She drew close to him. He cupped her chin in his hand, kissed her lips, lighting up every nerve in her body. Gently, he broke away. "See you tomorrow night." He hummed a Greek melody as he walked down the street. She lingered, breathing in the sweet evening air long after he had turned the corner.

Chapter 9

CARSON SAT AT HIS DESK and waited for his new trainee. He welcomed this break from a day crammed with meetings. It gave him time to switch gears and think about Bridget. She was unusual, different from the other women he had known. Her ideas about the cooperative housing were a bit idealistic, but they were clever. He had got what he asked for in his ad, but a few doubts had crept into his euphoria. Bridget was definitely a free spirit. Had he asked for more than he could handle? He worried about her ex, too. He seemed to enjoy watching the Coffee Bandit ruin their date. Was she really over him? If so, what had she seen in him in the first place? What did it say about her?

He heard a knock at the door and surveyed the office. Everything in order. Earlier, anticipating this meeting, he had cleaned his desk with polish he kept in the drawer, and dusted off the pair of navy blue wing-backed chairs that faced him.

His boss walked in, followed by a short young man with dark curly hair. Carson pegged the guy at around thirty. He wore a baggy, creased suit. From a distance, it could have been muddy brown or washed-out navy blue.

The kid looked like a wet rag. Either he was in the wrong place or had never heard about dressing for success.

"Here's the new trainee I told you about," said his boss. "Meet Mark Appleby."

Mark walked toward him, hand extended, an apprehensive smile flickering over his face. "I've heard a lot about you, sir. In the short time you've been here, you've made a hit in this company. I'm excited to learn the ins and outs of investment banking from you."

Carson shook Mark's hand and tried to discern sincerity in his face. He seemed pathetic.

"They tell me you're a computer whiz," said Carson. "Just what we need. We work very hard in this department. Long hours are the norm."

"Yes sir." Mark nodded. Carson's boss sat on the edge of the desk, signaling Mark to take a seat. Carson watched Mark scratch the stubble on his chin as he sat down.

"I'm expecting you to harness Mark's abilities," said his boss. "They're considerable. He's a raw talent."

Carson nearly groaned and glared at his boss. "Excuse me," he said. "May I speak with you?"

His boss nodded and followed him into the hall.

Carson tried to keep his voice calm, but it rose with each word. "What do you mean raw talent? I expected a fully trained assistant. I don't have time to baby-sit an unprofessional genius."

His boss shifted his weight from one leg to the other. "Don't get upset. He's part of the Welfare-to-Work program we've instituted. We bring Mark off the dole and the bank gets a tax credit. It's a win-win situation and you're the most, shall I say, compassionate of our young executives. I believe you can turn Appleby around."

The idea appealed to Carson in theory, but he didn't know how he could do his job and train someone who needed so much supervision. He imagined his brother Jack calling him a wimp. His voice took on an edge. "I appreciate the company's efforts, but I don't think I'm the person to do it."

His boss looked him straight in the eye. "I realize you're the most overworked person in the department right now. If you refuse, I'll understand."

Carson agonized. If he were in Mark's position, he'd want someone to give him a chance. "All right," he said. "I'll train him, but I need more secretarial help."

His boss clapped him on the shoulder. "That's the spirit. I'll see what I can do."

They walked back into the office. Mark sat slumped in his chair, scratching his scalp through unruly curls. Carson doubted he would make the cut.

Mark looked at him.

"So you're a genius run amok," said Carson.

His boss laughed. "Mark's a math whiz, but he's weak in organizational skills. That's where you come in. I'm sure you can shape up this bright fellow in no time."

"I'd appreciate the help, sir." Mark straightened his back.

"Be here tomorrow, eight a.m. sharp," said Carson. "We'll work out your schedule then."

"I love hard work, Mr. McAlister."

Carson squinted at Mark, almost expecting him to salute. "Just call me Carson."

"Here's Mark's file," said Carson's boss, handing him a thick dossier. "Read this and call me if you have any questions." He smiled tersely. "Okay Appleby. Let's go and finish your paperwork."

Mark rose and brushed the wrinkles at the knees of his suit. "See you tomorrow, Mr. McAlister," he said, before following Carson's boss out the door.

Carson opened the dossier and began reading. The kid had taken six government-sponsored training courses, but his work record was practically non-existent. There were a few odd jobs with bad progress ratings showing him as tardy and indifferent.

He flipped to the back of the file. On it was a one-page document. Mark's family had been on and off welfare since he was born. Mark had continued the trend after high school even though he had managed to finish a year of college on scholarship where he ended up on the dean's list before quitting.

Employees like Mark were expected to give the bank a two-year work commitment as well as attend college courses at night. Carson would give Mark a chance, but banking required more discipline than Mark had shown.

* * *

It didn't surprise Bridget to see David at Java High. He sat at the coffee bar, sipping a cappuccino, his eyes honing in on her.

She strode toward him, her knees shaking. Country-western music blared through the cafe. When she reached the counter, Edward made a face behind David's head and mouthed the words, "Athhole."

She held back a smile.

"You look like you've seen a ghost," said David. "Don't worry. I'm not here to harass you. We have something to discuss."

"We're supposed to stay apart, remember? You set the rules. So why are you here?"

He carefully pressed cappuccino foam against the side of his cup. "Did you tell your new boyfriend what happened in my apartment?"

"He's not my boyfriend and what I tell him is my business."

"Well, you'd better tell your mother."

"What are you talking about?"

"She called the other day pretending we never broke up. She said that your Grandmom was coming to town and invited me to dinner. I told her you'd explain why I can't make it."

Suddenly, David's sweet cologne made her nauseous.

"I haven't told her because she can't handle things like that." She pictured her mother's face contorting like an ugly cookie when she heard the news.

David sipped his coffee thoughtfully. "If you don't tell her soon, I'll have to. And by the way, you'd better tell your boss." He smiled cynically. "Remember? The married guy you had no trouble hopping into the sack with? Or maybe I should call him myself."

"Do whatever you want. I can't stop you." She longed to dump the rest of his coffee on David's head, send foam cascading down the front of his shirt. She saw the front door open. Carson walked in. She searched the tables, stacks, computer room until her eyes lit on the stairs to the basement reading room.

"I want you to leave me alone," she said. "Follow me and I swear I'll kill you."

"Threats like that can land you in a lot of trouble."

"I don't care." She caught Carson's attention and pointed toward the stairs.

"Just remember to call your mother."

When she reached the stairs, she saw Carson massaging his temples.

"Are you all right?" she said.

"I'm fine. Work got a bit complicated this afternoon." He smiled and raked his hand through his hair. "But I'm glad to see you."

She set her hand on the staircase's carved wooden banister. "I wanted to show you Java High's archives. Come on."

Carson followed her down the steps. "Isn't that your ex at the coffee counter?"

"Just ignore him."

They reached the bottom of the steps. Burled walnut bookshelves covered the walls. Three oriental carpets lay on the wood floor. Along the perimeter, small oak tables, each topped with a tall green glass-shaded lamp, waited for someone to sit in quiet contemplation or read. In the center stood a glass case filled with drawings.

"It's like a museum," she said. "The owner deals in rare books. He bought all the furniture at an estate sale. He even has his own curator." She led Carson to the glass case; her ears attuned to the din upstairs. A set of drawings were displayed in gold frames.

Carson read from a pewter plaque: "'On March 4, 1681, as payment for a debt of 16,000 pounds owed to his father, King Charles II of England granted William Penn a tract of land encompassing the states of Delaware and Pennsylvania.' That's better than winning the lottery."

She heard David's voice at the top of the stairs and flinched. What a horrible mistake, trapping herself in this dusty room.

Carson stepped back. "You look more jittery than I feel."

"I'm okay." She tugged at his arm. "There's something else I want to show you."

Startled, he let her pull him toward a dark corner where a print hung on the wall. He leaned his nose within an inch of the glass. "It's so dark here."

She scanned the room, picked up a heavy brass lamp from a nearby table, and struggled to point it toward the prints.

"Do you need help with that lamp?"

She staggered. "I'm stronger than I look. Here's Elfreth's Alley, it's the oldest residential street in the United States."

He seemed puzzled for a moment before returning to the print.

"Isn't it great down here?" she said, setting the lamp on the table with a thud. "Dry as a bone. They have a state-of-the-art dehumidifier. Want to see it?"

Carson put his arm around her shoulder. "Are you the Java High Building Inspector? Come on, let me buy you a cup of coffee." Gently, she pulled away and tried to listen for David's voice. She heard a low buzz upstairs, cups clinking against china plates. This was ridiculous. They couldn't stay down here all night.

*　*　*

When they reached the top of the stairs, she searched for David. He was gone. She took Carson's hand.

His firm grasp steadied her, gave her a surge of confidence. They found a table near the window. She set her handbag down and sighed with relief.

"What can I get you?" said Carson.

"I'd love a piece of baklava and a double de-caf latte."

He stood and straightened the creases in his pants. She was odd, but endearing. And really sexy in that long, clingy black skirt. "I'll be right back," he said.

On his way to the counter, he passed tables filled with trendy-looking people reading serious books, writing in journals, working on laptops. He liked the spirit of camaraderie.

At the counter, a young man wearing a wispy goatee and dread-locks grinned at him. Gold hoops hung from each nostril as well as his ears and eyebrows. A row of nine earrings hung from his lower lip.

Ouch, thought Carson.

"What can I get you, thir?"

Carson couldn't pull his eyes away. The kid also had four thick, gold studs piercing his tongue.

"I'll have a double de caf-latte. On second thought. Make it . . . No, never mind." What had Bridget ordered? He turned and saw her looking furtively around the room. The ex again, no doubt. What was going on with them?

"I'll have a double de-caf latte."

"Two double de-caf latteth?"

"No, not two. One double de-caf latte, a cup of regular coffee and a, a . . . something that starts with a b?"

Carson pointed toward Bridget. "She orders it."

"Yeth thir. Baked apple covered in puff pathtry. She loveth that."

"Perfect. I'll take one of those, a double de-caf latte and a cup of coffee."

"What kind of coffee, thir?"

"I said one de-caf and one regular!" He had thought this would be a great night, but his nerves were getting frazzled.

* * *

Bridget watched Carson thread his way back to their table. So far he was hanging in with her, but she wondered for how much longer.

He set the tray on the table and sat down. "I don't think this is what you wanted, but the kid with the studs in his tongue said you loved baked apples."

In the coffee bar, Edward pretended to wipe out glasses. Bridget smiled. "Edward means well, but he likes to confuse new people. I forgot to warn you." She pressed her fork through the pastry into the apple. It was tart and sweet and delicious.

"I should have ordered Sarah's Ugly Cookies," said Carson. "They look like someone sat on them, but they taste great."

She felt exposed hearing her mother's name. "Sarah is my mother. She's the Ugly Cookie lady."

"Your mother? I thought the woman on the cookie package was Amish."

"The ad agency did that deliberately. They said she looked too Jewish so they made her wear a bonnet. I think it's insulting myself."

"Sounds like your mom likes to win the marketing game. My dad was into that kind of thing." He paused. "Is this the family business?"

"Kind of. My father passed away five years ago. My mother founded the company, but Dad was her chief trouble-shooter."

Images of his own father flooded Carson's mind. "I'm sorry about your dad," he said softly. "My dad died, too. He had a heart attack a year ago. It was a real loss for my mother. They had a wonderful relationship."

He remembered his father cuffing his cheek out on the patio by the old red Weber kettle grill, remembered the complaints about indigestion after his father ate one too many hamburgers.

He tried to maintain his composure, force a smile. "It's been a little longer for you. How have you come to terms with it?"

His eyes echoed the sadness she felt at the mention of her father's death. Carson was seeking direction and she wanted to give it to him. But she had come to acceptance through her own weird channels choosing to remember the best thing her father gave her, the gift of humor.

"I handled my father's death very differently than my mother. She's the drama queen." She remembered her mother standing at the pulpit of the synagogue wailing as she read pages of notes giving the history of her father's family all the way back to the shtetl in Russia. When they lowered the coffin into the ground, her mother handed out dice to all the mourners to toss onto the casket instead of the customary handful of dirt.

"I've lost you," he said.

"Sorry." She folded her hands on the table. "I sometimes dream about my dad. He comes to me, ready to tell another joke." She took a deep breath. "My dad died at the gaming tables. Someone lost a lot of money on his lousy throw of the dice and shot him. His friends assured me that Dad would have thought of it as a just end. He loved Atlantic City. They even had a gambling theme at the funeral, grouping flowers in lucky combinations. The casino where he died comped the funeral luncheon. Dad would have howled over it. He bragged about every comp he ever got."

There were so many stories she could tell him. If he stuck it out through half of them, he deserved the Purple Heart.

Carson shook his head. "You're not going to believe this, but our fathers may have had some things in common."

"Like what?"

Suddenly, he regretted mentioning his father. How could he describe him and not present the wrong image? He stirred his spoon into his coffee creating a whirlpool.

"It sounds like they both lived on the edge. My father gambled on a few ventures before Mother gave him the start-up money for a business that turned into a chain of electronics stores." He shifted in his chair. "Dad tried a few other things, too. They didn't really work out."

She saw his uneasiness. It struck her that when people first learned about each other, they became extra cautious, tap-dancing around sentences, sensing the other's response, finally leaping into the fray. Each time they leapt, they sought solid ground, trying to establish links. If not, they went their separate ways. She yearned for the link.

Carson rubbed his temples. He sensed that they were entering a new place. "Dad started out as a photographer."

"An artist?"

"In a way. He specialized in filming, umm, funerals."

Bridget thought it sounded a little creepy, but who was she to judge?

"He got this idea that people wanted to memorialize the end. He even took artful shots of dead people in their coffins just like the Victorians."

She pictured Carson's father in a somber gray suit, filming her dad's wacky funeral. "Maybe we should team-up up when we retire and do theme funerals. I know a florist who can make flower arrangements in the shape of dollar bills."

Two mock creases appeared between his eyebrows. "It's not funny. I was very close to my father." He saw her stiffen, but he couldn't help laughing. It was all so ridiculous. He took her hand, held it tight. "When my dad filmed those funerals, some crazy stuff happened."

He curled his finger around hers. "Until now, I forgot that Dad sometimes joked about it. I hope we can laugh at the other skeletons in our closets." He dreaded talking about Anne. There was nothing funny in that story.

The pressure of Carson's fingers reassured her. He wasn't as perfect as she'd first imagined. Maybe he would keep his sense of humor when she told him about David. Right.

"On that cheery note," he said. "I've thought about your project. This morning, I asked someone at the bank to look into community loans and related stuff."

"That's sweet." She saw Edward pointing to the computer chat room. David sat at the first terminal watching her.

She withdrew her hand. "Let's take a walk. There's something else I want to tell you."

* * *

At river's edge, a pair of ducks slid by breaking the pattern of fading sunlight reflected on the water's surface.

Carson rested his arm on Bridget's shoulder, his face expectant. His cheeks were flushed, his hair damp from their long walk through the warm evening air. She saw the river's movement flickering in his eyes. The wind had died down, locking heat in the air, creating a dense space in which to pour her words.

She led him to an isolated bank shaded by maple trees and settled herself against a tree trunk. Through the soft cotton fabric of her blouse she felt the rough bark.

Carson sat down beside her, stretched out his legs and lay his head in her lap. She ran her hand through his damp hair. He closed his eyes and smiled. "What did you want to talk about?"

"It can wait."

He stroked the tender skin of her throat and brought her face to his. "Tell me," he said, brushing her lips.

She sifted strands of his hair through her fingers and looked away. If she didn't tell him now, David would. "It's about my ex," she said. "When he asked me to move out of his apartment, I made a spare key." Her words tumbled out, each faster than the next. "I couldn't believe the relationship was over so one night I used the key to get back in." She saw the muscles in Carson's jaw twitch.

A slight breeze wafted off the river. Carson thought of Anne. After their breakup, she had made no attempt to contact him except to Fed-ex the engagement ring to his office. He hated that cold cut-off, but he had deserved it.

Bridget smelled a faint odor of algae drifting from the river's edge. Her voice faltered. "I wanted to make things right in the worst way. I was so sure if we talked, we'd work things out. From what I could see, he wasn't involved with anyone else. I stupidly thought he was pining for me."

She saw that Carson's eyes had turned blue-gray in the gathering dusk. He sat perfectly still. "You don't have to do this," he said.

"Yes I do." She spoke quickly, hoping to gloss over the worst parts before Carson got up and bolted.

"When David came home with his new girlfriend, I, unfortunately, was trapped in his loft. I stayed perfectly still through dinner trying to plan my escape. The next thing I knew, they were making love on the sofa. I tried not to look, but the whole thing seemed so far away, like I was watching strangers in a movie."

He shifted his weight to see her better. She seemed so agitated that he lay his hand over her arm, offering his assurance.

She cleared her throat and continued. "I meant to get out of there, but when I found he'd plagiarized my work, I lost my cool. I tossed his manuscript and a reference book over the railing. I didn't aim to hit them. Next thing, all hell broke loose. No question I'd done something illegal. It was humiliating."

She gazed at the river. "We ended up confronting each other, me in my underwear, he in his birthday suit." She heard a chortle and looked down. Carson was smiling.

The story was funny all right, and the way Bridget told it made him laugh, but Carson still asked himself whether it had been a one-shot moment of insanity or part of her personality. What if they broke up? Would she follow and harass him? Yet, it struck a cord. He'd inflicted deliberate hurt on Anne. At least Bridget had meant no harm.

And she looked so forlorn, twisting a lock of hair around her fingertip as she described the aftermath. He sat up and hugged her.

She lay her cheek against the starched cloth of his shirt. "Why aren't you running away? Doesn't it bother you?"

"I've walked into bad situations myself thinking the outcome would be different." He pressed his lips to her earlobe, caught a whiff of sweet apple on her breath.

A current ran up her spine. Finally, an enlightened man.

He stroked the nape of her neck. "I imagine it could be exciting watching your ex make love to another woman. My dad could have started a whole new business."

She laughed and kissed his shoulder. "It's funny only in retrospect, especially seeing their hysterical gyrations, like two worms on a hot pavement."

Gently pulling away, she looked at him, saw amusement in his face. "I might as well tell you all my secrets. I once dated a married man who still happens to be my boss. It was your garden-variety affair: naive woman meets unhappily married man who doesn't tell her he's married until she's fallen in love with him. The last thing I wanted to do was break up someone's marriage."

He found it hard to imagine her stuck in those situations. It was a lot to absorb, but she looked so helpless. "Let's put this away for now." He eased her onto the grass kissing her softly.

She opened her mouth, tasted coffee and mint on his tongue. Soft stubble on his chin tickled her cheek. She grasped the back of his neck, felt her body respond to his.

Suddenly, from the corner of her eye she saw someone standing behind a tree. David. She flipped Carson over and sat up.

* * *

Carson flicked on the light in the foyer of his apartment, dropped his keys on the side-table and headed for the kitchen. He desperately needed a beer.

Had Bridget's ex followed them? She'd become visibly upset, asking him to search the woods for the ex. All he saw was a squirrel climbing a tree. Either her ex was extremely slick or she was paranoid.

He opened the refrigerator, grabbed a beer, flipped off the cap and tipped the bottle to his lips. The cold, bitter liquid soothed his throat. Bridget excited him, but he worried about her judgment. He believed that her intentions were good when she broke into her ex's apartment. But why hadn't she pegged her ex for the egomaniac he obviously was? The guy didn't have to hit her with a restraining order. Besides, if he had any compassion, he would have dropped it by now.

In the living room, he flopped on his new beige leather sofa. Already, he was in deep lust for her, but he didn't know if he could handle a triangle. Her ex held all the cards and wasn't about to leave her alone.

Across the room sat two tall boxes holding planks of teak waiting to be assembled into bookshelves. Once he got the place in order, he'd make it into a romantic hideaway. Trouble was, if he invited Bridget over he'd have to case the building to make sure her ex wasn't hiding in the utility closet.

In spite of everything, he couldn't wait to see her again. It wasn't simply to get her in bed although kissing her was like being drawn into the eye of a hurricane.

The phone rang. Bridget. He sprinted to his desk and snatched up the receiver.

It was his mother. She seemed cheerful enough, filling him in on the local gossip, telling him who won the latest golf tournament at the club, who drank too many martinis and flirted with the wrong wife or husband. He glanced at a silver framed photograph hanging on the wall taken on his parents' twenty-fifth wedding anniversary.

He remembered the party held on an Autumn afternoon on the back lawn of his parents' house. Couples danced to the music of a big band. Champagne corks popped. His mother and father presided over it all, smiling radiantly as they cut the anniversary cake.

How's Dad? he almost said, and caught himself. "How are things with Jack and Lisa?" He tried to make his voice sound light and carefree, but his mother's voice took on a different weight.

"They're still battling."

His heart sank. His mother confirmed what Lisa had tried to keep from him.

"It's affecting Sally and the children. Jack brings all the stress home."

"I don't know why Jack ever got married. The business has always been his real wife. He should chill and spend time at home with Sally and the kids."

"I've tried to tell him, but neither of you are good at listening to advice. You're stubborn mules, just like your father."

Anger had crept into his mother's voice since she returned from Greece. Why grow angry with Dad now that he wasn't around to defend himself?

He lifted his feet and set them on the desk. "The difference between Jack and me is that Jack spends all his waking hours with the business and I'm trying to have a personal life." He sighed.

"You'll have a chance to talk with him next week. He's coming east on business and arranged his flight so he would have a layover in Philadelphia. He wants to see you."

"I'm not sure I'm ready."

"I'm asking you to meet him as a favor to me."

Carson drummed his fingers on the desk. "Fine. Tell him to get me the details."

"I also need you to do something else for me. I've called a family meeting in August. I want you to come home for it."

"I don't want to talk about dividing up your estate, again. Splitting it three ways is fine. It's Jack who has a problem."

"This concerns all of us. And we'll talk about it when you get here."

"What's this about?"

"It's not terrible. But we need to be together."

"Okay." He closed his eyes. "Oddly enough, I was thinking about Dad today and the time I went with him to film a funeral."

"Don't remind me of that foolishness. Sometimes, your dad did the dumbest things."

"It's kind of funny when you think about it."

"Only in hindsight."

"My brother never thought it was funny."

"Stop it. Your brother was only twelve. Of course he told on you. Your dad shouldn't have tried to keep it a secret."

Carson picked up a pen. Dropped it. Picked it up again. "Dad took failure hard. I wish we had talked more about it. Maybe he would have been a little less driven."

"Wishful thinking. No one could stop him from proving himself."

"I miss him."

Catherine sighed. "So do I."

He smiled, remembering his father's hearty voice, the way his mother's face lit up when she saw his burly frame walk through the front door.

"Carson, are you there?"

"It's been a rough day."

Chapter 10

BRIDGET PUSHED THE third quarter budget aside, folded her arms on her desk and rested her head in the crook of her elbow. Andrew had ordered her to do the impossible, shave the operating budget by another five percent. That meant more starch at meals and, due to rising insurance costs, a cut in the extra-curricular activities she had organized. Hopefully, she'd find a way to keep the Befriend-A-Pet program going with the local Humane Society. The line item that accounted for the handler's fee was very small.

She refused to let disappointment get the best of her, but she had to find low-cost replacement activities. Without productive days, the residents faced boredom, which led to depression. Even doctors sometimes misdiagnosed depression in the elderly, calling it normal aging. But she knew better. Lack of mental stimulation became a self-fulfilling prophecy leading from depression to illness and senility.

Until now, she had kept the budget in bounds by maintaining low staff turnover and avoiding an overrun in the cost of temporary help. Survival of the nursing home depended on the loyalty of employees. But, she couldn't blame the aides when they left for better paying jobs.

She worried about the Grandparent Program, too. Her grant would run out in the Fall. Two years ago, she had met with the principal of the local elementary school and won the approval of the parents to bus a select number of children to the home for afternoon activities with the residents. The grant had allowed for transportation and an aide to travel with the children to and from school.

She had cajoled Andrew into accepting the extra cost of serving the children supper with the residents. He had agreed when she told him that the residents showed a decline in physical symptoms after bonding with the children.

The nursing home buzzed the day the children came. The residents chose stories and games, their faces flushed with anticipation. Losing the program would be a crushing blow to their morale. Andrew liked the program, but he liked the bottom line more and had refused to pick up the annual five thousand dollar bill when the grant ran out.

In the corner of her desk, beneath her in-basket, lay her cooperative housing journal. She withdrew it and opened it to a fresh sheet of lined paper. Despite David's put-downs, his theft of her idea proved its validity.

She picked up a pen and began making notes.

—*Mixed generations. Yes.*
—*Moderate physical challenges. Yes.*
—*A percentage of people with low incomes to exchange chores for rent.*
—*Small salary for Claire and me. Duties will include day-to-day management, trouble-shooting, accounting and ordering of supplies.*
—*Everyone will have a private room, but share baths. We'll have a common sitting room/living room, dining room and kitchen.*
—*A cooperative board chosen to make major decisions.*

She tapped the pen against her cheek. In the grand scheme, her vision would be nothing without Claire.

She made a set of parentheses. Inside, she wrote, Fantasy or Reality? And underlined Reality.

Before she went too far with her dreamy tangent, something more important loomed before her. This morning, she'd called Andrew and had set up a meeting for five o'clock. She'd decided to tell him about David and the restraining order. He was number two on her list. The hardest would be number three, her mother.

Andrew didn't need much incentive to fire her. She'd already defied one too many cost-cutting directives. This would only add fuel to the fire.

A noise at the door startled her. Edna stood on the threshold, her wizened face looking apologetic. She tottered across the room.

"Sorry to bother you, but a young lady's in the waiting room. She wants to see you." Edna leaned across Bridget's desk and whispered, "I remember her. She's the one who made Cupid's Retreat." Edna tried to swivel her hips.

Bridget stood up. "You mean Claire? She's not due back from Columbia until September."

She heard familiar voices in the hall.

"Miss Claire. Do you recommend any new exercises to get old pelvises into action again? Mine's a little creaky."

"I'll send you a diagram, Al. I'm banned from visiting rooms. Remember?"

Claire burst into the office, huarache sandals slapping the thin rug. "I'm home, Bridgie, she called. "And still in one piece." She wore a straw, Spanish-style cowboy hat, a white peasant blouse, and a purple hand-woven sash through the waist of her khaki shorts. Her caramel-colored skin had tanned to a milk-chocolate brown.

Four inches shorter and twenty pounds heavier than Bridget, Claire threw chunky arms over Bridget's shoulders in an affectionate bear hug. "You don't know how much I missed you." Her voice carried a weariness Bridget hadn't heard before.

Bridget pressed her cheek against Claire's herbal-scented hair before releasing her. "It's great to see you, but why so early? Are you in some kind of trouble?"

She remembered a hint of concern in Bev's voice when they last spoke on the telephone. "Claire says she's busier than ever down there, but it's impossible to get through on the phone and she doesn't always get my letters." Bridget knew that Bev missed Claire terribly. She envied their close relationship, often wishing that Bev was her own mother. "Claire and I have each other," Bev used to say. "And that's more than most people."

Bev and Claire even talked in a comfortable jargon, finishing each other's sentences in a way that Bridget wouldn't dare try with Sarah. And Bev's voice always carried a tenderness for Claire, no matter how much hot water Claire got into.

"It was tough getting mail to you," said Bridget.

Dark circles ringed Claire's large, brown eyes. "That's an understatement. Everything's unreliable there."

"Does your father know about this?"

Claire settled on the carpet, pulled her legs to her chest and rested her head on her knees. "I called him. He asked me to come down to Atlanta and stay with him for awhile. I'm not going. His proper wife doesn't like to be reminded about his bastard daughter."

"What went on in Columbia?"

"I mouthed off to the wrong people. Luckily, Boon-Dan-Tan, my spiritual guru, set me up with a medicine woman he met years ago. Madre Catarina saved my life, but the Peace Corps booted me out."

Bridget twisted a lock of hair. "Couldn't the Peace Corps transfer you instead of kicking you out?"

"I messed up pretty good. Training in Columbia was tougher than I expected. They assigned me to help a group of villagers replant farmland that had been used to grow cocaine. That and my big mouth almost got me killed."

Claire's eyes grew dreamy as she described the mountain peaks wreathed in wisps of cloud; the villagers in their worn, brightly colored clothes. Bridget had heard many stories like this about Claire's work in India, but Claire had never risked her life before.

Claire spoke with affection about her assigned village in Columbia. Once vibrant, it had become a gathering of aging huts. Yet the people were friendly. Women and men labored side by side in the fields, showing her how to use simple handmade tools. Soon, corn, beans and squash sprouted from the dark soil.

At night, the villagers played haunting melodies on flutes. Beat rhythms on drums. She taught them protest songs by Phil Ochs, Woody Guthrie and Pete Seeger, songs her mother sang to her when she was little.

One day, a renegade band of soldiers approached the village claiming to be part of a peacekeeping force, but the villagers knew better. "Cocaine," they whispered.

A week later, the soldiers began "borrowing" land for "military purposes." When Claire's frustration erupted into anger, she organized a meeting in an abandoned shack.

The night of the meeting, Carlos, one of the villagers, gripped her shoulders with his gnarled fingers. "Be careful," he said.

Two days later, a group of soldiers hauled her away, dragging her into the hills. She thought of her mother and father, of Catarina the medicine woman with the long braid down her back and skin that smelled of wood smoke. She thought of Boon-Dan-Tan who had blessed her before she left. And she thought of her stupidity. Putting herself and the villagers in danger wasn't the way to change the world.

Three men locked her in a hot dingy shed, fed her cornmeal mush and left her alone. She vowed to change her life if she survived. She'd return to Philadelphia and work with Bridget and Boon-Dan-Tan.

The following morning a man opened the door. His hair was matted to his head, his clothes smelled like horse manure.

"I ven aqui, carino!" He stumbled into the room, his breath stinking of tequila. He was so drunk he could barely stand.

He lumbered toward her, backed her into a corner and knocked her to the ground. They fell to the floor and rolled across the dirt. "Te quierro, hermosa," he whispered.

"Madre Catarina, help me," she prayed. The pit of her stomach filled with white-hot anger.

Suddenly, the man pressed a gun against her ribs. In a drunken stupor, he dropped it when he tried to unbutton her blouse.

She rolled away and grabbed it, the trigger cold in her hand. Trembling, she aimed at his shoulder, wondering if she'd have the guts to use it. When he lunged at her, all doubt evaporated and she pulled the trigger.

The bullet glanced off his shoulder making a deep gash. "Putana," he cried.

She wanted to laugh. "If you don't get help soon," she shouted. "You might bleed to death."

"No Doctore." He struggled to undo his belt buckle. "Si, te quierro."

She lifted the butt of the pistol, gathered her strength and slammed the handle on his head. He howled with pain, but the blow stunned him, giving her time to get out and run.

All night she followed voices in her head, villagers singing, chanting. The next morning, she found Madre Catarina who fed, bathed her, hid her beneath a sack of wool when the soldiers came. "This is not the place for you, my child," Catarina said. "Go to Boon-Dan-Tan. Your path is with him."

Through her connections, Catarina arranged for a jeep to pick Claire up and deliver her to U.S. headquarters. Two days later, by mutual consent Claire was dismissed and sent home.

Chapter 11

CLAIRE PLAYED WITH the cuff of her shorts.

"Are you really okay?" said Bridget, her breath tight in her throat."

"It's over, Bridgie," said Claire. "I learned a big lesson. I can't save the world by myself, but Boon-Dan-Tan and I agreed that it's time to shift my karma. I want to focus on things closer to home so he invited me to move into the Divine Guidance Center."

"Maybe I'll join you. By tomorrow I may not have a job."

Claire looked puzzled. "What's shaking?"

"Did you get my letter telling you what happened in David's apartment?"

"One of the few. What a mess."

"David's' been hounding me ever since, trying to sabotage my life. He's threatened to call Andrew."

"Andrew can't survive without you."

"Not necessarily. He's changed and I've ignored a few of his budget cuts. Plus, I have a criminal record so he has grounds to fire me."

"And I thought it was bad in Columbia."

"It gets worse. David might go ahead with his own plan for cooperative housing. Since he started writing that damned book, he's declared himself an authority. Worse, he follows me everywhere."

"Can you go to the police?"

"No. I'm the predator. He's the victim. All he has to say is that I'm stalking him and I go to jail. He's gone crazy since he saw me with this new guy I recently met."

"Does the new guy know the story?"

"I told him everything." Bridget felt her lips curve into a smile. "As a matter of fact, he kind of got turned on by it."

"You pick the weirdest boyfriends. One's about to fire you. One tortures you, and the new one gets turned on by learning that his girlfriend is a pervert."

"I'm beginning to wonder about myself, too." She glanced at the clock. "I have a few minutes to go. Isn't Boon-Dan-Tan the guru whose book you told me to read?"

"Right on. You'd love him Bridgie. He's gentle, enlightened and smart. Mom knew him in India. He's done a lot of good work around the world, but his headquarters are here in Philly near the University."

Claire unfolded her legs and stood up. "Be careful with Andrew. I'll call you later from the Divine Guidance Center and give you my number."

"Where are you off to now?"

"I'm taking this jelly butt of mine over to Java High's computers. Gonna check out the Spiritual Dating site. Maybe my true karma is to find the love of my life and set up cooperative housing with you."

Bridget laughed as she walked Claire to the door. "If only we had the money."

*   *   *

Bridget walked through the lobby toward Andrew's office trying to steal herself. If Claire, her rock, could start on a new path, so could she.

The tightly woven Kelly green carpet had just been cleaned, leaving an acidy odor of chemicals in the air. Three women sat in wheelchairs by the large plate-glass window staring blankly into the parking lot. One pressed her fingers together as though knitting.

"Knit one, purl two," she said.

"Hello, Miss Bernstein," said a woman sitting next to her.

"Hello Mrs. March," said Bridget. She noticed that Mrs. March's yellow flowered housedress was buttoned crookedly. A gap appeared at her breastbone while the top button waited to be fastened. Bridget kneeled in front the wheelchair. "Here, let me help you."

"Where's my daughter?" Mrs. March clutched Bridget's hand. "You seen her?" Her fingers felt frail as the bones of a bird.

Bridget released Mrs. March's hands to refasten the buttons of her dress. "Your daughter comes the first of the month."

Mrs. March's face collapsed. "Tell her I want to go home."

"I know." Bridget bit her lip. According to her medical records, when Mrs. March's husband died four years before she had been an outgoing seventy-two year old woman. Over the next year she had broken down physically and begun seeing three doctors, none of whom knew the others were treating her. She had ended up taking a combination of pills that Bridget suspected had contributed to her decline. Now they could do little to repair the damage.

Even in her demented state, Mrs. March responded to the Befriend-A-Pet Program becoming fond of a chocolate Labrador named Charlie, growing calmer after each of the dog's visits. It angered Bridget that Andrew would dare think about cutting the program.

The third woman began to howl.

"She makes so much racket," said Mrs. March.

"It's because she doesn't feel well today," said Bridget.

She motioned to a nurse who came over and comforted the woman. Then, she continued down the sterile hallway past bare walls and evenly spaced, identical doors. She bent down to pick up a candy wrapper, her hand brushing the waxy surface of the carpet. Beneath the smell of chemicals lurked a faint odor of urine.

She blinked against the dim lighting. No wonder the residents slumped their shoulders when they walked down the hall. She peered through the dining room doorway. The air smelled thick and starchy, of gravy and noodles.

At a table near the window, Al and Edna were absorbed in conversation. They made a funny pair, Al with his ebony coloring and booming voice. And Edna, her skin white as the lumpy mashed potatoes on her plate, her voice high and thin. Sparse hair sprouted from her pink scalp.

Bridget watched Al lean forward and touched Edna's hand, remembering when she and Claire had matched them up. Edna had been living at the nursing home for nearly a year, her easy wit vanishing as she fell into a funk. Al had arrived after a minor stroke and was sent to Claire for physical therapy.

"Al's got the same sense of humor as Edna," Claire had said.

One afternoon, Bridget brought Edna to Cupid's Retreat under the pretext of having her catalogue the record collection. Claire and Al were already there sorting through old magazines. After making introductions, Bridget and Claire left on their respective rounds.

Later, when they peered into the room, they spied the pair dancing a wobbly waltz to Johann Strauss on the stereo. From then on, Edna and Al were inseparable, growing increasingly impatient with the strict nursing home rules. She imagined how happy they would be living in a house full of movement and laughter.

"Eat, Edna," Al, was saying, when Bridget reached their table. "You need to keep up your strength. Just a few more bites and I won't nag you any more."

"You're as bad as my daddy," said Edna. "He made me sit at the table all night until I finished my peas."

"I'm not your daddy and you know it." Al winked at Bridget and lifted the fork to Edna's mouth. Edna tilted her head and allowed the peas to drop in.

"There," she said as she chewed. "Make you happy?"

"Look who's here." Al chuckled, patting an orange vinyl chair. "Sit down young lady. It's gourmet peas tonight. Right from the can."

"I can't," said Bridget. "I've got a meeting with the boss."

"You mean the warden?" said Edna. "Whatever happened to the idea you and Claire had about an alternative to this dump?"

"Yeah," said Al. "Miss Claire said it would be like a kibbutz in Israel. All the people working together."

"It's still on the drawing board."

"We'll do anything to get out of here," said Edna. "If there's some way we can help, let us . . ."

"Ms. Bernstein, you're late!" Andrew loomed in the doorway. "Didn't you set this meeting up? It's ten past five."

He was dressed in his uniform, a well-tailored Armani suit, the French cuffs of his shirt held together by cloisonné studs. She noticed he'd died his hair an unnatural shade of black, styling it to camouflage his receding hairline.

He scanned the room. "And how is everyone this evening?"

"We'd be better if you'd talk to Miss Bridget nicer," said Al. "If it wasn't for her, this place would be a stinkhole."

Andrew blanched. "We need our director to act responsible."

Bridget gritted her teeth.

"It also means taking time for the residents," said Al.

Edna dug her spoon into her peas. "Mr. Jacobson," she said in a singsong voice. "I have something for you."

"Not now, Edna." He stepped into the room and spoke with a syrupy lilt. "Are you coming Bridget?"

She saw Edna lift her spoon, pull it back, and let the peas fly.

"Stop!" Andrew raised his hands to deflect the green blobs that splattered against the sleeves and cuffs of his shirt. He glared at Bridget. "You've got ten seconds to get into my office."

"Send Edna back to her room immediately," he called to an aide. "And see that she stays there!"

"She's fine right where she is," said Bridget.

"Don't defy me," he said, and stormed down the hall.

Bridget signaled to the aide to leave Edna alone. The aide winked.

"You always get me into trouble, lady." Bridget smiled and wagged her finger at Edna.

"I'm senile. Can't help it." Edna grinned and linked her arm through Al's.

*　　*　　*

In the employee lounge, Bridget bought a bag of microwave popcorn from the vending machine. Her meeting with Andrew had gone too smoothly making her uneasy. He had been preoccupied with something and seemed more interested in wiping stray peas from his shirt than listening to what she had to say about the restraining order. Of course she had edited the story, eliminating the part about watching David and his girlfriend have sex.

She set the bag of kernels in the microwave and fiddled with the dial. She jiggled the handle, slapped the side of the microwave. The machine whirred on.

Exhausted, she collapsed onto an old plaid couch, set her feet on the coffee table and watched the bag expand. Confessing had its advantages. It had given her back an appetite. A buttery odor filled the air. She heard the kernels pop against the sides of the bag.

She liked to think that the place needed her. Hadn't she kept it running smoothly and done well by Andrew and the staff? She had a knack for hiring good workers who brightened up the place.

Her mind wandered back to Carson and the river. She touched her lips. What a thrill to kiss him. If only she could stop worrying about David.

Suddenly, Andrew, his face beet red, exploded into the room. "You lied to me. After everything I've done for you and you lie to my face."

"What are you talking about?"

"I returned David Angsdorf's call after you left my office. He refuted your story and told me how you sneaked into his apartment, watched him have sex, and tried to kill him with a baseball bat. He says you're unbalanced."

"It didn't happen that way," she said angrily.

"It doesn't matter. You're fired."

"You're using my personal life against me because I refuse to put the patients in jeopardy by cutting the staff."

"It's about insubordination and your criminal record. I can't put someone with a violent history in charge of frail human beings."

"I need at least a month to organize things."

"I want you out now. Don't think I didn't hear about Claire sneaking around earlier this afternoon. She probably wants to turn this entire building into a brothel. Now get your purse and go."

"I deserve proper notice."

"If you won't get out, I'm calling the police." He walked to the phone.

An acrid odor filled the room. Smoke poured through the crevices of the microwave door. Bridget leapt to the microwave and jiggled the handle. It was burning hot. She jumped back, grabbed a pile of napkins and forced the door open. Popcorn burst into flames. The shrill ring of an alarm startled her.

Andrew stood frozen, his face aghast.

Water splashed against her shoulder. In a panic, Bridget wondered how to get the patients out.

"What the hell did you do?" shouted Andrew. She heard a roar and looked up. Water cascaded from the ceiling. The smoke had set off the sprinkler system.

* * *

Bridget's clammy feet squished footprints into the wet carpet as she trudged down the hall to her office. A security guard stood outside her door. She brushed past him toward her desk. Andrew had given her fifteen minutes to leave.

She felt some consolation that the smoke damage had been limited to the employee lounge, and that the sprinkler system had only gone off in the lobby and the staff offices. By the time the fire trucks arrived, the janitor had put out the fire and the patients sitting in the lobby had been evacuated.

She rummaged in her desk through six years of accumulated calendars, stickers and notes, and hurled them across the room. Paper fluttered to the floor.

She wasn't surprised that Andrew had given her the ax, but she hadn't expected to float out on a raft.

She picked up a framed photograph. A few drops of water dripped from her hair and pooled on the glass. In the photograph, she was seven years old sitting on her mother's lap, her face serious. Her father wore his club sport coat, a deck of cards embroidered on the lapel. He smiled as if he'd hit the jackpot. She wiped off the frame and stuffed the photograph into her duffel bag.

Besides Claire, he was the only one who had ever accepted her imperfections. Maybe getting fired was the break she needed to take a deeper look into herself. She had already paged Claire at the Java High. They would meet at the Wu Fong Chinese restaurant in fifteen minutes.

She reached into the back of her desk drawer and found the single love letter she had saved from her relationship with Andrew.

A love letter that told her how strong she was, how she could do anything when she set her mind to it. Little did he know that she was ready to prove him right.

"Miss Bridget, your taxi's here," said Edna. She stood in the doorway wearing a yellow slicker. In her hand, she held two faded pink towels. "I brought you these so you could dry yourself off." She glanced at the guard.

The guard nodded to Edna who handed her the towels and a note. Bridget zipped her duffel bag closed and slipped the note into her pocket.

"We're with you," said Edna embracing her.

She hugged Edna's thin frame. "I'll find us a new place," she whispered.

In the lobby, the green carpet glimmered beneath a sea of water. Andrew angrily gestured at the fire chief. Black rinse dripped from his hair streaking his shirt collar. She held back a giggle, avoiding Andrew's gaze as she walked past him.

He grabbed her arm. "Get yourself some help before it's too late."

"Get a better dye-job." She glared at him and marched out to the taxi. "Wu Fong Restaurant on Spruce," she said, settling into the back seat on one of the towels Edna had given her.

The taxi pulled out of the nursing home driveway past urns of wilting impatiens. She withdrew Edna's note. The handwriting was a little shaky, but the message was clear. Written inside a lopsided heart, it said, "Al and I will follow you wherever you go. Break us out of here."

Next, she pulled Andrew's old letter from her pocket. "When I see how happy you make my patients, I'm turned on in a thousand ways. I love you." She slumped in her seat and remembered the December night Andrew broke up with her.

She had been living in her first apartment, a small efficiency with a tiny bathroom that contained a cast iron bathtub. She had turned on the taps, hypnotized by filigrees of steam gathering into frost at the corners of the bathroom window.

In the kitchen, the phone rang. She rushed to pick up the receiver. It was Andrew on his cell phone, his voice strained.

"I need to see you," he said. "I'm a few blocks away near Fitler Square."

She wished he'd come to her apartment. But, they had made a deal since he'd told her about his wife and the divorce. They would meet in out-of-the way places in case his wife decided to follow him.

"Come here tonight," she said. "I've just drawn a bath and . . ."

"I'm sorry," he said. "The bath will have to wait. This is important."

"Okay. I'll be there."

She turned off the water, got dressed, and put on boots, parka, scarf, hat and mittens. She was sick of this nonsense, sick of herself and Andrew and all the time she had wasted on him. She opened the front door, cold air stinging her cheeks, seizing her lungs. The moon hung brightly in the sky, turning crevices, footprints, snowdrifts, blue.

He had hired her fresh out of graduate school as a social worker in his nursing home. Given her a break. Groomed her for management and she had rewarded him with long hours and complete dedication. That counted for something. Didn't it?

She trudged up the street. The ice-clad tree limbs rattled like dry bones. Suddenly, a shock came over her. Was this it? Was he finally leaving the wife who made him so unhappy? But then he surely would have come to her apartment.

She had grown dependent on him, and he, in turn, on her. He had provided the solid foundation she needed to feel worthwhile, his love and support filling her up so that she was able to turn a blind eye toward the fact that he still hadn't separated from his wife.

Her fingers ached from the cold. Up ahead, she saw headlights shining. Her heart beat faster. As always, she felt a thrill in her belly at the prospect of seeing Andrew. He would wait for her in his old green loden coat, the brim of his fedora tipped low, the grooves at his mouth set firm against the cold.

The wind had picked up. But she could take the cold because later, she'd carry the scent of Andrew's skin home with her. She'd ask him to open his coat and she would warm her hands against his chest, against the thick wool of his sweater. She clapped her hands together. Despite the gloves, her hands felt like blocks of ice. Snow crunched beneath her feet.

Her anxiety evaporated when she opened Andrew's car door, smelled leather, wet wool and his musky cologne. She climbed into the car and shut the door before leaning across the armrest to kiss his lips.

He smelled faintly of spices. Something Middle Eastern. Prepared by his wife, no doubt. But her fingers had warmed up and he was beside her.

"My bright and clever girl." He hugged her shoulders, pressing his hands against her wool coat, against her back muscles.

Girl? The weight in the tone of his voice set her teeth on edge. "What do you want to tell me?"

He sighed. His hands remained still against her back.

A sharp pain struck the pit of her stomach.

"You've supported me through thick and thin," he said. "Inspired me, too. I admire your management skills more than anyone."

What the hell was he saying to her? The heater was blowing too hard. She began to sweat. The windows had fogged up. She wanted to celebrate this violent cold, but he spoke to her like a father, not a lover.

She pulled away from him. "What do you want to tell me?"

The green light from the dashboard illuminated his eyes and the creases at the corners of his mouth. "After all the love and care you've given me. After . . ."

Tears sprang to her eyes.

"I've admitted everything to Martha. I couldn't go on any longer. We've called the divorce proceedings off."

Her lungs burned. She remembered the wine-stained kisses, his promise of marriage and children. The car felt as if it were wheezing, puffing. He tried to put his arms around her.

"Leave me alone."

"I never wanted this to happen. If I could split myself, I would. It's just that I don't want to lose my kids. Please don't cry. It won't affect our work relationship at all."

What about the desire they shared? The business talks late into the night? And what about the child they might have had with Andrew's gray eyes and her long fingers, the child who would have been their future?

She edged toward the car door and thrust it open. Frigid air rushed in. She stepped out, slipped, caught herself.

He came after her, falling flat on his face. "Bridget. Please!"

The trees glittered and cracked in the wind. She didn't hear a car door slam or his car start. For a split second, she wondered what might happen to him. But the night was dangerous and she had to get home.

The cabdriver had turned up the air-conditioning. Bridget shivered, hugging herself. Up ahead, Claire paced back and forth beneath the restaurant's blue and white-striped awning. A row of mahogany-colored ducks hung in the steamy window, dripping golden fat.

Bridget balled up the letter and stuck it in the ashtray.

Warm air enveloped her when she got out of the cab. Claire rushed toward her. "What a disaster, poor thing. I thought Andrew might hold you hostage." She took the duffel bag from Bridget's hand.

"I nearly needed an ark to get out of there," said Bridget, thankful for the warm air and Claire's smile. "You've never seen a bigger mess."

"I'd have given anything to see Andrew in his fancy duds, soaking wet."

Bridget leaned against the brick facade and chuckled. "It was pretty funny. You should have seen the hair dye staining his shirt. He said I'm a menace to society."

"Maybe a menace to stuffed shirts." Claire pushed open the door of the restaurant. "After a glass of wine and some food, you'll think clearer. You might wind up thanking Andrew in the long run."

The smell of hot oil assailed their nostrils when they reached the counter. Above it, mushrooms of all sizes and colors hung from the ceiling: red mushrooms, large as lobsters; long floppy caps, mushrooms thick as a stevedore's fist.

"You get caught in rain? No rain," the clerk tittered. His blue-black hair shone in the fluorescent light.

Claire ignored him. "I phoned in an order. Johnson."

"Of course." He headed into the kitchen and returned with two brown shopping bags.

They left the shop and walked toward Bridget's apartment. "I know this looks like a lot of food," said Claire. "But you're on a tight budget from now on. If you eat right, it'll last you a week."

"I'm not destitute yet," said Bridget. They turned up her street. She stopped at the fruit display in front of her neighborhood greengrocer and picked up a bag of golden cherries, smelling their sweet scent before setting them down. She sighed. "I guess I'll have to learn how to save money from now on."

"Move into the Divine Guidance Center with me. Rent's only a hundred-fifty dollars a month." Claire followed Bridget up the steps to her apartment. "Get your vibrations balanced, and then we can start talking about the cooperative housing project. There's an architect living at the Center. I'm sure she'll help us with design plans."

"It might be time to take the plunge."

Claire paused at the top of the landing. "Right on, girl. But, we've got to make sure that David doesn't bring us down."

"Even with David out of the picture, I still have my doubts."

"What jive are you talking? Aren't you the one who says we should reach our highest potential and then aim higher?"

Bridget unlocked her apartment door. "It sounds better when one is gainfully employed. Although, you sure didn't let anyone stop you in Columbia."

"'Cause I believed in what I was doing. Besides, I'm off-the-wall nutso."

"And I'm not? We're quite a pair." Bridget held her hand up.

Claire grinned and gave her a high five. "I'll stick by you girl, even if we go right over a cliff."

In her bedroom, Bridget changed into a pair of shorts and a t-shirt. When she walked into the kitchen, Claire had set the cartons on the table along with two sets of chopsticks.

"You can tell a lot about a man if he knows how to eat with chopsticks," said Claire. "A man who uses only a fork is stuck in his ways."

"Come to think of it," said Bridget. "David and Andrew used forks."

"Proves my point."

"I wonder what Carson uses," mused Bridget.

* * *

"I'm stuffed." Claire bustled about the kitchen labeling food for future dinners.

"You've done enough," said Bridget, refilling their wine glasses. "Come into the living room." She settled into Grandmom's old rocker while Claire sprawled on the floor.

Rocking back and forth, Bridget remembered the first time Claire appeared at her school in the middle of seventh grade. She had just come back from India with her mother.

For Bridget, who was timid, Claire had been a stick of dynamite. Someone who motivated her. Claire wasn't afraid of anything or anyone, not the kids who teased her and called her a half-breed, nor the teachers who had trouble keeping her from speaking her mind.

Both only children, they had instantly felt a kinship, becoming best friends. By that time, her mother was practically living at her cookie factory, and Grandmom was preparing to retire in Florida. Bridget found herself spending most of her free time at Claire's house where Bev welcomed her like her own child.

"Remember Chuck, the class bully?" said Bridget. "I wonder where he is today?"

"I bet he's president of a giant corporation or a politician," said Claire. "He was good at stealing people's money. Remember the time he jimmied open my locker and stole the money I had collected for the homeless?"

"Yeah. By that time I'd learned a few tricks from you. I jimmied open his locker and got your money back."

"Which led you to your present life of crime," laughed Claire.

"Your mother might accuse me of teaching you the tricks of the trade."

"She still thinks we hang out at opium dens." Bridget pushed her foot against the floor and rocked faster.

"What about your grandmom? Does she still want to bust out of Florida?"

"I talked to her about buying Mom's convent. Mom's just using it for storage. Grandmom said she'd help me buy it if Mom agrees to sell it cheap." She sipped her wine. "But that was before I got arrested."

"Here's the game plan," said Claire. "You go to the factory. Lay it on straight. Act like it's no big deal. That way, you'll catch Sarah off guard."

The phone rang. Bridget's head began to pound. Her nerves

hung together by a single thread. One snip and she'd unravel. "It better not be Andrew or David," she said.

"Want me to get it?" said Claire,

Bridget shook her head. She rose and picked up the receiver. Carson's cheerful voice surprised her.

"You sound tired," he said.

She reached for a lock of hair. "I had a rough day." The last thing she wanted was to share another tale of woe with him. "My friend Claire's here hanging out with me."

"Can't wait to meet her."

Bridget smiled.

"I called to see if you were free for lunch tomorrow. We could brown bag it. I usually go to Rittenhouse Square."

"Sure. Is noon okay?"

"I'll be sitting on one of the benches near the 19th and Locust entrance."

"You're blushing," said Claire when Bridget hung up the phone.

"I like him," said Bridget grimly.

"You make it sound like a curse."

"He stayed through one catastrophe. Do you think it'll last?"

"Get on the upbeat. So far, he's hanging tight. Maybe getting fired will turn him on, too."

"Right." Bridget lifted the half-empty wine bottle from the coffee table and refilled her glass. "We ought to write a book about catastrophes that turn men on."

"Yeah," chuckled Claire. "Breaking into you ex's apartment earns an entire night of lovemaking. Breaking into your ex's and getting canned from your job earns a whole day in bed with your new man catering to your every desire."

"How about an eviction from your apartment and getting a bad reference from your employer?"

Claire writhed on the floor and stretched out her arms to an imaginary lover. "Man, that'll earn you a whole weekend of good lovin'."

Bridget tried to give Claire a dirty look.

"Ooooh-baby," Claire moaned.

"Cut it out," said Bridget. She stood up, hands on hips and burst into laughter.

Chapter 12

BRIDGET'S ALARM STARTLED her awake. Seven-thirty, and nowhere to go until lunch. She got out of bed, disoriented. Last night's hilarity with Claire had left her.

She stretched her arms over her head and tried to shake off the lethargy that had overtaken her limbs. On her dresser, pale blue delphiniums dropped their petals onto the lace dresser scarf that one of the patients from the nursing home had given her for her birthday last year. The corner of the scarf was bunched up beneath a pile of books.

When she stopped seeing David, she had set herself a lofty goal of self-improvement, choosing classics from Austen, Joyce, Mann. She lifted the books and straightened the edge of the scarf. Now that she had the time, she had no energy to read them.

She turned toward her oak nightstand, a flea-market find she had planned to refinish. But the job didn't appeal to her today. She decided to follow her normal routine and see where it led her. First, she took a shower, carefully blow-drying her hair. Then she brought in the newspaper. By the time she finished her bagel and coffee, it was eight-thirty. The day stretched loose and empty before her. Thank goodness Claire had invited her to a retreat tomorrow. She wasn't ready to spend too much time alone.

On the deck of the apartment below, her neighbor had set out a wrought iron table and two chairs. She imagined sitting in one of those chairs, her legs propped up on the other. She would wear a wide-brimmed straw hat and sip iced tea, whiling away the day with one of her books.

The thought dissipated as fast as it came. She got up, went into the bedroom and rifled through her closet. Guilt set in when she was idle. The old work ethic, she chided herself. It wasn't all wrong. It simply needed tempering. That's what living in the Divine Guidance Center with Claire could do for her. Help her slow down. She would set an objective to clear her mind so she could forge ahead with her plan for cooperative housing, use this time in her life as an opportunity to change. If she wanted to talk to Carson, she'd better sound like she knew what she was doing. She'd stop at the library before meeting him and see what kind of resources they had about foundations.

She settled on her favorite suit, rose colored trousers with a matching double-breasted jacket. From the research she'd already done, she'd determined that the kind of cooperative housing that interested her wasn't usually located in urban areas. It also catered to more conventional families with children.

She had followed a study conducted in Denmark where a group of families had tried to create the atmosphere of a small town, providing day-care as well as the choice to share meals, social and recreational activities.

Her target group was more diverse, although a single building would be cost-effective. Rural life wouldn't work well for the elderly who needed to be near doctors and relatives. And it wasn't ideal for younger people who wanted job opportunities and nightlife. She slipped on her blouse and fastened the buttons. Besides, her heart was in the city. Her model for successful housing in the city was at the center of David's book. She knew that the pressure to publish had made him terribly desperate. Still, there should be room for both of them.

An hour later, she left her building and walked toward the parkway, briefcase in hand. Inside, she had stacked fresh paper, folders and a notebook. She straightened her shoulders, held her head high. She always felt better when she had a purpose and an objective to accomplish.

Sunlight dappled the streets, warming the mild air. She hadn't planned to stop at the Rodin Museum, but the azaleas finishing their season of neon bloom lured her toward the high gate. Despite the day's beauty, she felt herself dropping into melancholy. She longed for Carson to hold her hand and tell her everything would be okay.

She followed a young couple past the bronze statue of The Thinker. His elbow rested on his knee. Chin in hand, he seemed immersed in a single idea, mulling it from every angle.

In the courtyard, she paused at an elaborate gate. Her eyes trailed up the length of the twenty-foot sculpture. Hundreds of angels, devils, couples embraced, twisting in metal up the walls.

She crossed the threshold. Light filtered through high leaded glass windows onto pale, creamy walls. The elegance of the space made her giddy. On a pedestal, a sorceress leapt from her rock, grasping air with the passion of her desires. Beyond, two bronze arms rose from another pedestal, reaching up, fingers and thumbs touching, light falling between.

A whisper of voices swirled in the air, motes of dust fell from the windows, translucent as gauze. In an alcove, a life-size bronze nude male stood with his hands on his hips, his eyes staring into the future. She could be strong as metal, too. She moved toward him and reached up, sliding her hand along the statue's cool hip.

She could almost feel the bone beneath, the pulse of veins. Something about the strong cast of the jaw reminded her of Carson. So far he'd held onto the handle bar while she took him along on her roller coaster ride. And what about his hang-ups? His unquestioned devotion to his father? She wasn't able to feel that way about her own mother. Overall, he seemed like the least neurotic man she'd met. She hadn't seen a dark side yet. Everyone had one, but if she laid down cash, she'd bet his was moderate.

She traced her finger along the smooth metal surface from the hip along the line of buttock and thigh. Her hand wandered to the stomach, flattening against hard metal. She expected movement, a quickening of breath. Gently, she lay her hand over the statue's penis and tweaked it. She wondered if she'd gone mad. Her mother would be appalled at her behavior.

"Harummph," came a voice behind her.

She dropped her hand and turned. A guard frowned. He was about her own age, hair clipped into a crew cut. "Did you see the sign?" he said, curtly. "No touching."

Blood shot to her face. "I was just on my way to the library," she said, and hurried past him.

*   *   *

"Did the guard say anything after that?" said Carson. He flashed a smile and set a white pastry box on the bench next to Bridget.

"I beat it out of there, fast."

They glanced at each other and broke out laughing.

"You're the wildest woman I've ever met. I'd be too scared of getting caught."

She felt her face flush. "The metal is unyielding. You kind of want it to be, uh . . ."

"More pliable?" He burst into laughter again.

She moved closer to him and smiled. A parade of people passed through Rittenhouse Square, businessmen and women in chic suits hurrying to lunch, nannies pushing strollers, toddlers chasing pigeons.

Near the 19th Street entrance, a man sat on the grass beating a syncopated rhythm on a garbage can lid. On the bench across the way, two old men in rolled up shirtsleeves had placed a chessboard between them and were deep in concentration. Taxis slid by on Walnut Street.

"Last summer, I came here almost every day," she said. She remembered how on his afternoons off, David would walk over from the University to meet her for lunch. A chill ran straight to her joints. She sensed David's presence like a damp fog and sank deeper into the bench.

She opened a container of yogurt and watched Carson unwrap a ham hoagie.

"How's work?" he asked. "Have the healthcare changes put your nursing home in the red?"

"Not Willow Tree." Bridget dipped her spoon into the container. "Andrew's got a knack for acquiring defunct homes and turning them around. He was constantly slicing the budget. We fought about it all the time."

He raised an eyebrow. "Why are you using the past tense?"

Bridget drew in a breath. "As of yesterday, I'm on the open market."

A quizzical look crossed Carson's face. "Don't you have to give notice?"

She twisted her spoon in the thick yogurt. "I got fired. I called a meeting with Andrew, and told him about the restraining order. At first he took it pretty well." She gauged the expression on Carson's face. It was neutral. She hesitated. "Andrew phoned David after our meeting. The rest is history. He had the police escort me out of the building."

Carson set his hoagie back on its wax paper.

She leaned forward and plucked a blade of grass. His silence made her nervous.

When he finally spoke, his voice had gone flat. "You've had a streak of bad luck. I'm sure you'll find a better job in a week or two."

She scanned the perimeter of the park. Distant figures hurried along the paths. A couple stood up, gathered their lunch wrappers and tossed them into a trashcan. "I'm not looking for another job."

"The housing idea of yours?" His voice took on an edge.

"Exactly. When I left the museum, I went to the library and searched their data-base for examples of how foundations are run."

He touched her hand, wishing he could feel more confident about her idea. "I hate to be a naysayer, but I don't think you're prepared for such a huge undertaking. I've found out some things at my bank about community loans, too."

"Remember, I've been in the field for eight years." She thought about the Saturday afternoons she had spent at the Penn library gathering statistics on aging and demographics. Then, she'd rush home to David and show him what she found. What she sought now was support from within the neighborhood she chose and from the city at large. With that in place, they had a fighting chance for success.

"Funding's your biggest problem," Carson's voice softened. "Community loans are out there, but they go to non-profit agencies with a solid track record. Even if you hooked up with one, you'd still need a building. I think your best path is to buy a building in conjunction with forming a foundation."

He touched her fingertips. "I know some of this stuff firsthand because I helped my sister run ours. Once you settle on a building, you could take a salary and the foundation could manage the assets."

She turned his palm upright, studied the folds and creases. He wasn't a typical banker, at least not the way she pictured a banker to be. She traced his lifeline, touched his wrist. "I see you have a big heart."

"It's easy to be generous when you have money." He closed his hand around her fingers. "Why don't you get a part-time job for a while with something connected to housing where you could get some good experience? I heard about a place in the city where a group has set up a residence for the homeless."

"But no one in the city's doing what we have in mind. Besides, if I get a job, that will be the end of it. I'll never have this kind of incentive again. Claire's putting all her energy into gathering support including an architect who can help make this happen."

"Will you two set up a senior citizen brothel paid for by Medicare?"

She smiled. "If I could, maybe I would. Claire believes we can do this. In Columbia, she defied a group of corrupt soldiers."

"I don't know if that was courageous or dumb." He let go of her hand, picked up his hoagie and took a bite.

She toyed with a button on her jacket. "I think you might be a bit of a weenie."

He choked and spit out the half-chewed bite into his napkin. "Me, a weenie? Tell you what, If you come up with something plausible, I'll help you."

"My mother has a building near the Italian Market. It's zoned for mixed use, commercial and residential. If I can get it cheap enough, my grandmom said she'd help me buy it."

"It'll still cost a lot of money."

"I have a small pension."

"You'll pay a penalty to take it out."

He was beginning to grate on her nerves. "The residents will pay rent."

"How many residents do you have?"

She paused, knowing how silly her answer would sound. "I've got a list of potentials. With my mother's building, we can house twenty." She saw a skeptical look cross his face. "Okay, I have two firm commitments, but I'll get more."

Carson lay his arm on the back of the bench and looked up

toward the lush leaves covering the branches of an oak tree. He admired her dedication. Maybe it took blind enthusiasm to go up against such odds. The leaves swayed in the breeze shifting the pattern of sunlight reflected on the sidewalk. He felt comfortable sitting with her. A bird swooped from the tree and landed in the grass. "Okay," he said. "Get me a proposal and your design concept and I'll look at it."

She smiled. "You've got yourself a deal."

He'd heard his father talking exactly the same way to his mother when he was a child. Hadn't his father stuck to his dream and finally succeeded? He leaned over and ran his hand across her temple smoothing back her hair. She tilted her face. He brushed her lips with his. Gently he pulled away. "I brought something for you." He lifted the box from the bench.

She unwrapped it, touched by his thoughtfulness. "Baklava. You figured out what I wanted."

"It wasn't too hard. I threatened to rip the earrings from Edward's tongue. Actually, he's a nice kid."

She stabbed the baklava with her plastic fork, lifting a layer of gooey nut-studded pastry. "Edward and his girlfriend might move in with us. And Claire has several friends from the Peace Corps who are interested."

"I'd kick out the first person who left hair in the sink."

"What if it was me?"

"You, I'd keep." He toyed with a lock of her hair, letting his fingers slide along its silkiness. "So how much rent would I be expected to pay?"

"For you, two thousand a month."

"You strike a hard bargain, but I'm sure in a few months you'll tell me it's all too overwhelming."

She wanted to be angry, but she understood. This project was over the top and promised to swallow up all her time. She gave him a feeble smile.

"Didn't your father start with a dream?"

He leaned over and kissed her cheek. No mistaking it, her tenacity reminded him of his father.

She took a deep breath. "Tell me how he got started filming

funerals. I'm really curious about why it failed. What made him get up and try again?"

Carson slung his arm over her shoulder and watched sunlight glint off the upper floors of the buildings across from the park. His father had been an optimistic man. Too optimistic. He wondered if his father had ever let the word failure cross his lips. "When my dad started out, he had unrealistic expectations. That's why I'm warning you to be prepared."

She was aware of sound, children shouting to one another, traffic passing by on the street. In the flowerbeds, the last of the tulips dropped their petals in the hot sun. "Tell me," she said.

He sighed. "My dad quit high school in his senior year to pursue his dream of becoming a great photographer. He moved to California, but never got a break. When he returned to Wisconsin, he got a job as a caddy at my mother's country club. I can just picture him soaking up everything, how the members dressed, what they ordered at the bar.

"Mother met him one morning when he caddied a round of golf she and her father were playing. Dad slipped her a note inviting her to dinner. They were never apart after that. After she married Dad, she offered part of her trust fund to invest in his own business, but he refused to touch it. He wanted to make it on his own."

"Maybe it takes someone so single-minded that they're able to block everything and everyone else out." She wondered why it sounded so rational now. She'd always hated her mother's self-absorption.

"At the time my father started his business, we lived in an apartment that was so small I could hear my parents' conversations. My mother didn't like the idea of Dad filming dead people, but she assured him that he had her support if he wanted to give it a try. I wanted to run into the hall, hug him, tell him I supported him, too."

"Your mother had faith in your father."

He heard a wistful note in Bridget's voice. If she only knew how much he missed his father, how he would have followed his father down any path he chose. He pressed his knee against her thigh. He'd never told anyone the story of his father's business, not even Anne.

"Anyway, I was ten when Dad forged ahead with his idea. Every day, I'd come home from school and hear him talking to funeral parlor owners, selling them his idea until he landed his first job with a hotshot widow. He decided to bring me with him as an assistant."

As he talked, Carson remembered standing on the stone floor of a church dressed in blue flannel pants and a short-sleeved oxford cloth shirt.

"Look up there, Carson," his father had said. "I'm panning those beams and the stained glass windows. Now, I'll focus on the casket. Don't be afraid. Just hold my equipment."

"Okay." Carson shivered. Fifteen feet away, sunlight streamed through a stained glass window on the face of Mr. Charles Denning. His waxen features reminded Carson of the monsters he saw in horror movies at the Saturday Matinee.

His father lowered the camera and whispered, "Mrs. Denning's here."

Carson heard the click of heels on the stone floor.

"Mr. McAlister," she said, holding out her hand. She studied Carson suspiciously.

"This is my son. He's my assistant."

Her eyes, the color of watery tea, bored into Carson. She turned to his father and lowered her voice. "I want my husband portrayed as the wonderful family man he was. Lies and rumors always circulate around successful people."

"We won't allow anything to taint this film," said his father. "You have my word."

"And another thing," said Mrs. Denning. "Certain undesirable people might show up today. I'm concerned about the effect on my children. I don't want these people filmed and I don't want a public spectacle by trying to keep them out."

His father rubbed his chin. "Even if you describe them, I might make a mistake."

"What do you suggest?"

"Splice them out later. That's the beauty of film. You can edit out the bad parts and leave in only the very nicest memories."

"Good. We're expecting some very important people today and

they'll want to see themselves at their best. Do an excellent job and I'll order at least twenty-five copies. I'm giving them out as mementos."

Carson saw his father's eyes widen.

Mrs. Denning knelt beside her husband's casket and lifted her tear-stained face toward the camera lens. "Chuck, I loved you so much. You were a wonderful husband. The children will miss you. Whenever I drive your Mazerati, I'll think of our wonderful Sunday jaunts into the countryside."

His father cued her to resume her prayer in silence. Mourners began to arrive. Carson and his father moved to the church entrance. His father attached the camera to a tripod and handed him a light. "I want you to point this at the people I interview," he said.

Two kids walked in with their nanny. His father whispered that they were Mrs. Denning's kids. He trained the light on them. The nanny glared at his father as he focused the camera on a boy.

The boy began to speak. "Mom used to yell at Daddy for coming home late. She says he killed himself in the saddle. I'm never gonna' ride horses."

The older boy stepped on the younger boy's foot. "Shut up!"

"Shut up yourself. I want to see Daddy."

The boys began pummeling each other.

His father motioned for the nanny to speak. "This is a disgrace," she said, and brushed past him.

Another guest stepped in front of his father's camera. "I can't believe my cousin's dead," he said, bobbing his head in front of the lens. "He got rich and I didn't."

He cupped his hands at the sides of his mouth. "For all you rich folks out there, I do good carpentry work. By the way, got a card? My father-in-law's about to knock off." The woman beside him grabbed his arm and pulled him down the aisle.

After everybody had entered, Carson watched his father pan the sober faces of the guests sitting in the pews. His father focused on a beautiful young woman who wore a smartly tailored black suit, her tawny brown hair pulled into a chignon. Tears slid from bright blue eyes over high cheekbones. She blew her nose into a delicate lace handkerchief. He saw Mrs. Denning grimace. Sweat had broken out on his father's neck, staining his shirt collar.

After the service, the pallbearers carried the casket out of the church. Carson sat down in the last row.

The young woman who had been crying approached them.

"Excuse me," she called to his father. "May I say a few words about Charles Denning?"

"Just for a minute, though. My son and I have to get to the cemetery." He raised the camera.

Mrs. Denning rushed toward them. "How dare you show your face here!"

The woman straightened her shoulders. "Chuck would have wanted me here because he loved me. "

"If he loved you so much, why didn't he divorce me?"

"He didn't want to lose the children."

"That's a laugh. He didn't give his kids the time of day."

"He was with me when he died," said the woman. She turned and walked slowly out of the church, the sound of her heals echoing against the stone walls.

Mrs. Denning dropped into a pew.

Carson felt sick to his stomach. His father had turned the camera off. They looked at each other.

"Maybe your mother's right," his father said, taking Carson's hand. "This isn't for me."

Outside, his father opened the camera and removed the film. Slowly he unwound it, the wind lifting a silver stream of ruined images in the sunlight.

"Son," he said. "Your old Dad will make you proud of him yet."

"What an awful group of people," said Bridget. "Still, it was brave of your father to try something innovative."

A bittersweet smile crossed Carson's face. "In the end, he needed a loan from my mother to start Ball and Jack's."

"Just like I'll need a loan from the bank." She playfully nudged her elbow into his ribs.

"There's a price to be paid for realizing your dream." Dad worked around the clock for years to get the business going. Sometimes, I think it killed him."

"I don't plan to work myself to death." She lay her hand over his wrist. "But in the beginning, it's going to take everything I've got."

He imagined Bridget working even harder than his dad. It seemed incompatible with a relationship. At least his dad came home for dinner most nights. Besides, if Bridget found a building, there'd be little privacy. What if he moved in, too? He doubted they'd have their own bathroom and he didn't like the idea of someone walking in on them while they showered together.

He was getting carried away. They hadn't even gone to bed yet and already he was taking showers with her. His skin tingled as he felt the pressure of her fingers on his wrist, imagined her fingers exploring the statue, exploring him.

He took a deep breath and checked his watch. "It's getting late. I've got to get back to work."

A breeze ruffled her hair as they stood up. "Would you like to have dinner tomorrow night?" he said.

"I'd love to, but Claire's taking me on a retreat for the next few days." She put her hands together and exaggerated a bow. "To heal."

He tugged at a lock of hair that had drifted over her shoulder. "How about Saturday morning? We could go to the Italian Market. I heard about a shop that makes fresh mozzarella."

She started to shake her head yes, than stopped. David shopped at the Italian Market on Saturday mornings so there was a chance she'd run into him. So what. In spite of his demands, the restraining order didn't include the Italian Market. Besides, the convent was a few blocks away and she wanted to show it to Carson.

He nudged her shoulder. "What's taking you so long to answer? Do I have bad breath?"

"I was, umm, thinking about my schedule."

"So, are we on?"

"Why not," she said, gathering her purse and the empty baklava box.

"I can't stay all day, though," he said. "I'm meeting my brother at the airport in the afternoon."

"The one you had problems with?"

"Yeah. We had a terrible fight the day I left." His face paled. "I accidentally punched him in the nose and broke it."

"You do have a dark side, after all," she chuckled. "I wonder what other skeletons you're hiding in that secret closet of yours." She tilted her head and smiled.

He thought of Anne, his broken engagement, and pulled Bridget toward him, holding her close. She'd understand better about Anne after they spent a little more time together.

She leaned her head against the curve of his chest and smelled his musky cologne. Reluctantly she pulled away. "Pick me up at eight. Things get going early down there."

"See you Saturday," he called as she walked down the path.

When she got to the corner, she looked over her shoulder. He stood by the bench, hands in pockets, watching her.

Chapter 13

WHEN BRIDGET TURNED OFF West Market Street and pulled her car up to The Divine Guidance Center, she saw Claire standing on the curb dressed in a saffron colored sari holding a paper bag, her battered gray backpack slung over her shoulders. Claire tossed her pack into the back seat.

"Great outfit," said Bridget.

"You like it? Before long you'll wear one, too."

"I don't think so." Bridget hit the gas, then slammed to a stop. A car honked behind her.

"Cool down, honey," said Claire. "You can wear anything you want at the Center. We'll take it slow. That's why we're going on this retreat, to break you in easy." She pulled a bagel out of the bag, orange filling oozing from the sides. "Gluten-Free with carrot-tofu spread. The Center's specialty. Want half?"

"No thanks, I'm not hungry." She watched Claire take a huge bite, her cheeks puffing out as she chewed. The morning sun beat against the windshield heating up the car. She turned the air conditioner up a notch. "Carson's not convinced that our co-housing idea will work."

"Most people wouldn't be. That's why you've got to empty yourself of static from unsympathetic voices."

"He came at me with the bottom line. He's right. Besides the hard work, it's going to take a lot of money."

"Carson comes from a concrete world. But there are other ways. Trust your inner guide."

"Will my inner guide write me a check for a million dollars?"

"IBM laughed at Steve Jobs and his personal computer. Look at your mother. With no money, she built a fortune out of a simple ugly cookie. Let everybody laugh. Boon-Dan-Tan's behind your idea."

"It had better work or I'll end up on my mother's assembly line smashing cookie dough."

* * *

Three hours later they veered off the interstate and followed Claire's handwritten directions until they found a sign for The Highlands–Divine Retreat and Conference Center.

"We made it," said Claire.

Bridget pulled into a long winding driveway that led to a small gravel parking lot overlooking the Hudson River. Mist hovered over the slate-gray water. Beyond, dark green hills shimmered in the late afternoon sunshine. She heard birds chirping to one another and felt the stress of the last few days seep from her pores.

Up the path through a grove of trees stood an elegant mansion. Flagstone steps led to a wrap-around porch where a woman sat in a rocking chair.

"Now listen," said Claire. "I'm going to follow protocol which means walking up the steps on my hands and knees. If you don't feel comfortable, you don't have to do it."

"Why didn't you warn me?" said Bridget.

"Because it didn't seem all that important."

They got out of the car and grabbed their bags. Bridget breathed in the heavy scent of pine. Needles crunched beneath her feet as she followed Claire up the path to the house.

Men and women in bare feet and white robes practiced tai chi on thick grass. Slowly, they moved their arms in tandem, gracefully thrusting them forward, lifting knees and balancing on one foot. A group of women sat at the base of an oak tree weaving daisies into necklaces. From within the building came the rhythmic sound of banging drums.

This was different from anything Bridget had experienced before. She remembered when Grandmom took her to the Orthodox Synagogue in the old neighborhood. The men, draped in shawls, sat in the front while the women sat in the balcony gossiping until the Cantor began the service. She thought, too, of Angel and the chapel at the convent where Jesus hung on a cross, arms outstretched, an arrow piercing his side.

Both the synagogue and the church had compelled and frightened her with their words and images. But here, as she watched the people gathered beneath the trees, she felt peace seeping into her bones.

At the base of the steps, Claire dropped to her knees and began crawling up. Bridget followed behind Claire.

The woman in the rocking chair rose. "Welcome to our home," she called as she sprinkled rose petals on Claire's head and back.

The woman's gauze dress billowed gracefully in the warm wind. She dipped her hand into the basket and tossed petals into Bridget's face. One flew into her open mouth. She wanted to spit it out, but to be polite she swallowed it, almost choking.

"Are you okay?" said the woman when Bridget reached the top step. She gently patted Bridget's back. "The petals are organic, filled with lunar energy. See the women on the lawn. Last night they held baskets of petals up to the full moon. The petals will help balance your yin and yang, giving you the strength to find inner harmony and the power to reach out to your fellow human beings. May the saints who passed before us bless you."

Claire stretched her arms skyward. "May the great Mother, guiding spirit of life, bring us peace."

"She will, my child," said the woman.

Claire ushered Bridget through the door and into the foyer.

"Can I get some of those petals for my mother?" said Bridget. "She needs them."

Claire squeezed Bridget's hand. "Maybe they'll hold the power you need to get the convent. Sprinkle them in her office and let their healing energy do their thing."

A tall man bowed. His ample belly stretched the material of a khaki Nehru-style jacket. "Welcome," he said, leading them to the check-in desk, then to their room.

The room consisted of two metal bunk beds. On a small wooden shrine stood a statue of the Indian god Shiva and the goddess Shakti entwined in a dance. A window shed bright light into the room. The communal bathroom was down the hall. It contained a long row of sinks and stalls as well as separate cubicles for showers. Bridget remembered a similar set-up in her college dorm.

"This isn't exactly a spa," she said, stretching out on the bed. "But it'll do."

"You should take a nap," said Claire. "We've got a full afternoon ahead of us."

*   *   *

Bridget woke to the sound of chanting. Claire sat across from her on the upper bunk, legs drawn into the lotus position. "Sita-Ram," she murmured and stopped when Bridget sat up.

"Sleep well?" she said, unfolding her legs.

"Yes," said Bridget, surprised at how rested she felt.

"Then let's check out the classes."

"The thing we did on the steps earlier," said Bridget. "They don't require it again, do they? I thought we were at Lourdes and you were going to throw your crutches away when you got to the top."

"Wasn't it great?" giggled Claire. "The lunarized flowers really relaxed me."

"Eating mine must have worked too," said Bridget. "I feel refreshed."

They wandered into a reception area ringed with doors.

Bridget read the titles above each door: Qigong, Living the Life Force, Transforming Stress, The Road to Holistic Well-Being, Come to the Kingdom of Nepal. She gave Claire a beseeching look.

"Let's start with Qiqong," said Claire. "Bon-Dan-Tan's leading the workshop. It's a great stress-reliever."

She followed Claire. "I was hoping they'd have the hex room, instead. I want to learn a good one for David."

"Come on." Claire pushed Bridget through a door. "Cleanse your soul. Think pure thoughts."

They paused to remove their shoes.

In the large, sunny room, pillows were piled in a corner. A small, frail-looking man with nut-brown skin, a long regal nose, and high cheekbones sat cross-legged on a mat in the center of the room. His eyes were closed. His hands rested on his lap. He wore a gray silk robe and a filmy silk turban over a long, black braid. He chanted softly, his face serene.

Claire picked up two pillows and motioned Bridget to sit in front of him. People filed in, some dressed in leotards, others in gym shorts and t-shirts. Still others wore loose fitting pants and tunics.

When a dozen people were seated, Boon-Dan-Tan opened his eyes. "Namaste," he said. "Peace and welcome."

"Namaste," the group replied in unison.

His velvety brown eyes encompassed everyone in the room. Bridget imagined him looking straight into her soul and felt a burst of energy radiate from within. All sound, except his high, reedy voice, faded away. She inhaled, exhaled, long and slow following his instructions.

"Qigong is a discipline," he said, "If you practice it regularly, you will find good health and strength. But more important, you will stay calm in the face of life's difficult decisions.

"You will lose your craving for crass material goods. Open your hearts and minds. Qigong requires that you reject the part of you that closes up to life. You must leave your inhibitions at the door."

"I will," whispered Bridget, lulled by the cadence of his voice.

"First, rotate your shoulders three times forward."

Bridget watched Claire and copied her movements. Then she closed her eyes and followed the voice of Boon-Dan-Tan.

"Now three times backward. Breathe deeply three times, inhaling and exhaling through your nose. This centers your chi or life force."

Bridget imagined exhaling negative energy from her system, breathing in, filling herself with peace.

"Now," he continued. "Think of nothing but your umbilical region, source of the life force which we call Dan Tian. Place your hand there. If your legs jerk, let it happen. Breathe deeply and keep your mind still."

Bridget opened an eye. People's legs were jerking. Claire sat perfectly still, her hand on her stomach. Suddenly, Claire's knee jerked once, then twice. Bridget squeezed her eyes closed, raised her head. she felt her leg jerk.

Following Boon-Dan-Tan's instructions, she massaged her elbow joints, her shoulders and kidney area, even her coccyx, watching everybody including Boon-Dan-Tan jerk their limbs. She smiled and felt like she was letting go for the first time in her life.

Slowly, the vibrations in the room quieted, except for an older man whose leg continued to jerk. Boon-Dan-Tan rose and went to him, massaging his shoulder blades. The jerking stopped.

Reseating himself, Boon-Dan-Tan began a rhythmic chant. Bridget swayed to his voice, feeling every muscle relax as if she could sink into the floor.

Finally, he rose. "Namaste," he said. "Go in peace and share it with the world."

He gestured toward Bridget and Claire. "Stay, my children." He waited until everyone else filed out, then trained his gaze on Bridget. "We welcome you. Claire tells me you'll be joining us at our center in Philadelphia."

"It might be temporary. Only six months or so."

"Claire has told me about your cooperative housing project. We can't offer you money, but should you need it, I extend our non-profit status. We will act as your conduit when you seek funding."

Bridget stared in shocked silence. Finally she spoke. "I don't know how to thank you."

"It is up to you and Claire to do the good work." He raised a finger. "One more thing. There's a new member on the Center's board who says he knows about you and your ideas. He has gathered much information and is producing a book which might prove helpful."

Bridget felt her neck and shoulders turn to stone. She glanced at Claire.

"And who might that be?" said Claire.

"An eminent professor. Dr. David Angsdorf. "At his request, I have made him available should you need advice."

Bridget sank to the floor.

Boon-Dan-Tan knelt before her, looking puzzled.

Bridget inhaled through her nose, exhaled slowly. "He's my ex-boyfriend and he stole my ideas to write his book."

Boon-Dan-Tan closed his eyes and lifted his hands. "You're going out into the world to practice what you preach. If Dr. Angsdorf's help is not needed, we will ask him to withdraw his support. Remember, The Divine Guidance Center is dedicated to helping you realize your goal."

"With all due respect," said Claire. "I have to tell you, David

Angsdorf's an asshole."

*   *   *

Bridget and Claire made their way to the dining room. The
scent of carrots, broccoli and garlic wafted toward them.

"How did David find out I was connected to the Center?"

"I think I know, Bridgie. I saw him at Java High the other day,
although we didn't speak. He passed by the coffee bar just as I was
telling Edward our plans. I didn't give it a second thought, but he
must have heard me. Promise you won't let it get you down. You're
on the right path and he can't stop you." They entered the cavernous cafeteria. "God I'm starving. Whenever something freaks
me out, I have to eat."

"Good for you because I just lost my appetite."

The steam table looked like an advertisement for the garden of
Eden's summer harvest. A tray of yellow squash sat next to a
bright green salad. And next to that sat a casserole of beans in
every shade from tan to mottled purple-brown to pure black. Rich
vegetable soups competed with bowls of yogurt. In the center
rested a silver urn filed with brown rice. Some of the people Bridget had seen on the lawn earlier had donned aprons, acting as
cooks and servers.

"Shh," whispered Claire, ladling beans into her bowl. "We eat
dinner in silence. Another thing they require is that everyone who
lives here be celibate."

"I wish I didn't qualify," whispered Bridget.

Claire tented her hands. "Oh great spirit," she whispered. "May
Bridget's words rise up and enter the libido of her new boyfriend."

*   *   *

As if trumpeting from a deep tunnel, a voice called Bridget's
name. A shape passed through the high window and floated to the
floor. "This is all Claire's fault."

"Mom?" whispered Bridget. She tried to get up from the bed,
but her arms and legs were numb.

Her mother's face glowed as though lit from within. Her mouth
curved into an angry frown. "Sure, you break off with David and

quit your job. I know what you and Claire are doing. You're running drugs from Columbia. You'll wind up in a dirty prison with rat
droppings on your bread if you're not careful."

Bridget's eyes flew open. She glanced at her travel alarm.
The digits turned over. Midnight. In the bunk above her, the new
roommate, a late arrival, slept restlessly. Springs pinged and
squeaked.

Her mother's image had vanished, but her presence hovered in
the humid air. The room had grown hot and smelled like damp
putty. Claire lay on her back, snoring lightly.

Bridget got up and walked into the lounge dimly lit by the red
emergency exit sign above the door. A dull ache pushed at her
temples. She made out the shape of a sofa and threw herself on it,
burrowing into velvety corduroy.

Perhaps her mother's bad vibes were out there amid the trees.
No doubt the housing idea would appall her. She hated anything
she couldn't control or understand. Bridget shuddered and stared
through the picture window at the moonlit lawn and the river flow-
ing by. Ripples glinted like quicksilver.

A figure emerged from the darkened hallway. It was Claire
looking like her old self dressed in her threadbare, moss green
terry cloth bathrobe.

"Hi sweetie. You had trouble sleeping, too? Our roommate must
have eaten a ton of gassy vegetables. That's the down side to vegetarians. Light a match and you'll blow this place up."

Bridget smiled as she made room on the sofa for Claire. Outside,
the crickets chirred their night song, an owl hooted a plaintive cry.
"My head's spinning," she said. "I can't get my mother out of my
mind. I dreamt she was in our room accusing us of being leftist
drug runners."

Claire raised an eyebrow. "Ah, you're gearing up for the onslaught." Her face grew concerned. "Sarah wants you to have her
version of the American dream, a house in the 'burbs and a husband who actually goes to a tenured job while you raise a brood of
perfect kids."

"Right now, it sure sounds good."

"You've got to stay calm. Think real careful about what you

want to say to Sarah. Then go for it. Ask her for the convent. The
worst she can say is no." Claire looked toward the river. "Tomorrow we'll take a long yoga class and meditation session. The psy-
chic energy here is dynamite. I guarantee your mother is no match
for it."

A breeze ruffled the curtains and drifted across the room,
cooling Bridget's damp neck. Her temples began to throb. None
of her thoughts followed a straight line. She imagined Carson sitting quietly with her by the river telling her everything would be
all right. Then she imagined David back at the Center bad-
mouthing her to Boon-Dan-Tan. She pressed her thumbs into her
temples.

"Come here, girl," said Claire. "Let me give you a good massage."

Bridget leaned her head back. The pressure of Claire's fingertips soothed the ache. She closed her eyes. "Remember when we
were kids how I always wished your mom was mine, too."

Claire smiled. "Bev's great. Only problem back then was all
her causes. We didn't settle down and stay in one place till I was
in seventh grade."

"But, you could always talk to her no matter where she was,
even if she was in a rice paddy in Thailand."

"For sure," said Claire. "She's my biggest supporter. I even told
her when I lost my virginity."

Bridget feigned a gasp. "I bet my mother still thinks I'm a
virgin."

Bridget remembered visiting Bev's house, the lunchtime talks
with Bev and Claire while they munched tuna salad sandwiches.
There were carved wooden bowls on the shelves, exotic masks on
the walls. Sunlight shone through a picture window onto a tangle
of plants. And Bev, in a peasant dress or worn blue jeans, hummed
along to Joni Mitchell or Neil Young while she cornrowed Claire's
hair. There was always a pitcher of herbal tea on the table, lots of
laughter, jasmine-scented incense floating in the air.

She thought of her mother's kitchen. Formica counter tops bare
except for a jar of peanut butter and a canister of chocolate chips.
She sighed. "My house was so different from yours. Dark. No one
ever home. The only nice memory I have is when I waited up for

my mom once in a while. She'd get in about eleven and if she was-n't too tired, she'd come into my room, sit on my bed and tell me the story of how she got started in business. Those were the only times I felt close to her. When she left my room I would lay in bed savoring every word, turning them over in my mind like a piece of chocolate melting in my mouth."

Claire's fingers grew still. "No doubt, Sarah loves you. But you keep wanting her to be someone she's not."

"I want her to be Bev."

Claire squeezed Bridget's shoulders. "You can't create a new personality for Sarah. But you can try to fill the gap. On the up side, you've got a hip new guy pursuing you."

Bridget smiled. "He keeps me grounded. Maybe he's a bit too cautious, but he's sensitive. And totally hot."

"I'd grab onto his butt and not let go."

Bridget remembered Carson's kiss in the park. She touched her lips and sighed. "I usually end up with the ones who look sensitive. Then I have to watch the door so it doesn't smack my back on the way out."

"Sounds like you learned enough to choose right this time."

"Carson's gutsy underneath his traditional veneer."

Claire raised an eyebrow. "Do you think he understands what we're trying to do?"

"I hope so." On the porch, a set of chimes picked up a melody in the breeze. Bridget twisted a lock of hair around her fingertip and listened to the melancholy notes. "I sense that my lifestyle has unnerved him a bit." She closed her eyes. "I think he might want more than I can give right now."

Claire finished massaging Bridget's temples. "You can't expect Carson to enter your radical world overnight. From what you've said, you two are more alike than not. You're both driven and dig the same things. Two sensible people ought to work that out."

Bridget lay her hand in Claire's palm just as she had when they were kids, two friends who knew each other's secrets. She smiled. "Who says we're sensible?"

Chapter 14

"MARK," YELLED CARSON into the intercom. "What are you doing?"

"Huh, boss? I can't hear you."

"Shut that damned CD player off and get your ass in here."

"Be right there," said Mark in a lilting voice.

Carson paced the length of the office and stopped when Mark came in.

"Did you finish the Thompson report?"

"In the middle of it."

"The report's due now." Carson's stomach burned. "No more music and personal calls until the report is finished, or I'll throw you out the window."

Mark looked over his shoulder toward floor-to-ceiling glass. On the parkway, traffic picked up as the first commuters made their way home for the evening. "You're going to throw me from the twenty-first floor? You'd commit a homicide over one measly report?"

"You have one hour."

Mark walked to the door and held the handle without turning it. "By the way. Did you say your family owns Ball and Jack's Electronics out of Madison, Wisconsin? That's a company on the move. They're in the Wall Street Journal this week."

"Schmoozing me won't earn you cool points."

"That's not it. I saw an ad. They're looking for someone highly skilled in computers and finance."

"Are you giving me the good news that you're leaving?" Carson nearly laughed knowing how much Mark hated hard work.

"No such luck, boss. Can't say it's not tempting. The job sounds ideal. I e-mailed a letter to them. A guy named Jack McAlister answered. That your father?"

Carson looked away. It stung hearing his father's name fall from the lips of a goof-off like Appleby.

"Jack McAlister is my brother. He doesn't care about the romantic aspects of computers any more than you care about working. He wants people who produce." For the first time Carson noticed a hurt look cross Mark's face. It surprised him.

Mark lowered his eyes. "I know I've been slow, boss. But you're gonna see, I'm really getting with the program."

Carson hesitated, then patted Mark on the back. "I know you'll do it. Remember, you can come to me for help any time."

"Thanks boss. That really means a lot to me."

He watched Mark close the door. In spite of everything he liked him. He hoped Mark could pull off the change he promised. Realistically, it would take a miracle.

After Mark left, Carson reached for his suit jacket. It was five o'clock. Mark was nowhere near finished with the report. He'd wander up to Java High for an hour or so and see if he could find Bridget. She should have come home last night from that retreat. Even though she'd only been gone for three days, he missed the sizzle she brought to his life with her crazy stories, her humor and ambition. It was like being inside a pinball machine, balls ricocheting from point to point, buzzers and bells lighting up. He cleaned his desk, turned off the office light and headed out.

*   *   *

At Java High's coffee bar, Carson ordered an iced tea with lemon. Edward waved to him and smiled from across the room where he was clearing tables. Carson waved back, happy to be recognized, glad to be part of the scene. He had Bridget to thank for that.

He squeezed lemon into his tea, inhaled the sharp acidic aroma and wondered what people did at a spiritual retreat? He pictured men and women with shaved heads and long robes playing drums and chanting. Whom had Bridget met? A guy exactly on her wavelength who would jump right into her project and her bed?

He squeezed the lemon to a pulp. She needed a lot of support for her project. What did a social worker know about business? Although her idea was noble, it was more complex than she realized. He gulped his tea nearly spitting it out. He had forgotten to sweeten it.

Ripping open a packet of sugar, he dumped the contents into the tea and watched the crystals sink to the bottom. In his world people took risks, but his world had neater parameters and a clearer path if you stuck to the grindstone and put in the hours. He understood that, but Bridget's world was more organic, filled with questions that didn't always have answers. It made him a bit uncomfortable.

Still, he almost felt her sitting beside him, her voice shimmering with intensity. He longed to kiss her, reach deep inside, absorb her warmth, her excitement. He scanned the crowd. The place seemed empty without her.

* * *

David twirled his cane as he headed up Pine Street toward Java High. He had spent the day working on his book and had run across some of Bridget's notes. He wanted to bump into her. If she were alone, he'd speak with her privately in the stacks, see if she had become a little more humble now that she knew he was on the Center's board.

What a stroke of luck running into Claire last week. She had ignored him, but not before he managed to overhear her tell Edward that she was moving into the Divine Guidance Center and that Bridget planned to join her.

Then a miracle happened. He had called Boon-Dan-Tan and casually mentioned Bridget's name. Within five minutes, Boon-Dan-Tan confirmed that Bridget planned to begin work on her cooperative housing project. That's when he volunteered to join the board.

He needed a diversion, anyway. Things weren't working out with Cecilia at all. The woman was gorgeous, rich and influential, but she had a big mouth, telling everyone they knew how Bridget had chased them around his apartment waving a baseball bat. He didn't want the situation played up now that he had a book contract. The whole thing showed him in a bad light.

Still, Cecilia wouldn't let it go. "We were almost killed," she argued. "People should know what an awful girlfriend you had."

Cecilia was right about one thing. It was important that Bridget not upstage him. Bridget had talent. If only she'd show a little humility, he'd give her credit for helping put the concept together.

He pushed open Java High's door. The air conditioning felt like a soothing balm. He'd worked up a sweat on the three-mile walk from University City. Chet Baker blew his horn mournfully on the stereo system. The cappuccino machine hissed steam into the air.

In the coffee bar he saw a familiar figure sitting on a stool, his perfectly cut sandy-brown hair brushing the collar of a well-tailored charcoal-gray suit. What did Bridget see in a buttoned down guy like that? She always went for the intellectual types. Rumor had it, they were an item now.

He grasped the cane, placed it firmly on the ground and limped over. Surely, she was angling to get a loan. That guy's bank financed community programs. It was his turn to be subtle if he wanted to get that loser out of her life.

*   *   *

Carson heard a chair scrape the floor next him. He looked up from his iced tea. Bridget's ex stared him squarely in the face. He wore a forlorn expression, as if he had lost something and didn't know where to find it. Somehow Carson didn't trust that look.

"How's it going?" said David, extending his hand.

Carson wondered what the guy wanted. He demanded that Bridget stay out of his turf, only to take over hers. Reluctantly, he shook David's hand.

"We haven't been formally introduced. I'm Doctor David Angsdorf." David emphasized the word "Doctor" as he flashed a smile showing off perfect white teeth.

"I know who you are, David."

Edward passed by carrying a tray of empty espresso cups and frowned in David's direction.

"How's Bridget?" said David. "I hope she's doing well."

"Terrific." Carson knew David couldn't have cared less. He wanted to push his fist through David's sparkling capped teeth.

David set his cane on the floor. "You two make a very, um, interesting couple."

"Is that right." Carson scrunched the empty sugar packet into a tight ball.

"You look more conventional than what Bridget's used to."

Edward watched them from behind the counter, a look of apprehension on his face.

Carson felt his own face heat up. "Maybe she got smart." From the corner of his eye he saw Edward give him the thumbs up sign.

David blinked. "I'm sure she bad-mouthed me, but the truth is, she never took the time to fully understand the housing concept. I taught it to her, but she doesn't really get it."

Carson swivelled in his seat and leaned forward. "Don't give me that bull."

David moved off his stool and thrust out his chest. "You don't know the truth about her or us. I can promise, you're in for some big surprises."

Edward slammed his empty tin tray on the counter in front of David. "Can I get you thomething?" he said. "Like arthenic?"

David's voice grew edgy. "Why don't you mind your own business and go clean out the coffee grinder."

Edward ignored him, turning to Carson. "Don't pay attention to thith athhole."

"Get lost, Edward," said David. "We all know that Bridget's bad news." He turned to Carson. "She'll get you into hot water at the bank before she's through with you."

Carson thought that David's tongue resembled the head of an ugly python slithering in and out with each syllable. "You're obviously still obsessed with her."

David clenched his jaw, swallowed, pressed his hands on his cane. "That's asinine. Bridget has some great qualities, but she's crazy. Why else did she break into my apartment?" His voice quivered.

Carson realized that David wasn't used to being confronted. He played his advantage. "You treated her like dirt. And you don't deserve her."

David's jaw dropped open, his teeth glinted. "You're a fool to believe anything Bridget says. One day, you'll realize you should have listened to me."

Carson ignored him. "See you later, Edward," he called as he made his way through the cafe toward the door.

He'd met fools like David before. They were so insecure, their only way to get attention was to create problems. When he reached the door, a young man wearing a dashiki and a wig of green dreadlocks walked in.

"Excuse me," he said.

Still shaken from his encounter with David, Carson tried to sidestep him.

The young man blocked the door. "Do you have a few bucks, sir? The management kicked me out and put me in the embarrassing position of having to buy coffee. What a waste. No one finishes what they have, anyway."

"You're the Coffee Bandit," said Carson, smiling in spite of himself.

"No, I'm the coffee recycler."

Carson dug into his pocket for some singles, pressed them into the Coffee Bandit's hand and left.

Chapter 15

TWILIGHT HAD SETTLED over the city when Bridget stepped over a stack of empty flour sacks on the loading dock of her mother's factory. She adjusted the waistband of her long, black skirt, smoothed the placket of her white linen blouse and checked her pumps for scuffmarks. Satisfied with her professional appearance, she rang the bell next to the battered metal door.

Her mind had been racing all day. All the years she spent trying to be independent of her mother's will. Now, she felt like a child. Her mother's decision about the convent would make a difference in how quickly she and Claire moved forward. On the way home from the retreat they had role-played dialogue. Nothing sounded right.

When Claire dropped her off, she had given her a bag of rose petals from the retreat. They were in her purse wrapped in tissue paper, crushed from nervous fingering.

She strived to understand how her mother might feel, her thirty-two year old daughter, single, unemployed, and about to give up her worldly possessions. There'd be no wedding plans, no grandchildren on the horizon. Her mother had liked David, how he popped into the factory from time to time to shoot the breeze, always flattering her.

Bridget pushed the bell again and held her finger on it. In less than a minute, the door swung open. Her mother stood before her wearing her factory uniform, a gray dress, white apron, and Amish bonnet.

"Bridget. Darling. Stop with the ringing. You won't believe what happened. One of my machines went kaput. I had to call in the whole crew to smash the cookies by hand. This disaster's costing me a fortune."

"Should I leave?" said Bridget, disappointed and relieved at the same time.

Her mother grabbed her arm. "I don't want you to leave. You said we have important business to discuss."

She tentatively followed her mother into the brightly-lit factory across the white-tiled floor past the assembly line. The crew worked diligently, pressing spoons into dough. Cookies moved in neat rows. The air smelled of chocolate chips and peanut butter, a scent Bridget associated with her mother.

Her mother paused at the end of the assembly line and opened the door to her office. Ushering Bridget in, she pointed to an old fashioned red-velvet armchair that faced her desk. "Have a seat."

Bridget brushed past her and perched on the edge of the armchair, the velvet pile had long ago matted into a dull sheen.

After shutting the door, her mother sat behind her desk. They stared at each other in silence, her mother's eyes expectant as she tapped her fingers against a pile of papers. Bridget rubbed her hands together, sure her mother was waiting for good news about David.

"So you're feeling alright?" said her mother. "What's up?"

If only once she could make her mother happy. "Claire's home," she said.

Her mother fidgeted in her chair. "Wasn't she off to South America? Does she need a job? Tell her I'm always hiring."

Bridget remembered the summers during high school when she and Claire worked on the assembly line weeding out broken cookies. Her mother had expected them to return after college and join the marketing department. "Claire's not a sales woman. And she was in Columbia."

"Oh. Save the rain forest and all that."

Her mother picked up a metal part and began wiping off the grease. An oily smell filled the room. Bridget noticed grease beneath the clear polish on her mother's nails. No doubt she had tried to fix the broken machine herself while Gordon gave her directions over the phone. When Bridget was a child, her mother often came home smudged with grease.

Her mother moved the rag methodically over the metal. "Grandmom's flight is due in at three tomorrow afternoon. Come for dinner Sunday night. I'm making a pot roast. Maybe you could bring a certain professor."

Bridget sighed. She remembered the dream at the retreat, how her mother stood by her bedside frowning. She touched a pearl button on her blouse. "Why did you call that certain professor?"

Her mother's voice brightened. "Oh honey, you saw him again. Aren't you happy I brought you two together?"

She looked up, tried to control the anger in her voice. It burst forth like steam from a boiling teakettle. "We will *never* get back together. Understand?"

Her mother set down the rag. "You two were perfect for each other."

"Listen to me."

"Don't be so stubborn, Bridget."

"Mom!" She sucked air into her lungs. "Last March, I broke into David's apartment. He brought his new girlfriend there, so I hid and watched them make love. It was all a dumb mistake."

She felt the weight of her mother's shocked silence. Her mother set the limp, greasy rag on her desk and folded her hands. Her knuckles turned white.

"David found me and got furious. We struggled. He fell down the stairs and hurt his leg. The police arrested me. He has a restraining order against me."

Her mother ripped off her bonnet and slammed it on the desk. "How could you do such a thing? What about your career?"

"No more career. I got fired."

"Police? Arrests? Fired?" Her mother rested her hand against her forehead leaving a greasy streak. "What man's going to want you after this? You could have been working here in the factory all these years, building up something important. Then you and David would have had a nice nest egg for a house and babies."

"That's your fantasy, not mine."

Bridget stared at the worn carpet. She took a deep breath, felt her chest rise against the fine linen of her blouse. She'd finish what she had to say and leave. "I'm moving into the Center where Claire lives."

Her mother's face froze into glassy stillness. "You keep hitting me over the head. What nonsense are you talking? Go back for another chance at your job." She pointed at the door as if Andrew stood behind it. "Now tell the truth, you didn't try something foolish like organizing the nurse's aids into a union? Workers don't need a union if you pay decent like I do."

Bridget's body slumped in defeat.

"And another thing. I don't want you moving into any religious center where they pray to rocks and crystals. I know about those places. You have to share unsanitary bathrooms and everyone walks around smoking pot. Feh. I won't have it."

Bridget tried to calm her pounding heart with the breathing exercises she had learned on the retreat. Slowly, she lifted her head, held it high, spoke calmly, "There's nothing more to say. I'm moving in."

"Stop the nonsense! You'll come and work for me. Meet the executives at the food companies. A beautiful woman like you can make out like gangbusters."

"What you've done is really great, but I'm going to open a special place where all kinds of people live and work together." She watched the color drain from her mother's face as she launched into her housing concept.

Her mother studied her as if she had just hatched from an egg of unknown origin. "What did I raise? It was all my fault naming you Bridget. First, you wanted to become a nun. Then you grow up to hang out with Claire the guru. Why can't you be a plain old American?"

Bridget focussed her breathing. She had nothing to lose. "You've got the old convent near the Italian Market. You only use it for storage. I'd like you to sell it to me at a reasonable price and then I won't have to stay at the Center."

"The city's interested in buying my building for a community center. They'll pay me two hundred thousand dollars. Where are you going to get the money to beat that, Miss Smarty Pants?" Her eyes bored into Bridget.

Bridget gripped the armrests in frustration. "It's to your benefit if I put the building to good use. You can make it into a foundation. You'd get a tax break and do something good for the community at the same time. We could call it the Ugly Cookie

Foundation."

Her mother's voice trembled with anger. "Your grandparents came to this country with nothing but the shirts on their backs. They slaved their whole lives to build for the future. Everyday when I see my factory, I remember their struggle. Now you want to throw it away on a foundation? Charity begins at home. You could take over this factory when I'm gone. But no. You want to cure all the problems in the world. Well, you can't do it without money."

Bridget banged her fist on the desk. "I'm so sick of hearing about money and profits."

Her mother picked up her bonnet and fiddled with the strings. "I'm charitable. Who do you think gives all their factory seconds to the soup kitchens in town? Me."

Bridget steeled herself. She'd try another tack. "You told me yourself that Gordon helped you start your business. I have people who want to help me, too."

"Like who? Claire?"

"Grandmom. She loves the idea."

"Why are you talking to Grandmom about these things? She's an old woman. You have no idea about the struggle you're in for. Look around. Do you think I got here overnight? I built this business from nothing with my own sweat and blood." A knock interrupted her. "Come in," she called sweetly.

A short, stout woman opened the door. "Hi, Bridget," she said. "How've you been?"

"Hanging in there, Alma."

"I'm sorry to interrupt you, Sarah," said Alma. "The mechanics are here. I've got some papers for you to sign."

Her mother instantly lifted her shoulders and regained her mantle of authority. She motioned Alma to the desk and slipped on her bifocals. Alma set the papers down. Her mother peered over her nose like a surgeon about to remove a tumor. "You tell them that I refuse to pay this until I see the work myself."

Bridget caught Alma's eye and smiled knowingly. From the stories her mother told, not only had she worked like a dog, she had managed every penny with an iron fist. In the final analysis, if she hadn't started in Gordon's bakery, the business might never have happened.

"Excuse me Bridget," said Alma. "I have one other thing to discuss with your mother."

Bridget played with the gold signet ring she wore on her right ring finger. Her mother had given it to her for high school graduation. On the front, Bridget's initials were engraved, and on the back was one word inscribed in Yiddish, "Baleboosteh." The translation had two meanings. Sarah intended it to mean an excellent homemaker. Bridget had chosen the second meaning as her mantra, one who manages well and assumes authority.

She watcned her mother talking to Alma, her full lips moving, remembered a winter night long ago, the cadence of her mother's voice when she first told the story of her business. Her mother had come home from work early, smelling of chocolate, sugar and butter. Wearily, she sat on the edge of Bridget's bed, removed her worn, white pumps, and set them side by side on the floor. "Would you like a bedtime story?" she had asked.

When Bridget nodded, yes, her mother's eyes grew dreamy, her voice distant. "It's time you know our family history."

Her mother began her tale by describing the dreary apartment she and Bridget's father had rented when they were first married. It faced a tire factory in South Philadelphia, a mile or so from the convent. They were almost broke, yet each morning, instead of looking for a job, Bridget's father snuck off to the racetrack. Five months pregnant, her mother was at her wit's end, unsure how they would pay the following month's rent.

Even though her mother worked for Gordon at his bakery concession in Skalron's Department Store, it wasn't enough to pay the bills. Gordon's business had hit a slump. To build it up, he had offered her extra money to give cookie-baking demonstrations.

Everyone knew that her cakes and cookies tasted good even if they looked ugly, but Bridget's father just laughed when her mother told him about Gordon's offer. "You can't make cookies in public," he said. "They'll turn out a mess."

"Says you." In that moment, her mother promised herself the cookies would be perfect.

Bridget remembered how her mother had smiled when she got

to the part about baking the cookies. Her mother was so nervous that day, she was afraid she'd go into early labor. Still, she stood tall behind the counter at Gordon's bakery, her fingers shaking as she tied an apron over her bulging waist.

Gordon removed bread from the oven, sweat dripping from his forehead. "You ready, Sarah?"

Her mother looked at him, a mouse in his own trap, his baker's hat slightly askew as he watched her measure sugar, peanut butter, flour. She would create perfectly formed peanut butter cookies. School children in plaid uniforms raced past, stopping when they heard the whir of her mixer.

Three little girls pressed close to the stage. Her mother could read their nametags: Maggie, Bridget and Colleen. She liked Bridget best. It seemed a solid, sturdy name. She decided if she had a girl, she would name her Bridget. She'd call on the luck of the Irish. It couldn't be worse than her own.

A small crowd gathered behind the girls. Her mother spooned the peanut butter into the bowl, cracked an egg over the creamy blob. She would make a beautiful batch of cookies for her unborn Bridget. When the dough was finished, she placed, rounded mounds on the sheet, sprinkled them with sugar and made criss-crosses with a fork.

After her mother set the cookies in the oven, she nervously watched the audience. It looked like they were having a good time. Suddenly, as if a spell came over her, she pulled the tray of half-baked cookies from the oven and set it on the table. She clenched her fists and willed them to stay closed. Her fists opened. She reached out and jabbed each cookie smack in the center. Hot dough burned her thumb. She winced with pain at each jab, but couldn't stop.

Some people looked stunned. The little girls in the front row giggled. Her mother smiled bravely and put the cookies back in the oven, then ran cool water over her fingers. Slowly, the pain subsided. When the cookies were done, she removed the ugliest batch she'd ever made.

"Voila," she announced, her voice quivering.

Everyone started laughing like she'd planned the whole thing as a joke. They all reached for samples, then clamored to buy everything she baked.

At the end of the shift Gordon stuffed something into her apron pocket. "You were great," he said. "Who would have believed ugly cookies could sell?"

In a trance, her mother walked the two miles to the apartment. She stopped when she reached the bridge that crossed the river to her neighborhood. Fifty feet below, the water rushed by, brown and muddy. Just the week before, she'd thought it might not be such a bad idea to throw herself off.

The walk had warmed her. She unbuttoned her old cape and reached into her apron pocket where a thirty-dollar cash advance seemed to give off heat. An idea hit. With Gordon's bakery as their first outlet, she and Gus would become a team of bakers. She looked down at her hands. Small blisters had formed on the knuckle of her thumb. Gus would never go for smashing hot dough. Maybe spoons would work. If he went for the idea, she'd have to take control of the paychecks. If not, she'd bake the cookies on her own.

Bridget glanced up at the wall behind her mother's desk. Awards covered it, including nine "Most Ugly But Delicious Cookie in Philly" awards. A five-dollar bill in a cheap wooden frame hung among them, a souvenir from the sale of her mother and father's first batch of cookies. All the years she resented the hours her mother spent at the factory. For the first time her own goals seemed similar to her mother's. Couldn't her mother see that they were both driven to achieve their dreams?

She smiled half-heartedly and wondered what her father would have thought about her buying the convent. Maybe he would have moved his gambling cronies in and set up a craps table.

Her mother gathered up the papers and handed them back to Alma. "Tell the mechanics I'll be out in a minute."

"They need an answer soon," said Alma.

"They'll have to wait. I don't make decisions without talking to Gordon." Her mother leaned back in her chair and gazed at Bridget. "See what it's like. You need a big reserve of cash for emergencies."

Alma quietly shut the door.

"I worry you're too much like your father," said her mother. "The two of you so impractical. You don't have a head for business. You don't even have a plan."

Bridget looked directly at her mother. Her anger had returned. "I'm getting it in place. With a foundation, you'd have a great tax deduction . . ."

"Stop! I don't need any more tax deductions. You've got to get yourself a job."

Bridget felt her mother suck energy from her bit by bit.

Her mother pushed a pile of papers aside. "You can't stay out of trouble. If you're not careful you're going to wind up with your picture in the post office!"

Bridget dug into her handbag until she felt the crinkle of tissue paper. "Here's a present." She leaned forward, avoided her mother's gaze and tossed the package on her desk.

Sarah ripped open the tissue paper. "What's this?"

"Rose petals. You make a calming potion. You could leave it in a dish or put it in your tea."

The petals had shriveled and crumbled into brownish flakes. Lunarized or solarized, nothing would help the situation.

"So. We add drugs to the list of offenses. I bet Claire brought this back. You two are smoking this stuff and having hallucinations. That's how you got your crazy ideas in the first place."

Bridget shot to her feet. "I'm leaving."

"It's bad enough giving everything away to the poor, now you're smoking drugs."

"Why would I give you drugs? Have you gone completely mad? They're dried rose petals. Smell them."

"Smell them and get high so I can give you my building?"

Bridget grabbed the packet and flung the petals in the air. They fluttered onto her mother's desk.

Her mother stood up and whisked the petals toward Bridget. "Did you fed-ex this to your grandmom, too? Both of you in cahoots behind my back."

"You're the only one who does things behind people's backs. You called David. Stay out of my business."

Her mother came around the desk and folded her hands across her chest. "I only called him because I know you're going through a bad time. It worries me. Promise me you won't get into anything like Prozac."

Bridget looked toward the door. "Thanks for the good advice, Ma. You just saved another future addict."

Out in the hall, the smell of baking dough overwhelmed her. Chocolate chip cookies passed by on conveyor belts. She flicked her arm out and knocked a row of them to the floor. They landed in a heap, warm chocolate oozing over tile.

A startled worker looked up. She walked past him, stepped out on the dock and collapsed on a flour sack. She pressed her hand to her heart and slowed her breath.

She imagined floating back into her mother's office, viewing the scene from above. The corners of her mouth curled up. Laughter rose from her belly. Too bad Claire didn't have a stash from Columbia. She could sure use it.

Chapter 16

A VEIL OF GAUZY CLOUDS sailed over the Italian Market on Ninth Street in South Philadelphia giving respite from the hot sun.

At fruit and vegetable stands vendors haggled with customers. Sides of deep crimson beef, whole pigs and ropes of pink sausages hung in the windows of butcher shops. Lace table cloths and linen napkins were arranged neatly in bins in front of a dry goods store. On the corner, a young girl sold sunglasses and striped beach chairs.

Couples from the suburbs dressed in khakis and sundresses walked past kids sporting spiky green and orange hair. Two women argued about the merits of brown sugar versus honey to glaze a ham. Carson bumped into a shopping cart. An old woman in a black dress cursed at him in Italian as she jerked her cart away. He apologized in a bad Italian accent making Bridget laugh.

At a produce stand shielded by a blue plastic awning, Bridget smelled the acidy-sweet scent of ripe tomatoes and realized how much she had missed the bustle and color of the market. After her frustrating meeting with her mother, it felt good doing everyday things, especially with a nice guy like Carson. Even if her mother had turned down her request for the convent, she hadn't completely given up hope. She wanted Carson to see it.

Before she could stop him, Carson reached past the cucumbers and pressed his finger against a tomato.

"Don't touch da tomatoes, mister," scolded the burly vendor. "You break, you buy."

"You heard the man," laughed Bridget. She playfully pinched Carson's arm.

"Ouch," he said in mock pain.

"Buy five pounds only two dollars," said the vendor. "A special deal. They're just right for gravy."

The vendor pulled his suspenders with his thumbs letting them smack against his chest, wrinkling his damp T-shirt. "Buy some apples. Look how red and gorgeous. You makin' dinner for this beautiful lady? Buy my stuff. She gonna marry you."

"You gonna marry me?" said Carson.

"Sure," she smiled. "You'll be the chef when we move into the convent." She liked the image of Carson wielding a soup ladle in a large kitchen and wondered if that would ever happen.

"Don't make fun. I'm a damn good cook." He handed her the package of tomatoes.

She held them as he looked over the apples, a tinge of disappointment washing over her. He hadn't directly responded to her teasing proposal about the convent.

Then again, this morning she had surprised him with the news that she had sublet her apartment to a woman she met at the retreat. She planned to move temporarily to the Center tomorrow. He had become sullen on their drive to South Philly. But as soon as they hit the market, he cheered up.

He took the overripe tomatoes from her. Juice stained the brown bag. He set it in his shopping bag.

Children darted between chicken coops, slipping on discarded lettuce leaves. The chickens squawked, flapping their wings. They gave off a sharp stench that mingled with the scent of cheeses, butchered meat, apples and garlic.

Bridget glanced through the throng of people. No David. If she bumped into him, he would surely fake a confrontation. She wouldn't take the chance. If she saw him, she'd avoid him.

She reached into Carson's bag, pulled out an apple, wiped it on her dress and placed it between his teeth. He took a bite. The hot sun broke through the clouds. Beads of sweat appeared on his forehead. The fruit smelled sweet and ripe.

They passed under the awning of the spice shop beneath a fringe of brick-red dried peppers. The aroma of garlic and basil lingered in the air. She imagined cooking with him, slicing onions, peeling tomatoes, the aroma of tomato sauce filling his apartment. She wished he didn't have to meet his brother at the airport in the afternoon.

Reaching into her handbag, she searched for her handkerchief, withdrew it and pressed it to his damp forehead. A smile crossed his lips. "How's your friend Claire doing with her lecture series?" he said.

"So far, so good. Nearly a hundred people attended the first one."

They stopped in front of his car. "Let me know when she's giving the next one. I'd like to go." He opened the trunk and set the bags inside.

"Are you suddenly getting the spiritual bug?" She settled against the warm metal.

He closed the trunk and pressed his hand against the window. Moving his face close to hers, he straightened his arm and leaned against the glass, boxing her in. "No, but I'm communing with the divine right now."

She pressed her index finger against his chest and felt his muscles tighten beneath the thin weave of his polo shirt. All she had to do was turn her head an inch to reach his lips. "I can't wait for you to meet Claire."

"Maybe she'll convert me, too."

"Not a bad idea Mr. Corporate America." She kissed his cheek. He turned and kissed her mouth, his tongue seeking hers.

His hand caressed her back. The street noise faded.

"Hey, yo, dude," a teenager called out. "Lovah boy needs a bucket of cold watah all over him."

They pulled apart. A group of teenagers stood across the street in a doorway watching them. Bridget lowered her head, trying to catch her breath.

"Time to split," said Carson.

The imprint of his lips lingered on hers. She took his hand and led him across Federal Street. "Come on. I want to show you my mother's building."

"Is she selling it to you?"

They reached the corner. "We had an awful meeting yesterday. Mom shot me down when I asked her for the building. She thinks I'm an irresponsible drug addict."

"You've got to be kidding."

Through the crowd, she recognized a tall, fair-haired woman. It was David's girlfriend. Suddenly, she saw David craning his neck, a police officer in tow.

Her stomach muscles tightened. She dragged Carson behind a stack of chicken coops. Chickens scratched and clucked as she flattened him against the doorway.

"Kiss me," she said.

"Now this is impulsiveness at its best." He pressed against her, kissing her lips, tightening his arm around her waist, his hip touching hers. She lost sight of David as her body responded to his kiss. Her heart raced, her skin tingled. Carson's hand swept over her back, lifting her dress, touching her thigh. The chickens squawked.

"Get outta there," shouted a man. "You're scaring my chickens." He stood at the curb wearing a blood-spattered butcher's apron.

They jumped apart. Carson ran his hand through his hair.

Bridget smoothed the front of her dress.

"My friend has something in her eye," stuttered Carson. "We're trying to get it out."

"My eye," said the man, sniggering.

"Come on, dear." Carson draped his arm over Bridget's shoulder. "Do you feel better?"

"I think so." She blinked, shielding her eyes from the sun as she searched the street for David.

*   *   *

The Police Officer pushed the brim of his hat over his forehead. "I want to help you. But tell me again. What exactly happened?"

"She threatened us with bodily harm." David folded the restraining order and stuck it back in his pocket. He knew he would find Bridget down here sooner or later. Watching her kiss that jerk in public was more than he could bear.

Cecilia opened her mouth to say something, but David cut her off.

"I told you, Officer, she's following us, making threats. And she's got her boyfriend doing the same thing. You have to arrest her. Right Cecilia?"

"So, Miss," said the Officer. "You agree that this woman threatened Dr. Angsdorf."

Cecilia hesitated and glanced at David. He kicked at a wilted head of cabbage laying in the gutter. "Uh-huh," she said. "But I don't see her now."

The officer scratched his chin. "If we can't find the woman in question, I can't help you. I'll be at Ninth and Christian." He turned and headed into the crowd.

David waited until the policeman was out of earshot, then hissed at Cecilia, "I thought you'd back me up. You sounded so lame. Where's that big mouth of yours when I need it?"

"You're the one who tells me to cool it every time I try to defend you. You can't make up your mind. You're obsessed with that woman and I can't take it anymore."

"I told you how her boyfriend insulted me at Java High."

Cecilia whirled around and pointed a finger at his chest. "I'm sick of your jealousy. This is all because you saw them kissing in front of his car."

"That's not true."

"I've had it with you. I don't need a phantom for competition."

*   *   *

"Let's go," said Carson. "That guy with the apron won't budge until we do. Besides, you look real tense."

She smiled wanly, scanning the street. "I just saw David, his girlfriend and a police officer. I didn't want to ruin our morning with a bad scene."

He leaned over and kissed her cheek. "I saw David at Java High, too, when you were at the retreat."

She sighed. "There's not much I can do if he's out to get me. Let's go to the convent."

He shielded her body as they turned the corner. It infuriated him that David wouldn't let up on her, but he wondered if she wasn't egging him on a bit. Then again, the guy gave her no real options.

Bridget pulled him to a stop at the corner. "Here we are."

He looked up at the building and read the words carved in stone above the door: Sisters of Mother Mary, Est. 1885. Stained glass windows flanked a thick wooden door. In a mosaic of blue, red and yellow glass Mary released a dove toward a beam of light. Above the stained glass, a number of windows were covered in rain-smudged cardboard.

Bridget touched his hand. "The building's great, don't you think? I want to show it to you. There's a place where we can hop the fence."

He wasn't so sure. Dirt and cigarette butts covered the marble steps. Trash was piled in the window wells. He followed her around the side of the building lightly trailing his hand along a chain link fence covered in vines. A stale, yeasty odor rose from the beer bottles broken and strewn along the edge.

"Mom usually keeps her trailer back here," she called over her shoulder. "If I had my hands on the property, I'd turn the backyard into a garden." She peered through the fence.

He noticed three abandoned buildings across the street, their windows broken. Two men and a woman sat in a doorway drinking out of paper bags.

"Do you see what's going on over there?" He watched her set a foot in the chain link. "We're three blocks from the Italian Market and already the neighborhood's marginal. This could be real trouble."

"I've lived in the city all my life." She began to climb. "I'm not scared."

"What are you doing?"

"Scaling the fence. Mom's caretaker works at the factory on Saturdays so he's not here."

"What if he took the day off? He could be sitting in a window right now with a shotgun."

"Move your butt. He doesn't have a gun." She hiked her dress up to her thigh. "Come on, put your foot right here."

He caught a glimpse of lace panties. His breath caught in his throat. With a leap, he landed in the middle of the fence, hoisted himself over and dropped down beside her. She touched his cheek and smiled. She was certainly strong-willed. Not an unpleasant quality. From the way she described her mother, no wonder the two of them butted heads.

They picked their way through weeds and rubble. An old bicycle frame was propped against the house next to a doorless refrigerator. Bridget climbed up the porch steps and looked into the kitchen. "When Mom bought the building, the nuns said they would pray for our souls. I hope they did. I need all the help I can get now."

She jiggled the kitchen window. "It's open."

"I think we should go," said Carson. "Someone might call the cops on us."

"Won't be the first time for me." She flashed him a grin and lifted the sash. Balancing on the sill, she climbed through the window into the kitchen. "Come on. Don't be a wimp."

By the time he squeezed through and landed on the kitchen floor, she was already rummaging through an open box, humming. Dust floated down from the high ceiling through dank air. He coughed and looked up. Elaborate angels were carved into the cornices. On the floor, boxes sat piled against a faded aqua blue wall, a cast-iron frying pan filled with water rested on the burner of an old Viking Stove.

"Why did your mother want this building?"

"She was going to open an Ugly Cookie Outlet near the market, but her friend has a building in Northern Liberties that she wants to use. All she keeps here are cookie labels and machine parts and the old furniture from my grandmom's apartment."

She led him into the dining room. On the pine-paneled walls, brass sconces, some missing light bulbs, hung at two-foot intervals. Below an ornate crystal chandelier, a large piece of machinery lay dismembered on the floor surrounded by tools. He imagined a polished oak table, nuns in black habits singing grace, vegetable soup in bowls, fresh bread on a cutting board.

"This building's perfect," she whispered. "When I was kid I used to come here all the time. I wanted to be a nun just like Sister Mary Elizabeth."

Carson leaned against the wall and laughed. "You a nun?"

"It's a stretch, but stranger things have happened. I know this building like the back of my hand. Look at these wide halls. It would be easy to build a wheelchair ramp. I can see it now. We'd put in a couple of skylights and a lift. I'd keep all the nice things like the angels and the moldings."

He traced the shadow of a cross on the dirty wall. The high ceilings gave the place a majesty missing in newer buildings.

"Truth is, I've never wanted anything so much in my life."

A sinking feeling hit the pit of his stomach. He sensed that her dream took precedence over him, yet he wanted to celebrate their adventure, take her in his arms, press her against the faded wallpaper and make love to her.

She led him up the staircase. The plaster walls were badly cracked. A large water stain covered the ceiling. Still, the house's serene character shone through, as if the house were resting, waiting for life to fill it up again.

At the top of the stairs, a door held a stained glass picture of Joseph working in his carpentry studio, his son Jesus watching him. It led to a large room, which looked out on the basketball courts in the playground on the opposite corner. There was a baseball diamond, too.

He watched her patrol the halls in her strawberry sundress. Light shone through the stained glass window burnishing her hair copper. She looked liked she belonged here. Unless her mother had a change of heart, she'd have a tough time finding the money to buy another building. For a split second, he hoped her mother held out, if only to slow her down a little.

"Come on Mr. Whale Vest," she called from the third floor. Check this out." He bounded up the risers, his footsteps echoing against the bare walls.

She kneeled over a cedar chest, rummaging through sheets and blankets until she pulled out a crocheted afghan, its rainbow colors layered in zigzag stripes. It had unraveled in a few places, but the colors were still bright and bold.

"Grandmom made this for me when I was eight years old." She closed the trunk and sat on it, hugging the afghan to her chest. "I slept with it every night. She's so bored in Florida. I think she's crocheted at least twenty more. I'd love to put an afghan on every bed in this place."

He sat down next to her and studied her profile, her fine,

straight nose, arching eyebrows, full lips and rounded chin. She looked like the stained glass portrait of Mary in the window down below. Now that he had someone terrific, he didn't want to let her go. She could get a job anywhere. Maybe, he'd ask her to move in with him. The idea scared and excited him.

Still, a small part of him wanted her to have this house. Fixed up, its clean white walls reflecting sunlight, people engrossed in activities, her idea could work.

"I think you're right about this place," he said wistfully. He moved his hand against the warmth of her arm, smelled the citrus scent of her perfume.

Her breath caressed his cheek as he drew her near. His fingertips touched hers. It struck him how often he'd felt lonely with Anne, but never with Bridget.

Slowly he slid his hand upward, his finger grazing her breast as if testing the wind. She turned to kiss him, easing her body against his. The curve of her hip pressed against his own. He longed to taste every inch of her.

She moved away and turned so he could unzip her dress, help her step out of it. She leaned forward to unbutton his shirt, caressing his skin with her cool fingers.

"This way," she said, picking up the afghan, touching him in the most exquisite places.

He followed her down the hall, trailing kisses along her neck, over her shoulder blades. She led him to a door at the end of the hall and opened it.

The room glowed with a golden light that shone from circular windows. In a swirl, she spread the afghan on the floor, then turned to him. Their mouths pressed together. They tugged at the remnants of their clothes, her panties, his pants and briefs.

His eyes swept over her porcelain skin, her full breasts, imprinting her beauty in his mind's eye.

Gently trailing her mouth along his neck, she planted tiny kisses from his chest to his belly. He felt as if silk scarves brushed his skin.

He pulled her close, melding into her body. "I don't ever want this to end," he said.

Suddenly, she stopped. "We don't have . . ."

"Wait." He reached toward his pants. "I've got a condom. It's pretty ancient." He felt his face grew red as he fumbled through his wallet. "If these things had expiration dates, we'd have to stop now."

"Do you want me to put it on for you?"

"Best offer I've had in a long time."

She ripped the packet open.

He lay back, hands behind his head, and closed his eyes. Slowly, she rolled the condom over his erection until he was sure he would burst. Then she was stretching across his body, her breasts against his chest, her lips warm and moist as she shifted her hips and took him inside. They moved together until he wasn't sure where he left off and she began.

He tasted the salt of her skin, felt her breath in his ear, the rise and fall of their bodies increasing his desire. When he heard her moan, he let go. Release came with a force that rocketed him into a wild free-fall.

*   *   *

He sat at the Sky-Top lounge inside USAir Terminal B and sipped a beer. His brother Jack would arrive any minute. He wished he were still holding Bridget in the mystical light of the convent. Maybe she was right about that spiritual stuff. He had never felt so in tune with himself or another person before.

Although the idea of meeting Jack was disconcerting, he missed him. For all his annoying habits, Jack had inherited their father's magnetism, something Carson knew he didn't possess.

He remembered sitting in his parents' backyard on hot summer nights splitting a case of Leinenkugel beer with Jack, telling jokes, aiming and tossing the dead soldiers toward the trash cans.

Did Jack want him to come home? They both knew that if their Dad had lived, he would have stayed. Still, he liked his job at the bank, and everything about this crazy city, now that Bridget was in his life. He even got a kick out of Mark.

He took another pull on his beer.

A hand slapped his back. Beer spilled over the lip of his glass.

"Hi Carson, old boy. How goes it?"

He turned. "Shit, you scared me Jack."

Jack grinned, his ruddy cheeks flushed. "I've really missed you, bro." He turned his face in profile and stroked the tip of his nose. "Look. The old schnozz healed up good as new."

Carson winced. A small bump protruded from the bridge of Jack's nose.

Jack settled himself on the barstool beside Carson. "All right, I admit it. I was wrong to pressure you when you had so much crap to deal with. You got so damned dreamy during the expansion. It shook me up. You faded away, and I didn't know what else to do. I always thought you loved Ball and Jacks like I do."

Carson sighed. Jack could have been his father, the way he leaned against the bar, propping the side of his head in his palm. He had even ordered the same scotch as their father, Glenlivet, neat, with a side of rocks.

Carson lifted his beer glass in a toast. "When all is said and done, I'm probably not suited to the business, anyway. There's real opportunity here."

"I know. Word's out that you're doing exceptionally well."

"Mother told you?"

"Someone else. I got an e-mail from your assistant, Mark Appleby. Seems he saw my ad in the Wall Street Journal. He says that everyone at the bank admires your work. You're a man on the move."

"Don't get too chummy with Appleby."

"Hey. I'm happy for you. Let by-gones be by-gones."

"I'm sorry I wasn't straight with you from the beginning. I never thought I'd leave. But with Anne and all . . ."

Jack playfully cuffed Carson's cheek. "It's behind us now."

Carson smiled. "How are Sally and the kids?"

"The kids are great. Sally's a little edgy. Since you left, I've been putting in fourteen-hour days. When I come home at a decent hour, it seems all I do is push aside the flower arrangement and spread my work across the dining room table. She gets pissed, but so far she's stuck it out with me."

"You'd better take care of her."

"Sally knows I'm there when she needs me." Jack dropped an ice cube into his scotch. "Since when did you become an expert on women?" He grinned suggestively.

Carson touched the cuff of his sleeve. The smell of Bridget's perfume still lingered on his clothes. "Knock it off. Now tell me what's up with you and Lisa."

"You were right, she's picked up a lot of slack. We're short-handed, though. And I still don't trust her like you do. I'm always watching my back."

Carson smacked the lip of the bar top. Jack's distrust of Lisa infuriated him. "You're crazy. She's more loyal than I am. I'm the one who jumped ship."

Jack sipped his scotch. "Calm down. I'm just trying to tell you that I don't think we can hire anyone and train them for her old job in the midst of all this. It's a long shot. But I've got to ask you. Would you consider coming back? You can have whatever you want."

Carson sighed. "It's not a good idea."

"I figured you'd say that. But you have to come home anyway. Mother told me that she called you about the family meeting. She's acting real strange and so is Lisa. They've been spending a lot of time together. When you look at them, their eyes are all red, as if they've been crying. Sally thinks they're trying to change the will. What I do know is that Mother can be influenced if Lisa pressures her."

Carson spread his hands on his lap trying to contain his impatience. Moving away from his sister had left a gap in his life. "Lisa wouldn't do that," he said quietly.

Jack swivelled his chair. "I overheard them talking about banks and lawyers and how Dad owed Lisa something."

"Have you asked Lisa what it's all about?"

Jack's face flushed. "About a million times and she gets real weird. She says we'll talk about it when you come home. Anything could happen between now and then. The problem is I'm dependent on her."

Carson wished Jack would stop with his paranoia.

Jack checked his watch. "Mark my word. Something's up."

"Time to get to my gate."

Carson fingered his beer mug. "Are we friends again?"

"Always were." With two swift swigs, Jack polished off the rest of his drink. He reached into his breast pocket for his wallet and threw a twenty on the counter. "I'm on the road for the next two weeks. See you the first part of August."

Carson watched Jack leave, a pall settling over him. Despite Jack's forgiveness, it felt as if the rift between them had grown wider. They were at odds about so many issues. Maybe things would be better when he went home. His mother wouldn't have called a meeting unless she wanted to clear the air about something.

He glanced at the bartender and considered ordering another drink. How pathetic hanging out at airport bars when he really wanted to see Bridget. Since she was moving tomorrow, he'd stop by her place and use the excuse that he wanted to help her pack. Besides, this whole thing was tough on her. She probably needed him.

He got up and searched for a pay phone, but first he stopped at a vendor and bought some flowers.

Chapter 17

OF ALL THE RECIPES in her mother's limited repertoire, Bridget loved pot roast best. Her mother had made it tonight in honor of Grandmom's visit. The three of them now sat at an elaborately carved dining room table in her mother's grand old Victorian house. Slices of tender meat rested in gravy on a serving platter. The aroma of garlic and allspice filled the air. Bridget's mouth watered.

From her perch at the head of the table, Bridget's mother scooped mounds of mashed potatoes onto gold-rimmed plates. Grandmom sat across from Bridget, her bulky frame encased in a too-tight, shiny, blue jogging suit. Although Grandmom had complained about the bumpy flight from Florida, Bridget thought she looked well and lively. Grandmom still took pride in her thick silver hair, pulled back into a French Twist, a style her hairdresser down in Florida had taught her.

Bridget fidgeted with the silverware. So far everyone had kept the peace. Her mother hadn't brought up their conversation at the factory or her move to the Center. Grandmom, on her best behavior, had complimented her mother on the newly decorated house. Thanks to her mother's over-enthusiasm, the exterior, its trim painted orchid-pink, looked like a child's version of a gingerbread house. Two-story high trellises trailed artificial ivy. Recently, she'd covered the dining room walls in glossy leopard print.

While her mother and grandmom politely debated the merits of paint versus wallpaper, Bridget thought about Carson. He had showed up at her apartment the night before to help her pack, and had taken her into his confidence, talking about the meeting with his brother. He still hadn't forgiven himself for hurting Jack.

When she touched his shoulder to comfort him, he had brought her hand to his lips. The next thing she knew, they were in bed making love. He had put her at ease, both of them laughing at the way they had groped for one another, as though they were practicing to become members of the Olympic wrestling team.

"Do I qualify for the gold?" she had said, when they finally collapsed into each other's arms.

He held her tenderly, kissing her forehead, telling her that from his perspective all her moves were spectacular. She couldn't think of a better way to say good-by to her apartment than spending her last night with him.

Her mother's voice cracked through her reverie. "How come you look so smug, young lady? What are they gonna do at that commune, turn you into the Dalai Lama?"

"Leave the child alone," said Grandmom. "You promised we wouldn't talk about this."

"This is the best pot roast you ever made." Bridget poked holes in her mashed potatoes with the tines of her fork. Her mother wasn't going to bring her down tonight. She thought of Carson's sweet face, remembered his lips pressing against her earlobe, the soft hair on his chest brushing against her breasts.

"Your Ma knows how to marinate the meat for good flavor," said Grandmom. "But look at that gravy, gray as your grandpop when he was laid out in his coffin."

"Please," said Bridget, dreamily. "No arguing."

"Why do you always have to criticize my food, Ma?" said her mother.

"I'm not criticizing. I'm just making a comment."

"Do you think she'll get better food in that boarding house she wants to open?"

"Never you mind. You're jealous because you won't be in charge."

"Can we talk about something else?" said Bridget.

"Like what?" said her mother. "That you're an unemployed jailbird?"

Bridget dropped her fork on the plate with a jarring clang. "A few days ago, I was a drug dealer. Which do you want?"

"Oy vey," said Grandmom. "It's not her fault David turned out to be a schmuck and that boss of hers an even bigger one."

"David's the schmuck?" Her mother pointed a spoon at Bridget.

"She broke into his apartment and watched . . . Oy vey, It's not normal."

Grandmom piled another slice of pot roast on her plate and waved the serving fork in the air. "Were you normal when you married Gus?"

"Don't insult my poor Gus. He's not here to defend himself, may he rest in peace."

Bridget felt her stomach churn.

"You still got the convent on Fitzwater Street?" Grandmom sliced her pot roast into tiny pieces.

Her mother's eyebrow twitched.

"I think you should give it to your baby," said Grandmom. "What you gonna do with all your buildings, sit on them like a hen hatching eggs?"

"I bought the building fair and square from the sweat of my own brow." Her mother glared at Grandmom. "I don't see you putting up any money."

"I put my condo up for sale and I'm giving the money to Bridgila. My profit could be as much as one hundred thousand dollars."

Her grandmom shocked Bridget. "I can't take that much money, Grandmom."

"Not to worry." Grandmom wagged her thick fingers back and forth. "My pension will cover me. Besides, I planned to leave it to you in my will. So let me see you enjoy the money while I'm still alive."

Her mother ladled gravy over the meat on Grandmom's plate. "One hundred thousand dollars will pay to fix up four rooms. Where you gonna get the money to fix the heating system and the floors? And what about the bathrooms?"

"She'll find a way. My Bridgila's very clever."

"Who's gonna be there? A bunch of dropouts with bells on their toes?"

Bridget set her elbows on the table. "There'll be fifteen to twenty lovely, decent people who care about each other." A few strands of hair had fallen over Bridget's temple. She twisted them around her finger. "I'll even make sure that the bathrooms have clean toilet seats," she said, a sharp edge in her voice. "And no one will have a communicable disease so you can come visit."

"If everyone's so nice and hardworking, why do they have to grab onto you to make their lives better? They're leeches. They want a free ride, dope and sex."

"You don't get it." Bridget stood up, knocking the chair over. "You don't really care about anyone except yourself. I've got to go. They're expecting me by eight."

"What about all the cookies I donated to the nursing home?"

"Just like manna from heaven." Bridget raised her hands toward the ceiling. "I'm leaving now. Thanks for dinner."

"Wait Bridgila," called Grandmom. "Is there room at the Center for me?"

* * *

Bridget set Grandmom's battered leather valise onto the back seat of her car. Grandmom had carried the same valise, buckled with an old leather strap, since Bridget was a child. Bridget stroked the cracked, dry leather as Grandmom bustled past her and settled into the front seat.

"Oy, that daughter of mine. Such a stubborn one."

Bridget planted herself behind the wheel. Grandmom pulled the seatbelt over her ample waist and snapped it shut. "Your mother is just like her accountant father. When she was little she wouldn't lend me money from her piggy bank without charging interest. So now she has a big house to rattle around in by herself. I'm glad to be out of there. Will I like this Center?"

A lump formed in Bridget's throat as she glanced over her shoulder. Her mother stood in the window watching them. The anger in her mother's face, the coldness in her eyes made Bridget wonder if her mother had cut her off for good.

This was turning into a fiasco. How would Grandmom fare at the Center? Bridget swallowed past the lump. "The Center's a very peaceful place, but awfully stark. If you don't like it, I'll bring you right back to Mom's."

"I'm no quitter." Grandmom winked. "Let's go for it."

Bridget laughed. "Then, let's burn rubber." Thoughts crackled through her mind as she turned the key in the ignition. It still seemed mad to drag Grandmom into this. She'd taken a chance asking her mother for the building, but she'd never meant to cause a rift between everyone.

"Maybe you should go back to Mom's," she said. "I know Boon-Dan-Tan will welcome you with open arms, but you'll have to share a room and bathroom."

Grandmom stared out the window, her jaw clenched. "Every time your mother insults you, it's like a knife to my heart. No. We go. A little bed and a little food is enough for me."

Bridget gunned the engine and pulled away from the curb.

Grandmom set her orthopedic shoes against the floorboards as though braking. Bridget slowed down. In the rearview mirror she saw the porch light of her mother's house snap off.

"So what kind of food do they have at the Center?" said Grandmom.

"Good food, but it's vegetarian. I can sneak you in a boiled chicken if you like."

"I can be vegetarian. If they have potatoes and flour, I'll make knishes. We'll get ourselves situated just fine. If your Ma won't give us the convent, we'll find another building. It's good for an old lady to have something to sink her false teeth into."

She touched Grandmom's hand. "You're smart and hip and you get great flashes of adventure."

"My darling, the only flashes I've had in my life are hot ones." She patted Bridget's knee. "I like the idea that they teach people to think better at the Center. The last thing I learned was how to set the thermostat for the air-conditioner in my condo."

Bridget felt her mood lighten. Never in her wildest dreams had she imagined that her grandmom would leave the comfort of her condominium and her mother's house for the austerity of the Center and the hard work of community living.

"You don't have to do all this for me. You've got a nice set-up down in Florida. The weather's good and you've got your friends."

"Friends, schmends. I think I'll live longer if I make a change. I'm damned bored down there. Remember my friend Rhonda? Her real name is Rachel. Well Rhonda-Rachel went and got the collagen treatment. At first she looked good, but the doctor pumped so much in her, she started to look like a dolphin."

Grandmom sighed. "After that, she started acting like a spring chicken, dragging me along to the dances. Next thing I know, she's marrying Mr. Klein. At first everything's dandy. They sit by the pool, play gin rummy. Then he has a stroke. Now she spends her days taking care of him. I helped her a lot and it made me feel good. But that's her life now. No more Early Bird Specials, collagen or dances."

"That's awful." Bridget thought of her grandmom living in the cooperative housing. They couldn't afford to set up assisted living, but they could set up a good prevention program. With a start, she remembered why Grandmom was here. "What kind of tests are they giving you at the hospital?" She hoped her voice didn't betray her anxiety.

"Just a routine check-up on my ticker." Grandmom gave Bridget's knee a reassuring pat. "Don't go around worrying, doll. I'm healthy as a horse. You'll take me to the hospital and they'll keep me overnight. It's no big deal. I just need more regular exercise."

Bridget pictured Grandmom taking yoga classes at the Center, eating healthy food and bossing everyone around. She nearly laughed out loud.

"So tell me," said Grandmom. "You found a new boyfriend yet?"

Bridget hesitated. "There's a guy I'm seeing. He's a goy."

"Makes no nevermind for me. You can find schmucks everywhere. Look at your father vanishing for days at the casinos. He bought presents for you, but he never protected you like a father should."

Bridget gripped the steering wheel. Something that had been nagging at her fell into place. Was that why she had fallen for David? He'd insisted on knowing where she was every hour of the day. Had she mistaken his obsession for the love and protection she desperately wanted? And Andrew. Hadn't he been her mentor, a strong authority figure? But Carson was different. Someone who could become a partner.

She turned onto City Line Avenue. The median strip glowed yellow beneath the streetlights. Traffic picked up. Grandmom had grown quiet. Her head bobbed toward her chest. A light snore escaped from her lips.

Besides Claire, Grandmom was the only person in the world she could turn to in a crisis. Grandmom was always there for her when she needed comfort and a safe haven.

After things fell apart with David, Grandmom had invited her to Florida. In less than twenty-four hours, she had packed a bag and boarded a plane.

She merged onto the highway, remembering her first day at Grandmom's condominium in Boca Raton, how lonely she had felt without David. She had leaned over the balcony and stared at the ocean. Waves whooshed against the sand. She was angry with herself for avoiding conflicts with him, for not pressuring him about children, angry with him for pouting when he didn't get his way.

Yet, she missed him. He loved walking with her in the warm sand, collecting shells, watching the moon rise over the water. The hot Florida sun bore down. A tropical wind blew across her face, but she felt no warmth.

She heard Grandmom calling her from the living room. "I've always wondered what kind of name is Bridget for a Jewish girl?"

Grandmom slid open the screen door. "Just because your mother loved those little Catholic school girls who bought her cookies when she started her business. She could have picked a nice Old Testament name like Judith."

Bridget joined Grandmom in the living room, blinking until her eyes adjusted to the dim light. She flopped into a chair and drummed her fingernails against the glass coffee table. "Your house is so pretty."

Grandmom swept her arm in a circular motion. "Too bad your poor Grandpop never lived to see it. He had to drop dead at the settlement and stick me with the mortgage. He always had bad timing in life."

Bridget knew her grandmom's sarcasm hid her sadness, a family trait. Her grandmom removed a white hanky from inside her ample brassiere and dusted a hollow lamp filled with seashells. Paintings of seagulls punctuated the wheat colored walls completing the Florida look.

"You stay right where you are and relax," said Grandmom. "I'm making a special breakfast for you."

When Bridget was small, her mother would drop her off at Grandmom's apartment on the way to the factory. After breakfast, Grandmother would sit in her freshly waxed rocking chair, lift Bridget up, and set her on her lap. While they gazed out the window, Grandmom rocked back and forth, telling stories of her childhood in Russia.

Now the air in the condominium smelled of sizzling butter and potatoes, a smell forever linked with Bridget's childhood.

"Come," Grandmom called. She carried two plates into the dining alcove and set them on the table. "I made your favorite, eggs over-easy and potato pancakes."

The plate overflowed with food. Bridget sat across from Grandmom, pressed her fork into the yellow yolk and watched creamy liquid run into the potato pancakes.

"Eat. You're too skinny."

She stared at Grandmom's wrinkled face. A few white hairs had loosened from the French Twist at the nape of her neck. Her once clear eyes were milky blue. For a moment Bridget felt as if she had caught a glimpse of her own future.

"So, you gave up a week of sex to come see me? Such a sacrifice."

Bridget choked on a piece of potato. "There's more to my relationship with David than sex."

"Oh yes. Meaningful relationships. That means free sex. In my day if a man wanted a nice girl, he had to marry to get it. I only did it to make babies. Your grandpop was no big deal in the sex department."

Bridget studied her grandmom's stocky frame. Grandmom had never broached the subject of sex so openly before. What had gotten into her?"

Grandmom swept her hand over the tablecloth, gathered crumbs and dropped them on her empty plate. "My friend Adeline dates lots of men. I think she likes to do it. Feh."

Bridget pressed her lips together to keep from laughing.

"Down here, there's one man for every thousand women. They're like gold if they can dance, drive and get it up. Even two things out of three gets them lots of women. Women do anything for the old cockers. Me, I wouldn't cook for them, let alone do what Adeline does."

A wicked grin spread across Grandmom's face. "I shocked you, didn't I? You seem so troubled and I wanted to make you laugh. I never talked to your mother much. I should have."

Bridget cleared her throat. "Maybe people didn't talk so much about these kind of issues back then."

"Who had time for issues? Now I have too much of it. Old people at the supermarket take forever to write a check and find their coupons. So I read the sexy articles. They tell personal secrets to the world. I read them to learn what this new world is all about."

Grandmom folded her creased hands tightly together. Blue veins protruded.

"I taught your mother that she had to be a virgin to find a good husband. That's all the personal talk we had. She never learned to express herself and it's my fault. I didn't know how to do it myself."

Through the screen door, palm trees rustled in the breeze. Bridget set down her fork and plucked a pink tulip from the silk flower arrangement in the center of the table. She wondered how long since Grandmom had made love or been held in a man's arms. Grandmom had once been a vital woman, yet she still had the needs and fears of someone younger.

"Now, let's hear about you," said Grandmom.

Bridget paused, lay the tulip on the table, then blurted out the truth. "I ran away from David because I'm afraid to marry him. He doesn't know if he wants children, but I do."

"If you love this David, go back. If he's worth anything, he'll talk it out with you."

"But you don't understand some of the problems."

"Maybe not. I should just play mahjongg and go to the Early Bird Specials with the women and forget it."

"What is it you want Grandmom?"

"What I didn't get. Survival was hard enough. Your grandfather worked like a dog. Who knew from magazine talk with their erotic zones and sexy spots and organisms."

"Orgasms." Bridget giggled.

"Orgasms, shmorgasms. Your grandfather and me, we didn't talk." Grandmom stared at the tablecloth and smoothed it with her thick fingers.

"My head woke up too late. It forgot my body is nearly dead. You're lucky to be living in this new world, but more important you understand how to live it."

Bridget winced. She hoped Grandmom was right.

"All of my life I was afraid. I hate to see the same thing happen to you. Look at this place. It's pretty, but they don't let poor Mr. Becker who had a stroke, sit outside on the lawn. They said sitting in a wheelchair ruined the decor. No unapproved ornaments allowed. So now I'm just an ornament. Is this a life?"

Bridget snapped her fingers. "You said that an old guy who can dance, drive and do it is hot property down here. Let's find one."

"I love you truly, my Bridgila." Grandmom rose from the table. "Forget all this for a while, doll. Go cover your tushie with that piece of string you call a bathing suit. The beach is waiting."

She let Grandmom shoo her toward the bedroom.

When she reached the door, she turned. From a distance, Grandmom looked luminous and youthful.

A loud snore startled Bridget. Grandmom shifted in her sleep and leaned her head against the window. Bridget exited the highway and passed the zoo. Soon they'd reach the Divine Guidance Center.

She mulled over what Grandmom had said in Florida about her fear of making changes. Grandmom had always done her duty to her husband and daughter. How many dreams had she set aside along the way? Now, she was opening herself up to a new life.

Her spirits rising, Bridget turned onto Market Street. Grandmom's belief in her was the catalyst she needed most to make her housing dream succeed. After all, Grandmom had taken a big risk long ago when she came from Russia to marry Grandpop. Although Bridget never knew the whole story, Grandmom's marriage had carried an undercurrent of unhappiness. Grandmom deserved some fun now.

Bridget pressed her palm against her forehead, chest, abdomen, and thought of David. The pain she had carried since the night in his apartment had gone. This was the closure she'd been seeking.

She glanced at Grandmom, her face serene as she slept. Her heart filled with tenderness. She longed to close her eyes, too, and drift away. Perhaps, tonight, she'd sleep soundly.

Chapter 18

BRIDGET PULLED INTO the front entrance of the Divine Guidance Center and shut off the engine. She sat quietly for a moment and watched Grandmom sleep, her breath deep and regular. Doubts replaced euphoria. Grandmom didn't know what she was letting herself in for. The residents were at least half Grandmom's age, wore different clothes, ate different food and certainly had their own way of communicating. She sighed and gently shook Grandmom's shoulder.

Grandmom's eyes fluttered open.

"We're here," said Bridget.

Grandmom leaned her head back and gazed at the Center's symbol, a brass lotus hanging above the door. "Ah Bridgila," she sighed. "Just like my old apartment building. Remember how the neighbors put mezuzahs on their doors? Maybe it's all the same in the end."

"Stay the night," said Bridget. "We'll figure everything out in the morning." She opened the car door and led Grandmom into the lobby.

Grandmom set her suitcase on the floor and stared at the young man who stood behind the desk. His head was shaved except for a thin braid hanging down his back. The braid was tied with a red cord that matched his cotton tunic. Silver bangles jingled on his wrists as he stepped from behind the desk and bowed. He waited while Bridget explained Grandmom's unexpected arrival.

"No problem," he said, turning to Grandmom. "We're honored to have you."

Grandmom bowed back. "So can I get my hair cut like yours?"

The glimmer of mischief in Grandmom's eyes reminded Bridget of a kid about to empty the cookie jar.

The young man offered Grandmom his arm. "If I had your beautiful hair, I'd keep it."

"A monk who knows how to flatter." Grandmom hooked her arm through his. "I think I'll be fine here."

Bridget smiled with relief. It was a good start.

The young man led them down a hall, opened a door and ushered them into a simply furnished lounge. Thick jute mats covered the polished wood floor. Three futons piled high with dark blue pillows lined the walls. In an alcove two statues, male and female, stood on pedestals, their hands clasped together. They were Kala-Das and Utara-Das, the Center's early Twentieth Century founders.

Claire sat on the floor. Eyes closed, she leaned over a small brass table. A stick of incense burned in a small brass holder. The woody scent drifted toward Bridget.

Grandmom wrinkled her nose. "Smells like the stuff Rhonda-Rachel used to light for her husband before he had his stroke."

"Shhh," said Bridget. "Claire's praying."

"Aum," Claire chanted. She seemed unaware that anyone had entered the room.

Two bundles of sheets, one striped, one floral, lay before Claire. Bridget wondered if Claire was blessing the laundry. The idea of chanting while washing and folding sheets soothed her. She imagined the sweet scent of fresh cotton, making neat creases and perfectly matched corners.

"Why are those sheets moving?" whispered Grandmom.

Bridget squinted. Through the open window, a light breeze stirred the fabric. "It's just the wind."

Grandmom touched her shoulder. "I think I see a hand."

Bridget hoped the place wasn't spooking Grandmom too much. "It's just a pile of sheets they've recycled to make clothing."

A puff of hair poked through the striped sheet like a tiny, white cloud. Bridget wondered if she was hallucinating? Edna? A dark-skinned face fringed with steel-gray hair poked up next through faded yellow tulips. Al?

Bridget leaned against the wall. What were they doing here? Slowly, they stood up and adjusted sheets tied around their waists and looped over their shoulders like saris.

"Namaste." Claire tented her fingers toward her heart before rising. A grin spread across her face. "You finally made it, Bridgie. And Ruth? What's shakin? You checkin' us out or what?"

"I'm giving up mahjongg to join your club." Grandmom imitated Claire, tenting her fingers and bowing slightly.

"Great," said Claire. "If you want, I'll teach you to throw the I Ching."

"What's everyone doing here?" interrupted Bridget.

"We finally busted out," said Edna. "Al and I were dying in that place."

Bridget felt a nervous twitch tug at the corner of her eye. "What about your families? And what about your medication?" She looked at Claire. "Does Boon-Dan-Tan know about this?

"It's A-OK for as long as it takes to set up our housing."

Al picked up a carpenter's belt fitted with tools and fastened it over the sheet. The tools clanked as he walked toward Bridget. "Now don't start preachin' to us, young lady. We're here to help you. I'm sick of nurses telling me when to take my high blood pressure pills. I know what to do."

"You betcha," said Edna. "We were level one in the nursing home and you know damn well we're healthy as horses. Most days we had more energy than the staff."

"What about Andrew?" said Bridget. "He'll be furious."

"We aren't prisoners," said Al. "We went to Willow Tree of our own free will and left the same way. I only moved in 'cause I didn't want to burden the kids."

"And you know I don't have kids to take care of me." Edna paused to catch her breath. "We want to take care of ourselves and each other. We don't need Andrew and his fuckin' rules."

Claire snickered. Grandmom applauded.

Beyond the picture window, Bridget saw the Willow Tree's Para-transit bus pull into the parking lot. The driver stepped out and helped an older woman walk down the steps. She wore a multicolored serape over her shoulders and carried a large package. The driver seemed frantic. The minute the woman walked off the bus, he bounded back up the steps and tossed a suitcase to the asphalt.

"Who is that?" said Bridget.

Al turned to the window. "Molly's here."

"Another one?" Bridget buried her face in her hands and rubbed her temples.

The woman appeared in the doorway, carrying a portable sewing machine. Braids the color of eggshells looped around her ears. "May I come in?" she called softly.

"You made it, Molly," said Edna. "Meet Miss Bridget."

Molly set her sewing machine down, held out a tiny, vein-webbed hand and pressed bony fingers into Bridget's palm. "I'm from Mr. Andrew's nursing home in Germantown. I've known Edna for years. When she told me about you and your project, I wanted to get in on the ground floor."

Bridget glanced at Edna, then back at Molly. "Did they warn you that we don't have a place yet? We've still got a struggle ahead of us."

Molly smiled. Wrinkles criss-crossed her powdery skin. "Piece of cake, my dear. You're looking at a woman who worked for the garment industry most of her life. I'm not afraid to put up a fight." She lifted her shoulders and puffed out her chest like a drill sergeant. "You see, when I first came from Ireland, I worked the sweatshops fourteen hours a day. People were fired if they sneezed. We learned to stick together. Have you ever heard of the International Ladies' Garment Workers Union?" she said wistfully. "Once upon a time, you could find our initials on the labels of most clothes."

"We're gonna do just fine," said Grandmom.

Claire crossed the room and threw an arm around Grandmom's and Molly's shoulders.

Grandmom pinched Claire's cheek. "My granddaughter's giving me a second chance at life. And this time around it's gonna be fun."

"I knew you were one of us, Ruth" said Claire. "Remember when you helped out at our Woman's Health Center Fundraiser a few years ago?"

"Of course," said Grandmom. "That old guy who served the punch. He flirted like crazy with me." She looked Claire up and down. "Is that a designer sheet?"

"Sure is. From the Hadassah Thrift Shop down the street. Wait till you try one on. They're real comfortable."

"I don't know about wearing sheets." Grandmom turned to Bridget. "But your friends are nice and none of them's got Styrofoam pumped into their faces."

"Collagen, Grandmom," laughed Bridget.

"Remember the good old days when we had a purpose greater than worshipping the almighty dollar?" said Molly. "People used to take pride in their work." Molly pointed a finger at Grandmom. "Your granddaughter's given us something to strive for."

"I haven't done anything yet," said Bridget.

"Oy vey, am I proud of my Bridgila," said Grandmom. "You can count me in one hundred percent. I'll cook. Show me some tempeh and I'll show you the best casserole you ever ate."

"How do you know about tempeh?" laughed Bridget.

"I saw it in one of the rags in the supermarket. They said it cures cancer."

"Cool with me, Ruthie," chimed in Al. "And I'll show you how to make the best hush puppies this side of the Mason-Dixon line."

Molly leaned over and hugged Grandmom, her arms reaching half way around Grandmom's ample waist.

Bridget saw her dream solidifying in front of her eyes.

"Oh, we intend to build this from the ground up," said Molly. "Edna even brought her hairdressing equipment."

"We've gone the route," said Claire. "They have social security and their pensions to pay expenses. And dig this. It's cheaper than a nursing home."

"You did a bang-up job at the nursing home, Miss Bridget," said Al. "We all trust you." He looked to Edna and Molly who nodded in agreement. "We can call our new place Habitat for Old Farts."

"Let's join hands and offer a chant of thanks," said Claire.

A knock interrupted them. Boon-Dan-Tan entered the lounge. "Excuse me," he said. "We have a visitor." A slim woman in a gray, tailored pantsuit stood next to him. The crisp collar of her white blouse was fastened with a sky-blue paisley scarf. She had slung a large black bag over her shoulder.

A nervous hush settled over the room.

Boon-Dan-Tan's usually serene face looked strained. He adjusted the black cord tied around the waist of his forest-green robe, pressed his hands to his heart and bowed. "This is Ms. Majors from the Department of Aging. She's investigating a report that several elderly people were lured here from the Willow Tree Nursing Home under mysterious circumstances. She's here to see that they remain in a safe environment."

Bridget's stomach lurched. She wasn't sure whether to laugh, cry or run.

Al hoisted his tool belt up on his waist. "Excuse me Mr. Boon-Dan-Tan, I don't mean disrespect, but no one tells us where to live. You see, with your permission, we choose to live here."

The woman knitted her eyebrows together and scrutinized Al before opening her bag. She rummaged through it, pulled out a pair of tortoise-shell reading glasses and set them on her nose. Next, she brought out a large leather-bound notebook, rifled through the pages and stopped.

Peering down her nose, she spoke slowly and clearly, "I'm looking for Albert Johnson, Edna Coomber and Molly McDonald." She looked up. "I imagine you're Mr. Johnson."

"I sure don't look like Edna," snapped Al.

The woman's nostrils flared. "It's my job to see that you remain in a protected environment and this place . . ." She peered beneath hooded eyes at the pillows, the statues, the burning incense. "This place hardly seems appropriate. Do you realize how worried your families are?"

"Never mind about Al's family," chimed in Edna. "They ignored him the minute he needed a little help. They were too busy to cook him a few meals or bring him to the doctor once in a while. Heaven forbid they'd waste a Sunday afternoon taking him out for a spin."

"You all need assistance and that's the bottom line."

"Excuse me Madame Bottom Line." Molly picked up her sewing machine and hoisted it over her head. "Are you trying to tell us that we're helpless?" Slowly, she lowered the machine to the ground. "Thirty pounds of metal." She smiled triumphantly and bent her arm, contracting her bicep into a small bulge.

"The Divine Guidance Center isn't equipped to monitor your medications or your finances," said Ms. Majors, tersely.

"We don't need monitoring," said Edna. "We can take our meds ourselves. As for staying in the nursing home, we can pay rent anywhere we choose. We're not crazy or senile. "I can show you a perfectly balanced checkbook any time you want to see it."

Bridget wished she could hug them all. Even if they didn't win this battle, they sure defended themselves well. "Ms. Majors." She felt her voice crack, cleared her throat and began again. "Al, Edna and Molly have a few medical problems, but so do younger people. They're as capable of taking care of themselves as you or me." Bridget looked pointedly at the tiny, precise handwriting on Mrs. Majors' notepad.

Claire linked her arm through Bridget's. The jasmine fragrance of Claire's cologne mingled with the heat in the room. Bridget heard Claire breathe deeply through her nose and exhale slowly.

When Claire spoke, her voice was gentle, her words measured. "I respect what you're trying to do, Ms. Majors. Picture yourself in thirty years. You feel good, but you're living in a place where you have to conform to strict rules and regulations designed for people with serious problems. You don't need someone to give you pills. You don't want them giving you something to keep you quiet when you raise a fuss. You want your freedom." Fist balled, she thrust her arm in the air.

Bridget bit her cheek to keep from laughing at Claire's defiant salute.

Ms. Majors studied Claire. "It's my job to address safety issues, not analyze the future."

Boon-Dan-Tan held up his hands, palms forward. "If I may interject. This is a spiritual house. We care for all who live here. No one falls by the wayside. Our community is especially cognizant of those in need. For us it is a way of life, not an afterthought."

Ms. Majors held up her notebook. "I don't . . ."

Boon-Dan-Tan pressed his hands forward. "I take full responsibility for everyone within these walls. We have a registered nurse on duty in our dispensary and a doctor on call. Allow our guests the dignity of their own decisions."

"The Willow Tree Nursing Home claims these people were brainwashed by a cult for their money." Ms. Majors removed her glasses and sighed. "That doesn't seem to be the case here."

Bridget gritted her teeth and waited.

"I can't force you to come back if you're competent and making independent decisions, which you seem to be." Ms. Majors looked like a tired schoolteacher. "Mind you, I'll check in to see that there's no abuse or infractions of the law."

Al high-fived Molly and Edna.

Bridget felt the muscles in her body relax. She realized she was digging her fingernails into Claire's arm and let go. Indentations appeared on Claire's skin, but Claire seemed oblivious.

"Don't worry none," said Al. "Edna's full of the dickens. Nearly killed myself keeping up with her on the treadmill."

"It's time for my evening meditation," said Boon-Dan-Tan. He turned to Ms. Majors. "I've asked our spiritual guides to give everyone, including you, safe passage on our life journeys." He turned to the group. "You all may take new names if you wish. I have given Claire the name Claire-Barunga, and Bridget may take Bria-Barunga. Together, their names mean, One Heart Helps the other."

Boon-Dan-Tan led Ms. Majors toward the door. He turned and nodded to Bridget. "Please come to my room when you have free moment." Bowing to the group, he led Ms. Majors into the hall.

Molly lowered herself onto a pillow and pressed her palms to her back. "That gave me a scare. I was sure my lumbago had kicked in for good."

Al knelt down to massage her shoulders. "You showed her pretty good, Molly. How about I get you a cup of tea?"

*   *   *

In the lobby, Bridget dropped coins one by one into the pay-phone slot, heard the line engage, and waited.

Andrew picked up on the third ring, his voice sounding jittery. Bridget guessed that he expected to hear from Ms. Majors.

"It's me," she said.

He inhaled sharply. "I have nothing to discuss with you."

"Oh I think you do." At the end of the hall, a woman turned on a vacuum. Bridget covered her free ear and raised her voice. "The lady from the Department on Aging was here tonight. Just so you know, she isn't bringing anyone back to the Willow Tree."

"Stop screaming at me."

"I'm not screaming." She collapsed into an old wooden chair next to the phone. The woman saw her and turned the vacuum off. She lowered her voice. "Your attack didn't cut it. Leave us alone."

"That was no attack." His voice had turned saccharine sweet. "I've talked with David Angsdorf. He's convinced that you've slipped over the edge."

Bridget's back stiffened. "You should take a better look at your source."

"Don't act so arrogant. He's updated me on your ridiculous plan. Given our own experiences with you, we agreed that you're in no emotional shape to run an enterprise of that magnitude."

Bridget felt giddy with fatigue. "Agree on whatever you want. The enterprise, as you call it, isn't yours to run."

*   *   *

When Bridget stepped over the threshold of Boon-Dan-Tan's room she felt a measure of peace return. The walls, painted a soothing beige, were hung with bamboo-framed pictures of ornately jeweled gods and goddesses. From a small CD player, a sweet melody issued from a flute, notes rising and curling in the air covering her like a blanket. In an alcove next to a futon, two bamboo chairs sat side by side. Between them rested a small brass altar. She wondered if Boon-Dan had a partner.

He sat on a cushion, legs drawn up in the lotus position. "Sit down and rest," he said, patting a gold silk cushion in front of him. Compassion radiated from his eyes as he spoke. "Claire tells me that your grandmother is rooming with Molly. A good match."

Bridget sat down and crossed her legs. "They have more spunk than me."

A hint of a smile crossed Boon-Dan-Tan's lips. "Don't be so quick to doubt yourself."

She wished his tranquility would surround her forever. "I feel like my whole life has led me to this, but now I'm paralyzed."

Boon-Dan-Tan smiled an acknowledgement. "You are following your karma now. Your path is a challenge you must accept as a gift.

True problems come to those who see their path and ignore it."

"Well I see it plain and clear, but my feet are dragging."

Boon-Dan-Tan laughed. "If you weren't a bit wary, you might run the risk of becoming arrogant. Arrogance has derailed many who have chosen a difficult path."

Bridget folded her hands and rested them on her lap. "Some people want to see me fail."

"You must put negative influences out of your mind."

"I'm trying."

He pointed to a chair covered by a gold and red silk shawl. "That chair belonged to my late wife Charmala," he said. "We met in India at the Divine Guidance Ashram of the great Guru, Kala-Das whose name means lover of Kala, god of eternity. Charmala was very ill when we married. But we had a dream to establish the Divine Guidance Center here in America. People said we were crazy, especially with my wife's bad health. But our love and commitment was stronger than death. To this day, I feel her presence. She has guided me in everything I do. When I hear negative comments, when people write lies about the Center, I pray to her. She reminds me to follow my karma. Wherever I go, I take her chair and loving spirit with me."

Boon-Dan-Tan closed his eyes. "Let us meditate together." He drew his hands in prayer. "Take time each day to rest and focus. Your Inner Light will guide you when you pay attention to it."

*   *   *

In the simply furnished room that Boon-Dan-Tan had blessed with a sprinkling of rose water, Bridget lay on her palette and tried to sleep. She thought of the devotion he had shared with his wife. How blessed they had been to connect so deeply. Even though she and Carson weren't exactly on the same track, she wanted to believe that they weren't that far apart either.

She listened to cars pass by on the street below. Strange shadows crossed the floor. She closed her eyes. The room spun. She was dropping into the mass of a black hole.

Doubts plagued her. She could afford to be impulsive by herself, but not for a fragile group of people. From the hall she heard a voice chanting softly. She understood why some people stayed inside the Divine Guidance Center and never left. Focus, she told herself. Focus. She was drifting, drifting into sleep.

A stand of coconut palms rustled their fronds in the morning breeze. Ten feet away, foam-flecked water licked the shore. On the horizon, a pirate ship lay anchored, its sail fluttering in the breeze.

"If you ever loved me, you'll free me," a voice shouted.

Bridget turned her head. Andrew was chained to a palm tree. "Look what they've done to me." He pointed a finger toward the beach.

From a stand of scrub pines, Grandmom led a group of people toward them. The group drew closer, removing pieces of paper from their pockets.

"No more sticky mashed potatoes and congealed gravy," shouted Grandmom. "I didn't give up the Early Bird Specials in Florida to eat this dreck."

"You tell him," said Edna. She wore a neatly starched house-dress and carried a bowl of peas.

"The food might be bland, but we save a lot of money," shouted Andrew.

"We want the Cupid Room back," said Al.

"You know the rules," said Andrew. "No visitors after eight."

"I want to spend the night with Edna." Al shuffled toward Andrew, kicking sand in his face.

"What are you doing?" sputtered Andrew. Sand stuck to sweat that had broken out on his forehead.

"We're gonna surround and torture you with stories of what really goes on with us," said Grandmom. "My friend, Rhonda-Rachel, over here can't wait to give three hours worth of details about her wild sex life."

"That's right," shouted Rhonda. "X-rated all the way."

"And you, Bridgila," said Grandmom, pointing to the pirate ship. "I put you in charge of that boat. Get your tushie out there and rescue it. We're all heading out to open sea. No zoning. No busybodies."

"But how am I supposed to get there?"

"In that little rubber boat. They call it a dinghy. Now go. We have work to do."

Bridget walked through the sand into shallow water. "Don't leave me," shouted Andrew. She ignored him and climbed into the dinghy.

As she rowed toward the ship, she noticed a tall man wearing a pirate hat and a black Speedo bathing suit standing on the ship's prow. Face obscured, he watched her through a spyglass.

She angled the dinghy to the side of the ship and climbed up the ladder.

"Who are you?" she said, jumping over the railing to the deck.

He stood at least six feet tall on strong, muscular legs. From his narrow hips rose a thick chest covered in a mat of curly hair. He lowered the spyglass.

"Carson?"

He moved closer and pointed toward the flagpole. "I've been searching the high seas for you. This is my new logo. I figured you'd recognize it."

She squinted. On the flag, was a whale. It matched the whales on the crazy vest he wore for their first date. "Have you talked with my Grandmom?"

"She sent me a Morse code message and said that you were in trouble. I fought off a band of pirates to find you." He leaned forward to kiss her.

Her knees went weak as he lifted her into his arms. No one had ever risked anything for her before.

"Let's go to the bed chamber and make little pirates," he whispered.

"But I'm not ready for . . ."

"Oh hush, darling.

She felt herself waking up and tried to stay in the dream. She wanted to make love to Carson. When she opened her eyes, the room was still dark. The air smelled faintly of rose water.

Boon-Dan-Tan had warned her that her subconscious might play tricks. But she hadn't expected her world to splinter into pieces. She cared deeply for Carson, but she didn't want to think of him as a safety net. She had only one option. Focus on the present.

* * *

"Claire, it's Sarah Bernstein. I understand you just got back from Guatemala."

"Columbia, but you're close enough." What a shock hearing Sarah's voice on the Center's pay phone. Sarah never took time for personal calls.

"It's one thing to do a little march in New York City or Washington, but why go all the way to South America?"

"What's shakin' Sarah?"

"What's all this spiritual nonsense you're filling Bridget's head with? She was a respectable person. I don't understand what happened. Her life fell apart and now she's into a cult. Tell me the truth. Is she taking drugs?"

"Relax. We don't do drugs or anything like that unless you count herb teas. Bridget wants to live here until she gets things going. We're together on this all the way."

"You're together with her to burn incense and fill your head with new-age garbage. You want to be big shots so what happens? You end up alone in some cubicle in a commune. No wonder men don't want you."

Claire held her tongue. She felt sorry for Bridget. Sarah was a formidable opponent.

"I want to talk to my mother," demanded Sarah.

"She's making knishes right now."

"She's due at the hospital tomorrow morning. Tell her that she should be resting."

Claire twirled the phone cord in the air. She watched Edna walk up the hall, her sheet dragging on the floor.

"Say something," demanded Sarah.

"I know you work hard. But so do a lot of other people, only they give back to the community. It's time you did too."

"Who gave me anything? You're just another mushugana who talks nonsense to my daughter."

Chapter 19

CARSON BURST THROUGH the doorway of Mark's empty office. He needed some documents immediately, and Mark hadn't answered his calls. Keeping track of Mark had forced him to stay late the past several nights. It didn't really matter, though. Bridget was completely tied up at the Center.

He had taken a short break on Tuesday to visit her. The old folks were flourishing. It surprised him how quickly they'd left tradition behind. The sheets they wore, strange as it seemed to him, seemed to signal a break with the past.

When Bridget introduced him to her grandmother, he had been impressed with her vitality. She seemed much younger than her eighty-two years, bustling around, serving them tofu knishes and green tea. He had to admit that Bridget was talented at organizing people. She looked like she belonged there. But she also belonged with him.

Her contentment alarmed him. She had made him sit on the floor of her room with her friend Claire while they went through a number of real estate listings. She had been so intent on explaining her renovation plans, including special showers, ramps and elevators, that he might have been a contractor instead of her lover.

Hopefully, things would settle down in a couple of weeks. Right now he had a problem that needed immediate attention. Mark had slacked off, leaving work early to hang out at the Marwick.

He'd have to get the damned papers himself. Mark's computer screen glowed, turned to the internet. That meant Mark was somewhere nearby.

Carson strode to the file cabinet, opened the first drawer, then the second, hoping to find the needed documents. Nothing. The third and fourth drawers were locked. He remembered specifically telling Mark that all records had to be accessible to him. He kicked the wastebasket over. Two empty coke cans, an assortment of candy wrappers and a condom wrapper fell out.

Who was Mark screwing in this office? He went to Mark's desk and looked for the key. In the bottom drawer, he found several sets of underwear. Taped to the side of the drawer was a key.

He returned to the files and opened them, then stepped back. The first drawer contained a pile of folded white shirts. Beside the pile, lay ties, socks and handkerchiefs. The next drawer produced an array of toiletries, which included shampoo, soap, deodorant, an electric razor and shaving cream.

Startled, Carson wondered why Mark's office was so well equipped. All he ever kept in his desk was mouthwash, an extra shirt, and an electric razor.

He buzzed the receptionist and told her to locate Mark immediately. Next, he went to Mark's supply closet. With the key, he opened the door. Supplies were piled haphazardly at the bottom of the closet. On a metal bar at the top, hung three suits, a sport jacket, slacks, polo shirts, a raincoat and a windbreaker. He heard someone clear their throat and spun on his heel.

Mark stood in the doorway. "Hi, Carson," he said, sheepishly. "You've discovered my closet." His face looked nonchalant, but his voice trembled. "I keep extra sets of clothing because of my workouts."

"Come on Mark. This is your complete wardrobe. I've never seen you wear anything else around here." Carson scratched a nagging itch on the back of his neck. Something clicked. "You live here, don't you?"

"What?"

Carson stared at him.

Mark sank into his desk chair and looked up, defeated. "You found me out." He removed a handkerchief from his pocket and wiped his hands. "I kind of live here. I come back late at night when everyone's gone."

"Why?" Carson closed the closet door and sat on the edge of Mark's desk. How the hell had Mark pulled this off? "You get a decent salary. Are you in some kind of financial trouble?"

"I was. I'm coming out of it now. I was playing a few stocks on the Net, trying to get ahead. But, I kept losing and couldn't afford an apartment."

"Don't tell me you use the showers in the gym and sleep on the sofa in the employee's lounge."

Mark's face brightened. "You got that right. All the comforts of home. The management almost begs you to live here. They've got vending machines for sandwiches and soups. Then there's the refrigerator and stove in the kitchen. Ever since they installed the cappuccino machine, it's better than home. Sometimes I put the gym mats together and sleep on them in a sleeping bag. It's good for my back."

"You have to stop."

Mark shot up from his chair. "Why? I'm on the internet most nights anyway."

"God knows how much money you've lost so far. Quit the e-trading, and you'll have money for an apartment."

Carson paced the length of the office. If Mark would only harness his street smarts productively, he had a shot at bigger and better things. It infuriated Carson. He felt like a surrogate father with a bright, errant child in need of straightening out.

He sighed. "I'll make you a deal. I'll lend you two month's rent for the Y. After that, find yourself an apartment."

Mark hung his head. "The funny thing is, this place really turns women on. You have to admit we've got a terrific view of the city."

Carson kicked the condom wrapper over to Mark's foot. "I'll bet you tell them you're the president of the company."

"I'm not that stupid." Mark picked up the wrapper and stuck it in his pocket. "But if they suggest something like that, I don't correct them."

A forlorn expression settled on Mark's face. Carson checked an urge to fire him on the spot. "Here's the deal," he said, pointing an index finger at Mark's nose. "Take my offer and move out of here. Next, get your ass in gear and start working. When I give you an assignment, do it in a reasonable amount of time. No more internet or personal e-mail during work hours." He folded his arms over his chest. "If you don't agree, you're out. And I don't give a damn about your so-called Attention Deficit Disorder. You pay a lot of attention to the things you like."

Mark groaned.

Carson held out his hand. "Do we have a deal or do you pack up and leave?"

Mark's shoulders slumped. "Deal." He weakly shook Carson's hand.

Carson walked to the door. "Get me the file on Dorchschmit right away. And stop e-mailing my brother."

"Right," said Mark, turning toward his computer.

"Shut that machine off. I don't want to see anything on it except business."

"Okay." Mark reached over, then stopped his hand in mid-air. "Hold it."

"Now Mark, I mean it."

"I just want to check out this web page one more time. It's from this really cool place called the Divine Guidance Center. The woman who writes about the Center is so passionate. Her name is Claire-Barunga. She's making me reexamine my life. I'm gonna change, boss."

Carson recognized the strange name. Bridget told him that she had one too. He hoped he never had to use it.

Mark stared at the screen. "The Center has a whole series of lectures coming up. Here's the schedule."

"I don't care. Turn the damn computer off and get to work."

Carson rubbed his aching temples as he headed out the door. The cool, gray walls and quiet corridor soothed his jangled nerves a bit, but he missed Ball and Jack's more than ever. Lisa would have appreciated the humorous side of Mark. He remembered the corporate meetings, how when they got boring, he and Lisa would pass notes back and forth making up names for the members of Ball and Jack's Board of Directors. He had once called a guy an orangutan and Lisa had wrote back that he shouldn't insult the animal.

He knew that Bridget would enjoy the story, too. But she was so preoccupied these days.

When he entered his office, he flopped into one of the chairs that sat across from his desk, remembering the day Mark showed up for his interview. He should have hung Mark out to dry after his first week. With the constant pressure to deliver better numbers every quarter, no one could show an ounce of slack. Just his luck getting stuck with the worst goof-off in corporate America.

On an impulse, he dialed Lisa's private number at Ball and Jack's, barely giving her a chance to say hello before he launched into the story about Mark. When he finished, he heard a long silence and waited for Lisa to commiserate with him. She laughed heartily.

"Lisa, talk to me." Now he was smiling.

She guffawed.

"You're hysterical. Stop it. I called you for advice and all you can do is laugh. Help me."

He heard her catch her breath. "It's the funniest thing I've heard in awhile. Send him out to me. I'll shape him up."

"Don't make a promise you can't keep."

"Boy, do I miss you," she said.

"I miss you, too. If you were here right now, I'd take you out for a beer.

"What about the new girlfriend?"

"You'd like her. She reminds me of Dad and you."

"That could be both good and bad. You can tell me all about her when you come home."

"Jack says you and Mother have been acting strange lately."

Lisa paused. "Don't let it worry you. In the meantime, threaten your assistant with a round-the-clock job in my office. He wouldn't survive for a week."

Carson smiled and hung up the phone. He had always thought of Philadelphia as a conservative city. But he had met the oddest assortment of people. Even Bridget marched to a different drummer. The farther out on a limb she went, the more endearing she got. But the qualities that attracted him to her also led her into sticky situations.

He set his feet on the desk. Everything was a trade-off. Bridget would move forward in her search for a building no matter what he said. As long as she made time for him, he was willing to stick around. He pictured her mingling with his old country club set back home and laughed out loud. He had never really fit in there himself. As a couple they'd be better off in the anonymity of a big city. He'd grown accustomed to walking to museums, galleries and movies whenever the mood struck. And raising kids in the city would put children face to face with a diverse group of people.

He thought back to his interlude with Bridget in the convent. His heart beat faster when he remembered speeding up Interstate 95 from the airport to her apartment. It was as though she had expected to see him. He dropped his feet from the desk and sat bolt upright. What was she doing now? Was she thinking of him, too?

Chapter 20

BRIDGET DROVE A CIRCUITOUS route to Thomas Jefferson Hospital, veering off Market, heading toward Bainbridge, then doubling back up Eleventh. She knew it was ridiculous to feel paranoid that David would follow her to visit Grandmom. But, she had recently seen him hanging around the lobby of the Divine Guidance Center and wasn't taking any chances.

She tried not to look over her shoulder as she walked from the hospital parking lot to the entrance, managing a single backward glance. Medical students in green scrub suits hefted backpacks on their shoulders. Two women carrying oversized shopping bags waited at the bus stop while a few hospital employees stood outside the entrance smoking cigarettes.

At the nurse's station, she showed her pass. The odor of disinfectant and bleach reminded her of the infirmary at the nursing home, often the first step before hospitalization and death. When she called the hospital this morning, the Doctor had assured her that Grandmom was in good health and would be released in the morning. But the prospect of losing Grandmom shook her to the core.

So many losses. Even the fragile thread between her and her mother had snapped. Hard to believe they hadn't spoken since that awful dinner.

She stepped into Grandmom's room. Grandmom lay in bed imprisoned beneath a tightly tucked-in sheet. Bridget gently sat on the edge of the mattress. "What a relief. They said the test results were fine."

"I'm not dead yet, doll, so don't get hysterical. Did you call your mother?"

"I left your room number with her secretary. She still isn't talking to me." Bridget leaned forward and stroked Grandmom's fleshy arm.

"That selfish daughter doesn't even bother to call."

"I've never seen her this mad." Bridget brushed a strand of springy white hair from Grandmom's face.

Grandmom lay her hand on Bridget's lap. "Maybe it's time we all made up. Your mama's a good woman underneath."

Bridget nodded in agreement. Although her mother drove her nuts, they'd never stopped talking for this long.

Grandmom sighed. "I'm spending too much time thinking about the past." She raised a finger and pointed it toward the ceiling. "Grandpop Nathan's breathing down my neck, asking me to come join him."

Bridget clutched Grandmom's hand. "You shouldn't talk that way."

"Don't worry. I'm too mad at him to listen." Grandmom pinched the sheet. "Laying here like this, crazy memories fill my head. I never told anyone. It's been eating me up all my life and I kept it inside."

Bridget looked at Grandmom's tired face, the puffy shadows beneath her eyes. "You hardly ever talk about your past. You're always protecting me."

"I try to forget, but it doesn't work."

"Tell me about you and Grandpop." Bridget held Grandmom's chubby hand to her cheek, the skin smooth as a young girl's.

"Ah, Nathan. What a schmoozer. We grew up together in Russia. I was maybe fourteen and he was nineteen when he proposed. Not a bad thing in those days. We dreamed about going to America. He promised to marry me and bring me there, but first he had to go and get a job. He said to wait three years. He'd send me money to come.

"I wrote him every week. The three years passed. In his letters, he wrote back to say how hard things were and how he went from job to job, not saving a dime. So I waited another year and another. I had dreams, too, of living in America with him. Finally, in the fifth year he calls for me." Grandmom stared at the wall for a long time, her eyes glazing over.

"Talk to me Grandmom."

"Okay. I talk. When I get off the boat, he's not there. Some schlepper picks me up in New York City and puts me on a train to Philadelphia. Such a train ride. Conductors talking to me and I don't speak a word of English. Finally, I see your grandpop at the station in a beautiful suit with a fancy car no less.

"He gets me a room and I stay there. He visits me two times a week. But when I get up the nerve to ask when we're getting married, he says we have to wait. Work is slow.

"I can't stay in my room all day, every day, so I do a little snooping. I find out where he lives from the Russian grocery store. So I go there. What do you think? He's shacked up with his goyisha girlfriend. He swears he's getting rid of her, but she helped him start the accounting business and does the books. How can he put her out on the street?"

Tears ran down Grandmom's cheeks. Bridget reached for a tissue from the nightstand and wiped the tears away.

"'I'll get rid of her slowly,' he says. 'So she doesn't hurt the business.' I pack my bags and tell him I'm going back to Russia where a man waits for me."

Grandmom closed her eyes. "There was no man back in Russia, so I took a chance. What can I tell you? Suddenly, your Grandpop dumps the girlfriend and within a week we're married. You see, he was an Orthodox Jew. He knew I would keep a kosher home.

"Years later I found out the girlfriend stayed in his life for twenty more years until she finally moved away. So Grandpop had his matzoh and ate it too."

Tears sprang to Bridget's eyes. "You didn't deserve to be treated that way." She remembered times when Grandmom blew up at Grandpop for nothing it seemed, screaming in Yiddish. Her mother still had a tendency to bad-mouth Grandpop. Bottled-up anger crept from generation to generation. Had she stayed with David and knuckled under, she'd have been no better.

Grandmom forced a smile. "When all is said and done, it worked out okay. I got my Sarah and you out of marrying Nathan." She nestled her head into the pillow. "I'm glad you brought me to the Center. For the first time in years, I have a real home again."

Bridget felt her throat close, but tried to smile. "Edna's arranging prayers for you around the clock. After all those notes she's taken, she's thrown together a program–Sufi mystic poems, verses from the Song of Solomon, a speech from Ghandi."

"It sounds like a recipe for one of your mother's ugly cookies."

"That's a ticket to success," laughed Bridget.

A voice interrupted her. "Are you girls saying bad things about me?" Her mother stood in the doorway, holding a huge box of cookies wrapped in bright red cellophane.

Bridget's body grew tense. The laugh she had shared with grandmom dissipated in the close air. Her mother walked to the side of the bed and set the cookies down.

"So," said Grandmom. "My daughter took time from her busy schedule to visit her sick mother."

"Stop with the guilt-trip, Ma. It won't work."

Bridget bit her tongue.

Her mother bent over to hug Grandmom then gave Bridget a brusque hug. "Have you two been crying? What's going on? The doctors said everything's fine."

"But I can't have any stress. And it would go away if you'd just give Bridget the convent."

Her mother's mouth thinned to a tight line. "That's between Bridget and me." She tugged on Bridget's sleeve. "We gotta talk."

*   *   *

Bridget followed her mother down the hall into the visitor's lounge. She leaned against the wall and crossed her arms. Her mother still looked angry.

"Sit," said her mother, smacking the sofa beside her.

Bridget thumped down, stretched out her legs and waited for another lecture.

"My caretaker told me that someone was in my building. He found an afghan sticking out of a trunk. When he said nothing was taken, I figured it was you."

"Look Mom . . ."

"I'm not here to fight. You've already made my life topsy- turvy, giving up your apartment to live in a commune. And your Grand-mom turning into a hippie. The two of you are making me crazy."

"What do you expect when people sit around smoking dope all day?" Bridget dug her fingernails into her palms.

Her mother touched her shoulder. "Now that you've made your little joke, let me talk. I was up half the night getting advice from Gordon. He convinced me you're not on drugs and he wants me to tell you something." Her mother folded her hands on her lap and stared out the window into a small courtyard where a group of doctors had gathered to eat lunch. A wistful smile settled over her face.

Bridget knew the smile well. It meant that her mother planned to tell her another factory story.

"You know about Gordon's bakery," said her mother. "But you never really heard about the early years in my factory before I had the cookie-smashing machine. Boy, did I fight with your father back then. He was never satisfied handling our customers even though they loved him. He never realized what a big charmer he was. When a shipment went wrong, he'd have the customers eating cookie crumbs out of his palm in no time. But that wasn't enough. He wanted to run the company."

Bridget twisted a lock of hair and remembered how her Dad bragged to his gambling buddies that he was the real brain behind her mother's business.

"On top of everything else," said her mother. "Your father was jealous of Gordon. He knew that I counted on Gordon for advice, but never behind your father's back. Except for one time. I need to tell you about it now.

"One morning everything blew up. Your father told me that he wanted to take over the Finance Department effective immediately. 'Don't get me started,' I said. 'The only kind of credit you could get is an extension on your gambling debt.'

"He slammed his coffee cup on the table. 'At least I can get it. Look at your big-shot Gordon. He's nothing but a bus driver since he lost his business.'"

Bridget sighed. After Grandmom's story, she was in no mood to hear this one.

"So I got dressed," continued her mother. "Dropped you off at Grandmom's and went to my private spot in a little park beneath a train trestle along the Schuylkill River."

Bridget listened to the urgency in her mother's voice as she talked about an event that had happened thirty years before. Wrapped in her old cloak, her mother had gone to sit by the river to feed cookies to the birds. She had ordered a new set of ovens for the factory. They hadn't been hooked up yet. In all the uproar, the shipping room had gone to hell. Gus was her right hand man. Even though they fought, she needed him.

She had just tossed a handful of oatmeal cookie crumbs to a pair of ducks when the screech of brakes broke her reverie. She looked up and saw sunlight reflecting off the chrome sides of a chartered bus.

Startled, she realized it was one of the buses Gordon drove. What was he doing there?

The door swung open. Dressed in a uniform and a matching cap, Gordon came down the steps. "Hi Sarah," he said. "I was looking for Parker Street when I got lost and realized how close I was to your favorite hideout. I took a chance you'd be here."

He removed his cap. She noticed new strands of gray shooting through his receding hairline. The furrows in his brow had grown deeper.

"Actually," he said. "I stopped by every day this week looking for you. You sounded so sad last time we talked. Are things better at home?"

"Same old stuff. Gus and me, we're like oil and water. So how are things with you?"

His eyes flickered. "When I'm on the road, I almost forget my troubles."

"Wish I could go with you. Just stay on the bus and forget everything, too."

"Better find yourself a smarter bus driver. I can't even find the Cityview Diner on Parker Street. That's where I have to pick up my passengers."

"Don't you have a map?"

"I'm embarrassed to say I don't. This is a fill-in job. Had to take it at the last minute. I'm grabbing any extra work that comes in. Got a notice from my bank last week. They're threatening to fore-close on my house." His face had turned ashen.

"That's awful. Why don't you let me help you out?"

"Absolutely not. You're in debt up to your ears. I'll find a way." He checked his watch. "I'm already twenty minutes late."

"I'll get on the bus and show you how to get there. You can drop me off at the factory on your way to the highway. She climbed up the steps behind him into the bus. It was clean as a whistle like his old bakery. "Sit yourself down," he said.

She sank into the velour seat behind him. He pulled a lever and started the engine.

They bounced along the road toward Market Street. "How's your little Bridget?"

"Doesn't give me a minute's trouble."

"Wish I could say the same. My kids are out of hand. Oldest son thinks shoplifting is a competitive sport. The wife isn't handling it too well. She knows we need the money, yet she wants me to be at home." He shook his head. "I don't mean to dump on you."

"Any time. You were the first person to believe in me."

She looked into the rearview mirror. Gordon glanced at her, his face anxious. "There's your group up ahead," she said. "Waiting in the parking lot."

Gordon pulled the bus to the corner and stopped. His eyes glazed over, his hands shook as he stared out the window.

"Don't you think you should open the door?"

"All of a sudden I'm so tired."

It scared her. She'd never known Gordon to give up on anything.

They heard a knock on the door. A man called in. "What's going on?"

"Help me Sarah."

An idea struck her. "You have to bring me to my factory, anyway," she said. "I'll make you a quick cup of coffee and we'll talk. Tell those people to go get a bite to eat. You're having brake trouble and need to fix the problem. Then call your boss. So what if your people get to Florida a little late."

Gordon stared at the door.

"Move!"

He pulled a chrome lever. The doors swung open. He bounded down the steps and talked to the group. One guy kicked his suitcase, then limped away. An older woman in a fur-trimmed coat shook her finger in his face. But the rest seemed to accept what he said and shuffled across the lot to the Diner.

Back on the bus, Gordon radioed the dispatcher. "The brakes are making weird noises. I need about an hour to get them checked out."

"Roger," a voice crackled through static. "Stay in touch."

Ten minutes later, they pulled up to the loading dock.

She led him through a side door into the packing room. Equipment, boxes, and furniture littered the floor.

Gordon removed his cap and mopped his damp forehead with his sleeve. She noticed a hint of color returning to his cheeks and pointed to a folding chair surrounded by a tall stack of cartons. "Have a seat. I'll get some coffee."

When she returned with two mugs, he was staring into space. He sipped thoughtfully. "You've done all right for yourself."

"Without you, I'd be nothing." She set her mug down and patted his knee. "Come on Gordon. This isn't like you. You always pick yourself up."

"Believe me, I'm trying."

"You just need to work for yourself again. Listen, I know of a business that's going real cheap. It's an old guy with no kids. He sells wholesale goods to baking companies. It's perfect for you."

He gave her a half-smile. "Don't tempt me when I'm broke."

She watched him drink his coffee. Lately, she'd been wracking her brain to find a way to make Gordon accept a business loan from her without Gus finding out.

An idea had been whirling in the back of her head for weeks. Gordon had a technical mind.

"I've got a problem," she said. "I need a machine that smashes cookies. The spoons aren't working anymore. I never expected the business to grow this fast."

He perked up. "I bet I could design one for you."

She smiled to herself. Good old Gordon could never resist a challenge.

He scanned the room. She pointed to a high-backed desk chair that stood in the corner and asked him to bring it into her office.

He hoisted the chair over his head and followed her down the hall.

In the office, he skirted the desk, set the chair behind it and sat down. "Don't mind me. I wanted to see how it feels to be my own boss again."

"You'll be there soon. I know it."

Across the room, a sofa sat at an angle in the corner. Foam padding covered its legs. Nuts, bolts, screws, a hammer and screwdriver, lay on the floor.

"What's wrong with that?" he said.

"It's a sofa bed that's broken. I need it to sleep on when I work real late."

He rose from behind the desk, walked over, bent toward the sofa, removed the pillows and set them on the floor. "Here's the problem. You're missing a row of screws beneath the frame."

Dropping to one knee, he picked up the screwdriver and bolts. In ten minutes he had finished. "Let's give it a try," he said, triumphantly.

Together, they flung open the bed.

He stared at her.

She felt suddenly shy, like a girl on her first date.

Neither blinked. Finally, they both looked away. He checked his watch. "Time to go."

"Do you know how to get back?"

"I'll manage."

On the loading dock, she watched him climb the bus steps. He waved as he pulled out of the parking lot.

The bus glinted like a silver medallion as it turned the corner. In a week, she'd give him a call and convince him to design the cookie smashing machine. She'd pay him a fair price, enough money to start his own business.

A phone rang inside the factory. Gus. When it came down to brass tacks didn't he and Gordon want the same thing, self respect? Once she and Gus made up, she'd tell him about her plan to have Gordon design the machines, but only under one condition. Gus would run them.

Bridget looked out the window into the courtyard. Daisies bloomed in a small garden near the picnic tables. Her mother had always been attached to Gordon. Of course she'd offer to help him in a time of trouble. But, what did her story mean? Her mother hadn't shown the same generosity at home.

"Say something." Her mother's voice sounded giddy.

"If you're trying to tell me that you and Gordon had an affair, that's your own business."

"What nonsense are you talking? I was a faithful wife and mother. Can't you understand what I'm saying? Look at me." Her mother beamed. "Have you figured it out yet?"

Bridget shrugged her shoulders. Was her mother asking her to work in the factory again?

"Why are you so thick? Gordon thinks you have a good head for business and believes with the right help and planning, you'll succeed with your commune project. With Gordon as my advisor, I've created the Ugly Cookie Foundation. Now, I need someone to act as trustee. Come Monday, I'm officially making you that person. Do you hear me? I'm giving you the convent and taking the tax break after all."

Bridget froze, then willed herself to speak. "With no strings attached?"

"Maybe one. In the future, I'd like you to speak nicer to me." Her mother smiled. "You and me, we're ... well, different. But I love you more than my own life. Don't they talk about karma at that crazy place where you live? I just gave you karma."

The air in the room felt suddenly buoyant. Bridget jumped up from the sofa. "This is more miracle than karma." She pulled her mother to her feet and waltzed her around the lounge.

"Slow down. You're making me dizzy," laughed her mother.

Bridget whirled her mother to a stop, saw dimples breaking into her cheeks. "I love you, Mom," she said.

* * *

David jotted names and numbers in his notebook from a list that had been tacked up to the Divine Guidance Center bulletin board. Already fifteen people had signed up for Bridget's Convent Renovation Project.

Sarah Bernstein must have lost her mind, giving Bridget the convent. Bridget had deliberately snubbed him, asking everyone on the Divine Guidance Board except him to serve on the convent's new board.

One name on the volunteer sign-up sheet struck him, Mark Appleby, a former student. It had to be the same kid who spouted an off-the-wall theory on how keeping the welfare system benefited capitalism. He could easily gain the confidence of an idiot like that.

Back at his desk, he dialed the number Mark had written on the board. "Carson McAlister's Office," a woman answered.

David hesitated. The name caught him by surprise. "Ur . . . I'm looking for a Mark Appleby. Does he work with Mr. McAlister?"

"He's Mr. McAlister's assistant. One moment please."

David knew he had to stay cool. In the long run, Mark could prove invaluable.

The line clicked. "Appleby here."

"Mark, this is Doctor David Angsdorf from the University."

"Who? Oh yeah, the hip professor with the great parties. How ya doin?"

"Sounds like you've given up the welfare system for full-fledged capitalism."

"I learned the hard way that you can't have it all. I lucked out with a great job and a great boss. I'm just an assistant, but I'm moving up the ladder."

"I hear you're interested in volunteering for the convent project."

"Yeah. Claire-Barunga's web page got me interested. Whatever she says makes sense to me."

"We can talk about her later. But I have a question? Did my lectures on alternative housing appeal to you?"

"You were brilliant. A genius."

"Good. I'd like to propose that you join the Divine Guidance Center's Board."

David heard a pause. "Are you interested?"

"Of course, Prof."

* * *

Boon-Dan-Tan gazed at the ten men and women that made up his advisory board. They sat at a low table on pillows passing around a pot of ginseng tea. Two new people had joined, an old friend of his, Richard Lipinski who headed up a soup kitchen in the city, and a banker named Mark Appleby.

Hair tucked beneath an aqua turban, Mark sat next to David Angsdorf, his sponsor. Mark seemed quite young for the credentials David had given him, but appeared serious about the work ahead.

Boon-Dan-Tan smiled. "I am pleased to announce that the Divine Guidance Center has committed itself to help Bridget Bernstein and Claire Johnson in their quest to bring people together in a cooperative, energizing way of living.

"Bridget's mother, Mrs. Sarah Bernstein, has begun a new foundation and donated a building perfectly suited to her daughter's goal. Because of Mrs. Bernstein's heartfelt generosity, we have sought the blessing of several ashrams in the area. While money is scarce, we have pledged to provide all of our expertise to see the project through. Our connection to the young women and their new community is sealed in the grace of divine energy."

David knocked over his tea and quickly wiped it up with a napkin. All eyes turned to him.

He smiled sheepishly. "Revered Boon-Dan-Tan. I respectfully ask you to reconsider. In the past, Ms. Bernstein has proven herself to be careless and therefore dangerous. She was the instigator of a serious altercation at her workplace where she became violent."

Boon-Dan-Tan motioned for David to stop speaking. "Bridget has explained the situation to me and has asked for guidance."

"But enlightened one, you don't understand. Bridget's not qualified. I know her mother and I'm sure she'd want me on Bridget's new board. Besides, even with a building, a great deal of money is required. In my position, I'm in touch with several government housing agencies. I'm sure I can get the proper funding."

Boon-Dan-Tan's face registered no emotion. "I praise your desire to help those in need. I'm sure the women will thank you for your good words."

David wanted to smack the complacent grin from Boon-Dan-Tan's face. "Excuse me," he said. "If I offer the board proof that this project can't get off the ground, or that it's seriously flawed, will you reconsider?"

"Only if you have absolute proof."

"My esteemed colleague Mark Appleby echoes my opinion."

Mark bowed his head, the tip of his silk turban touching the table. "Thanks for putting me on this esteemed board, and thanks to Dr. Angsdorf for proposing that I join. I have nothing but admiration for him. I suggest that you push full-steam ahead with the Convent Project and appoint Dr. Angsdorf as advisor. He could share his expertise and in so doing our goal will be unified."

David snapped his binder shut, annoyed at Mark and the way he mimicked Boon-Dan-Tan.

"I will speak to the women," said Boon-Dan-Tan.

David stood up and bowed. "Excuse me," he said. "I have a faculty meeting. If the women need me, they know where to find me. Namaste."

In the musty lobby, he leaned against a white plaster wall. Luring Mark to the committee had turned into a bust and now he was stuck. If nothing else, maybe he could use Mark to get information about Bridget's boyfriend.

He punched his fist into his palm, then brightened. He'd get Mark to deliver a message to Bridget. She needed to know that he still had clout. Besides, she snapped pretty easily when pushed to the wall. Look how she'd run out on a marriage proposal.

He walked out of the building. Hot, sticky air enveloped him. A fragment of thought, sharp as glass, cut through his brain. So far, she showed no signs of running out on this project.

Chapter 21

THE PIANO PLAYER IN the tearoom of the Dilworthe Hotel launched into a Gershwin melody. Crystal prisms refracted light into rainbow colors across white tablecloths. Carson was glad Bridget had met him here for tea in another beautiful dress. It gave him hope.

Through the filmy weave of pale green fabric, he traced the outline of her slip, anticipating the apple-sweet taste of her lips, the warmth of her skin. He smiled and pointed toward the ceiling where plaster angels circled an elaborate chandelier. "Remember the angels on the ceiling of the convent?"

"The angels sang that day." She felt his stare burn through her as if he were undressing her. She missed him more than she liked to admit. Because of their busy schedules, she'd hardly seen him since he stopped by the Center a week ago. When he called yesterday, she hadn't had the nerve to tell him about the convent. No doubt he'd be upset.

He moved his chair closer, leaned forward to kiss her, his hand grazing her thigh.

She touched his fingers and held them against her knee, brushing her lips against his.

The waitress walked toward them, stopped at their table and poured water into crystal goblets. "Are you ready to order?" she said.

"If they don't have Lipton tea, I'm lost." Carson nodded to Bridget. "Why don't you order first."

The waitress stood, pen poised, a professional smile on her lips. "Madame?"

Bridget withdrew her hand and opened the menu. "I'll have the Lapsang Souchong. And, oh yes, the assorted tea sandwiches."

"Sir?" said the waitress.

"This Lapsang Souchong. Is that a new breed of dog?" He

chuckled.

The smile faded from the waitress's face. Bridget turned her head away and tried not to laugh.

"It's a smoky sort of tea, sir."

"From China," said Bridget, in a serious voice.

Carson lowered his own voice into a baritone. "Okay. I'll have the Gunpowder Black Tea. From China. And the tea sandwiches with a bowl of mayonnaise on the side."

Bridget stifled a laugh.

"Yes, sir." The waitress backed away.

Carson turned to Bridget. "You have a problem with the mayonnaise?"

"If you're trying to annoy me, it won't work." She slipped off her shoe, ran her toes up the length of his calf.

He reached beneath the tablecloth and caressed her ankle.

Warmth spread from the pit of her stomach radiating through her body. She hoped he'd invite her back to his apartment. They would make love. After, he would hold her in his arms and she would tell him about the convent.

The waitress returned with two china pots and the sandwiches. She set them on the table and placed a crystal bowl of mayonnaise in front of him.

Bridget poured tea into her cup, then dabbed mayonnaise on a cucumber sandwich. She took a bite.

Carson smiled. "Back home I put mayonnaise on everything including steak."

"Yuck." She munched her sandwich contentedly and watched a wedding party filter into the lobby. The groom whispered something into the bride's ear. The bride kissed him and laughed. Bridget remembered attending a friend's wedding with David. "They have a great ballroom upstairs," she said. "David thought it was the perfect place to get married."

"Don't remind me about weddings." Carson removed the lid from the sugar bowl, spooned sugar into his cup. "I really messed up in that department."

"Oh?"

Just last week he'd received a postcard from Anne. Imprinted on it was a large red heart. A jagged white line bisected the middle. "Your brother told me you're coming home for a visit," she wrote. "Please don't call or come near me, you coward." The words had stabbed him like a knife in his stomach.

Bridget watched him tap his spoon against the saucer. You've never told me much about your ex-fiancé," she said.

"Because the breakup was awful."

"Want to tell me what happened?"

He bit his lip. "I'm embarrassed."

"It's your call."

He saw curiosity in her eyes. "Anne is a nice person, but I should have broken off with her long before I asked her to marry me. Everyone assumed we'd marry and I went along with them. I fell into a pattern and never questioned it." He looked away, but forced himself to continue.

"I wasn't happy and blamed it mostly on Jack, but I knew it concerned Anne, too. I settled for her, thinking life would be different once we married. Pretty naive on my part. After Dad died, my relationship with her and my career at Ball and Jack's began to disintegrate. That's when I knew I had to leave. Without telling anyone, I applied for the job here in Philadelphia."

Bridget wondered if they had something in common, the tendency to run away from difficult situations.

"I should have told Anne first, but the words wouldn't come out." He clanked his teacup into its saucer, then stroked the rim. "You see, Anne was happy living in Madison running her interior design business, seeing her parents every day, having Friday night dinner at the country club. I cared about her. She loved me in her own way, but our relationship revolved around our work and families, not us. We hardly ever talked about anything intimate. I didn't want to hurt her, but I knew she wouldn't leave Madison unless she truly loved me. Call it a cowardly test or whatever you want, but I had made my mind up." He noticed that Bridget had shifted her legs away from his.

"The wedding was three months away," his voice faltered. He balled his fist. No matter what happened, he would finish the story.

"I had to be out on the East Coast in six weeks. That's when the idea struck. I would invite Anne to my place for a special dinner that would make or break us. If she understood the meaning behind it, I'd stay and see my obligation through. If she didn't, I'd know it was time to go."

As he talked, he remembered standing in the kitchen of his old apartment back in Wisconsin. Anne had quietly let herself in, breezing into the kitchen to join him at the stove where he was melting chocolate for the mousse he had planned for dessert. "Hi darling," she said.

"There's an open bottle of wine in the fridge." He lifted his cheek for a kiss.

She poured wine into two glasses. "I'm tired," she said.

While she talked about her day, she rearranged the glasses in his cabinet. He gritted his teeth as he whipped eggs for the mousse. Every time he set up the glasses the way he liked, she came over and moved them.

He slid the beef bourgoignon from the oven. "Dinner's ready."

She followed him into the dining room and let him pull out her chair.

"You're always so thoughtful," she said. "I'm the luckiest woman in the world."

Her skin reflected in the overhead light had a milky sheen. She looked at him as though they belonged together, would in fact live happily ever after.

He opened the champagne and filled their glasses.

"Mother and I went house hunting today," she said. "I think I've found our dream house. Can you see it with me tomorrow? It has a great nursery." She leaned closer and held her glass up for a toast. "We should think about starting a family right away."

He clinked the rim of her glass, spilling foam on the carpet. "Let's eat."

Anne set her glass on the table and lifted the casserole lid. "Smells great. This is a step up from hamburgers on the grill."

Carefully he sat down, his plate still empty. "I had help with the dinner."

Anne looked puzzled.

"Dad and I made it together."

Anne's face paled. "What are you talking about? Your dad is

dead."

"We cooked it the day before he died to celebrate our engage-ment." His breath caught painfully in his throat.

Anne dropped her fork on her plate, chipping the rim. "Is this some kind of ghoulish joke having your father reach out of the grave to spook me?"

Blood pounded in his ears. His Dad had liked teasing Anne, which annoyed the hell out of her.

She fingered her diamond engagement ring. "Something's wrong. I've never seen you act so weird."

He pressed his hand against his chest trying to slow his heart-beat. "Sweetheart, I'm not suited for Ball and Jacks. Things were different when Dad was alive, but there's no place for me now. I have a job waiting on the East Coast. It starts in six weeks. I want you to come with me."

Tears sprang to her eyes. "You did this behind my back?"

"I have to take this job."

"What about me? Our families are here. Our friends. We have everything we want. Why would we leave?"

He took a deep breath. "If I don't establish my own career, I'll go crazy. You don't have to give me an answer tonight." He knew he didn't sound enthusiastic.

"The wedding's in three months. I can't go." She sat quietly, tears snaking down her cheeks.

He felt dishonest and dirty. Picking up his napkin, he leaned across the table and tried to brush her tears away.

"Don't touch me. You might as well have left me at the altar." She threw her napkin on her plate and rose from the table. "The answer to your bogus offer is no!"

"Let's be reasonable," he said.

But Anne was already out the door. She was right. He had writ-ten his own ticket to freedom.

Carson stared dejectedly into his cup. "It was a damn cowardly thing to do. But, I spent most of my life trying to fit an image and underneath I hated it. I was always trying to do the right thing. After Dad died, I saw my future more clearly."

"It was sad for both of you," said Bridget, folding her napkin into pleats. "But Anne couldn't help who she was and you didn't give her a reason to believe you weren't on the same wavelength."

Carson set his cup into its saucer. Of course Bridget would sympathize with Anne. She been dumped in a nasty way, too. "I promised myself I'd be brutally honest in any relationship from now on."

"I hope you're not practicing on me."

"Believe me, you're not another dress rehearsal."

He reached for her hand. She lay her fingers stiffly across his palm. He wanted her reassurance and the warmth he'd felt earlier. "You must think I'm a jerk."

She heard the piano player launch into "I'll Build a Stairway to Paradise." Carson looked distraught, yet the way he had broken up with Anne bothered her. She tried to gather her thoughts. "It's fine that you started a new life, but it came at a big cost to Anne." She saw him wince and softened her voice. "At least you're not denying what you did."

He smiled wearily. "I don't want to make another mistake. We've got a chance to start over with clean slates."

She pressed her fingers into his palm and smiled. "At our age, we can't totally clean our slates. Whether we like it or not, we've got baggage: suitcases, overnight bags, steamer trunks, attache cases. You name it. We've both packed them to the brim."

"We've already emptied a few suitcases. Why not a small garment bag?"

A shadow crossed the table.

Carson let go of Bridget's hand.

She looked up to see a young man dressed in jeans, tasseled loafers and a rumpled navy blue blazer. His dark hair hung down his neck in limp, curly clumps. He gave her a lopsided smile. In his stubby hand he held an attache case. Something about him seemed familiar.

Mark lifted the attache case and tapped it with his index finger. "Sorry to bother you, boss. I'm on my way home from work. I found the Pearson papers you were looking for. When I went to set them on your desk, I noticed you had written your schedule on your calendar. I thought this might be a business meeting and rushed over in case you needed them."

"Why are you working on a Sunday afternoon?"

"It's my new commitment to the bank, boss." Mark avoided Carson's eyes. He set the attache case on the tea table nearly knocking over the vase of flowers. He smiled at Bridget, opened the case and removed a manila folder.

The way Mark studied her set Bridget's teeth on edge. Where had she seen him before?

Mark shut the case and handed the folder to Carson.

"Thanks Mark," said Carson, curtly. He turned to Bridget. "Bridget Bernstein, meet Mark Appleby, my assistant."

"Bridget Bernstein?" Mark snapped his fingers. "I know you. You're David Angsdorf's old girlfriend."

Bridget felt her cheeks burn. "And you're one of his former students."

"Right on. I met you at one those swinging parties he used to have in his loft. Not that you'd remember me. I used to be a slacker." Mark leaned toward her. "I was going to call you."

"Why?" she said, coolly.

"I don't know if McAlister's filled you in on me. I've done some ugly things, but I'm turning over a new leaf personally and professionally."

Carson stared coldly at Mark, willing him to disappear.

Mark ignored him. "Anyway, I'm trying to build my spiritual life, so I've started seeking direction at the Divine Guidance Center. Last night I was at the Center's monthly board meeting. David invited me to join. He wants to create a steering committee for volunteers to help you renovate the convent for your intergenerational housing project. David says you're not capable of doing the project on your own. He's trying to stop you. I'm real sorry. I think it's a grand idea and you've got my backing."

She gripped the arms of her chair.

"Glad you're here with McAlister, though." Mark winked. "He's a bit straight-laced, but you can't have a better guy in your corner.

Try to loosen him up. Gotta go. See you tomorrow, McAlister."

Carson stared at Bridget.

She avoided his eyes.

"When were you going to tell me about the convent?" he said, abruptly.

"I planned to tell you today." She reached for her water, swishing ice against the side of the glass. "My mother surprised me and gave me the building. She's started a foundation and made me trustee, just like you and I talked about."

He folded his hands in his lap. "You should have called me right away."

"I was scared. I know you have reservations."

"Who wouldn't? Realistically, you need at least a year of planning before you begin renovations." Maybe the timing was bad but he had to ask her. "Move in with me. I've got a great apartment. There's beer in the fridge and all the hot water and privacy you could want. A trustee doesn't have to live on the premises. You can hire a manager."

Part of her longed to say yes. She was already in love with him. But another part feared that he was manipulating her.

"Anyway," he continued. "The mess of renovation will wipe you out. And you've still got David on your case."

His face looked hopeful. She measured her words. "I know you mean well, but I'm tired of running every time someone tries to shoot me down. Moving in with you isn't the answer."

"What about our future? Don't you want to raise kids? You have to think about the schools." He knew he was rambling and felt desperation creep into his voice. "Move in with me. You can work nine to five and still manage the convent."

"You're asking me to run out on people who risked their own futures."

"I need you. What is it that makes you want the whole world to love you?"

She rested her head in her hand and closed her eyes. He had hit too close to home. "If I live with you, how do I know you won't run out when the going gets tough like it did with Anne?"

Her rebuke stung. "Let's turn the cards around for a minute.

Didn't you act impulsively no matter what the consequences when you broke into David's apartment?"

"Look who's talking. You had no trouble breaking off a relationship to pursue your goals." She stirred her tea furiously. A few drops spilled on the tablecloth staining it dull, amber-brown. "You left a woman standing at the altar in the middle of her child-bearing years. What was she supposed to do at the last minute with no other options?"

"Does that mean you want to break this off?"

"You're twisting my words. You sound as controlling as David."

His fist hit the table. "Don't compare me to your ex-boyfriends."

"Shh." She clenched her teeth. People looked at them, cups poised in mid-air.

"I won't be quiet. We have something great and you're screwing it up."

"You knew my plans from the beginning. Now you're trying to wreck them."

"I'm willing to help if you'll just slow down. What's the big rush?"

The piano player struck a chord and began stringing a series of notes together.

Bridget pushed her teacup away. "You're going full steam ahead in your work. I don't see anyone asking you to slow down."

"It's easier for you. You're in the driver's seat."

"You set your own rules when you left Ball and Jacks." She watched his face turn crimson.

An English couple sitting at a table near the piano called out a request. The piano player struck up a cord.

"God bless America," sang the couple.

"We should go," she said.

"No." He looked up at her and folded his arms across his chest. "I'm staying for the sing-along. God bless America," he sang.

A second table joined in. Bridget rose. He raised his voice and glared at her. "Land that I love."

Anger spread through her body.

She reached for her purse. "From the mountains, to the valleys and damn all the selfish men in between," she sang before marching out of the room to the rhythm of the song.

* * *

In the dream, she stood in the middle of a cavernous banquet room dressed in a white satin gown sewn with so many sequins she could have sworn she was encased in tiny blinking lights.

Thick red-flocked wallpaper covered the walls of the room. Brightly lit chandeliers hung from the ceiling. On the banquet table stood an eight-foot high ice sculpture of a bride and groom.

Grandmom lumbered toward her. "My sweet Bridgila. You look gorgeous on your wedding day, I could cry." She pointed toward the foyer. "Did you see your grandpop laid out in his coffin? That crazy goy you're marrying is taking videos of him."

"It's Carson's job to film dead people."

"I wasn't criticizing. I'm surprised is all. Who invited your grandpop, anyway? And tell me, how did they get him here?"

"I don't know."

"Ruthie. Good to see you." Her father strutted over from the bar, wearing a tuxedo jacket embroidered with a deck of cards in red, black and white satin thread.

"Here comes the gambler bum," said Grandmom.

"He's not a bum," said Bridget. "He's helped Mom in a lot of ways."

"I don't care if Ruthie insults me," said her father. "This is the happiest day of my life."

He turned to Grandmom and withdrew a blank notebook and pencil from his breast pocket. "So Ruthie, I'm making book on my future grandchildren. What's your bet? Boys? Girls? How many?" He touched the tip of the lead against his tongue.

"Leave me alone, you no-Goodnik." Grandmom's head swerved toward the entrance. "Look who's here. Grace Kelly." She leaned on Bridget's arm and whispered, "She looks good for a dead lady. Do you think she had the collagen treatment?"

The woman wore a green sheath, pearls and white satin gloves buttoned at her wrists. In her hands, she carried a small box wrapped in tissue paper. It dawned on Bridget. The woman was Carson's mother.

"What you got in the box, Gracie?" said Grandmom.

"I brought a little something to welcome Bridget into the family." She glided toward Bridget and handed her the box.

Bridget tore off the tissue paper and opened the box. Inside were two airplane tickets to Greece.

"For your honeymoon," beamed Carson's mother.

"It's a lovely gesture. I'm sure we'd love Greece, but Carson and I haven't made honeymoon plans."

"Take the tickets, dear. It would mean a lot to Carson."

From the corner of her eye, Bridget saw Carson chatting with David. "Excuse me," she said. Carson smiled. David smirked. What on earth were they talking about?

"Don't go anywhere," shouted her mother. "I have present for you, too."

Grandmom took Bridget's arm and guided her past the melting ice sculpture. Dressed in a beaded apron and bonnet, her mother stood on a stepladder. She leaned over a white sheet.

Like a magician, she whisked the sheet into the air. "See everyone. My masterpiece. An ugly wedding cake!"

A collective gasp silenced the guests. Before them stood a giant cake in the shape of a volcano.

From beneath the table her mother turned on a switch. The floor rumbled as the cake erupted whipped cream, sending miniature statues of brides and grooms into the air. "Ugly is beautiful," she shouted.

Bridget stared at her ankles. Something strange was happening. The ice sculpture had dissolved, filling the room with water.

"Carson," she called. "Help me!"

* * *

"Wake up, Bridgie!"

She felt cool water dripping over her temples into her hair. When she opened her eyes, she saw Claire pressing a washcloth to her forehead.

"You were talking in your sleep, yelling Carson's name," said Claire. "I heard you all the way down the hall. You looked so feverish, I didn't know what else to do."

Bridget sat up and removed the washcloth. "I had the weirdest dream."

"Do you want to talk about it?"

"In a few minutes."

She thought about Carson, the anger in his eyes when she left the Ritz. She had acted like a jerk. She should have stayed and talked it out. Some social worker. She had the ability to help everyone but herself. And what was the dream about?

Chapter 22

"I'M NOT GOING IN THERE for a drink until you take off that skull-cap."

"But boss."

Carson wondered what had ever possessed him to say yes to Mark's invitation to grab a beer after work.

Mark removed a bobby pin that attached the embroidered yarmulke to his hair. "It's important that I keep my chakras protected so I don't lose spiritual energy. You won't let me wear my yarmulke at the office."

"You're not Jewish."

"I pay homage to all religions."

They reached the entrance to the Marwick Bar and Grill. "I was here for Happy Hour once before and I didn't like it," said Carson.

Mark folded the yarmulke, stuffed it into his pocket and grabbed Carson's arm. "Come on, it's Friday night, You haven't heard from Bridget in over a week. Let's check out the fabulous women looking for rich bankers like us."

In the dimly lit bar, tepid, smoky air assailed Carson. A handsome, cocoa-skinned man sat on a small stage plucking a guitar, scatting jazz. Several well-dressed elderly people stood in a semicircle and lifted martini glasses in a toast.

He traced the shape of an embroidered whale on his vest feeling Bridget's absence in every bone of his body. Why would she want anything to do with him? He'd upset her with his story about Anne, then overwhelmed her by pushing her to live with him.

"I don't know what I'm doing here," he said.

"Stick with me, boss." Mark pulled Carson toward a group of women standing near a hand-carved oak bar, its gleaming surface studded with drink glasses. "You need to keep dating. Maybe you won't attract the quality of women I used to, but you'll be okay."

"What do you mean by used to? Isn't looking for women the only activity you care about?"

"Not anymore, boss. I told you, I'm in a transitional stage."

A redheaded woman smiled at them. Carson ignored her. "I don't get it, Mark. You seem different lately. Even your work's improved." He shook his head. "What's up? A religious conversion?"

"Exactly. I'm touched by the Divine now."

They pushed past the crowd at the bar and found two seats.

Mark placed his attache case on the bar top. "I've been going to lectures around the city, hearing about karma and ecological yoga and transforming through transition. It knocks my socks off. I realize how lost I've been."

"And now you're found." Carson ordered two Samuel Adams beers and tried to keep exasperation out of his voice.

"It's more than transforming. I'm crazy about Claire-Barunga, the woman who gives the lectures."

Carson spun in his seat to face Mark. "You've fallen for Claire Johnson?"

"Yeah. I go to every lecture she gives. She takes my breath away. She's beautiful both inside and out, from the tips of her toes to the thousand petal lotus chakra at the crown of her head. All I dream about is that she loves me back."

"Did you tell her how you feel?"

"No." Mark stared at the bar. "What does she want with a jerk like me? Sometimes we talk a little after her lectures. I offer to do stuff for her like photocopying fliers."

"I guess you use the bank's copy machine."

"Of course. It's blessed now. It talks to me and tells me what to do. It's even given me business advice. Every deal you and me work on from now on is sure to succeed. The copy machine also told me that Bridget's project will succeed."

"Knock it off or I'll have you committed." Carson took a long pull from his bottle of beer.

"You should listen to Bridget. Maybe you don't want to date her, but she has great ideas. She and Claire-Barunga are real women. No artificial values."

"Values? What about the way you've lived? Setting up house-keeping at the bank."

"I told Claire about it. She says it was a case of the rich giving to the poor so I could find my inner life. That's what she and Bridget are after too."

Carson scraped the damp label from his beer bottle. He had no quarrel with Bridget's personal values. Her zealousness for the Convent Project had simply overtaken their relationship.

Mark snapped open his attache case and held his hands reverently over the stack of books. "Claire asked me to read these before we meet again tomorrow night at her next lecture. It's a test to see if I'm really sincere. I finished them all, boss, *The Tao Te Ching, The Bhagavad Gita, The Tibetan Book of the Dead.*"

"You and Claire would seem to be from completely different planets." Carson traced a scratch on the bar top. "But who am I to know what turns people on? I fell for a woman who devotes her entire life to helping people. She's practically living the life of a nun."

"Bridget's a humanitarian." Mark's expression became dreamy. "And Claire's magnificent."

Carson reluctantly glanced at the books. "What are they really about?"

"Here's something you'll like." Mark handed Carson a pamphlet. "It's called The Spiritual Focus. Claire wrote it. It talks about inner peace through mindful living." Mark craned his neck. "I'll be right back. There's somebody I want to say hello to."

Carson ordered another beer and watched Mark walk up to the redheaded woman he had noticed earlier.

Mark whispered something into her ear. The woman's expression darkened. She tipped her glass forward, spilling wine on Mark's shoes. Mark jumped back and bumped into another woman who accidentally spilled her drink on his shirt. He gestured an apology and walked back to the bar.

"What was that all about?" said Carson.

"I don't get it." Mark grabbed a handful of cocktail napkins from the counter top and dabbed at his shirt. "I met that woman a couple of months ago. All I did was point to you and ask her if she wanted to meet someone who would give her inner peace. She exploded."

"Sit down," said Carson, shaking his head.

From the corner of his eye, Carson saw a blonde woman at a nearby table smile at him. His heart pounded. Through the haze of smoke she looked like Anne.

The woman got up and came over to the bar. Her hair was shorter than Anne's, falling just below her shoulders. Her eyes were pale blue.

"I noticed you when you walked in," she said. "May I buy you a drink?"

She seemed nice enough. "Let me buy you one, instead."

"Okay." She smiled. "I'll take a Kettle One Martini, dry, with two olives."

Carson signaled the bartender.

"You look like a sensitive guy." She picked up her glass and primly sat on a barstool. "I see you like beer from micro-breweries. Handcrafted. I don't drink beer, but I'm quite fond of good vodka."

"I'll be seeing you, boss," chimed in Mark, putting his books back in his attache case. "Got some more work to do." He snapped the case shut and popped the yarmulke back on his head.

They watched Mark thread his way through the crowd to the door. "That's my assistant," said Carson. "He's wacky, but okay. My name's Carson McAlister."

"Cecilia Cummings. You make the most outstanding impression. I love those whales swimming across your vest."

He tried to work up some enthusiasm. "I'm just coming off a relationship. I don't usually hang out in bars."

"Then we have something in common. Neither do I. This is the first time I've been here since my relationship ended. I prefer the Dilworthe."

Carson winced.

Cecilia fingered the strand of pearls at her neck. "My mother is a patron of a number of museums. My favorites are the Museum of Art and the Rodin Museum. Have you been to them? They're across the street from each other. We could visit them together sometime."

He imagined Bridget sitting next to him on a barstool. She'd lift her head, her chin tilted toward him, her voice husky as she retold the story of her encounter with the statue in the Rodin Museum. For a second he almost laughed out loud.

Cecilia lifted an olive from her glass and popped it into her mouth. She eyed him as she chewed and swallowed. "What kind of work are you in?"

"Banking. I handle investments for private clients."

"A growth industry. Clients only get older and richer. Take it from me. In our law firm, we deal with the bluest of blue bloods."

Blue bloods. She sounded like the typical woman back home at the country club. Someone Bridget would peg as his type.

He watched Cecilia reach into her handbag and remove a tube of pink lipstick. As she dabbed pearly color on her thin lips, he imagined Bridget's full, sensuous mouth.

"I live over on Delancey Street," said Cecilia. "In a fabulous condominium. I moved there to be closer to the guy I just broke off with. He's a college professor, incredibly self-centered. He had this maniacal girlfriend who broke into his apartment after making a copy of his key."

Carson gripped the sweating beer bottle.

"She's also a pervert. She watched us, um, make love. Then she chased us with a baseball bat and knocked David down the stairs. There he was at the bottom, his leg crushed and this insane creature starts kicking him in the stomach. She punched me a few times, too, before I had a chance to call the police. When they arrived, she threw up all over us. What a nightmare. The worst part is, he's obsessed with her. I finally had to end it."

Carson broke into laughter. This whole conversation was ludicrous. He couldn't escape Bridget even when he tried.

Cecilia patted a stray lock of hair into place. "It's nothing to laugh at."

"Of course it isn't." Carson swallowed, but hysterics overtook him again. He quickly took a swig of beer and choked.

Cecilia sipped her drink and stared at the bar top.

"Do you know what Lapsang Souchong is?" he said, kicking the chair rail.

She smiled smugly. "Of course I do. It's a small, ugly dog."

*   *   *

Eager to be rid of Cecilia, Carson walked her through the warm evening air to her parking garage. Although he let her hook her arm through his, he longed for the moment when they reached her car and said goodbye.

"You're a very nice man," she said, moving closer to him, pressing her breasts against his arm.

Car fumes mingled with the odor of Chinese food. It made him feel sick.

They reached the entrance to the garage. She brushed his cheek with her lips before opening her purse and removing a ticket. He pulled out his wallet.

"I've got it," he said, taking the parking ticket from her hand. He gave the ticket and a twenty-dollar bill to the cashier.

"You're such gentleman." She snuggled close. "There's a lovely little restaurant on my street. I've been dying to try it. I'm inviting you. Expense account, you know. I can write you off. But I'd rather write you in."

"Let me . . ." He was about to say, "Let me call you," knowing he was simply placating her. He'd never call.

"And after dinner, we could go back to my place. I have a whirlpool that accommodates two just perfectly."

He lowered his eyes and stared at her blue and white spectator pumps. "You're a nice person. But I don't think we're suited for each other."

She pulled away.

He heard the sound of an engine roaring down the ramp.

A steel blue BMW screeched to a stop in front of Cecilia's toes. The parking attendant jumped out and grinned, jangling keys in his hand.

Cecilia glared at the attendant. "How dare you treat a fine car so recklessly?"

The attendant's grin froze on his face.

"Please don't be upset, Cecilia," said Carson. "The car's okay."

He put his hand beneath her elbow and tried to steer her toward the front seat of her car.

She jerked her arm away and stormed past the attendant.

Jumping into the driver's seat, she opened her purse, reached inside, dug out a quarter and aimed it at the attendant. "Take some driving lessons, jackass." She threw the quarter out the window. It whizzed into the attendant's chest, bounced off his shirt and clinked against the concrete floor.

Carson watched her gun the motor and speed away.

The attendant shrugged his shoulders.

"Here." Carson withdrew his wallet again and pulled out a five-dollar bill.

* * *

On the street, he found himself wandering toward Java High. Maybe his brother was right. He should have stayed in Madison. If he'd married Anne, he'd be settled in a mediocre, but comfortable life by now.

He could have worked his butt off all week, played golf with Jack on Saturdays at the Country Club, retiring to the clubhouse to complain about Anne and the noisy kids like everyone else. After a few drinks, he'd go home, watch the ball games and fall asleep on the couch. He began to sweat and loosened his tie.

Up ahead, he spotted the six foot, neon Java High coffee cup blinking on and off. Java High had a back room where people bought computer time. Half-smiling, he remembered how disdainful he had felt when Mark urged him to go online to find a woman.

The idea of an electronic courtship had some appeal. His luck had failed him in face to face situations. Why not write to women without smart-assed patter? You'd know if you were compatible right up front, no chemistry to mess up your brain.

At Java High's entrance, a group of kids rode skateboards over the sidewalk, skimming the edges of the wall. A local band stood on the stage by the window, their music thumping out onto the street. He made his way to the back and the bank of computers lining the wall. At the counter he bought an hour of computer time.

"Can you recommend a good chat room?" he asked the clerk.

The clerk grunted. A line of people stood behind Carson.

Drumming his fingers on the desk, the clerk said, "Look pal, if you want to surf for romance, plug into the Instant Bulletin Board. Select any category you want. If you find someone you like, take her into a private room. Now I don't mean a real room."

"No kidding," said Carson.

The clerk leered at Carson. "There's a shitload of love waiting for you. Anything else you want to know?"

Carson felt his face flush. "Never mind."

He found computer number three and slumped into his seat. First, he'd invent a new screen name and a brief description of himself. Before turning on the machine, he doodled on a pad of paper. What should he call himself? Asshole? He was an asshole who couldn't keep a romance going to save his soul. Why not take off on that? Assoul? An ass with soul? That didn't feel right.

He had to cool it. That was it, Coolbank, the Cool Banker. He wrote the word on a piece of paper. Coolbank. A guy who ordered mayonnaise with corned beef. How would women feel about a mayonnaise guy in New Orleans? Gumbo with mayonnaise. Dallas? Ribs with mayonnaise. Chicago? Hot Dogs with mayonnaise. Maine? Lobster with mayonnaise. That was it. Maine. Cold lobster tasted great with mayonnaise. There had to be a woman for him in Maine.

He selected Romantic Singles Under Forty in Maine and scrolled through his choices. Some women desired walks on the beach; others, intimate dinners and fireside chats. The hotter ads got more detailed. They specified breast and penis sizes, sexual aids, unusual apparel, and various combinations of people and positions. One had to be a mathematical genius to wade through this limitless maze of human desires.

Something caught his interest. "Intelligent, robust, athletic woman from Maine."

"Sex is environmentally friendly here," she wrote. "We make love in the woods, meadows and on top of mountains."

When he thought about making love in the woods, he remembered a friend who had contracted Lyme Disease that way. Another sexually transmitted disease to worry about. Forget it. He'd advertise himself.

He typed in his bio: "Banker who is just short of being a worka-
holic, likes skiing, art, camping and lobster with mayonnaise.
Looking for long-term commitment."

Within minutes, a dozen responses flashed on the screen. He
eliminated all but one, plugged in the name and brought up the
description.

At twenty-nine with a master's degree in biology, attractive,
petite, brunette Helene from Portland, brewed and sold her own
beer. After a hard day in a biology lab, she loved sculpting classes
and a leisurely home-cooked dinner. She enjoyed skiing, hiking
and ice-skating. A one-man woman, she wanted to mate for life like
Canadian geese and was willing to relocate.

"Please respond quickly," she wrote. "Tell me more about yourself."

"I'm a thirty-four year old banker," he replied. "Recently trans-
planted to the East Coast. Love the big city but miss the closeness
of a small town. I seek a dynamic, intimate relationship with no
pretensions. If we hit it off, we can fly south in the winter and
north in the summer."

He propped his elbow on the table, plunked his chin into his
hand and waited.

Just then, an instant message appeared.

"Hey Coolbank, What's your horoscope? I'll bet it's Gemini. I'm
a Gemini. Forget the Maine woman. I live right here in Philadelphia and am very attractive, sensitive, and nurturing. Look behind
you at terminal number eight."

Carson spun his seat around and craned his neck. He saw people busily working the keys, heads bent in concentration. Then he
spotted number eight. A young woman with clear, gray eyes
behind wire-frame glasses got up and came over to his terminal.

"Hi, Coolbank."

"How did you do that?"

"I was behind you in line. You seemed like a nice guy."

"But . . ."

"When I passed by your terminal, I saw your screen name written on a piece of paper. "I cut in on your babe in Maine."

"I congratulate you on your creativity whatever your name is."

"Maggie." She held out her hand.

From the corner of his eye, he recognized a couple sitting at a table near the window of the coffee bar. Bridget and David were deeply engrossed in conversation. David's hand rested on a stack of papers an inch away from hers.

Carson's heart sank into his stomach. The scumbag was trying to get back with Bridget. Why else would he look at her so intently?

"Would you like to have some coffee?" said Maggie.

"I'm sorry, but I've got to go." He left through the service entrance that led to an alley out back. He remembered that Mark was attending Claire's lecture tomorrow night. He hadn't planned on going, but now, after seeing David leering at Bridget, he changed his mind.

Chapter 23

BRIDGET WATCHED DAVID rip open a packet of Sweet n'Low and pour it into his cappuccino. He had called this morning saying he wanted to show her something important. Mark Appleby had told Claire who told her that David had been snooping in the neighborhood surrounding the convent. She needed to find out what was up.

He pushed a sheaf of papers toward her. "This petition will stop you dead in your tracks."

She stared at the well-thumbed pages. Across the top of the first page she read the bold letters, COMMITTEE TO SAVE THE CONVENT. Signatures lined the petition on both sides of the page.

"Who are you saving the convent for?" A cynical smile crossed her lips. "Me or you?"

"Don't get smart with me. The neighborhood wants a legitimate community center not a bunch of nuts playing house. And face it, from what I've seen, those old farts you recruited look like escapees from a mental institution."

She drummed her fingertips against the papers and let him wait for her reaction. Even when he was at his nastiest, he carried a haunted look in his eyes. She sensed he might be at odds with what he had set in motion. She leaned toward him. "Why do you want to hurt these people?"

He sipped his cappuccino. "You're the one who's hurting them." His eyes hardened. "Leading them into this mess. Andrew's planning to sue you and your foundation for endangering their welfare."

She almost laughed. In this war, no prisoners would be taken alive. "You talk like we're dumb cattle naively entering the slaughter house. Andrew's already sent his inspector to the Center twice. She's talked with Boon-Dan-Tan and the residents. So far she seems rather impressed."

He snorted. "Then she's lost her mind, too. How can she turn a blind eye to those ridiculous clothes Molly made with that army surplus material? Camouflage saris for everyone. And what's with the Army boots?"

"At least Molly's not destroying herself with a vendetta like you."

"I'm only concerned about the welfare of these people and the community. Don't think I haven't reminded the board how unstable you are."

"The board's getting sick of your tirades. If you think I'm not capable, why have you used every idea I've shared with you?"

"That's bullshit. This is my idea and you know it."

She tightened her hand around her teacup.

He thumped his index finger on the petition. "You're incompetent and impulsive. This is for the big players. You'll have a converted building, and nothing else if the community doesn't want you there. All I have to do is send these signatures to the State's Attorney General. He'll open up an investigation. With all the skeletons in your closet, there's a good chance you'll lose your nonprofit status."

She fought the urge to shout and lowered her voice. "We're turning a portion of the convent over to the community. When the plans are complete, I'll make an announcement. I'm sure the neighbors will be more than satisfied."

He rolled his eyes. "You still have to get past the zoning board. Our case against you is strong."

She pushed the petition back toward him. Her little finger hooked into his cappuccino cup, tipping it over, spilling coffee over the signatures. She began briskly rubbing the papers with her fist.

"Oh dear," she said. "All the names are smeared. Your karma must be off today."

*   *   *

Andrew Jacobson watched his son Edward amble up the street. What a disgrace. His future Harvard-trained doctor looked like the front man for a Rastafarian band. How could Edward drop out of college for a job at a ratty coffeehouse?

Andrew remembered when Bridget Bernstein had dragged him to places like this. He'd been utterly crazy about her, changing his habits just to please her. Maybe he didn't handle the breakup up well, but Bridget never understood the kind of pressure Martha had put on him.

"Yo Dad," said Edward. He waved his hand and shook his dreadlocks before joining Andrew beneath the blinking neon Java High Coffee cup. Three boxes were set up in front of the window for the weekly Saturday Soapbox Lecture Series.

Andrew reached into his pocket for his Tums, slipped two from the pack and popped them into his mouth. Edward had continued his body-piercing program. He had stuck at least fifteen gold hoops into each ear, four studs in his nose, a multitude in his eyebrows and nine in his lip. God knew where else he had them. But what upset Andrew the most were the thick studs plopped into the middle of Edward's tongue.

"Edward. Do you realize how ridiculous you look?"

"The name ith Mamu-Barunga."

"Sure Mamu-whatever."

"Before you thtart in on me, Dad, I already told you. I'm not going back to college next themethter."

"Let's leave college alone for a second. Why haven't you called me?" Andrew fingered the packet of Tums. "Look Mamu . . . Teddy . . . Edward." He shook his head. "I'm worried. You've mutilated yourself, destroying your tongue and your speech. And now you've dropped out of school."

Edward checked his watch. "Thorry Dad. Can't talk now. I thtart work in five minuteth, and then I want to attend thith lecture tonight."

"What's it about? Maybe we could go together?"

An impish grin crossed Edward's face. "It'th about the thpirit within uth all."

"For God's sake. You need a few spirits in your wallet when it comes time to pay the bills. I won't support your lifestyle."

"I don't need your money. I have my job, and I'm moving into cooperative houthing where everybody shareth."

"Cooperative housing? Andrew dropped against the brick wall. "Who's running it?"

"My friend Bridget. There she ith."

Pain shot through Andrew's stomach as if he'd swallowed a razor blade. Bridget hurried up the street, hugging a stack of flyers to her chest. She was dressed in white cotton jeans, a black t-shirt and had tied a scarf made of camouflage material around her neck. Behind her, dressed in matching camouflage saris, walked Al, Edna, Molly and Claire.

As they crossed the street, Bridget noticed a red Mercedes blocking the bus lane at the corner. Who would be so arrogant?

Then she recognized the man leaning against the brick wall. She stopped in the middle of the street.

Edna nudged her. "Move along, honey. We're blocking traffic."

They reached the curb. "Look who's here," said Claire. "The probation officer."

"Hello warden," called Edna.

"How's prison life?" chimed in Al.

Andrew pursed his lips.

"Hey Bridget," called Edward. "Come and meet my dad."

Edward's dad? She slowed down her pace. Blood drained from her face making her dizzy. She remembered a photograph on a shelf in Andrew's office of a tow-headed little boy whom Andrew called Teddy.

"Don't let this throw you," said Claire. "I'll grab Edward and tell him that you used to work with Andrew." She waved to Edward. "Help me set up for my lecture, Mamu-Barunga," she called.

Bridget handed the flyers to Edna. "Let's get to work everyone."

Andrew walked toward her. "What are you doing to my patients now? Putting them out on the street to work. They should be in a protected environment."

"As you can see, they've never been better." She studied Andrew's face looking for signs of Edward. There was a resemblance in the cupid shape of their mouths. Both of them had a cleft chin, but that was it. Edward's face was softer, more cherubic, while Andrew was all angles.

"You've caused a mutiny at the home. I've got patients trying to get out. Their families deluge me with calls night and day."

"Have you stopped to think you might have brought this on yourself?"

Claire's voice boomed from her soapbox. "Are you bogged down with the stress of accumulating more and more material goods? Have you lost your way? Come to the Unitarian Church at eight o'clock. Join in fellowship as we raise the building blocks of our souls together. One by one, from alpha to omega, we will forge a path to enlightenment."

"This is what you left the nursing home for?" said Andrew.

"You fired me, remember?

He grabbed her arm. "I know there's another Bridget inside of you. You simply had a breakdown. I'm willing to take you back on Monday along with Al, Edna and Molly."

She was puzzled. Why would he want her back after all that had happened?

He looked down at the pavement. "It's strictly business," he said quietly. "The patients miss you."

She saw a squad car approach, its lights flashing. "I'm sorry."

"What about all I taught you?"

She shook her head as she studied the pattern of bricks lining the sidewalk nestled into themselves like the wings of birds. She was through taking lessons at such a high price.

A tow-truck sped past.

Andrew's face grew dark. "You'd like to think you're so nice. Remember how you left me laying on that cold, freezing sidewalk? You never let me explain everything and you didn't even know if I could get up. I could have died!"

"If you had, your wife would have thanked me." She shook her arm free.

He looked up. "What are they doing to my new car?"

She turned. Halfway down the block, Al was sticking a flyer into the windshield wiper of a red Mercedes as a man busily hitched a winch to the front bumper.

*   *   *

A faint, musty odor arose from the ancient red carpet in the small auditorium of the Unitarian Church. Fresh paint covered cinder block walls. Bridget and Molly sat in folding chairs waiting for Claire's lecture to begin.

Molly crossed her combat boots at the ankles. "I'm glad Ruthie's back from the hospital. She looks so good."

"Tests came out A-OK," said Bridget. "Grandmom's a real trooper."

"You don't know what you and your grandmother have done for us, Miss Bridget." Molly clasped Bridget's hand between her warm, dry palms. "There we were at the end of the downward slope of our mediocre lives. Now, we're so busy we don't know what to do next. Everyone at the Center loves my camouflage outfits. And Al, he's building shelves for the library."

Bridget smiled. "Edward's gang loves the way Edna shaves their heads."

"And Miss Claire, her lectures inspire me." Molly dropped Bridget's hand and pressed her right palm to her heart. "The last time I heard someone so fiery was when I joined the Communist party. Who'd have thought the Soviet Union would turn out like that. All those politicians sold their people down the river, don't you think?"

"Good to see you again," said a voice. Bridget looked up. Mark Appleby leaned toward her chair. A cream-colored muslin shirt fell loosely over matching trousers. He had cut his hair short and had pinned a silver and blue yarmulke to his head.

"Sit down, young man." Molly patted the chair in front of her.

"No thank you Ma'am. My boss is coming. We're sitting over there."

Bridget felt sweat break out at the back of her neck, her senses suddenly alert to every nuance in Mark's face. She saw no ulterior motive in his good-natured smile.

The noise level had risen. Edward and a group of kids from Java High sauntered through the door dressed in an assortment of tie-dyed t-shirts and low slung shorts.

"By the way," said Mark. "I've gone to every board meeting on your behalf and I've attended all of Claire's lectures. She recommended a reading list to me."

"That's great, Mark. Even Boon-Dan-Tan's noticed your devotion."

He leaned over and whispered in her ear. "Got a secret to tell. I'm crazy about Claire-Barunga."

Startled, Bridget looked at him. She wondered if Claire knew about his feelings.

Claire, her hair braided into a regal crown, walked on the stage, stepped on a footstool and lowered the mike. She adjusted the hem of her black tunic and nodded to Bridget.

Mark almost swooned as he stumbled to his seat.

"My message isn't new," began Claire.

From the corner of her eye, Bridget noticed Carson slip into the seat beside Mark. Her heart pounded. He looked so self-assured in his charcoal-gray suit.

"Together," continued Claire. "With new insight and the aid of modern technology, we're making changes at the grass roots level and rebuilding the spiritual system through cooperation among people in our own communities."

Carson turned, acknowledging Bridget. Seeing him again only underscored how deeply she missed him. She longed to sit beside him, his arm around her shoulders; her back pressed against the muscle and sinew of his chest.

Claire's words brought her up sharply.

"It's time to put our spiritual values to work. Go out into the community with your knowledge and skills. Teach a child to read, teenagers how to earn a living, educate the community about changes in technology and communication."

For the next fifteen minutes, Bridget tried to focus, but Claire's words faded in and out. She heard some key phrases signaling the lecture's end.

"Reach out to your families, your neighbors. Share your wealth. Only then can you become enlightened. Do I have your support?"

"Yes," yelled the crowd.

"Join with the community of the Divine Guidance Center. Our weekly outreach meeting is held here on Friday. We'll see you then." Claire pressed her hands together and held them to her breasts. "Namaste. Go in peace," she said, and stepped down from the lectern.

Bridget moved with the crowd. In the foyer, people had already gathered around Claire.

Carson walked toward her. She held her breath, her pulse quickening. The foyer light shone behind him, outlining his body as if he had been painted in fine ink. "Are you here with Mark looking for spiritual women?" she said.

"Sure am. I was eyeing Molly. She's got wisdom written all over her face. And her combat boots. Damn sexy." His arm brushed her shoulder. Goosebumps arose on her skin. "Can we go outside and talk?" he said.

She led him out the door to the front steps and sat down. The trees rustled in the breeze. The concrete step felt cool through the thin cotton of her skirt. She cleared her throat. "I'm sorry I left you so abruptly at the Ritz." She studied the pattern of fleur-de-lis embroidered on Carson's socks as he sat down next to her. "If you haven't already noticed, I tend to run when the going gets tough. It's not a nice trait."

The hem of her skirt had settled against his pant leg. He traced the stitching. "At least I know you have a talent for marching." He tapped his feet on the steps.

"I should have called you and apologized." She held out her hand.

He took it between his palms and kissed her fingertips. "I've been dying to call you, too. I've wanted to tell you something. I met Cecilia Cummings last week."

"David's girlfriend?" She pulled her hand away. Was Cecilia trying to steal Carson? Or had David set this up?

"She and David broke up. I met her at a singles bar."

"Do you like that kind of woman?" Her voice took on a chill.

"Absolutely. Cecilia's got an expense account. She invited me to an exclusive restaurant and then to her apartment to check out her whirlpool bath." He broke out laughing.

Bridget sighed. "We have decent, communal showers at the Center if you're interested."

"Sounds good if we could have a shower stall to ourselves." He looked at her expectantly. "I don't want to scrub Molly's and your back at the same time."

"What did Cecilia say about me?"

"Nothing much, short of telling me that you tried to commit murder. I thought she was the most pretentious bullshitter I ever met. She thought I was a jackass, so we got along great."

"It serves you right for picking up women in bars."

He traced his finger along her shoulder blade. "I hated every minute of it. I compared all the women there to you and nobody came close."

She leaned against the step and sighed. His words were like a rope being thrown to her as she struggled to get out of a deep pit.

His face grew serious. "There was one thing Cecilia said that alarms me. David's obsessed with you. It's worse than you thought." He paused. "I saw you with him last night at the Java High. Now if you two are thinking of getting back together, that's your business. But I felt I should warn you."

"Back together? He couldn't wait to tell me how he's sabotaging the zoning for my building."

"Look, I'm still not a hundred percent sold on how you're going to live, but I'll do what I can at the bank to help with any loans or community grants that might be available."

She kissed him on the cheek.

He smiled. "Are you hungry? Let's pickup dinner and eat at my place. You never saw my apartment."

"Sure, I'll call my friend Connie at the supermarket and have her put something together for us. It's on the way to your place."

Chapter 24

THE SUN DIPPED INTO the western sky, bathing the brick buildings in a warm glow as Bridget and Carson walked up Pine Street. Most of the antique stores lining the sidewalk were closed. Ornate iron gates guarded treasures behind glass windowpanes. On the corner a pretzel vendor packed up his cart for the evening.

They stopped in front of a window filled with porcelain dolls. "Madame Alexander," said Bridget. "Aren't they beautiful? My dad used to buy them for me when I was a kid."

Carson leaned against her shoulder. "You loved your dad in spite of everything."

"I have lots of nice memories. He loved giving tours at the factory, putting on a show. When I was a kid, about once a week after school, he'd leave work early and pick me up at Grandmom Ruth's. We'd go to fun places, amusement parks, skating rinks." She smiled cynically. "Sometimes he snuck me into the track, kind of like your dad taking you to film funerals."

Carson nodded. "Guess they needed us for moral support."

She remembered her mother screaming at her father after he brought her back from one of their outings. "Go waste your money. But you won't teach my daughter any of your rotten habits. If you think bringing a doll home makes everything normal, you're sick."

"Maybe our backgrounds aren't so different," said Carson. We had goofy dads who loved us. To me, Dad could do no wrong. He was unusual, that's all."

"I see why my dad aggravated my mother." She pressed her arm against his ribs. "I sometimes think that my parents worked things out in the end by settling into a fatigued kind of love."

"I don't remember my parents fighting. You had to see Dad in action. He was a hoot."

Bridget admired Carson's sincerity, but she guessed that on some level, his mother had resented his father's self-destructive lifestyle. She glanced at Carson's face. He looked so content. She didn't want to burst his bubble. "I'm glad you surprised me like this," she said.

"I shamelessly used David as an excuse to see you. I was sure if I called, you'd refuse to see me."

It felt right walking down the street with him. If only she could find a way to make her dream work and keep him in her life.

They reached the entrance to the Forever Fresh Supermarket.

Reluctantly, she let go of his arm. He went inside to get the order she'd called in from the church. Connie, who worked in the fish department, had promised to pick out some nice shrimp and fixings for a salad. "Send only your boyfriend in," Connie had said. "I have a surprise for you."

Bridget thought of Connie, how she had kept herself and her three kids going after her husband deserted her. Bogged down with financial and family pressures, Connie never complained about working extra shifts.

Sometimes Bridget would baby-sit when Connie got the opportunity to work on the weekend. She loved Connie's kids, especially the youngest, two-year-old Carmella who would cuddle on her lap and try to read storybooks to her.

Ten minutes later, Carson emerged into the gathering dusk carrying a bag of groceries. He held up a smaller bag, peeling back the brown paper to reveal a bottle of Dom Perignon champagne.

"Your friend wants you to have the champagne as a gift for all the favors you've done for her."

Bridget looked through the window trying to catch Connie's attention, but saw her own reflection instead. "We should take it back. Connie really can't afford it."

"Hey, this Connie's on the ball. She said you'd say that. She also said you should use it to seduce me."

Bridget felt her body grow warm. She took the bottle of champagne as they began walking. Connie could read her like a book.

Carson looped his arm around her waist. "I made plans to visit my family next week. My mother wants to see me. Something about Dad's estate. I think Jack's agitating things."

"Would you go back to Ball and Jack's if your mother asked?"

"Not at this point." He stopped in front of a mid-rise, gray stone apartment building and swung the wrought-iron gate open. "Here we are." He led her up a cobblestone path through a small garden. Pale, yellow roses climbed a trellis framing the doorway. She breathed in their sweet scent as they entered the building.

His apartment was spacious and still retained a working fireplace and original oak chair rails. Sunflowers sat in a blue glass vase on the dining table. He owned an interesting mix of old and new furniture including an ancient, carved walnut desk tucked into an alcove of the living room across from a black leather sofa and love seat. In the center of the living room lay a pair of barbells. His bedroom was down a narrow hallway.

In the kitchen, she set the champagne on the counter. Carson followed her and unpacked the grocery bag, removing a head of romaine lettuce, Belgian endive and radicchio.

"I'll make the salad," she said

He reached into the cabinet for two champagne glasses. "First, let's have a toast."

It seemed so natural, like they'd always been together.

He took a towel from the sink, wrapped it around the cork and neatly popped it out of the bottle. "Tell me. What can we do to stop David from turning the neighborhood against you?"

She liked his use of "we." "I'm taking the gang down to canvass the neighborhood. We'll tell them who we are and what we're trying to accomplish."

Light glinted through cut-glass facets in the champagne glasses. "You're determined, but so am I. No wonder we sometimes go head to head." He poured champagne in her glass, and stood so close she could feel his body give off heat.

She tried to look away, but his eyes pinned hers. Suddenly, she felt something cool and tingly roll over her fingertips.

"You're spilling champagne," she laughed.

He quickly set the bottle on the counter and took the glasses from her hands. Bending over to kiss her damp fingertips, he lifted his head. She smoothed back the hair from his forehead.

"If we don't fix dinner now, we may never get to the table," he said. Moving to the counter, he opened a drawer and rummaged through it. "I bought these sets of ebony chopsticks in Chinatown. They're perfect for shrimp."

"Do you use them?"

"Yeah. They're fun."

* * *

Claire hurried along the darkened street toward the Divine Guidance Center. She felt edgy walking alone down Walnut Street so late at night, but traffic hummed along and an occasional pedestrian passed by.

By all accounts, the lecture was a success. An odd assortment of people had shown up. She thought about what she might have said differently, how she would improve her lecture next time by using meditative techniques to focus the audience's energy.

Up ahead she saw the Walnut Street Bridge that crossed the Schuylkill River and led back to the Center. Suddenly, a shadow loomed across her own in the light of the street lamp. Her heart pounded. She picked up her pace.

"Please," a man's voice called. "Don't be scared. It's your faithful servant Mark Appleby."

She was on the bridge now, the river reflecting the golden lights of the city.

Mark caught up to her.

She turned to face him, her heart still pounding. "You scared the daylights out of me." His face looked drawn beneath the orange glow of the streetlight.

"I wanted to tell you that tonight's lecture was the best I've attended. The point you made about how life's quest doesn't truly begin until we find our own path really hit home. I think I've found mine. Remember that book you gave me about that guy, Parzival and his quest for the grail, or should I say his inner consciousness?"

Claire's mouth dropped open.

"If I read that myth right, all of us have our own grail. I thought mine was at the bank bamboozling the likes of my boss. You know, steady paycheck, trying to get around the rules."

"If you're serious about making a change, you shouldn't be screwing up at work."

"I know. I want to walk the straight and narrow more than anything else in the world. See, I've got ideas of my own. Once you get the convent going, I want to live there if you'll have me."

They stopped at the end of the bridge. He set his hand on the railing. "Meeting you and reading those books has changed my life. Watch this." He pulled a blue and red-striped tie out of his pocket. With a flourish, he dangled it over the stone wall before letting go. It caught a current of wind, rising before falling to the water below.

Claire smiled. "I guess you are serious if a bit naive."

"Naive, I'm not. From the time I was a kid, I've seen every con. The streets taught me about survival. But this spiritual stuff and the way you express it hit me in a place I never knew existed." He stepped toward her. "Plus, I think you're beautiful."

Claire stepped back onto the curb.

"Can we get a cup of coffee somewhere? I promise it's all on the up and up. I'll spring for it."

She paused and focussed on his aura. The colors surrounding him pulsed yellow and orange. He was ripe for a change. "Okay," she said. "I know a diner where we can talk."

*   *   *

Bridget pushed a piece of shrimp to the side of her plate with her chopstick.

Carson watched her through the flickering candlelight. What had happened between the kitchen and the dining room table to make her so distant?

"This is delicious," he said. "Why aren't you eating?"

She sighed. "I've lost my appetite."

He moved his chair closer to hers until their thighs touched. "You're worried about your project."

"It's more than that. I'm worried about us."

Candlelight softened her face, yet her eyes asked him for something he wasn't ready to give. He was glad for the dim glow. He'd keep his voice upbeat, but he didn't want her to detect any doubt in his eyes. "Maybe, we've both learned something." He hoped she'd be willing to compromise on her dream. She could work at the Center during the day and live with him.

He picked up a shrimp between his thumb and forefinger and held it to her lips.

She set her teeth firmly on the tip of the shrimp and bit. When he moved to pull his hand away, she held his wrist.

Each bite brought her lips closer to his fingertips. His fingers opened. The tail of the shrimp fell to her plate.

"Glad you got your appetite back," he said.

* * *

In his bedroom, she unbuttoned his shirt, loosened his belt buckle. His pants fell to his ankles.

"Whales," she smiled. "Swimming across your boxer shorts."

"You like them?"

She looked down appreciatively. "I love that giant sperm whale swimming toward me."

His breath caressed her neck like warm fingertips. She helped him unzip her skirt.

"I missed your beautiful body," he said, tracing the outline of her ribs, hips and buttocks.

She pressed herself into his belly, rotating her hips like a match head striking flint.

He flicked his tongue against the satiny skin of her throat and lay her across his bed. Taking her fingers one by one into his mouth, he licked them very slowly, enjoying the look of elation that crossed her face.

Her breath quickened as his tongue flicked over her navel, along her hip, shifting below her belly, between her legs. She concentrated on the place where he kissed her. "I like the way they do it in the Midwest," she whispered.

He pressed his lips against her thigh and laughed. "This is serious." He rolled on his back beside her.

She kissed his stomach. "I'll show you how we do it on the East Coast." When she took his erection into her mouth, his body arched. Each time she ran her tongue along the length of him, he felt as if his muscles were breaking out of his skin.

*　*　*

When he opened his eyes, it was morning. Streaks of pale pink light brightened the sky. Bridget had fallen asleep on his chest.

Gently, he shook her shoulder. "Wake up, darling. Would you like a bath?"

She roused herself and sat up.

"I don't have a fancy Jacuzzi, but I've got a big old cast iron tub."

She watched him walk toward the bathroom, enjoying the way his butt muscles flexed with each step. Soon she heard the water running. She hugged herself. He had held her in his arms so tenderly last night, as if she were a fragile china doll. She closed her eyes, imagined them living together at the Center.

"Your bath awaits you princess," he called.

She got up and moved to the bathroom door. The air smelled of lavender. She reached for him, holding him close. "Now I'm really a Jewish princess."

"And I'm your goy prince." He eased her into the tub.

"How do you know that word?" she said, laying her head against the tub's lip.

"I used to go with my dad to a deli in Madison." He gently massaged lavender-scented shampoo into her hair. "The owner taught me a few words." He leaned over and kissed her nose, cheeks, lips. "I've knocked off quite a few corned beef specials in my day, with mustard, not mayonnaise. That makes me Jewish, right?"

"Grandmom would say so."

"I really admire your Bubbie for making a change at her age. She's full of energy." His lathered hand slipped from the nape of her neck over her breasts and into the water, resting for a moment between her thighs before gliding toward her knees.

"Older women seem to turn you on."

"Yup." He arched his eyebrows. "But I'm most excited by you." He turned on the faucet. How elegant she looked lying in the bath, prisms of water sparkling in her eyelashes, her skin lustrous. He stroked the soap from the crown of her head.

Clear, warm water fell over her eyes and face. "It feels as though you're making love to my hair," she whispered.

Shutting off the water, he helped her stand. He picked up a towel, wrapped it around her shoulders and pulled her toward him.

Water splashed to the floor. She lay her head on his shoulder wishing she could stay with him all day. Although it was Sunday, she had a meeting at the Center at noon.

"I've got to get back soon," she said.

He held her against his chest. "At least stay and have coffee with me."

"Sure." She splashed back into the water and pulled him over the lip of the tub.

Chapter 25

WRAPPED IN CARSON'S plaid terrycloth robe, she sat on the sofa and watched him pace back and forth in front of his desk. He'd been relaxed before he slipped on his jeans and went into the kitchen to make coffee. By the time she joined him in the living room, his demeanor had changed.

"What's up?" She lifted her legs onto the sofa, curling them beneath her.

His coffee sat untouched on the desk. "I got a letter from my mother yesterday which I forgot about as soon as you agreed to dinner. I reread it while I waited for you. She's weirded-out about my Dad. It's strange. She never lost her temper with him when he was alive."

"Never?" Bridget pulled the robe tighter.

He shrugged. "Maybe irritated, but not angry."

"My mother doesn't hold anything back." She smiled. "Both ways are extreme, don't you think? It sounds healthy that your mother's expressing some anger."

He picked up the cup and cradled it in his hands. "What's the point?"

Bridget looked away. The sunflowers on his dining room table shone deep yellow in the morning light.

He sat down on the floor next to her and leaned his weight against her knee. "Maybe I'm overreacting. I'd like your opinion. Can I give you a little background, then tell you what she wrote?"

"Okay." Apprehension settled over her.

"It's hard to talk about this." His voice caught in his throat. He set the coffee cup down.

She kissed the nape of his neck. "Go on."

His voice fell into a monotone. "After Dad died, Mother became seriously depressed. She moved into the guestroom and wouldn't let anyone into her and Dad's bedroom. Not even to vacuum or dust. The only thing she took care of was Dad's golf clubs. She polished them every day, setting them by the front door as if he would come back and claim them." He gave Bridget a wry smile.

"The whole family worried about her, but we didn't have a clue how to help. Except that we knew she had always wanted to go to Greece. At the office, when we were cleaning out Dad's desk, we found a stack of brochures advertising the Greek Islands. We got this brainstorm to send her. We thought it would bring her out of her funk. Lisa even arranged to go too, but at the last minute Mother decided to go alone."

He sipped his coffee and sighed. "The letter is about her time at the Artemis Hotel on Santorini."

Bridget watched the digital clock on Carson's desk flip over to 10:30. She'd be late for her meeting, but this was important.

He settled against her arm. "My mother loved the island of Santorini, loved the cliffs, the rocks, the light and the smell of chamomile. But she couldn't sleep at night. So she sat at a little table in the courtyard waiting for morning when she would walk into town for breakfast. On the way, she would pass by a young honeymoon couple, obviously deeply in love. Mother would exchange a few friendly words with them, but their affection for each other pained her. She decided that she shouldn't have catered so much to Dad's business, she should have yanked him from the office and made him get on a plane with her.

Carson shifted away from Bridget and stared at his hands. "I get where she's coming from. But she knows it wasn't easy running the company."

Bridget twisted a lock of hair around her fingertip.

"In a little garden on the edge of town Mother stopped to say hello to an old man who lived there. She had seen him delivering eggs to the restaurant near her hotel. He spoke good English and Mother accepted his invitation to share a cup of coffee. The morning was so pretty and she couldn't stand to be by herself anymore.

"In his kitchen, above the cupboard hung a heavy, silver framed photograph of a young man standing in a stiff old fashioned suit. Next to him, sat a dark-haired woman in an elaborately decorated costume. The old man touched a heavy gold ring he wore on his finger and told Mother that he'd been married for forty-five years. His face registered a longing she immediately recognized.

"She looked out the window toward the sea and saw sunlight cutting through the mist, striking the far cliff. For a moment, she felt Dad's presence. White-hot anger rose up inside her. Why had she let Dad be so careless with his health? Why hadn't she spoken up when she had a chance?

"She wanted to get up and run, but she stayed and drank her coffee. The old man told her about his life on the island, about his children who lived in Athens. When it was time to go, Mother let the old man guide her to the door.

"She patted his hand and strode through a field of chamomile to the stone wall that marked the point where the path met the sea. Poppies glowed in red bunches. She stooped to pick up a handful.

"One by one, she plucked the petals and threw them over the wall. It was time to admit the truth. Dad had been irresponsible to her and us.

"Far below, where the petals fell, she saw the young couple walking the path, engrossed in conversation. For a moment, she imagined they were she and Dad. She would hold Dad's hand, tell him she forgave him. He would kiss her one last time, and assure her that she was finally free to get on with her life."

Carson rose and went to his desk. Bridget sat quietly on the sofa, her face deep in concentration. Her silence unnerved him. Forget the whole story, he wanted to tell her. Forget it and come running with me on the River Drive. He knew when she spoke, he wouldn't want to hear what she had to say. "Okay. Talk. Tell me I don't understand women."

She shifted, rearranging her legs. "I think your mother's telling you that until your father died, her life revolved around him. She didn't dare interfere with his agenda. The trip gave her the distance to come to terms with what she missed."

"What do mean? You're blaming the poor guy for dying?"

She sighed. "It's hard for me to say this, but it sounds like your father was a great guy, but also self-destructive."

Carson flattened his hand and chopped the air. "No more analyzing."

"You asked for my opinion." She drew in a breath. "You're in denial about him. Maybe that's what your mother's trying to say." She held her body still, not wanting him to misinterpret any gesture she made. "Your mother loved your father, but when she saw that young couple in Greece, she knew how much she'd lost."

"I hear what you're saying, and I'm trying to understand. But, you're confusing me. Aren't you doing what my father did? Your ambition is driving us apart."

She steadied herself. It was important they worked this out in a calm, rational way. "First, this conversation isn't about us, but you need to understand that I've found my life's work. In a year or so when things settle down, I can back off a bit."

He knelt by the sofa, his head touching her knee. "I'm in love with you. Don't do this to us."

She ran her hand through his hair, the fine, glossy strands slipping through her fingers. "I love you, too. But I can't stop what I'm doing."

He looked out the window. The sky was overcast. A light drizzle fell onto the windowsill. "You can accomplish your goal without giving up your life. I've taken a cue from you. I've signed up to coach a basketball team across the street from the convent, but it doesn't mean I have to live there."

"Don't make decisions for me," she said softly.

"I'm asking you one last time. Move in with me."

"I can't under your terms."

"If you really loved me, you'd say yes."

She got up from the sofa. "Can we talk about this after my meeting?"

"Sure. Run out and hide behind your commitments. We talk now or forget it."

In the bedroom, she pulled on her skirt, wishing they could go back to last night and start over, wishing he hadn't tried to manipulate her. When she reached the living room, he had disappeared.

She looked into the kitchen. He stood at the sink watching her, the dishes from last night's dinner piled next to him on the counter. She stepped into the doorway.

His eyes had hardened. "I'm sorry. This isn't working out."

A lump formed in her throat. "But . . ."

"Don't say anything else."

Through the open window she heard two birds calling to each other. Carson had focused his eyes on the door behind her. Reluctantly, she turned and let herself out.

On the street, the drizzle had turned to rain. A car backfired. She looked up toward his window and felt the sting of raindrops pelting her face.

Chapter 26

CLAIRE FINGERED A DRESS in a crushed cardboard box that sat on a table at the Belle Epoque Thrift Store. "Sounds like Carson's family problems have totally zoned him out."

Bridget lifted a silk scarf from a bin, let it drop and watched it float to the table. "Last night we made the most incredible love. I felt so close to him. When he talked about the couple walking the beach in Greece, I pictured us."

Claire held the dress against her chest. "Look, if you want to move in with him, do it. We can run the convent during the day and I can recruit some people from the Center to run it with me at night. I'll cut out my lecture schedule for awhile."

Bridget imagined living in Carson's apartment, cooking dinner together after a hard day's work, sitting on his leather sofa across from him, toes touching as he figured out the crossword puzzle and she read a novel. It wrenched her to set that dream aside, but it wasn't fair to drop everything on Claire.

"I can't change my life just to suit a man and neither should you. Now go try on that dress." She held the dressing room curtain open and sighed. "I wore a dress that came from here when I first met Carson at Java High."

Claire unzipped the back of the dress. "Love sure messes life up."

"No kidding. I told him my secrets. You're the only other person who knows me like that." She watched Claire slip out of her jeans. "Plus, he's the best lover I ever had."

"That's a drag." Claire squeezed herself into taut satin. "I've had a real dry spell myself, but maybe that'll change tonight. After Mark and I pick up a cookbook at Java High, we're going back to his place for dinner."

"He's sure smitten with you."

"I've jumped too fast in the past, but Mark's a hip dude. Sensitive too. Plus, he wants to help us with the convent."

Bridget remembered how Mark's eyes had lit up when Claire took the stage at the church, then remembered Carson's cold stare when she left him standing in the kitchen.

Claire turned her back to Bridget. "I know you're sad, girl, but stick with your dream. It'll bring you happiness in the long run. Now, zip me up."

Bridget slowly inched the zipper up the back of the dress as Claire sucked in her stomach. The zipper stuck.

Claire flattened her palms against the splintery wooden wall and jerked herself taller in an attempt to give Bridget more slack.

"I think you might need a different dress." Bridget forced the zipper until it stopped two inches short of the top.

Claire released a barrette. Cornrows cascaded over her back covering the unzipped section. She turned to face Bridget, her eyes dreamy. "I've got to have this dress. It's green, the color of my heart chakra. Besides, it's sexier than my sari."

*   *   *

Outside the thrift shop, the late afternoon sun had heated up the pavement. Bridget felt the soles of her feet warming through her thin sandals.

In what had become a habit, she scanned the street. "I haven't seen David at the Java High or the Center since he showed me that ridiculous petition."

"Because he's spending all his free time agitating the neighbors near the convent," said Claire. "Mark's keeping an eye on him. The Board Members at the Divine Guidance Center are onto him, too."

"I heard. But that won't stop the damage he's already done." They had reached the Java High.

Claire opened the door. "We got to get our butts out there and show the neighborhood the architect's plans."

Edward waved to them as they entered and found a table.

Claire waved back. "I love Mamu-Barunga. He's really grooving on my lectures and gets it in a heartbeat."

"Maybe you're his guru. He hasn't deliberately messed up an order since you got back in town."

Claire glanced toward the book section and adjusted her dress.

"It's time for me to meet Mark." She picked up the brown paper bag holding her street clothes.

Bridget folded her hands together and watched Claire disappear into the stacks. Loneliness settled over her. People sitting at nearby tables laughed, talked, sipped tea and coffee. Finally, she rose. She'd stop and say hello to Mark.

The stacks were unusually quiet. She walked toward the cookbook section. A few regulars leaned against the bookshelves reading books they had no intention of buying.

She spotted an unkempt man who appeared every afternoon, talking to anyone who braved his foul breath and body odor. Dirty shirt, buttons missing, he walked through the store with a book in one hand, expounding on a variety of subjects, while the other hand grasped the waistband of his pants to keep them up.

That was the beauty of Java High. There was room for everyone. She reached the back of the store. Claire's voice drifted toward her. She stopped.

"Two cups of sugar, half a cup of heavy cream and five egg whites beaten stiff. Then bake for half an hour. Mmmm, sounds good."

"Here's another one we can try." She heard Mark's voice. "Rub garlic over a peeled medium sized zucchini. Slice lengthwise and saute in butter. Put aside. Caramelize onions and toss with zucchini." He spoke quickly.

Bridget peered around the stack. Claire and Mark sat huddled together in a darkened corner bent over a large cookbook sprawled on the floor in front of them. Mark wore a camouflage sheet tied with a belt around his waist. His hand was hidden beneath the hem of Claire's dress while Claire's hand rested high up on his thigh.

Obviously, they'd fallen hard. Hooray for them.

*   *   *

"These bathrooms are in pretty good shape," called Al from the third floor of the convent. "'Course, you'll need new fixtures, but the pipes are solid."

"Stop with the pipes and come down here," called Grandmom. "Bridget needs help setting up her office."

Al thudded down the steps. Bridget saw him dragging a rug, dust billowing in the air.

"What's that schmata you're bringing in here?" Grandmom slapped her hand on a stack of flyers.

"It's a good piece of carpet, Ruthie."

"Of course it's good. It came from my old apartment, but it's been sitting up there with all that filth and bugs. I won't have it in my Bridgila's office."

"I'll beat the dust out of it."

"Forget the carpet, we gotta clean up my old roll top desk so Bridget has a place to do her paperwork."

Bridget coughed and opened the window. Across the street, kids ran down the basketball court. Their shouts and laughter drifted through the heavy air. She noticed a tall, well-built man standing at the end of the court wearing black shorts and a t-shirt. Her heart pounded. Carson. She had been checking out the basketball courts for the last five days. He lifted the basketball and tossed it to a group of kids, then made a break down the court.

A kid in baggy gym shorts passed the ball to Carson. She watched the fluid movement of his body as he dribbled down the court and passed the ball back to the kid. For a split second, he turned to glance at her building. Her hands gripped the windowsill. She backed away. No way would she let him see her watching him.

The kid jumped, made his shot. The ball swished through the net. Carson blew the whistle.

She fought an urge to run down the steps and out onto the court. Even from this distance she could tell that the kids enjoyed him. A boy slapped Carson five before he dribbled the ball toward the net, hooking his arm, releasing the ball in an arc through the air. The ball hit the rim and fell through. The kids cheered.

"Bridgila," said Grandmom. "Time to knock on doors."

Startled, Bridget turned toward Grandmom who gave her a funny look. "Are you okay, doll? You look a little pale.

Bridget fussed with the papers on her desk. "I'm fine. What about you, Grandmom? Are you up to walking?"

"The old ticker's doing great. Nothing like a little tune up to

give an old lady a jump-start. These boots Molly gave me pinch my
toes a little, but they're good and solid."

"So what's the game plan?" Al brushed dust from the sheet he
wore over an old pair of coveralls.

Bridget smiled at his effort to fit in at the Center. "You can take
off the sheet, Al. We don't want to alarm the neighbors so we're
wearing street clothes. They already think we're a cult."

He untied the sheet and folded it as she explained the game
plan. "Al, you'll canvass block four. Grandmom and I will take
block two. Edna and Molly will take block three. Here's the pitch:
We tell the neighbors that we're making a commitment to the
neighborhood by planning a free community resource center and
day care center. And remind them that they're welcome to stop by
any time."

"Don't forget about the weekly street clean-up," said Al.

"And with our zoning," said Grandmom. "I'll make sure this is
a drugless zone."

"Drug-free zone," corrected Al.

"You get the point," said Grandmom, indignantly.

Bridget took a stack of flyers from Grandmom. "Time to go.
Molly and Edna are downstairs waiting for us in the chapel."

In the muted light, Molly sat in a pew attempting to pull her
legs into the lotus position. Edna kneeled and prayed, clicking her
rosary beads before a dusty statue of the Virgin Mary. Bridget, Al
and Grandmom filed into the front pew and bowed their heads.

Silence fell over the group. Edna straightened the jacket cuffs
of her lavender pantsuit. Grandmom toyed with the belt of her
wrap-around housedress. The daisies were faded, but she had
carefully ironed the dress this morning.

"Oh great spirit," chanted Molly. "In honor of the good nuns who
helped this community, we pledge to carry on their great works."

"Pardon me, Ruthie-doll," said Al. "You want to say something
in Hebrew?"

Grandmom raised her head, "Baruch atoi adonai, elu-henu mela
choilum asher vitsu vana shell neighborhood cooperative housing."

"You tell 'em Ruthie," shouted Al.

* * *

"I thought we'd have better luck than that," said Bridget as she and Grandmom trudged up Tenth Street.

Beads of sweat had broken out at Grandmom's temples. She waddled unsteadily. "Such rudeness. Imagine slamming the door in my face. That David, he did this to us."

"We're not down yet." Bridget wished she believed her own words, but she was beginning to think that maybe her mother had been right all along, maybe this was more than she could handle.

Ahead, Edna and Molly dragged their feet, still carrying a stack of flyers. Bridget smelled sausage cooking. Although, she had no appetite, it was time to get everyone back to the Center for dinner. Across the street, the basketball courts had emptied.

She saw Al pacing back and forth in front of the convent. "Look at this," he shouted.

Graffiti swirled up the convent's facade in crude, bold loops: Get the fuck out of our neighborhood.

A dozen kids stood at the corner laughing and jeering. A mix of races: white, African-American, Hispanic, Oriental, banding together just to chase them out. Bridget marveled at the irony of it all. No one cared about the benefits to the neighborhood and this was supposed to be the easy part.

"I put up with worse thugs in the sweatshops," shouted Molly at the kids. "You're all a bunch of wimps!"

"Let's get inside," said Bridget. "Para-transit's on the way."

She climbed the grooved marble steps and fumbled with the keys.

"We ain't afraid of yous," shouted a kid.

"It's you, not yous," shot back Edna. "And don't say ain't." The kid looked at her, momentarily disarmed.

Bridget swung the door open and herded everybody in. Harsh light poured into the foyer from high windows hurting her eyes. She heard a stone hit the door. She felt dizzy. David had won the first round.

Chapter 27

DAVID WALKED PAST Java High, one of his old suits tucked into a plastic bag beneath his arm. His life was falling apart. He had blown it with Bridget, been burned by Cecilia. His teaching had lost its edge and now, he had just learned that some of the members of the Divine Guidance Board were seeking his removal. When it came down to survival of the fittest, he had no choice but to go to extremes.

If his plan worked, Bridget's morale would hit rock bottom. Then he'd become her champion, even relent a bit with the neighbors near the convent. She had valuable experience and no doubt still loved him. He'd make her see that she needed him.

He turned a corner and stopped at the opening to a small alleyway. A scruffy man sat on a wooden box. The man wore ripped cotton shorts and a t-shirt. In his hand, he clutched an empty coffee cup. On his face perched a pair of dark glasses and a slightly skewed fake mustache.

The man looked up, an expectant smile on his face. "So how much?"

David smelled rotting garbage. "A hundred bucks, plus new clothes and a haircut."

"Not too shabby." The man slapped his hands on his thighs. "That'll buy a lot of coffee."

David leaned against the brick wall. He hated dealing with weirdoes like the Coffee Bandit. "Do you understand what you have to do?"

The man grinned and gave a thumbs-up sign.

David reached into his pocket and withdrew fifty dollars and a piece of paper. "Get a haircut and shave at this address. These are the directions to the Unitarian Church where you'll meet me at seven. I'll give you the rest of the money when you show up. Got it?" He noticed how the Coffee Bandit's hands shook when he helped him to his feet.

"Thanks, buddy," said the Bandit, holding his trembling hands in front of him. "Caffeine withdrawal. Ain't that a bitch? You saved my life, buddy. Thanks."

*   *   *

A subdued buzz electrified the air in the crowded sanctuary of the Unitarian Church. Men removed their jackets and tugged at knots of ties. Smartly dressed women in ice cream colors of peach and vanilla intermingled with the crowd from the Center who wore brown-striped sheets, star-spangled sheets and fancy floral sheets.

David leaned against the doorway inside an alcove talking to the Coffee Bandit. "Bridget Bernstein's over there." He pointed toward the pews. "In the reserved section with that white guy wearing a skullcap and that black woman with the braid. Third pew. See her? She's wearing the cream-colored dress. I reserved the aisle seat next to her for you. You know what to do."

David counted out five ten-dollar bills. Before handing the money to the Coffee Bandit, he brushed lint from the Bandit's shoulders. "My old suit fits you well."

"Yeah," said the Coffee Bandit. "Gotta keep up that corporate image. Now where is she again?"

*   *   *

Bridget sat beside Claire and Mark. The scent of perfume and aftershave lotion floated through the overheated air reminding her of a funeral parlor. She scanned the sanctuary and saw David standing in the back. Quickly, she turned to face the altar.

Mark leaned across Claire and touched her shoulder. "I hope you won't be angry, but Carson's coming to the lecture tonight. You should talk to him. Just a few weeks ago the guy was on top the world. Yesterday, he almost flubbed a deal."

She felt blood rush to her face as she checked the sanctuary. She wasn't in the mood to fight. If he wanted to see her, why hadn't he picked up the phone and called?

A man squeezed into the aisle seat next to her. Dressed in a black, double-breasted suit, white shirt, and a simple red and black striped tie, he seemed dazed by the heat. He patted his neatly cut hair in place.

The way he tilted his head, he looked vaguely familiar. He shifted away, his hand trembling slightly. Maybe he was shy or hurting from a broken romance. The idea attracted her, a wounded bird longing to fly again.

She smiled at the soap-opera scene she had concocted. This man had to have an enlightened side or he wouldn't have come to the lecture.

"Boon-Dan-Tan's here," whispered Claire.

He appeared on the podium wearing a dark blue robe embroidered with lotuses. A filmy, white turban covered head. His eyes focused on the audience.

Bridget saw Mark reach for Claire's hand.

Boon-Dan-Tan raised his arms.

"Welcome fellow saints." His clear voice seemed to lift him toward the ceiling, compelling Bridget to listen closely.

"Many of you feel separated from the other. Alone and disconnected. Some of us think we are better than others. And go to great lengths to prove it. Such is the absurdity of humankind that we search for gratification, artificially inflating our egos.

"Why are we willing to accept the low opinion others attach to us? Why do we feel a deep sense of failure in terms of society's demands?" He paused and surveyed the audience, a peaceful smile crossing his lips.

"We must remember that we are all contained within the great cosmic egg. And within the egg is a shared electro-magnetic mind field. When we feel that vibration, we find connection and vibrate as one."

Bridget saw Claire lean against Mark's shoulder. Her feet hurt and she slipped out of her sandals. The man next to her repeatedly crossed and uncrossed his legs.

Boon-Dan-Tan lowered his voice. "Follow me on a quest to honor ourselves, the yin and yang of our great Mother Earth." He held his arms out in front of him.

"Soul mates, spiritual ones, we shall rise and connect. Leave your bodies. Let your souls soar. Look down at those around you. Embrace them. Rise above individuality. Shock the part of you that won't let go. Take my spiritual hand." He closed his eyes and rocked on the balls of his feet.

Bridget took Claire's hand. She, Claire and Mark raised their clasped fists into the air along with the audience.

"We have left our bodies," said Boon-Dan-Tan. "We love with one spirit. We kiss with one soul. We copulate with one zest. We are love Gods and Goddesses. We shall go forth and change the world."

A moan issued forth from the audience.

"Our minds eternal. Our spirits everlasting," Boon-Dan-Tan whispered into the microphone.

"Our brains mindless. Our spirits shallow," the man next to Bridget mumbled.

"Beg your pardon?" Bridget wasn't sure if the man spoke to her. He swivelled his head, his eyes like amber granite, then slipped to his knees and grabbed her legs.

"Graceful insteps and toes eternal." He bowed his head and licked her ankles.

Bridget screamed.

Boon-Dan-Tan leaped in the air. The podium and microphone crashed from the altar onto the stone floor of the church.

People rushed toward the exit as though a crazed gunman had fired bullets. Others stayed, but kept a distance. The man clutched Bridget's foot and nibbled her toes. Bridget tried to pull her foot away. The man held tight. "Let go," she screamed.

Suddenly, Mark bent over and yanked her foot free, accidentally elbowing the man in the face. Stricken, the man looked up like a hurt child. A red blotch appeared on his cheek.

"What do you think you're doing?" Mark grabbed the man's arm.

"I was just kissing her feet." The man jerked away and dodged through the crowd.

"I'll get him," said Mark.

"Leave it alone," said Bridget. She felt her body go numb.

"What a lunatic." Claire removed a tissue from her pocketbook and wiped Bridget's foot. "Have you had a tetanus shot lately?"

"I've got to get out of here." Bridget put on her sandals and stood up. A crowd formed around her.

"Are you all right?" someone asked.

At the back of the church, she saw Carson. Her knees buckled. "Steady," said Mark.

David walked toward her, his eyes boring through her skin. "I warned Boon-Dan-Tan that something like this would happen. You create havoc wherever you go. What a way to get attention."

"Cut it, David," said Claire. "The crackpot sitting next to her attacked her."

"I don't believe that."

"You've been hounding her from the get-go," said Mark. "I think you set this whole thing up."

"Arrest her," David shouted to the group of people surrounding them. "She's stalking me."

"The hell I am," said Bridget. "You're not worth it."

Bridget caught Carson's eye. His face looked startled. She pushed her way past David. Carson turned, bounded down the steps and into the night.

*   *   *

Pencil in hand, Carson sat at his desk and tried to concentrate on the Hoover spreadsheet. The numbers floated past him like fish swimming in a tank.

What a ruckus in the church. Bridget might have been wonderful and dazzling, but she was a magnet for trouble. If he wanted to live a normal life, he had to forget about her.

He felt more anxiety now than when he had left Ball and Jacks. A cracking sound startled him. He looked down at his pencil and realized he had snapped it in half.

Maybe he should throw in the towel, go home and forget about Philadelphia. The idea repelled him. Screw everyone. He aimed the pencil pieces at the window and hurled them toward the lights of the city below. They bounced against the glass and landed on the floor.

*   *   *

SWM—34—Are you a normal person with a normal job? Do you like mundane activities like jogging and watching the late show on t.v.? Do you want to raise well-adjusted children? Me, too. Let's go for a run together on the River Drive. Box 5786.

Chapter 28

CARSON STOOD BESIDE Louise in her kitchen peeling potatoes. He had called her the day she answered his ad. They had just spent an exhilarating afternoon rollerblading along the river. Now, he watched her open the oven door, bend over, and baste a turkey. She was sweet, had a great body, and could obviously cook. He knew what she had in mind for the three hours it took to bake the turkey. Sounded good to him, although she didn't attract him the way Bridget had.

Louise closed the oven door and brushed past him. He felt the full imprint of her muscles against his back and caught his breath. He would give this a fair chance.

He picked up another potato and peeled it. From the corner of his eye he saw Louise lift two cocktail glasses from a shelf. He liked watching her move. Her butt was perfectly firm and rounded. He squeezed the potato and dropped it into a bowl of ice water.

She turned, holding the glasses in her hands. "We could make this a regular Saturday date."

"Let's drink to that."

"Sure," she said. "I don't have hard liquor. But there's a bottle of Campari on a shelf in my bookcase. Why don't you go into the living room and get it. There's a lemon in the fridge. I'll cut some wedges for an extra dose of vitamin C."

"No wonder you're in such great shape," said Carson.

"Same to you," she said.

He walked down a narrow hall. Her apartment was spare and sleek. The living room contained a chocolate brown love seat, a chrome chair, and a glass-shelved bookcase.

At the bookshelf he reached for the Campari. He wondered if Bridget was at the convent today. Last week he'd noticed a crew scrubbing some nasty graffiti from the building. He hoped she didn't stay there by herself.

By the time he reached the kitchen, Louise had filled the glasses with ice and a wedge of lemon. A bottle of club soda waited on the counter.

"You're the nicest guy I've met in a long time," she said.

Carson opened the bottle and poured a bit of ruby liquid into each glass. He filled the glasses with club soda and handed her a drink. Her face was soft and pretty. Freckles dotted her nose. Her pale brown hair was pulled back in a ponytail. He sipped his drink.

She smiled and took the drink from his hand. Her long eyelashes fluttered against his cheek when he kissed her.

"You're easy to be with," he said.

"And so are you." She pressed her mouth against his lips, running her hands over his hips. He reached for the clasp that held her hair in a ponytail. With a flick of his finger, he released the clasp. Hair cascaded over her shoulders.

In the hall, she untied the string at the waist of his gym shorts. He remembered Bridget's fingers grazing his skin, her fine white teeth nibbling his ear. This didn't feel right.

"Carson," whispered Louise. "I'm losing you."

"Uh, I'm sorry." He dropped his arms and leaned against the wall. "I guess rollerblading wore me out."

She stroked his cheek. "Maybe you need a little nap. I could use a shower myself."

"I'll be all right," he said. "I think I'll sit down for awhile. Why don't you take your shower, and I'll wait in the living room."

"You sure?"

"Yes. Go ahead."

He waited in the kitchen until he heard water running. Quickly, he lifted the telephone receiver and dialed Mark's number.

Mark picked up before Carson heard the phone ring. "Yo," he said.

"I'm glad you're home," whispered Carson. "Can you help me out? I'm in a jam with a date, and I want you to call me in fifteen minutes to tell me we have a work emergency."

"You mean she's not so nice?"

"No, she's wonderful. She's in the shower right now waiting for me, and there's a turkey roasting in the oven."

"And you want to leave? Are you crazy?"

"Don't ask questions. Just get me out of here."

"No problem. I'll do it. Do you think you could grab me a drumstick, I'm not quite used to all the vegetarian food Claire's been feeding me."

"Shit Mark. This isn't the time to make jokes."

"I'm serious, boss."

Carson heard the water shut off and gave Mark the number. "Did you get it?"

"Yeah, I got it. Don't forget the drumstick."

Chapter 29

BRIDGET POKED HER HEAD into the lounge. "Excuse me, Mark."

"Yo, Bria-Barunga."

Mark kneeled on a cushion reading the Divine Guidance Center newsletter. His silk turban glowed in the lamplight like an aqua jewel.

She entered the room. "What did you find out about the foot-kisser?"

Mark folded the journal and set it on his lap. "Richard Lipinski, one of the board members, was at the church the night the foot-kisser assaulted you. He thinks he recognized him as the Coffee Bandit."

She leaned against the wall and snapped her finger. "The guy looked familiar, but I've never seen the Bandit without a disguise."

"Yesterday I went to see him myself. He turned tail and ran. Just before he got to the door he shouted that you had the most beautiful corn on your toe."

"I don't have any corns," laughed Bridget.

Mark pressed his right thumb and forefinger together and held up his hand in a meditative gesture. "You should talk to Richard. He's a tax attorney by day, but runs the soup kitchen at Project Dignity at night. Seems the Coffee Bandit shows up there most nights. Richard said that all he has to do is give the Bandit extra coffee and he'll fess up."

"What does Richard have to do with David?"

"He saw David talking to the foot-kisser in the back of the church. He's had a couple of run-ins with David himself and doesn't trust him. Besides, he hates the way David's tried to squelch your project."

Anger rose up inside Bridget's belly.

Mark shifted on his cushion. "If Richard finds proof that David was involved, Boon-Dan-Tan will remove David from the board."

Bridget rubbed her temples. "We're supposed to help each other. How did this turn into a hostile corporate takeover?"

Mark stood up. "When it comes to weak egos, you have to watch your back." He shrugged. "Just call Richard. He's waiting to hear from you."

*   *   *

Richard lived near the Center in a Tudor style house on a tree-lined street. Bridget lifted the lion's head knocker. A deep echo resounded when she struck it against the door.

She heard footsteps, then the door swung open. "Come in. Come in." Richard swept his arm toward the hall. Black hair swooped over his forehead in a shiny wave. Dark brown eyes peered at her from behind horn-rimmed frames. He wore an immaculate blue and white-striped shirt, tucked into neatly pressed khakis.

A stuffed hyena stood in the corner staring at her with beady, glass eyes. Startled, she stepped over a fox and shook Richard's hand. "You have quite a place." Her voice cracked.

"Thanks." Richard warmly grasped her fingers. "The house was built in the twenties and belonged to my grandparents. I've lived here all my life. Mother willed it to me when she passed on." He bowed his head. "May she rest in peace."

He led Bridget into the living room. Thick beams held up a white plaster ceiling. Two wrought-iron chandeliers dangled from elaborate cords. The antique furniture was covered in dark, red brocade. A stuffed armadillo filled an alcove near a massive, stone fireplace. She shuddered.

Curled in a ball on the sofa lay a white cat. Was it real or stuffed? Cautiously, she leaned closer looking for movement. Relieved, she saw its abdomen rise and fall.

Richard knelt before the fireplace grate and tried to light it. "I know it's summer," he said. "But I thought it would be fun to make a fire."

She cleared her throat. "Do you live here all alone?"

"Yup." He struck a match. "I'll never move. I feel my mother's presence every day." He looked wistfully at a stuffed ocelot sitting by the fireplace tools."

"You certainly have an interesting collection of animals." She nearly choked. She hated the idea of killing animals for sport and then stuffing them.

Richard blew at the flames. "Thank you. They're examples of my work."

"Your hobby?"

"No, my job."

"But, Mark told me you were a tax attorney."

Richard slapped his thigh and laughed. "Tax attorney? Mark sure got that wrong. I'm a taxidermist." He lifted his head proudly. "I've done work on all the continents except Antarctica. Next month, I'm off to Nairobi for a conference on better techniques in preserving big game, especially endangered species."

Bridget sank into a claw-foot chair, confused. How could a person who did so much good for the homeless involve himself with animal killers?

Richard got up, sat next to the cat and rubbed its belly. "You have a weird look on your face. You don't think I had a hand in killing these animals?" He smiled. "Don't worry. I consult with environmental agencies working to stop poachers. When we find slaughtered animals, we preserve them to show the public how magnificent they are. Our goal is to stop wanton killing."

"I never thought of taxidermy in that light."

"The world's full of surprises. That's what keeps it interesting." He clapped his hands. "Now down to the unpleasant business of dealing with our friend David and the Coffee Bandit. After an extra slice of cherry pie and three cups of coffee I got the Bandit to confess. David paid him a hundred dollars and cleaned him up just to disrupt Boon-Dan-Tan's lecture and blame it on you."

The cat climbed into Richard's lap. He gently stroked its back, lost for a moment in reflection. Slowly he raised his head. "Sad commentary on the human race when a person takes advantage of the mentally ill to do his dirty work."

She twisted a lock of hair and sighed.

"Don't worry. I already talked to Boon-Dan-Tan. He's taking

David off the board, but not before he spends some time alone with him."

"That should be interesting."

"I've got an idea. Let's cheer ourselves up with some dinner. I baked a great squirrel meat lasagna."

Bridget jumped out of her chair.

"Just kidding," he chuckled.

*   *   *

In the Divine Guidance Center's kitchen, Bridget stepped on a footstool and reached into the cupboard for a bag of flour. From her perch, she surveyed the kitchen. Large copper pots hung from a metal rack above the stove. At a steel table near the sink, Mark spooned mashed potatoes over a sheet of dough.

"Pay attention," barked Grandmom. "The secret of a good knish is a light hand!"

Claire took eggs from the industrial-sized refrigerator, looked up and winked at Bridget. Mark and Grandmom had been bantering about recipes all afternoon, Mark bragging about his mother's baked beans with ketchup, and Grandmom about her secret ingredients for borscht.

"What are you looking at?" Grandmom waved a wooden spoon at Bridget and Claire. "Mark's a good boy. He'll learn how to cook right. You young women don't take the time to learn because you're always too busy."

All that had changed since Bridget moved into the Center. Everyone was required to perform kitchen duty. She enjoyed chopping vegetables, slicing potatoes, paring apples, scouring the large copper pots until they gleamed. From a wooden shelf, she removed a stainless steel bowl. In the bowl's curved reflection, she saw Boon-Dan-Tan enter the kitchen carrying his harmonium.

"Namaste," he said and bowed before seating himself on a prayer rug on the green-tiled floor. After a brief meditation, he struck the harmonium's keyboard. Soothing sounds filled the air.

Bridget hummed along. Boon-Dan-Tan's presence filled every corner of the room. Calm settled over her as she prepared her dessert ingredients for the ritual blessing. She loved this time of day. It reminded her of helping Grandmom in her old kitchen, mixing dough in a big yellow milk-glass bowl, cranking hand-held beaters while listening to Yiddish folk tunes on the old record player. Later, when Bridget's mother and father came to pick her up and have dinner, she'd fall asleep in her father's lap during reruns of the Dick Van Dyke Show.

The music stopped. Boon-Dan-Tan spoke, directing his gaze at Bridget. "Happiness eludes the man who tries to destroy others. He will always roll into his own gravel pit."

Bridget smiled at Boon-Dan-Tan's funny metaphor. She wondered if he'd spoken to David yet, but it didn't really matter. This was her cue to begin the evening prayer. She gathered cloves, cardamom and lemon.

Boon-Dan-Tan rose and walked to the butcher block in the center of the kitchen. While the group gathered around him, Bridget arranged the ingredients on the wooden surface.

Boon-Dan-Tan lifted his arms. "We are here today to bless the cookies our sister Bria-Barunga is baking for tonight's dinner. Each ingredient bears special significance: flour, the earth's staple; eggs, the regeneration of life; butter, the gift of the sacred cow."

Bridget heard Grandmom grunt.

Boon-Dan-Tan continued as if in a trance. "Cloves to stimulate our first chakra, our seat which must always remain firmly rooted to the earth; cardamom to open our senses to the spiritual realm; lemons to remind us that a touch of sour ultimately leads to sweetness; tofu, one of the earth's best proteins."

"Tofu in cookies?" shouted Grandmom. "Feh. We already have it in the knishes."

"Excuse me, Ruth," said Edward, hiking his apron up over his cut-off shorts. "But, I think it's a great idea. The people who come to our kitchen need all the nourishment they can get."

"Oy vey." Grandmom glared at Bridget. "And your mother's coming for dinner tonight. What will she think?"

"She won't know if you don't tell her," said Claire.

Three bells signaled the end of evening prayers. Boon-Dan-Tan bowed and left the kitchen. Everyone returned to their tasks.

Bridget dumped butter into the bowl and tried to smile at

Claire. "Guess what the Coffee Bandit told Mark?"

"Can't wait to hear this one."

"He has a fetish for my corns. Too bad Carson's not even interested in my hangnails."

Claire cracked an egg over the bowl. "Don't bet on it."

"You know what really makes me mad?" Bridget added a cup of turbinado sugar and a teaspoon of vanilla to the eggs. "I saw a personal ad last week and I'm sure Carson wrote it. He advertised for a 'normal' woman as though I'm deranged or something. He didn't have the decency to choose a new box number."

"I know it hurts," said Claire. "But it's better that he gets on with the life he understands. Otherwise you'd have even bigger problems down the line."

Bridget glanced at Mark and Grandmom. Mark watched intently as Grandmom pressed a floured rolling pin into dough. At the eight-burner stove, Edna busily stirred vegetable soup in a large cast-iron soup kettle while Molly folded the napkins she'd made out of the last of the camouflage material. A group of teenagers laughed uproariously at a joke as they cut celery and carrots. Thank goodness for the warmth of community. It kept her from falling into despair.

She sliced a chunk of tofu, beat it into the butter, then added flour, baking powder, salt, cinnamon, cardamom, clove and lemon peel.

After she had mixed the dough, Claire stuck her finger in the bowl and tasted it. "Far out. The people who eat at the soup kitchen are sure lucky."

Bridget smiled. "I had a great teacher. Baking with Grandmom was like working with a precision drill team. Even the chocolate chips stayed in place." She rolled balls of dough, dipped them in sugar, set them on a cookie sheet and flattened them with the bottom of a glass.

When the baking sheet was full, she crossed the kitchen, past Mark who expertly cut rows of knishes apart with the side of his hand. She slid the cookies into the oven. The fragrance of baking dough reminded her of spending afternoons in Grandmom's apartment after her father died. She had drunk milk from a jelly glass and munched on perfectly round homemade, cinnamon cookies. Later her mother would rush home from the factory with a pizza and a bag of ugly chocolate chip cookies.

She opened the oven, smelled the aroma of half-baked cookies. Across the room, Molly and Grandmom slid knishes onto a platter. She pulled out the tray, lifted her finger, held it in the air. She thought of her mother all those years ago in Gordon's bakery smashing that first batch of cookies with her bare hands. Bridget touched the top of the cookie. It was burning hot. Her mother must have been half out of her mind to smash them. Yet, out of despair had come success.

She lifted the spoon, mashed it into a cookie, mangling the half-baked dough, then mashed another, down the line of neatly arranged mounds.

"Hey Bridget," called Edward. "Are you smashing cookies?"

Grandmom rushed over to the stove. "Stop this nonsense. You don't bake ugly."

"I can't stop," laughed Bridget. "It's karma."

"Or genetics," Claire broke out into peals of laughter. "Ugly tofu cookies?"

"I didn't raise you to be like your mother," said Grandmom.

Bridget slid the cookies back into the oven. She couldn't believe what she had done. She'd spent so many years distancing herself from her mother. Now the lines had blurred.

When the cookies finished baking, she pulled them from the oven, waited for them to cool slightly and slid them onto a plate.

"Grandmom," she said. "Try one."

Grandmom's face grew serious. Deep wrinkles appeared on her forehead as she furrowed her brow, blew on the cookie and bit into it. As she chewed, the frown lines relaxed. "Not bad." A hint of a smile tugged at the corner of her lips. "By the way," she whispered. "Your mother's cookies aren't bad either."

* * *

At five-thirty, Bridget and Claire stood behind the steam table in the soup kitchen dining room. Doors would open in fifteen minutes. Claire spooned humus into a bowl. "Gotta hand it to you,

Bridgie. Your tofu cookies are a hit. Who knows. Maybe you should open your own cookie factory."

"And compete with Mom?" laughed Bridget. "No way." She heard familiar voices in the hall, saw the doors swing open.

Her mother strode across the room followed by Gordon. "Here they are. The revolutionaries." Her mother beamed and held out her hand. A large, square-cut diamond glittered on her ring finger. "Come, give your mother and her new fiancé a hug."

"Fiancé? Since when?" Bridget hurried around the table and rushed toward them. She never thought her mother would give up an ounce of independence to marry Gordon.

Gordon embraced her in a bear hug. "Ah Bridget. Always your mother pooh-poohed my proposals. Finally she comes to the warehouse and says, 'Where's the ring?' So I go up to my office and open the safe where it's been sitting for three years and I say, 'Sarah, I want to look after you.' And she says, 'Okay.' Just like that. Believe it or not your mother likes it when I take care of her."

Bridget blinked back tears. She was happy for her mother and Gordon, but surprised at herself for feeling envious. She pushed the emotion aside.

"Let's not get all excited before dinner," said her mother, brushing at her own eyes.

"Bridget's got something new, too." Claire held up a large metal tray.

Her mother peered at the tray and clasped her hands to her chest. "You made ugly cookies?"

Bridget nodded.

"Here, try one," said Claire.

Tentatively, her mother picked up a cookie and studied it carefully. "They're even uglier than mine." She bit into it and handed half to Gordon.

"These are fantastic," said Gordon. "I taste a hint of lemon. You should use some Meyer lemon rind for real depth. I can get them for you wholesale."

"See, Gordon," beamed Sarah. "She's her mother's daughter, after all."

Gordon smiled. "I'm getting two strong-willed women for the

price of one. Bridget, in celebration of my engagement to your beautiful mother, I'm donating a new van to your endeavor at the convent. I'd also like to offer my service on your board. I've got a lot of experience and I want to share it."

Bridget tried to find her breath, but could only mouth the words, "Thank you." She touched Gordon's shoulder, noticing how her work-roughened hands were beginning to resemble her mother's.

"Where's that grandmom of yours?" said her mother.

Bridget pointed to the kitchen.

"Ma!" Her mother burst through the doors into the kitchen.

"Bridget, honey. Get on it," Claire smiled broadly. "We've got about a minute till they open the doors."

They watched two students help Molly set dishes and flatware on the far end of the table.

Mark brought out the mashed potatoes. "Here come the troops." He pecked Claire on the cheek.

A line began to form filled with scruffy-looking men and women. Hair matted, faces lined and weathered, they wore layers of ragged clothes that hung from their bodies. Some carried packages wrapped in smudged newspaper. A few held the hands of children.

Bridget's heart went out to them as she set a casserole on the steam tray and picked up a serving spoon. A tall man wearing a tattered baseball cap stepped out of line and came toward her, plate in hand.

"You'll have to get back in line, sir," said Claire.

The man shuffled closer to the table.

"You know the rules," said Bridget. "Please follow them." She stared at him. Greasy hair stuck out beneath the cap. She recognized the narrow shape of his jaw. The Coffee Bandit.

"I won't hurt you," he said. "Please don't be afraid."

He dropped to floor and crawled beneath the table. "I love your feet. I love your feet. Marry me and have babies with beautiful feet."

Bridget backed away. "Take it easy, fella."

"Mark," shouted Claire. "Come quick."

Chapter 30

IT WAS A CRYSTAL BLUE, open-sky day. The air smelled clean, free of the car exhaust and bus fumes Carson had grown used to in the city. He hiked up the fabric of his pants, sat down on the step and leaned against the white pillar on the porch of his mother's house. A perfect expanse of green lawn rolled toward the street. Across the way, large custom-built houses stood in an elegant line protected by tall hedges.

The scene would bore him in a few days, but for now the predictable uniformity of his old neighborhood felt soothing. There were no second-guesses here. Not long ago, he and Anne were headed for just this kind of lifestyle. Now, he didn't know what he wanted.

"Carson," called his mother.

He rose, opened the screen door and walked into the house. His mother sat in the living room in her favorite blue and white silk-striped chair. The French doors were drawn open to the garden. Geraniums and zinnias bloomed in a tapestry of color. A warm breeze floated into the room billowing the curtains.

A pitcher of lemonade, two empty glasses, and a plate of cheese and crackers rested on the carved mahogany cocktail table beside her. Although she wore a white polo shirt and an orange golf skirt, her bearing was elegant, as though she awaited a formal gathering.

"Sit down and talk with me for a while." She lifted the pitcher and poured.

He sat in his father's old wingback chair and set his feet on the hassock. "Should I be nervous about the meeting this afternoon?"

A worried expression crossed his mother's face. "It's not a financial meeting, but it's complicated and I need to discuss it with all of you at the same time."

276

"That's reassuring."

She sighed. "Sometimes your dad did strange things."

"Can't we let him rest in peace? Dad did the best he could for the family." Carson heard the annoyance in his own voice.

She paused. "I'm not condemning him, but he had flaws like the rest of us. I didn't stand up to him the way I should have. Back when I was young, lots of women devoted themselves to their husbands and their careers. I harbored a lot of resentment. There was always one more meeting, one more dinner, one more round of drinks he had to buy for the guys."

What had gotten into her? She seemed driven to the topic. "I don't know what you're talking about. I had a great childhood."

"I'm glad you feel that way." Her voice held a tentative note.

He folded his arms across his chest. It was that damned letter that had set up this conflict between them.

His mother stirred the lemonade in the pitcher. "Our family tends to sweep things under the carpet. I guarded your father's image at a huge cost and I was wrong. That was my message to you in the letter."

Carson imagined Bridget sitting beside his mother, nodding in agreement. Had Bridget seen a more realistic picture of his family than he ever had?

Suddenly, a memory surfaced. He tried to quash it, but it grew stronger. He was twelve years old, the last game of Little League Season. He stood on home plate, bat in hand, the sun blinding his eyes. Bases loaded.

The pitch came in fast and hard. He swung and connected with a perfect hit. The ball whizzed into the outfield, soaring over the back fence. The crowd roared as he ran the bases and slid. He had hit his first and only home run.

Rising from home plate, he brushed dirt from his pants. His thighs ached. He scanned the stands, hoping his Dad's meeting had ended early and this time would be different. Everywhere he looked he saw other kids' dads. Finally, his eyes lit on his mother. She wore the team colors and waved a banner. He remembered scowling at her before turning to walk off the field.

He hated that memory. Until now, he had managed to block it

out. He thrust himself out of the chair and strode to the picture window. Across the street a workman lifted long shears and pruned dead twigs from a maple tree.

His mother joined him. "I'm sorry I upset you."

Carson shrugged. "Forget it. What time are we due at the store?"

"One, but let's get there early. I want to show you the new lay-out. I think you'll be pleased."

*   *   *

Carson and his mother walked through aisles of shelves laden with the latest computers, video equipment and electronic gadg-ets. Rock music blared from overhead speakers. Neon lights flashed different manufacturer's names from four corners of the store.

On a huge TV screen dominating the center of the store, a life-size image of his brother materialized. "Ball and Jacks guarantees the lowest prices for all the best brands," blared his brother's voice. Carson stopped and watched Jack demonstrate the use of various pieces of equipment with the help of a bikini-clad model. "I bet Sally's isn't thrilled with his assistant."

"That's the least of it. Sally's not a happy camper these days." His mother checked her watch, then smoothed a non-existent wrinkle from the skirt of her beige, Chanel suit. "Come on. They're waiting for us." She tugged Carson's sleeve.

He followed her into the conference room, threading his way past empty tables to the back where a table was set for lunch. As soon as he saw Jack engrossed in conversation with Lisa and Sally, he felt his tension ease. The hell with the fights. They were all together again.

His mother tightened her grip on his arm.

Startled, he saw that Jack and Lisa were dressed in gray power suits. They resembled each other physically, like an old married couple, and their tastes in clothing had grown similar. Were they finally getting along?

Jack jumped up and shook Carson's hand. Lisa held him in a tight embrace. Sally remained seated, her hands folded together.

Carson guided his mother to a chair, then kissed Sally's cheek. Her skin felt stiff and cold. He couldn't blame her for shutting herself off. She hated surprises. In this family, she got them often.

He didn't expect her to speak first, but she did. "I'm glad you're finally letting us in on the secret," she said. "I told Jack if we don't get this thing resolved, I'm packing my bags and taking the kids."

His mother's shoulders sagged. "I don't to want upset you anymore, Sally. Things should get better after today."

Carson leaned toward his mother. Her face was pale, but composed.

Sally's knuckles had gone white. "Then please get on with it."

His mother looked at each of her children. "You all know that your sister was adopted." Her eyes searched Lisa's face for assurance.

Lisa nodded.

"But your father and I held something back. When I told Lisa last month, we agreed you should know the truth, too. Lisa's your biological half-sister."

"How can that be?" Carson kicked the table leg.

"Your dad is Lisa's real father."

"Dad never cheated on you," said Carson.

"Of course he didn't."

Lisa shifted in her chair. Her blue eyes, duplicates of both Jack's and Carson's, scanned the table without blinking. It seemed to Carson that she was afraid if she blinked and lost sight of the scene, it would all disappear.

"I won't deny that I'm in shock too," Lisa said. "Recently, Mother explained everything to me."

"Does that mean Lisa gets one share of the estate for being adopted, and one for being biologically connected?" said Jack.

"Knock it off," said Carson.

"If you're going to change how you divide up the estate, give Carson's share to Lisa." Jack laughed nervously.

"Typical," said Sally. "You're acting just like a three year old."

Lisa turned to Catherine. "If it's all right with you, I'll tell how it happened."

Catherine gripped Lisa's hand and nodded.

"Growing up in California," said Lisa. "I never doubted that the man who raised me was my natural father. Everything was fine until he died when I was twelve. Then my mom got sick. After she died, I learned she'd already arranged for a family to take care of me."

Carson saw his mother let go of Lisa's hand and bunch a piece of the tablecloth in her clenched fists. Silverware, set neatly for lunch, rattled as it jumbled together. His stomach twisted. In his bones, he knew the story was true. They were traveling another of his father's bizarre paths. He looked at Lisa. "Are you one hundred percent sure that Dad's your real father?

"Let her talk, honey," said Catherine.

Jack cleared his throat. "I've watched you for years, Lisa. It drove me nearly nuts how your gestures, everything reminded me of Dad, reminded me of Carson. I always thought you were imitating Dad so you could fit in. But I still don't get this whole thing."

"Would you tell them the rest, Mother?" said Lisa.

Catherine's hands relaxed. "Before your father and I married, he went to California to become a photographer. He had a certain flair, but it wasn't enough. In no time he was broke, living on the streets. In a last ditch effort to get home, he sold his sperm to a sperm bank. He told me all about it on our wedding night. We never talked of it again until I got the phone call from Lisa's mother."

Lisa's lip trembled. She lowered her head. Carson put his arm on her shoulder.

"Before Lisa's mother died, she located your father's name at the sperm bank. They called us with her number. Your father and I fought for days before I finally convinced him that he had to talk with Lisa's mother. She asked if we would take Lisa and raise her as our own. Your father worried that things wouldn't turn out so he swore me to secrecy. Once Lisa came to us, he grew to love her as much as he loved you boys. By then, he insisted we forget about it so no one would be hurt. I always planned to tell you, but time just slipped away. I hope you'll forgive me."

Carson scanned Jack and Sally's shocked faces, watched Jack's face relax before regaining its familiar determination.

"I'd like to officially welcome you to the family, sis," said Jack. "You've not only picked up Carson's job, you've shown a real knack for marketing, just like Dad."

Carson leaned back in his chair, almost tipping it over. "So what are you saying, Jack?"

"I'm saying I'm glad you have your job in Philadelphia. You're happy there. I saw it in your face when we met at the airport. I came back and told Lisa we didn't have a choice, you were there to stay and it was up to us to make it work."

"You know how much I admire you for taking a risk, Carson," said Lisa.

She leaned over and hugged him, her hair brushing against his neck. He remembered how she had always laughed at his jokes, how she fell off her bed in a fit of giggles when he told her about Dad taking him to film funerals. "You'll do a great job for Ball and Jacks," he whispered.

*   *   *

Carson held his mother's arm as they crossed the parking lot.

"I know this was a terrible shock," said Catherine. Her voice trembled slightly.

"It was a shock all right." Carson squinted into bright sunlight, searching for the car. He wondered if she understood how much this whole thing upset him. What had been the point of leaving everything behind? He'd only created another mess in Philadelphia. Ahead, the ball and jack revolved round and round its pole in an endless loop.

They reached his mother's old green Mercedes.

"Don't be too angry at your father. He was a bullheaded man." She settled herself into the car. "I loved him more than my own life. We worked hard to keep it all together, but it was a loose seam we wove."

Carson gunned the motor and turned the air conditioner on full blast. Hot air hit his face. "If Dad had told us about Lisa right away, there would have been more peace between us. Maybe I'd have stayed."

"You don't know how long I've blamed myself for keeping this from you."

They drove in silence. Carson turned down the air conditioner. Outside the car window, strip malls gave way to cornfields.

"Understand," said Catherine. "Your father was a troubled man. His own father sent him to work when he was ten and then criticized him constantly. I'm trying to fit all the pieces together."

Carson wondered if he was turning out like his father, the kind of man who needed to control other people and their lives.

His mother leaned against the headrest and closed her eyes.

He longed to be a child again, sitting on the edge of her bed. "Tell me a story," he would say.

And she would smile indulgently. "Did I tell you the one about how I met your father?"

He turned down their street. It would be different now. She'd begin like this, "Jack and Jill went up the hill to deposit sperm in the sperm bank . . ."

Chapter 31

THE FISH DEPARTMENT of the Forever Fresh Supermarket was unusually quiet. Most of the locals were at the final Saturday afternoon concert of The Waterfront Summer Series.

"I'll take a small piece of salmon," said Bridget.

"I thought you were all vegetarians at the Center," said Connie. She reached into the case, brushed the ice aside, and picked out a fleshy piece of fish.

"My grandmom's sick of tofu."

"Are you going to stick with a vegetarian diet when you move into the convent?"

"No. The older folks find it hard to give up their eating habits. And I like fish too much." She realized she was talking like she had already moved in. "Truth is, I'm having second thoughts. The neighbors staged a protest at the first Zoning Board hearing."

Glassy fish eyes stared at her from their bed of ice. She cringed. "The protests have completely unnerved me. I've got people relying on me and now everything's in jeopardy."

Connie took a sharp knife and sliced a thick piece of salmon. "Don't give up. It's hard to do the right thing when people don't listen." She lay the salmon on a piece of waxed paper. "But I think you'll make it kiddo."

Bridget thought of David. Boon-Dan-Tan had kicked him off the Board, but he'd only gotten worse. She'd heard reports that he was in the neighborhood almost daily.

"I want to ask you something," said Connie. She folded the wax paper over the fish. "I'm sure you'll get the zoning. And when it happens, do you think you'd have room for a single mom with three kids?" Connie taped the packet of fish closed. "I love your idea. When Bob left, shoot, I didn't even have a minute to cry over him. Your set-up sure sounds good to me."

"We'd love to have you if we ever get going. Some of the older folks will be certified in child care."

"Great." Connie smiled and handed Bridget her package. "My kids could use some grandparents. I'm all they have. Hey, how's that handsome boyfriend of yours?"

"We broke up." She hoped her tone of voice sounded nonchalant. "He couldn't take my new lifestyle."

"Too bad, said Connie. "But, the kind of life you're leading sure ain't for sissies."

"Maybe I expected too much from him." Bridget checked her watch. "It's late, I've got to back to the Center."

"Let me know if you need any help."

"Will do." She pushed her cart down the cookie aisle. Up ahead, she saw her mother's familiar face beaming from beneath its bonnet on a cardboard display. She had to admit that her mother was remarkable, a woman who took control of her life despite all odds.

Suddenly, David rounded the corner. She turned her cart and headed back to the fish department.

"Wait."

"I don't want any more trouble," she called over her shoulder.

He pushed past her and blocked the cart. "I saw you leave the Center."

Her hands tightened on the handle. "So you follow me and then accuse me of stalking? I'm calling the Manager."

"Please. I want to talk to you."

"After all you've done?" She thrust the cart at him.

He jumped back.

She edged toward him as he backed down the aisle. This time she'd run him over.

He braked the cart with both hands. "Calm down. I just want to tell you a few things. First, I've lifted the restraining order, effective Monday and I'm leaving the neighbors alone."

She had imagined this moment for months. Now, instead of elation, she felt empty. "What you've done at the convent is worse than slapping me with a restraining order."

"I've been meeting with Boon-Dan-Tan. I admit it, I've been ill, but I want to get better. He's agreed to help me. I want to start on my new path by dedicating my book to you."

"I'd prefer that you didn't." He seemed so harmless now, but she knew better. "What's really going on with you?"

"Listen Bridget. Everything I did was selfish. I was wrong. Jealousy got the best of me. All I want is a second chance to start over."

"After what you've done?"

He stepped closer. "I can't pass by Rittenhouse Square without thinking about you."

She tried to push past him. "Then find a new route."

He blocked her way, his face pained. "Let's go someplace and talk."

"No."

"Think about it. I've already made some big changes. Let's talk again about having children. You'll make a great mother."

Laughter rose from deep within her. She doubled over the cart. The scene was beyond surrealistic.

"Go ahead. Make fun of me. But, I know you still love me. You can't predict what the future might bring."

"It won't include you." She wheeled her cart in the opposite direction past the smiling face of her mother. She wanted to call Carson. Then again what did it matter? Carson needed the kind of woman he had described in his last ad. And it certainly wasn't her.

Chapter 32

"FORTY SEVEN," WHEEZED Carson. "Forty-eight, forty-nine." Sweat poured down his face. His muscles and lungs burned. He sucked in air. "Fifty."

Dropping to his knees, he clanked the barbell to the floor of the corporate gym and pressed a hand against his aching diaphragm. He still had a hundred strokes ahead of him on the rowing machine.

Unable to concentrate, he'd taken a long lunch hour and tried to lose himself in exercise. He had wanted to call Bridget at least five times a day since he got back, but there was nothing left to say. If she had any compassion at all, she would have called him. What was the point of spirituality if she couldn't sense that he needed her?

He watched two women in matching fuschia leotards talking with each other as they pedaled their stationary bikes. In the corner, the head of the International Unit, his face contorted in pain, ran on the treadmill, his potbelly bouncing along in rhythm.

"Yo, McAlister!"

Carson turned to see Mark bound into the gym. He looked better than ever, full of vitality even though he'd had his head shaved. Today, he wore a yellow tie embossed with black and white interlocking yin-yang symbols, two fish chasing each other's tails. A pointed contrast to the dingy rep ties he used to wear.

"Hey boss. You look awful. Trying to give yourself a heart attack?"

"Look who's talking. With that tie and shaved head, you're pushing the corporate envelope."

"At least I'm not killing myself."

"I'm trying to get back in shape."

"You're already in shape. You haven't been yourself since you came back from your vacation." Mark tapped his Birkenstock sandal against Carson's white sneaker. "You've got to get with it boss, 'cause I got something heavy to tell you."

Carson glanced at the man puffing away on the treadmill. "You're leaving, aren't you?"

Mark dropped to the floor next to him. "Yup. Sorry about that."

"You've been working your butt off and just when you start climbing the ladder, you quit."

"Timing's right for me. Bridget just got the zoning for the convent." He pointed a finger at Carson's chest. "She also got a loan. Don't worry, she told everyone that you were a big help to her."

Carson looked up. "Aren't I the hero."

"What are you talking about? That woman cares about you."

Carson slammed his fist into the mat. "Like hell she does."

"Let go of your anger, boss. Group housing is her destiny. Your spirits collided for a brief, shining moment so you could inspire each other. You'll always have that."

"Cut the cosmic crap, please. If she wasn't so stubborn, we could have worked it out." He stared at the mat. "I guess I'm stubborn, too."

"That's too bad, boss. You gotta get more love in your heart. This inner soul stuff is liberating. As soon as the convent's ready, I'm moving in, too."

"Are you going to give me the usual two weeks notice?"

"At least a month boss, until Bridget gets back."

Carson gripped the rowing machine, his muscles frozen. "Back from where?"

"She's going to Israel. Boon-Dan-Tan's sending her to a kibbutz for training. Now don't get mad. I'm sure she was planning to call you."

Carson glared at Mark. He imagined Bridget meeting some tofu-loving idiot assigned to kitchen duty with her. She'd invite him back to the states. They'd set up their futon in the convent and make love beneath her grandmom's afghan, oblivious to the commotion around them. His gut clenched. "Listen Mark, I don't care about convents or kibbutzes. As long as you're here, we're focussing on work. Meet me in my office in fifteen minutes."

He repositioned himself on the rowing machine and set the resistance level to its highest notch. Grabbing the bar, he pulled back, pushed forward, pulled again. His muscles burned. Let Bridget go ahead with her dream. And she could take Mark with her.

* * *

The three aspirins Carson swallowed when he got home from work hadn't loosened the hold of a nasty headache.

He needed to talk to someone about his family. In spite of his resolve to forget her, Bridget's name kept popping into his head. He knew the reason why. She'd understand how cut off he felt from everyone. He reached for the phone, then snatched back his hand as if the receiver was made of hot metal. She'd already forgotten him with her big travel plans. Holding a cold wash cloth to his forehead, he went into the living room and stretched out on the sofa.

He closed his eyes and fought the pain throbbing at his temples. Thoughts crowded his mind like branches littering a path in a forest. Lisa had called him earlier. Although she was putting up a good front for the rest of the family, she had admitted to him that she was angry with their father, too. By not giving her a rightful heritage, he had allowed their brother and others to treat her like an outsider.

Numbness overtook him as he drifted off to sleep. He was sitting in the mahogany pew of a church holding an invitation from his mother. The church looked familiar. He recognized the elaborate stained glass window casting blue and red patterns on the floor. Mr. Denning's funeral had taken place here. Below the vaulted ceiling, in a balcony, a choir sang God Bless America to the strains of a pipe organ.

As his eyes adjusted to the dim light, he realized that the pews were filled with people. Next to him, sat his mother. His brother sat behind him, squeezed between Sally and Lisa. Lisa looked glum; Sally, sullen. At the pulpit, stood the minister dressed in a black suit and white collar. Suddenly, Carson recognized him. Dad?

His father looked robust and healthy, not bloated. His face had lost the red splotches that appeared on his cheeks when he drank too much.

His father raised his hands and the room went quiet.

"Thank you my fellow congregants."

"We're not your congregants!" Carson turned toward the voice. An apron-clad woman wearing a bonnet stood up.

Sarah Bernstein. She looked just like the woman on the Ugly Cookie package. Next to Sarah sat a man dressed in a white suit, black shirt and striped tie. His eyes looked cunning as if he had just placed a bet and planned to win. It had to be Mr. Bernstein.

"Congregants," the minister began again. "I have a sermon for you."

"You can't preach," said Carson. "You're not a real minister."

His mother stood up. "You look good, Jack. What have you been doing with yourself?"

"Well, Catherine, I finally realized what you were trying to tell me. Since I didn't change my way of living, I've changed my way of being dead. I wish I had done it earlier. We even have social workers and therapists in heaven to help those of us with unresolved earthly issues."

"Dad," called Jack. "Look at what happened to me. I'm following in your footsteps and Sally's furious."

Reverend McAlister stepped forward. "I don't know what to say to you except that I was wrong. All I can ask is that you forgive me and try to change your ways."

"What about me?" Lisa stood up and walked to his side. Accusation filled her eyes.

"Help me, Catherine," said his dad.

His mother straightened her shoulders. "I told the children the truth, honey."

"It was our secret. I didn't want to tear the family apart."

"Well it has," said Catherine. "We should have done it sooner. Maybe you wouldn't have eaten all those fatty steaks and killed yourself."

His dad raised his arms. "Can you forgive me, Lisa?"

"I want to," said Lisa. "But it'll take time."

Carson looked at his father, trim in his suit jacket. "This is all very nice," he called. "But, you're a coward. You got your act together after you died."

His father put his arm around Lisa's waist. "Please understand. I was a flawed human being doing the best I could."

"It wasn't good enough," said Carson. "Why did you come back?"

"I want you to accept me so that you, Jack Junior and Lisa don't make the same mistakes."

"Don't you have any remorse?" said Carson.

"You can't have a life without remorse."

"That's a cliche." Carson slammed his fist on the back of the pew.

His dad winced. "If you'd only look around, you'd see that you still have our family to depend on."

"Like hell he does," said Sally. "Carson deserted us. This whole family is a bummer."

"It's a bummer all right," said Carson. "No one wants me back."

His brother stepped into the aisle. "That's not true. Call me sometime, Carson. I need your advice more than ever."

"Enough of this," said his father. "Now where's your new girl-friend?"

Carson rose from his seat, searching the pews. "She doesn't want me back, either."

"Yes I do," called a voice. "I'm right here."

"Where? I don't see you. Why can't I see you?"

"For heaven's sake. I'm up here."

Carson followed the sound of Bridget's voice. She was sitting on a rafter.

"What are you doing up there?"

"I'm waiting for you."

"Bridget," he whispered, but she was gone, fading into white mist. His eyes fluttered open. Shadows moved against the wall. Turning his head sharply, he half expected to see his father stand-ing in his living room wearing clerical robes.

He wanted to scream at what he couldn't see. He got up, his head pounding. His damp shirt clung to his back as he walked to the kitchen. He turned on the cold water full blast and dunked his head beneath the faucet. There was no one left to count on, not even Mark. He couldn't believe he'd miss him, too.

He lifted his head. Droplets of water splashed onto his shoul-ders. There were other options. The bank had branches up and down the East Coast. He wondered what Boston was like.

Chapter 33

BRIDGET ROSE FROM HER DESK, adjusted an ancient metal floor fan and let it blow across her damp skin. The late summer heat wave showed no sign of letting up.

As soon as she finished the budget report, she'd lock up the convent and get back to the Center to finish packing. Her flight to Israel didn't leave until tomorrow evening, but she had a training session in New York beginning at eight a.m. and she needed to catch an early train.

She fingered the silver pendant Claire had given her. Cast in the shape of the Indian elephant god, Ganesha, it symbolized overcoming obstacles. She would need to become a spiritual athlete to leap over the hurdles she had set before herself.

This morning, Claire and Mark had left for an overnight retreat at the Highlands. She remembered her weekend there with Claire, wondering how Claire and Mark would cope with the celibacy requirement. She chided herself. That was her own frustrated libido talking.

On the wall, an old, frayed poster of Lourdes lifted slightly in the fan's breeze. She scrutinized it, wondering if the waters cured romantic losers.

At her desk, she checked the flight schedule for the tenth time. Twenty-four hours from now she'd be in the air. She was tempted to call Carson, ask him to drop everything and join her, if only for a few days. In Athens, they would have lunch in a taverna near the Acropolis. Then, she'd change her flight plans, leave for Israel a week later so they could fly to Santorini. Maybe Zorba would show up as their guide.

She'd already thought of a good excuse to call Carson. She'd pretend to have problems with the budget, ask him if she could run the numbers by him. On the other hand, he'd probably wonder if she'd secretly made a copy of his apartment key. If only she had given him a key to the convent, instead.

They made a fine pair the way she hid behind her work and he behind a false illusion of a perfect family life. Now she sat alone, Sister Bridget willing to give a piece of herself to anyone who knocked on her door, except her lover. Wasn't that what her mother had done for so many years, working at the factory day and night? How easy to avoid intimacy by hiding behind responsibility.

She got up and went to the window. A single lamp cast a blue glow on the darkened basketball courts littered with empty beer bottles, candy wrappers and crumpled newspapers. She remembered Carson dribbling a ball across asphalt, shaking sweat from his hair. Maybe the day would come when her heart stopped falling into her stomach every time she thought of him.

Beneath the broken streetlight on the corner she saw the glow of three cigarette butts and the shadows of the local kids who hung out there. They seemed harmless enough, but just this morning she'd found more graffiti scrawled on the building demanding that she leave. Tonight, she'd write a note to Claire asking the volunteers to keep an eye out. Maybe they could organize a movie night or sports activity to keep the group off the street.

One of the kids got up. She saw him stamp out his cigarette. "Hell no, the bitch gotta go," he shouted. The other kids joined him, chanting in unison. His arm looped back in a pitch. He let something fly through the darkness.

Pebbles spattered against the window screen. Although, tempted to yell at them, she was out of patience and didn't want a confrontation tonight. She turned off the fan, gathered her papers, put them in her backpack and snapped off the light.

Stealing a last glance through the window, she saw someone running through the darkness toward the kids. The gang leader. Hair prickled on the back of her neck. Had David organized this? She hadn't trusted his sweet-talk for a minute.

On the stairs, boxes and tools littered the risers. She picked her way over wrenches, hammers, nails. Since she couldn't leave through the front door, and Al had taken the broken knob off the back door, she'd get out through the kitchen window.

She hurried through the dining room into the kitchen. A patch of moonlight glowed on the floor. She lifted the sash, rattling the windowpane. It was stuck. She heard someone pound on the front door. She was about to break the glass when the window popped open. Climbing through, she breathed the humid night air. Quickly, she scaled the fence, hoping no one saw her run down the street and turn the corner.

*   *   *

"Bridget. Let me in!" Carson pounded on the front door, opened the mail slot, peered in and listened. Silence.

"Bridget. Are you in there?" He heard the harsh sound of his own breath, smelled the mustiness of the building. Livid, he turned to the kids, some of whom played on his basketball team. "What's the matter with you idiots? Was a lady in there?"

"Yeah, Mr. McAlister," said a kid in low-slung jeans. "This professor guy gave us ten bucks apiece to scare her. We didn't mean no harm."

"That's a hell of a way to have fun. You guys need to grow up." He turned to Angelo, one of his star basketball players, saw him drop his head, stick his hands in the pockets of his baggy pants.

"I want the whole team back here tomorrow, twelve o'clock sharp. We're cleaning up this place. No complaints or I'm calling your parents."

He breathed hard. Sweat trickled over his forehead. He wiped it on the sleeve of his t-shirt.

If only he'd called the Divine Guidance Center earlier. When they told him Bridget was leaving tomorrow, he had rushed over, hoping to catch her.

Where were her street smarts staying here alone so late without a telephone? And David's ghost always dogging her. She couldn't keep out of trouble to save her life. What did she do to attract these fools? If it weren't David, it would be someone else.

Come to think of it, he was just as bad as Bridget, screwing this whole thing up beyond repair. He and Bridget might as well live on opposite sides of the Grand Canyon. It was time he got on the horn to see what other options the bank offered.

Chapter 34

BRIDGET STEPPED OFF the plane, momentarily blinded by the Athens sunlight. In the distance, mountains, tawny as a lion's coat, rose toward a dark blue sky. On the sea, islands floated in dreamy shapes. She thought of Carson, how his eyes matched the fragile color of the water.

At the baggage carousel, she retrieved her luggage, found her gate. The plane was delayed longer than she had expected, almost six hours. She heard the musical staccato of Greek voices punctuating the air. A thrill lit up her body. Even the dingy airport seemed brightened by sunlight. She stopped at the snack bar, bought a coffee and a feta cheese pie. She had enough time to take a cab into Athens, but somehow it didn't seem right.

An English couple lounged at a table next to hers, sharing lemonade, kissing between sips. "It was a marvelous holiday," sighed the woman. "I wish we didn't have to go home."

Bridget bit into the warm pastry, imagined Carson's mother alone in the airport, and on Santorini walking a rocky path toward a whitewashed village.

She saw herself and Carson strolling along the beach, their toes warm in the sun-burnished sand. He would tell her stories about his family. She would listen to the soft intake of his breath as he moved to the next sentence.

She thought of her upcoming apprenticeship in Israel, of people bustling in narrow city streets, farming on the kibbutz where tomatoes and cucumbers grew in fields carved from desert. She looked forward to her stay in Israel, but her enthusiasm had waned.

An old man set a cardboard box on the floor, smiled at her and lit a cigarette. She thought of Carson's mother finding comfort in a stranger's face.

Carson's voice echoed in her mind. "It could be us." She stared at the pastry crumbs on her plate.

When she looked up, the English couple had gone and the old man had unfolded a newspaper. A tour group stood nearby, chatting about their trip to Santorini later that afternoon.

It could be us.

What was the name of the hotel where Carson's mother had stayed in Santorini? She wracked her brain. Something that began with an A.

She checked her watch. It was a little past five a.m. in Philadelphia. Claire, back from the Retreat, was probably in the Divine Guidance Center kitchen on breakfast duty. She fished her calling card from her purse. At a bank of pay phones, she dialed the Center, waited until they put her through. Claire answered, her voice upbeat as always. "How are things going?"

"So far so good, but . . ."

"Man, I was hoping you'd call. Guess who was at the convent yesterday afternoon when Mark and I got back? Carson."

Bridget's heart somersaulted.

"Someone on duty told him you were at the convent the night before you left. He came to see you, but you must have just missed him. He saw the kids throwing rocks at the building. The next day, he got the kids to clean all the graffiti off the building. He was annoyed that you'd hang out at the convent alone. I told him to chill."

"I don't want to hear anymore." Bridget tried to keep her voice neutral.

"He babbled some crazy stuff about transferring to Boston. Maybe we've sent him over the edge."

"He'll manage." Bridget twisted a lock of hair. It was probably better that he left the city.

"I've upset you."

"No." She sighed. "Maybe a little."

"Forget him. Go have a blast on the kibbutz. Meet a handsome sabra. Man, I wish I were there with you. Send me an e-mail when you get to Israel."

Bridget hung up and strode through the airport out the door.

Oleander bloomed in pink sprays along the driveway leading to the busy main road. The air, though buoyant, smelled of diesel exhaust. She checked her ticket again. Listlessly, she thought about visiting the Acropolis.

It could be us.

An idea nagged at her. She touched her pendant.

Back inside the terminal, she found the ticket counter, waited in line. When she got to the front, the attendants smiled at her. "I'd like to change my flight to next Monday," she said. Her own voice startled her, but a surge of energy shot through her veins.

While the attendant changed her ticket, she wracked her brain. Finally, it struck her. The Artemis Hotel.

Next, she called Boon-Dan-Tan. "You've been through much stress," he said. "Have you thought carefully about your actions?"

She assured him that she had, but she needed space and time to rest her mind. When he gave her his blessing, she relaxed. She could almost hear Claire's reaction. "You're crazy, girl. But go for it."

She pulled her luggage past foreign faces and the seductive lilt of foreign languages. "Domestic Terminal," she said, when she reached the cab stand.

*   *   *

In the small courtyard of the Artemis Hotel overlooking the Caldera of Santornini, Bridget sipped milky ouzo with ice. On this, her second night, she had staked out a table in the corner. She watched the sun begin its descent and nibbled an olive. She'd already ripped up two letters she'd written to Carson.

She wanted to tell him that one of the maids remembered his mother. The maid carried a small key-chain sporting a ball and jack on her big ring. Bridget had recognized the symbol and mentioned it.

"Neh, Kyria McAleestir," the maid had said. "A strange, but kind woman."

The maid had told her that each night at sunset, Carson's mother had retreated to her balcony alone to drink a scotch and water. Yet, in the morning, when the maid came to straighten things up, she would find a full glass of scotch sitting next to an empty one on the table.

She also wanted to tell him about the people she'd met since she'd arrived, an older Italian gentleman who drove his motorbike at top speed along curvy roads to the sea. And a couple in their late twenties who whined about how the sun was too hot, the cheese too salty, and the wine too thin.

Quickly, she had retreated into a cocoon of silence. Even the waiter knew when to leave her alone.

This morning, she had ventured along the path that led into town and was pretty sure she'd found the old man Carson's mother had met. She wanted to say hello, but he looked right through her as he clipped his grapevines. She was a blip on his screen, unlike Carson's mother whose eyes spoke his language.

She looked toward Nea Kameni. The dormant volcano floated like an island in the sea. The sun had turned the water surrounding it fiery orange. Strains of a lilting Greek melody floated through the courtyard.

The waiter, a young boy, with a shock of thick, black hair, stopped at her table. "Madame, is a man who ask for you."

She looked up. An older gentleman sat at the bar. He lifted his glass to her. She half-smiled and turned away.

The waiter laughed. "*Oxi. stin porta.*"

She tilted her head toward the courtyard gate, the alcohol heightening her senses. A mirage leaned against the frame, his face bathed in the surreal light, his eyes asking a question she recognized.

The air almost carried her as she got up, took a step toward him. Waning light brushed his hair with amber highlights. His eyes had darkened to dusty blue beneath tawny lashes. The tilt of his hip was soothingly familiar. When she reached him, he turned away as though her presence burned his skin.

"Carson, what are you doing here?"

"Claire told me where I could find you."

She touched his hands, felt the weight of bone beneath skin. A vein pulsed in his neck, beating in time with the rhythm of her heart. Words formed in her throat, but she couldn't speak. Her heart repeated the question in his eyes.

Do you think we can make it?

The sun enveloped them in a last flush of light. Here, suspended between sky and sea, she hoped they'd find the answer.